If you feel battered by the Christmas season, resentful of its mindless cheer, isolated by its phoney inclusiveness, this book is the antidote. These fine writers and poets hold a mirror to the dark side of the season, show us we are not alone — and then gift us with a generous measure of insight and humor to get us through. If I'd had this book ten years ago, I wouldn't have blown a thousand dollars on a trip to Algiers just to escape the season.

— Mary Edwards Wertsch, author of **Military Brats**

Never was an anthology more aptly named. Proof of the adage, "Misery loves company," this compilation exposes the raw feelings behind the statistics that warn of the increased dangers of homicides, suicides and all the other 'cides that burgeon during the holiday season. When all else fails to ignite the holiday spark, besieged optimists will find that the reading of fiction provides its own rewards.

— S.L. Stebel
author of **The Boss's Wife** and **Spring Thaw**

◇

Before you wish anyone a "Merry Christmas," you should read **Christmas Blues.** *There are legitimate reasons others do not share your feelings. The slices of reality behind the works in this anthology include the pain of loss at Christmas, the suffering caused by the perversions of tradition and the fact that Christmas is not everybody's holy day. We can understand a little more about our neighbors, if we have the courage to listen to the many voices outside the popular religion of our culture.* — Royal F. Ewing, pastor, retired

CHRISTMAS BLUES

Behind the Holiday Mask

An Anthology

Edited by

Zelda Leah Gatuskin

Michelle Miller

Harry Willson

Printed in the United States of America
First Printing, 1995
ISBN: 0-938513-18-4
Library of Congress Catalog # 95-79549

Credits:

"Christmas Is Special," an article by Dorothy M. Ainslie, first appeared in the winter, 1993-94, issue of *Prime Times*, a publication of The Monroe Publishing Co., Monroe, Michigan. It is reprinted here with permission.

"Exorcism," by Peter Cooley, was published in *New Collage*, Vol. 4, No. 192, 1972-73.

"Christmas Eve," by CB Follett, was previously published by *Parting Gifts,* March Street Press, 1994, Vol. 7, No. 1.

"My Secret," by Jan Nystrom, originally appeared as, "The Keeper of Secrets," in *The North American Review*, March, 1990.

"Silent Night," by Miriam Sagan, was originally published in *Artful Dodge*, Fall, 1989.

AMADOR PUBLISHERS
P. O. Box 12335
Albuquerque, NM 87195

Table of Contents

Art Work:
   Mark Funk — illustrations: pages 38, 84, 160,
        175, 185, 230, 274, 295, 320
   Zelda Leah Gatuskin — cover collage
   Claiborne O'Connor — cover layout, calligraphy
        and illustrations: pages 31, 105, 112, 182,
        223, 290, 317, 330
   Evan Smith — "The Snak.s Crismis," page viii

The SNaks Crismis

The Snaks Crismis
Was Good But
Not Good a noF

Evan J. Smith

Age 6

Introduction

"Nor was it any satisfaction to be shown the Mask, and see that it was made of paper, or to have it locked up and be assured that no one wore it. The mere recollection of that fixed face, the mere knowledge of its existence anywhere, was sufficient to awake me in the night all perspiration and horror, with, 'O I know it's coming! O the mask!'"

Charles Dickens, "A Christmas Tree," 1850

Despite my resolve to ignore the season, I sat by the fireplace that Christmas Eve, acutely aware of my aloneness. Haunted by the image of crackling hearths in the homes surrounding me, I felt pressure to at least build a decent fire.

I was not alone in my ambivalence. One friend had left gleefully for the Bahamas to escape Christmas. A co-worker, chronically depressed, had announced with dark vigor that if things hadn't improved by Christmas Eve, she was going to kill herself on New Year's. I believed she was serious until, at the last minute, she maxed out her credit card for a sudden trip back east to be with her family.

The problem remained: Many of us wanted desperately to love Christmas, yet, in truth, we dreaded and loathed it as a dark passage we were forced to endure. Once a year. Every year. For the rest of our lives.

Staring into those lonely flames, I decided someone should collect the stories and do a book on this "Christmas Blues" phenomenon. On the back of a Christmas card I made a list. What were the essential elements to fulfill the myth of a perfect Christmas? 1. You had to have love, both familial and romantic. 2. You needed a fair amount of money for gifts, decor, feasting, traveling, entertaining and a general sense of well-being. 3. The holiday must have personal, spiritual meaning for you, preferably of the Christian variety.

That night I felt none of these elements were in place in my life. A harsh light was focused relentlessly on my failure as a human being — failure to have garnered my fair share of love, wealth and spiritual meaning. Christmas to me represented an unfair hope that, at the stroke of midnight, Santa Claus would come down the spiritual chimney and heal everything: familial pain, torn relationships, shattered ideals, global disharmony, my bank account. I expected more than Christmas could possibly deliver. I needed to lower my sights to some simpler and survivable expectation — something like the innocence of tiny tree lights or falling snow.

I tossed my list into the flames and watched the fire die out.

◇

Our editorial intention is not to negate or attack Christmas, but to take a good hard look at the painful and ambivalent aspects of the season. When a group of people admit harsh social truth together, they create an experience of cultural bonding, which is a powerful antidote to cultural alienation. As Jewish co-editor Zelda Gatuskin said at one of our editorial meetings, "Because of this anthology I feel less alienated from the whole Christmas thing. I *care* now; I want people to have a good Christmas!" Co-editor Harry Willson told me, "It did me good to wallow in it, out of season, and to find so many kindred spirits." It is no coincidence that I myself have had not only survivable but enjoyable Christmases during the two holiday seasons which have passed while we put together this anthology. I believe that is largely due to the empowerment I have felt in reading the Christmas Blues stories of other people and knowing we are helping to put these stories into the culture. In a way, this is our own Christmas carol, collectively sung in a minor key.

◇

Film director Tim Burton's 1993 animation film, *The Nightmare before Christmas*, combines the seemingly opposing elements of Halloween and Christmas. A well-meaning Halloween Santa leaves gifts for the children which, when opened, frighten and attack them. We found that such Christmas ambivalence is not a purely contemporary development, however. From 1837 through the turn of the century, Charles Dickens, Henry James and other writers commonly associated fear and horror with the "cheerful discharge" of Christmas and thus entertained readers with a genre known as "the Christmas ghost story," which they claimed was an ancient tradition. The opening lines to James' *The Turn of the Screw* (1889) describe the ensuing story as "gruesome, as, on Christmas Eve in an old house, a strange tale should essentially be..." Dickens, who is attributed with inventing the image of the cozy-by-the-hearth Christmas, also wrote of the dark side and unreasonable expectations of Christmas, as in his 1851 essay, "What Christmas Is As We Grow Older."

"Was that Christmas dinner never really eaten, after which we arose, and generously and eloquently rendered honour...then and there exchanging friendship and forgiveness...That Christmas when we had recently achieved so much fame...when we had won an honoured and ennobled name, and arrived and were received at home in a shower of tears of joy; is it possible that that Christmas has not come yet?"

And it is Dickens who describes Christmas toys from his childhood as "horrible," "sinister," "ghastly," and "demoniacal." He has particular difficulty reconciling to a mask given him one Christmas, and suggests that his dread was caused by the mask being too serious a reminder of "that fixed and set change coming over a real face...the universal change that is to come on every face and make it still..."

It is significant that these writers connect death images to a holiday associated with birth, and that their audiences so willingly join them in making this connection. My Pagan friends remind me that the celebration of Yule and Winter Solstice predated the Christian celebration of Christmas. Yule takes place at the darkest time of year, when it is our physiological inclination to hibernate. Obviously, hibernation is a mimicry of and metaphor for death.

There is a clue in our holiday fascination with light. Christmas is, after all, associated with soft, subtle light which selectively illuminates while keeping much hidden — tiny electric bulbs, candles, luminarias, firelight — not with bright or harsh light. By our holiday preference for soft winter lights, are we bowing to the fact that winter's dark is our natural and undeniable environment for that time of year? Does our attempt at gathering for holiday joviality and mirth actually go against the grain, in the deep recesses of our collective unconscious, and is this why we get the Christmas Blues? Perhaps our Christmas rituals are in part motivated by an unspoken need to huddle together and perform magic — be it the Pagan practice of magic or the Christian celebration of miracles — against the specter of our mortality. The wearing of the holiday mask may be an attempt to evoke power over, or to deny, our darker aspects. A good, honest look at the history and traditions of both

Christmas and Yule, Christian and Pagan, suggests another "meaning of Christmas," one which relates to a time when we confront and try to reconcile these forces of dark and light.

Whatever the explanation behind the Christmas ghost story phenomenon, our *Christmas Blues* collection finds a distinct place in this strange tradition, as our tales are about exposing and expunging our inner holiday ghosts and demons.

◇

A note on the diversity of our contributors: We did not focus on soliciting "known authors." Gathered by a simple call for manuscripts, these stories represent a stunning and undeniable cultural statement both from professional writers and first-timers who had something strong and personal to say on the subject. *Christmas Blues* is a daring collection of dynamic truth-saying which pulls the holiday hype-&-media mask aside.

Filled with recurring themes of alienation, alcoholism, disenchanted childhood memories and unattained ideals, this book is a brave reporting of a significant social condition. A potential healing tool, *Christmas Blues* is rescued from despair by the discovery of our common humanity, the creative solutions of holiday survivors, and a lot of bittersweet humor.

This collection will find its home not only on "literary anthology" shelves but, perhaps more importantly, in sociology, self-help and psychology sections as well. Most of all, we expect to see it in those Christmas book displays, along with the other holiday classics, right between *The Night before Christmas* and *A Christmas Carol*.

Christmas Blues is about giving ourselves and each other permission to feel and express *all* our feelings. Or, as Charles Dickens wrote in 1851: "Welcome, everything! Welcome, alike, what has been, and what never was, and what we hope may be, to your shelter underneath the holly, to your places round the Christmas fire, where what is sits open-hearted!"

Michelle Miller, March, 1995

TRADITION

Our mass-media culture has a way of absorbing whatever comes along, making a fad of it and synthesizing various symbols into what it then calls "tradition." Scrooge and Grinch, reindeer with red noses, candy canes, going home and overeating are all part of Christmas today.

Tradition can hold society together, but when society is beyond that point, what's left of tradition can be a painful hindrance to an individual's getting on with life. We're trying to hold ourselves together in the face of the fact that things aren't the way they used to be. Traditions that once felt affirming may now come laden with doubt, guilt or regret. Like the branches of an overdressed tree, our holiday spirits droop under the weight of so many memories and expectations.

Contributor Karen Ethelsdatter asks in a letter: "Are there any answers here? Perhaps not to hide from the memories, but let them and the tears come. And the solace of nature that a tree provides. And the steadying influence of ritual: seeking a tree, decorating it, taking it down, and being present to each moment."

A remarkable number of our contributors chose the tree as the symbol which needed attention of one kind or another. The concern seems to have little to do with the old Nordic tree-worship. Perhaps this section is really about memory and what to do with it, more than trees or food or old-fashioned department stores.

We include here a parody on the annual duplicated family Christmas letter. We have a statement from a card-carrying Grinch, and also a fresh analysis of "Grinch-ness," as embodied in the person who thinks of Christmas as a production that creates obligations, which can then mistakenly be called love. Finally, an allegory of talking body parts helps clarify what's really going on here.

Getting a Christmas Tree

Karen Ethelsdattar

Anticipating it.
Walking by the little markets of trees
on the streets as the weeks
walk closer to Christmas,
breathing in that resinous odor,
small forests
punctuating the city's winter air,
lingering luringly in your nostrils.

Consider
not having a tree this year,
shutting in a drawer
the photograph album
of memory & your senses,
pretending,
leaving the living room as it is
most every day of the year.

Pretending
you never saw your mother in her evening gown,
or clattered up & down the stairs
in her high-heeled shoes...

Leaving the living room as it is
most every day of the year.

Pretend you never went with your twin sister
& those two Swedes, your father & his friend Sam
who died last year or the year before,
to cut Christmas trees in the woods in the canyon,
& pine branches, fir boughs, Oregon grape for the mantels
& doors & buffet & table...

Leaving the living room as it is
most every day of the year.

Pretend
you were never the mother
of two small children, now grown & living elsewhere,
who tore into their presents with innocent greed
& wailed to sleep with the tree lights on all night
& could never bear to dismantle the tree in January.

Leaving the living room as it is
most every day of the year.

Wake early
on Saturday, December 13
to call your dentist about a broken tooth;
to carry to the post office with its noon closing hour
the package for Mother & Dad.
Walk by the tree market
just for a look
the way you walked by a shop window
again & again to look at that dress you couldn't afford
& then did;

Inquire in an uncommitted sort of way
the prices
& then find yourself
carrying a tree home in your arms,
its full skirt roped in,

balancing it,
feeling its still live weight
like the weight of the child you once lifted;
beginning to make its acquaintance,
reveling in its presence —
its nearness, its familiar smell, its beard-like prickle.

A tree before ten in the morning,
& nearly two weeks before Christmas.
Are you really a nonbeliever?

Then erecting it
just a little off-center
& filling the room in its scent.
Sitting in its presence.
Watching the cat on its hind legs
nibbling & browsing in its branches
like a giraffe among the tree-tops.
Delaying to decorate it.
Living that way the whole day.
Encountering it each time you walk into
or through the now magic room...
gazing at it, drinking it in —
the forest, your childhood, your mother years
come home.

Burial

Catherine Couse

Even before Thanksgiving they started setting up for the Christmas trees. One night when she walked through the empty lot the trailer was there, parked a few yards back from the street, propane tanks at one end, charcoal grill at the other, just like last year. There wasn't anyone in the trailer, then or for the next few nights, but soon the fencing showed up, wooden slats for the trees to lean against, and the sawhorse where the wreaths would hang. The neighborhood did not have sidewalks but there were a few pedestrians, older people who no longer drove, small children, joggers and walkers with headsets on, enough people to have worn a path across the lot. She cut through the lot twice a day, walking the dog, once on the way to the cemetery, once on the way back home.

She did not have the grave of a friend or relative to visit in the cemetery, although sometimes now she would speak to certain headstones as she passed. "So, Anna May," she would say to the headstone at the bottom of the hill. "I see they planted a fresh one over the weekend." She would nod toward the mound of dirt in the row behind Anna May. "Hope you two are getting along." Then she would continue on, back out to the road, whistling to the dog, who would run up, tail wagging, tongue dripping, and allow herself to be put back on the leash.

In the old neighborhood there had been a park where people walked their dogs. Four or five people might have been there on an evening after work, leaning against the fence or sitting around the picnic table, while the dogs ran back and forth across the softball fields and tried to take sticks away from each other. The

6

dog walkers called each other "Dasher's mother" or "B.G.'s father" and talked together about leashes and flea collars, kennels and veterinarians. She became friends with the mother of a Golden Retriever named Buster, and she and Buster's mother would walk to the park together, filling each other in on the events of the day, as though each were a diary for the other. Susan had talked about paint and spackle while Buster's mother relayed the details of her pregnancy.

"I'm saving the master bedroom 'til last," said Susan. "Mark won't tell me what color he wants to paint it. I guess I'll wait until after he moves in."

"Is he moving in soon?" said Buster's mother, "When are you getting married?"

"I don't know," said Susan. "We haven't set a date yet."

When Susan first left the neighborhood she went back sometimes to the park, driving down in the car after work. Now and then she would run into Buster's mother, walking along pushing a carriage, Buster trotting obediently by her side. Susan would park the car and join her, smiling in at the sleeping baby, who never woke up as long as the carriage kept moving, but she could only listen to so many stories about the baby's accomplishments, and when it was her turn to talk she couldn't think of anything to say. Gradually she gave up going, and she hadn't been back for a while.

There weren't any parks in the new neighborhood, so she ran the dog in the cemetery. The dog was good at weaving her way in and out of the headstones, running at top speed, as though she were herding them, like sheep. It was pleasant there in the warm weather, green and peaceful, and full of rabbits for the dog to chase. Sometimes she would let the dog off the leash and sit down for a while in the warm evening sun. Now the ground was frozen and the cemetery was dark, except for the gleaming of headlights on the stones from cars going by on the road.

At work all the talk was about Christmas. Somebody had all their cards in the mail, somebody else hadn't bought them yet. This one had wrapped all her presents months ago. That one was stringing popcorn to put on the tree, the other one favored candy canes, but nobody bothered with cranberries, which rotted.

"What about you?" someone asked her. "Have you put your tree up yet?"

"I'm not doing a tree this year," she said. She would do the minimum necessary to avoid inviting comment. Next year she would fly away to some hot, sunny island, preferably near the equator, where the days never got any shorter and the natives weren't even Christian.

Trees had arrived in the empty lot by then, row upon row of them, standing up in clumps against the wooden slats. The smell of pine hung in the air for fifty feet in either direction, greeting her as she came and went. Now there was a man inside the trailer, watching a small t.v., right there behind the lighted window, inches from the path. He sat at a table littered with dirty dishes, newspapers, and empty styrofoam cups. Often when she walked by he was eating dinner, sitting there with his coat on, and sometimes a woman sat there with him, sharing his meal. On those evenings the smell of charcoal and grilled meat mingled with the scent of the trees.

"You wish I'd grill a steak, don't you?" she said, as the dog strained forward on the leash, nose high in the air. "You'd like some leftovers, wouldn't you?"

Back at the house she put her frozen dinner in the microwave and ate alone in the quiet at the kitchen table while the dog huddled at her feet and waited for food to fall on the floor. There were never any leftovers from the frozen dinners, but she always saved at least a spoonful of sauce or a couple of noodles to put in the dog's dish.

Christmas drew closer. The man in the vacant lot no longer sat in the trailer. Now he could be found outside holding trees upright for people to look at, or tying them to the tops of cars. She kept the dog close to her side as they crossed the path through the vacant lot, away from the customers. Every evening she and the man would nod at each other and say hello.

At work there were cookies and candy on every desk, Santas

perched on file cabinets, and an artificial tree in the conference room. "I can't believe you don't have a tree yet," her colleagues said to her. "You always get those great big ones."

"Not anymore," she said. "That was in the old house," and let it go at that. Most people didn't ask any more questions, or bug her about the party she wouldn't be throwing this year. Christmas was a series of chores that you did for other people, children with wide, excited eyes, husbands or lovers that you sat up late at night with, sipping eggnog in the dim glow of the colored lights from the tree. The dog didn't care about colored lights. Dogs saw the world in black and white.

The old house had been large and rambling, with spacious, high-ceilinged rooms. There on a busy corner in the middle of the city Susan would sit in the summer on the wide front porch in the shade of the maple trees. Her house was a twin to the house next door, except for the color, and except that as hard as she tried, she could never take care of things as well as Steven and Kathleen, the elderly couple who lived there. If her porch sagged a little theirs was solid and even, and where her house needed a coat of paint on the side by the driveway, Steven spent the summer taking care of his side, canvas dropcloths laid carefully down.

"He actually wipes the paint off the driveway with a wet cloth," she told Buster's mother as they walked along with the dogs. "Drip by drip. I can't wait 'til Mark and I are married and I don't have to do everything myself."

"Did you set a date yet?" said Buster's mother.

"Not yet."

"Mark's no dummy," said Buster's mother. "By the time he moves in you'll have the whole place redecorated."

Steven and Kathleen had lived in the house next door from the time it was built, some sixty years before. Steven was often outside working on the house or the flower garden in the back yard. On summer evenings he came by her porch to chat, and in winter when he got out his snowblower to do his walk, he did hers too. Kathleen, who suffered from dizzy spells, appeared on

Sundays for church and rarely otherwise.

That first Christmas in the old house Mark was busy a lot, working out of town. Susan bought a tree in proportion to the rooms, ten feet tall to reach the ceiling. Steven helped her carry it up the stairs. She put up the tree in the living room corner, where there were windows on both sides, to give the best view from the streets.

"Your tree will be even more beautiful once you have decorated it," Steven told her. "You must come over and see ours. Come and have a highball with us."

"I'll come right now," she said, and followed Steven home. He opened the door and ushered her up the steps, beaming. The house was as immaculate on the inside as it was on the out. Stopping off in the kitchen, Steven mixed her a highball in a tall glass.

"Kathleen," he called. "Where are you? Susan is here to see the tree."

Susan stopped short in the doorway to Steven and Kathleen's living room. "Oh," she said, "I had no idea."

The tree and the miniature city beneath it took up half the room. The city was laid out perfectly to scale, with stop signs at the corners and lamp posts lining the streets. Lights shone in the windows of every tiny house. There was a library and a school, a court house and a supermarket, and a hospital with an ambulance parked in the driveway. The doors to a small firehouse stood open to display two hook-and-ladder trucks with a pole between them. A train ran along the edge of the city, passed through a small forest, crossed over a bridge, and came to rest in the railway station.

She looked up at Steven and Kathleen, standing in the doorway with their arms around each other, children's smiles on their faces.

"This is incredible," she said. "How long does it take you to set this up?"

"Oh," said Steven, "it's really quite easy. Look here." He lifted up a farmhouse and a barn with a silo behind it and pulled back a corner of the display. "The whole set-up is drawn on this mat underneath. The wires are run along this pattern I've drawn. Each house has a number, and there is a bulb that comes up under each one. Of course each year we add something, and I have to change things a little bit. But it only takes me a couple of evenings."

"Your grandchildren must love to come here at Christmas," she said.

"Oh, yes," said Steven. "They get quite excited about it. They move things around so, it takes me a while to straighten it out when they leave."

The three of them sipped on their highballs while Steven and Kathleen gave her a tour of the tree, pointing out special ornaments collected over the years, gifts they had received from their children, and the bubble lights they had bought when they were first married.

"Someday you and your young man will have your own Christmas memories," said Steven.

"When is your special day, my dear?" said Kathleen, patting her hand. "You will be such a beautiful bride."

"I don't know," said Susan. "We haven't set a date yet."

She swayed just a little going down the steps on her way home.

"I'll tell you one thing," she said to Buster's mother the next day as they walked the dogs to the park. "The man knows how to make a highball."

For a short time in the new neighborhood, she had found a dog-walking companion to replace Buster's mother. Tony was a young man who lived down the street, the only other single person in the neighborhood. On Spring evenings when she and the dog passed his house Tony would be sitting on his front porch, or working on the lawn, or washing his car. At first she and Tony just said hello, and then it got so that she stopped to talk for a minute, and pretty soon Tony was walking with her and the dog all the way to the cemetery and back. Sometimes they drank beer together and listened to rock and roll, and in the early summer when the nights were long they went for bicycle rides together after dinner.

"I was hoping to meet a beautiful girl from the neighborhood," Tony said.

"Thank you," she said, "but I'm not exactly a girl. I must be ten years older than you."

"Age doesn't matter if you like each other," Tony said.

Tony had never been inside the cemetery until she brought him there. "It's nice here, don't you think?" she asked him after their fourth or fifth visit. She and Tony sat on the ground in the shade of a tree while the dog raced among the headstones and chased the squirrels. "It's so secluded."

"It's definitely a cool place," said Tony, grinning at her. "Last weekend I was partying with my friends Mark and Valerie and I brought them down here, and it was awesome, really dark and kind of foggy. It was pretty late at night. I waited until Valerie had walked a little ways away from us and I sneaked up behind her and kind of put my hand over her face and scared the shit out of her. She screamed really loud." Tony grinned more broadly. "It was pretty funny," he said.

By the end of the summer she had gone back to walking the dog alone. She and Tony stayed friends, stopping to talk if they met on the street. Every now and then they got together for a beer. One night on her way through the vacant lot she ran into him, picking out a Christmas tree with his girlfriend. Tony introduced her to the girlfriend.

"That's a great tree," she said to them. "Have a wonderful holiday."

"We're spending Christmas with my family," said Tony's girlfriend. "Tony's the headline act." She put her arm through Tony's and looked up at him. "Everyone wants to meet him," the girlfriend said.

"I'm sure he won't disappoint them."

"Did you put up your tree yet?" Tony asked her.

"I'm not having a tree this year," she said.

On her first Christmas in the new neighborhood she had

bought a tree too large for the rooms in the house. She had borrowed a saw from Tony and cut the bottom off. The new house was practical, built of brick for easy maintenance, with the lower ceilings and smaller windows of homes built after the war.

"It's a different sort of house," she had said to Steven and Kathleen. She had gone next door to visit, to tell them she was moving. "You know, built in the fifties. It's a quiet little neighborhood kind of off to itself. The streets aren't busy like they are here. There isn't really any traffic except for the people who live there."

"It sounds very nice," said Steven. "Sometimes the neighbors here are so noisy they keep me awake all night."

"It'll be a lot easier to take care of," she said. "And I can afford to pay for it myself." She didn't mention that the house had one less bedroom and half as many windows, or that now she could pay Mark the money he had loaned her, the down payment on the old house, plus interest, of course, the check she had written each month which she no longer handed him but sent off through the anonymity of the mail.

"Someone like you won't be alone for long," said Steven. "We'll miss you, but we hope you'll be very happy. You deserve to have good things."

He went out to the kitchen to mix them all a highball. Steven and Kathleen raised their glasses to her.

"We wish you a wonderful life in your new home," Steven said.

The forest of trees in the empty lot began to thin out, leaving more room to walk between the rows. Christmas was less than two weeks away. The weather grew cold and windy. She wore her mother's old fur coat to walk the dog, with plenty of tissues in the pockets for her watering eyes. The man in the vacant lot nodded at her as she passed, his scarf pulled up over his face. Now there were wreaths for sale in the lot as well as Christmas trees, and wrapping paper on a table in front of the trailer. The lot was crowded with people, wandering up and down the rows of trees, holding them up for each other, turning them to study every side.

At work little presents began to appear on people's desks. She started her shopping, running out on her lunch hours, or stopping off places to do errands after work. One evening she headed down to the old neighborhood, picking up wine for friends from the office and books to send to her sister and her family out on the west coast. Books were heavy and expensive to mail, but worth the trouble if she could get through the season without a single trip to the shopping malls, especially the men's department, which still set her off balance, a leftover from worrying about what to buy for Mark. She had pretty much stayed out of the men's department since she and Mark broke up.

That last Christmas together she had agonized over his gifts, the gold-toed socks that claimed to be hole proof, a robe to hang next to hers on the bathroom door, the pale blue sweater he had specifically requested. At least he had been happy with the socks.

"This sweater is all wool," Mark had said, trying on the sweater with a pinched expression on his face. The sweater fit perfectly and brought out the blue of his eyes. "I won't be able to put it in the dryer."

"I'll wash it for you," Susan had said. "Why don't you try on the robe?"

"I don't wear robes," he said. "I thought you knew that."

She had opened her own presents in order, largest to smallest, saving the tiny square box for last. She had ripped off the paper, and opened the box to find a gold necklace with a dark blue stone, much like the one from last year, only last year's stone had been pink, and the one from the year before, turquoise to match her favorite earrings. Late that night, sitting up by the glow of the Christmas tree lights, Mark asleep in the still unpainted master bedroom, she had thrown the necklace into the fire.

She stopped at the drug store for wrapping paper and ribbon. If she got the books into the mail by morning they might arrive on time. She drove by Steven and Kathleen's house on her way home. Christmas tree lights shone brightly from the windows. Too late in the evening to stop in for one of Steven's highballs. By now he and Kathleen would be getting ready for bed.

The Saturday before Christmas was sunny and very cold. She wrapped some presents and stacked them on the floor in a corner of the living room. She went and got the mail and sat down at the table to read the Christmas cards. At the bottom of the pile she found a card addressed in Steven's old-fashioned, elegant hand.

"Dear Susan," he wrote. "It is not a happy Christmas for me. My very dear Kathleen passed away last month. I miss her terribly. Nothing will ever be the same again. We miss you in the neighborhood. The new owner doesn't take care of things the way you did."

She rubbed her hand over her eyes, and read the card again. Then she put her head down on the table and sobbed. The dog sat on the floor and wagged her tail. With a cold, wet nose the dog pushed at her elbow. After a while she got up and took the dog for a walk to the cemetery. She stopped and spoke to the headstone at the bottom of the hill. "You're lucky, Anna May," she said. "What do you care if it's Christmas?"

The man in the vacant lot was stomping his feet and rubbing his hands together when she passed back through. "How's it going today?" he said.

"Fine," she said. "How much are your trees?"

"Forty and under," the man said. "What do you need?"

"A blue spruce, a small one."

The man led her to the back of the lot and pulled a tree away from the wooden slats. "This one's marked thirty," he said, "but I'll give it to you for twenty-eight."

"Fine," she said. "Let me go get my car."

She took the dog home and came back with her car. The man went and got her tree from its hiding place at the back of the lot. He cut the bottom off for her and stuffed the tree into the trunk of the car.

She put the tree up in front of the living room window. The tree was perfectly shaped on every side. It stood straight up in the stand on the very first try. The lights shone through the window where they could be seen by her, coming home from the cemetery with the dog, and by the paper boy when he came to collect his money, and by an occasional neighbor driving past. One evening she called Steven's number, but a child answered the phone and she hung up without asking for him. She took the tree down even before New Year's, packing up the decorations and the cards on the mantel, and hauling the tree outside to the curb.

A few days later it began to snow. There were already a few inches on the ground when she took the dog out for a walk. By now the trailer and the wooden slats were gone from the vacant lot. Snow covered the pine boughs and the pieces of ribbon that littered the ground. Snow masked the scent of pine that still hung in the air.

In the cemetery the snow fell on the headstones, and the plastic poinsettias on the tops of people's graves. By the time she and the dog cut through the lot on their way back home the snow had filled in their footprints. All that night in the quiet street the snow continued to fall. In the morning when she got up and looked out the window the snow had turned the Christmas tree into a large, frozen mound, covered over with fat white flakes, like the petals of flowers, that floated softly down.

All Your Brother-Branches

Geraldine Gobi Greig

> *All your brother-branches*
> *Palms up to the sky,*
> *Some crooked in struggle,*
> *But blossomed out and growing upward...*
>   Luvsandambyn Dashnyam

I've grown to feel it a barbaric custom to murder trees and drag them into our homes to celebrate birth and beginning. I last bought a Christmas tree on my own steam in 1980. Buying poinsettias, I noted the small tree lying against the nursery wall, still bound with twine; kicked aside, abandoned, straight from pillage to garbage its apparent lot in life. Of course I had to salvage it. Bound for so long, its arms never straightened to the standard of stateliness but swirled in a spiral about the trunk and, loving it, I thought: the Burning Bush. I took the small, special tree to the office and set it up on the desk and named it "Luther." One and all were welcome to honor it with finery, and during slow moments we of the night shift strung strands of popcorn and cranberries to adorn it.

I brought "Luther" home in time for Christmas, waking around 2 a.m. in the Eve to decorate him with sacred ornaments found by chance or fate on an errand earlier that Season, and fresh popcorn/cranberry garlands; no lights that year since the Burning Bush quality seemed radiance enough. After adorning him for the Day, I drove to the countryside where a truly mystic, prophetic experience blessed me. Back in the city, the Day was especially luminous and holy, with warmest fellowship after the world at large awaked and friends dropped from the sky, bringing new friends. From his place of honor against the window, Luther blessed our gathering with his living benevolence, his lifted arms open wider in the warmth of the Day.

Skip eleven eventful years: someone else in the household insisted, a *real* tree this year, no arguments. One was brought in for *me* to decorate. I turned from the televised light of "The Little Matchgirl" remake to behold a scruffy midget tree, chosen, it seemed, in equally dim light, for it had mysterious, unsightly gaps in its branches, bare spots, and so called to mind a case of mange rather than stately elegance. No sooner had I scorned it than I felt chastened, ashamed, for it also had presence. I felt a breathing being shared the room, and I hugged it and cleared a table for it. Ten days later, I dressed it in the last hours of Christmas Eve, procrastination the personal custom. The night was overcast and, busied at my task, I longed for visibility. I finished untangling the lights and switching bulbs to space colors, etc., shortly before the stroke of midnight. Those who had found the tree were leaving my work in peace from the house in back of the main abode, so they were summoned for pie and coffee to celebrate my effort and, rejoicing in the reason for the new member of the household, to hang the final ornaments. As I stepped out to fetch them, the eyes lifted to the heavens and I gasped with pure joy to behold: the skies had cleared and the full starry host were magnificent, just as they should be, proclaiming The Night. Without thinking, I shrieked with delight that inspired the local canines to chime in.

I sensed that tree was something special; and so it was. It became family. It reigned from its table *the entire year* of 1992. I fed it plant food; I talked with it from time to time; I opened the blinds each morning to give it the light of its window. On special occasions, I turned on its lights to sit quietly in the otherwise darkness loving it; loving the fact ancient Chinese fancied stars were celestial elms; loving the actual ancestral elms in the land of my dead beloved; loving the fact the Mongolians called Jupiter the "wood star" (and now a British astronomer claims shining Jupiter itself, not a comet or planetary configuration, was the Christmas Star); and loving the tree imagery of renewal of life in the Yom Kippur readings that had snapped my soul into sanity. The same readings I later would prayerfully study as the last light of Yom Kippur bathed the large tree of our front yard, as the beloved lay dying half the world away and I prayed so fervently for him, though I had no rational knowledge he was dying in those hours. It all adheres, and coheres, colors and comforts, so despite the random fallow Seasons we stumble through, I do praise, and praise again, the Father of the Gift of the radiant place in the year called Christmas.

Came Christmas of '92: some in the family, encouraged by my strange fervor of the preceding year, bought a new tree for the Season, but I could not bring myself to dishonor the "old" one by removing it, for it was *still* up, *still* mostly green, still fragrant. It had lost a bare minimum of needles since its original Christmas with us. So the new tree sat out the Season in its tub on the patio, a gift to the local birds, until it was carried away to the cruncher for its new incarnation. I lamented its waste as a tree, for I'd loved it too; but the special 1991 tree, a true gift, is *still* with us, still mostly green, still somewhat fragrant. Where the green has dimmed, the dry needles have not fallen, nor are they brown. My sister noted they have a *golden* cast.

Before typing these words, I turned its tiny lights on and sat loving it, and it seemed eternal. Its sole ornaments otherwise are small wooden plaques decoupaged with Scripture, the same ornaments Luther wore an orbit of Jupiter ago. There is no doubt they've inspired its mystic longevity.

Christmas Trees

D.C. Berry

When dragged out to the street,
they lie there like blind sea monsters
left stranded on the beach,

some still with angel hair
and fringed with tinsel, which the wind
will flash into a quivering silver

flame. Ours is still out there
gaudy as the Grand Old Opry. If a heart
could have a hangover,

my eyes would ache,
the thing all huddled at the curb like it
is a Baptist date-rape

the morning after, though right through the last
verse of "Silent Night" it had been perfect.
Now, lying out there like a stripped rocket.

Peas for Christmas

Jo Stevenson

I remember it well, that Christmas, even now. And yet I was barely beyond the toddler stage. I was trudging beside my mother on a Melbourne suburban street toward the tramstop junction.

It was almost noon and the fierce Australian sun, relentless in its intensity, made me feel sticky like the pavement beneath my feet. From time to time my flimsy sandals would stick as they sank into the rubbery asphalt.

"Mommy, I'm tired. My legs hurt," I said, pulling away from her hand. Sinking to the curb with my feet in the gutter, I saw my white sandals were smeared with the blackish tar. "Joanie, get up at once," Mom said angrily. "You'll get your dress dirty. You know I was up early this morning ironing it. I washed it last night, dead tired as I was after work." Helping me to my feet, she spoke more gently, "Come on now, Pet, only two more stops to go and then we'll be at the junction. I have enough money for the fare from there. The tram will take us to the terminus and then it's an easy walk on the dirt road to Auntie Nan's. She'll have a nice Christmas dinner for us."

The thought of Christmas dinner — a hot, heavy meal in the middle of the day — did little to inspire me to continue the weary journey. But I knew there was only enough money for the last two sections. My dream was to one day have enough pennies to buy a tram and let all little girls and their mothers ride free.

As we walked beneath the merciless blue sky a tram passed and stopped ahead of us. We had almost reached it when it took off again. "No matter," Mom said. "Another will come." I saw my mother looking at the wet patches on my tight bodice. But there was no shade; just a wooden bench seat.

At last another tram came. We climbed inside, welcoming its protection. As it swayed on its way, I wished I could stay on it forever. But all too soon we arrived at the terminus and were walking in the sun once more.

Relief at reaching my aunt's house mingled with a sick feeling in the pit of my stomach, for I was scared of my stern Uncle Bill. He not only believed that children should be seen and not heard, but that they should eat everything put before them and thank God and their generous relatives for it.

I guessed that they were waiting for us, for my cousins were already seated at the dining table. My uncle lifted me onto a cushion on a chair at the end of the table and then sat at the head of it. I looked at the enormous platter of food set in front of him — a large leg of dark gray lamb, thickly covered in pale, yellowish gravy, congealing as I anxiously watched him serving the food. Surrounding the lamb were floury-looking potatoes and peas — piles and piles of peas — bright green, hard and shiny. My plate was the last to be filled by my uncle: slab of gray lamb, thick with lumpy gravy, large floury potato and two huge ladles of those shiny, hard peas. I forced down the greasy meat and dry potato. I tried hard to chew those peas. I gagged and gave up.

I sat quietly hoping no one would notice. But Uncle Bill looked over at my plate. I could see his eyes glinting before they narrowed as they fastened on my uneaten peas. "Eat them, Joanie," he said, or I will force them down your throat with an iron pipe I keep in the garage."

I never did see that pipe. My throat contracted as he spoke, making it even harder to swallow those peas; but swallow I did.

Then Uncle Bill sat back, raised his wine glass and smiling at everyone said, "Happy Christmas."

[From a novel in progress]

Bateman's

Linda Pinnell

Emily shivered as she bent down to pick up the morning paper. It wasn't freezing cold — the temperature was still in the thirties. But it was cold, that kind of a damp, bone-chilling cold that could only be attributed to a West Virginia December. It was easy to forget those things when you'd been living in the Sun Belt, with its Chamber of Commerce title implying an abundance of warmth and prosperity.

Yes, it was easy to forget the gray, drizzling Decembers that refused to snow for Christmas, stubbornly waiting to incapacitate the mountain roads with January blizzards.

She stepped back inside to the warm, bright buzz of her sister's kitchen. It was almost overwhelming, but it blocked out her more recent memories of Miami, a secure but unsatisfying job, a barren fifteen-year marriage that had just petered out. She smiled grimly. The marriage hadn't even had the decency to end in a final blaze of drama. It had just slipped quietly through her fingers, and she hadn't even cared enough to clasp them closed.

And so she had come home. Home for Christmas. She hadn't been home for Christmas since college. Her decision to come back had been impulsive, but right. She couldn't stand the present, couldn't face the future; that left only the past.

Her sister Margaret, in one of her weekend-rate phone calls, had invited her for Christmas. At the thought of being part of a family, Emily hadn't even hesitated but had caught the next flight out. As her plane had circled Greater Pitt, she realized she had done no Christmas shopping. That had been three days ago. Today was Christmas Eve.

23

"Let me see the paper," Missy said, flipping it open to the comics page.

Lisa stared over her shoulder. "What's my horoscope say?"

Both girls were gulping down Pop Tarts and coffee. Last night Emily had spoken to Margaret about the propriety of teenagers drinking coffee. Margaret had merely chuckled, "Oh, Em — if I could only be sure it stopped with coffee."

The subject had dropped there. Somehow the years had smoothed the rough edges of sibling rivalry, but at a cost. Neither would risk disagreements now — it was simpler just to let a subject drop.

"I need to do some last minute shopping," Emily said, stirring Cremora into her coffee. Emily hated Cremora, but one made concessions when visiting a home where everyone drank their coffee black. "I'm thinking of going to Bateman's."

"Oh, god! Auntie Em, you can't be serious," shrieked Lisa.

Auntie Em. That had been her nickname since the first time the girls had watched *The Wizard of Oz*.

"Why not?"

Missy snorted derisively. (Another gesture Emily found unattractive in a teenage girl, but hadn't broached with Margaret.) "Boy, you can tell you've been gone a long time. Everybody shops at the mall."

"I know Bateman's is open — I saw their ad in the paper."

"Yeah," Missy snickered, "they're open all right."

A car honked and without even a good-bye the girls scooped up their coats and bolted out the door.

Margaret sighed. "It's changed, Em. It's not like you remember. Maybe you should just go to the mall."

"I'm not going to the mall, Margaret. I've always hated malls. They're so homogeneous, so impersonal."

Margaret, practical as ever, asked, "Why don't you just give cash, Em? Mom and Dad could use the money. My kids will spend it on things that you and I would never dream of buying them; and with Will laid off, I don't want you to buy us anything when we can't reciprocate the favor."

"Favor! Really, Margaret, you are my sister. Besides, having me here for Christmas is your gift to me. But — as for everyone else, you know I'd rather give something more personal."

"Suit yourself. Just don't forget, we're supposed to pick Mom and Dad up for Mass tonight."

Emily smiled. Some things never changed.

◇

Emily would never have admitted it, but she was glad she hadn't shopped yet. George and Edna, who now lived in the high rise, seemed pale imitations of her parents; Margaret and Will, depressed beyond what a layoff would constitute; Margaret's daughters grown to total strangers. She wondered if they had used any of her Christmas gifts of the past five years. Their tastes did not even faintly reflect her own. Perhaps Thomas Wolfe was right. Or perhaps it was only an attack of post-divorce/pre-Christmas melancholy.

Since the rental car had good wipers and an efficient defroster, the drizzle was of little consequence. Bundled in a heavy bouclé jacket, Emily drove around town for an hour. Some landmarks were intact: the high school, an ecumenical mix of churches, a small pharmacy. Some changes were disorienting. What used to be the post office was now an office building. Mailmen had set up shop in a brick and glass monstrosity a few blocks south. Finally she came to the main street she knew so well.

She couldn't believe her good fortune. A parking space in front of Bateman's. As she started to parallel park, she noticed for the first time that there were plenty of places in front of Bateman's, in front of any store. Curious, she decided to circle. Scanning the four-block main street, she realized there were few other stores.

Bateman's, the Liberty Grill, Faulkner's Sporting Goods, the News Stand. Punctuation marks in a long sentence of boarded store fronts.

She made the loop by the Greyhound terminal. Did anyone really get off there anymore? Or did people only board, eager to escape the dusty, dimly-lit depot, populated by the occasional winos who moved in from the bridge in inclement weather?

She came back to the original parking spot and pulled in. Her mouth was stubbornly set. She would buy at Bateman's.

As Emily viewed the store, a rush of memories came over her. Her parents had always brought her and Margaret here a few weeks before Christmas to "talk to Santa" while they divined what the girls hoped to find under the tree.

On later Christmases, she and Margaret would come to town right after school on Fridays to grab a wonderfully high cholesterol dinner at the Liberty and shop till all the stores closed. Now there was only one real store, Bateman's.

Emily put her money in the meter and walked to the entrance. The display windows were decorated exactly as she had remembered them. Although he was a little chipped in places, there was something reassuring about watching Mickey Mouse trim his tree. But Minnie's dress looked drab and faded next to a new line of women's holiday wear. The incongruity was disturbing.

Then there was the foyer. Bateman's had always advertised the town's tallest Christmas tree — and first artificial one to boot. It still boasted its twelve-foot height, but for the first time it showed its substance more as errant bowl brushes than blue spruce boughs. As the lights shone brightly on the tarnished silver ornaments, the eye followed the natural line upward to the tinsel star which now, alas, served only to point out a dingy ceiling badly in need of replastering.

The first floor passed inspection, acceptable but unexciting. She was drawn toward the elevator. One of her fondest childhood memories had been Bateman's elevator. It ran not by means of buttons, but by means of a heavy brass hydraulic lever mounted waist high. The lever had to be pulled to exactly the right position in the arc to line the elevator up with the proper floor.

Emily's favorite elevator operator had been a tall, Black woman with heavy gold jewelry and magenta nail polish. She always ran the elevator smoothly, with no jerks or stops or jimmying to get it lined up with the outside floor. It was always perfect. She wouldn't have even needed to say, "Watch your step, please," but she always did, in a clear, confident voice.

And that had been why Emily had always loved the elevator. It had represented power to her. In fact, and she had never told anyone this, except her best friend Sara Jane Lawson, that had been her grade school ambition: to run the elevator at Bateman's. Of course, that had been before college and the MBA. But even in this day of radical feminism, Emily could think of few jobs that afforded such power.

She reached the elevator and pushed the gilt-framed UP button. The doors opened to reveal Bateman's most expensive renovation, an automatic elevator spouting Christmas Muzak. Disgusted, she took the stairs.

On the second floor she stopped to look for trendy sweaters for her nieces. She had leafed through *Glamour* and *Vogue* to arm herself with ideas of what was fashionable. Apparently few people at Bateman's read *Glamour*. The generic sweaters looked like they had been on the edge of fashion for a decade; possibly they had been hanging around for that long. Nothing here for the girls.

She decided to go to the toy department on fourth for old times sake.

"May I help you?" asked an elderly clerk. It was like *The Twilight Zone*. She was the Bateman's clerk of twenty years ago — blue, polyester print dress, black orlon cardigan sporting a circle pin with single pearl.

"Are toys still on fourth?"

"Why, dear, fourth floor's been used for storage for ten years, since we did away with furniture. Children's goods are on third with housewares."

"How appropriate."

The clerk looked unsure whether to laugh or be insulted, so she did neither. Emily took the elevator this time, still ruing its modernness and Christmas Muzak. The ride was blessedly brief.

The floors were still uncarpeted, but not with the basketball court sheen she had expected; more the dusty, oiled look of floors in a country grade school. She stared at the barren territory, remembering when even people who didn't have children would venture there to see what a real toy department looked like. Now a few shabby teddies and imitation Cabbage Patch dolls sat perched above the towels, sheets, and baby clothes.

She whirled to leave and bumped into another clerk — the same clerk?

"I was looking for the toy department, for Santa."

The clerk looked puzzled at the absence of a child, then seemed to identify Emily as the toddler as she kindly explained, "But, dear, Santa doesn't come here anymore."

"I'm not surprised," Emily mumbled before she fled down the three flights of stairs.

Outside she sat rigidly in the car, careful to let it warm up before pulling out. There was still time to go to the mall, but she decided against it. She flipped on the radio, only to be assaulted by a Chipmunk's Christmas song. She instantly quelled Alvin and his melodic fraternity. She took a final look at Bateman's.

The past had no purpose except in reverie. It was never like you remembered it, but only gave a sense of false security when the future took too much courage to contemplate. Emily knew now that she had that courage. She had sought that safe haven and found it tarnished, lacking. Better to remember it like some childhood Christmas ornament — gleaming, shimmering, slightly out of reach.

By the time she pulled into Margaret's driveway, Emily had mentally balanced her checkbook, subtracting each cash gift, and figuring the first available flight back after Christmas.

Margaret met her at the door and stared at her empty hands. "Still hiding things before Christmas?"

"The mall was crowded."

"I thought you were going downtown." Emily smiled wanly and said, "I never really made it downtown."

A Christmas Letter

Betty Wald

In the midst of a very stress-filled holiday, I was receiving some happy Christmas letters in which only wonderful things were happening in the families of friends. Since I was going slightly crazy at the time, trying to prepare for a Chanukah celebration for my husband's family, which included gifts for seven children, spouses and grandchildren, plus Christmas festivities for my four children, also with spouses and babies, these letters seemed unreal. I decided to write a realistic letter and send it along with our holiday cards. I had fun writing it and it helped relieve some of my stress.

Dear Friends,

Every year I vow I will go into the City to see the tree at Rockefeller Center, gaze at the Tiffany windows, hear *The Messiah* sung at Carnegie Hall. I will have tea at the Plaza and listen to Christmas hymns at St. Thomas' Church. I will go on candlelight tours of historic homes and attend midnight mass. And most of all, I will be calm.

Every year I cut out articles in *The Times* that review all the store windows, all the places to hear music, all the restaurants that have brunch along with fireplaces and garlands. I buy magazines that have features like, "Ten Ways to Beat Holiday Stress." I vow to be merry and calm.

And here it is, three days to our Chanukah celebration, two weeks to Christmas and I am gritting my teeth, crossing out items on lists and adding new ones. I am still shopping for gifts, still planning menus, still unpacking ornaments. The menorah is out, the crèche is in its box, and somewhere a tree is waiting to be picked.

"Can we have shrimp cocktail before dinner Sunday or is it a no-no?" I ask my husband. "What color do the menorah candles have to be? Should I make chicken soup?"

"Where is the wrapping paper? Did you hide the scotch tape?" he asks me in turn. "Will you pack the gifts for my son David in a box and take it to the post office? Can you pick up a cake or something for the office?"

We pass each other in the hall, going opposite directions, tossing reminders over our shoulders.

"Don't forget the holiday party at work Thursday and the dinner dance next week," my husband says. "Take my fancy shirt to the cleaners, please. Did you get a gift for the head technician?"

"Both my daughters and their families will stay over Christmas Eve," I tell my husband. "I'll have to buy sheets for the pull-out couch downstairs. Leave me some money. Do you think you can make potato pancakes for my family for Christmas brunch?"

"Ask me later, I can't think now," he says. "Can you make real applesauce for Sunday? Don't buy Motts and dump in some cinnamon."

"Ask me later," I say and we blow kisses and get in our cars. My radio blares on, Christmas music fills the air. "Oh shut up," I say and turn it off.

I will be calm, I tell myself, damn it, I will be calm.
                    HAPPY HOLIDAYS!

My letter seemed to sound the right note for a lot of people during the holiday season. Not only did I blow off steam by writing it, it was fun to get calls from friends like the one who said, "I got such a kick out of your letter. I think it was the first time I've laughed since the holiday decorations went up. I know we're supposed to be happy but I'm stressed to the max." And then I'd hear the friend's story and we'd laugh about the craziness of it all.

Others told me how much they disliked those upbeat photocopied Christmas letters. "My kids are okay but gee, when I read the exploits of some families, I start comparing, and mine always come up short. Your letter was a relief."

Some people never mentioned the letter and I didn't hear from my friend Millie in Boston — you know, the one whose daughter worked with Mother Theresa over the summer and whose son interned in Senator Kennedy's office. I wonder if she'll send me her annual letter this Christmas. I hope not.

Credo

Anonymous Grinch

I repudiate the Christmas traditions which I remember and know about.

I reject and dedicate energy to oppose and weaken and discredit the belief system which underlies these traditions.

I do not believe that Jesus was born of a Virgin on Christmas and died on the cross and was raised on the third day to save believers in him from sin and damnation. I believe that that idea is both stupid and immoral.

I do not believe that Santa Claus brings gifts to good children.

I believe we should try an economy which does not depend on the exchange of gifts at the end of the year. The invention, distribution and sale of items that do not correspond to what humans need or want amounts to waste and stupidity.

I do not believe that trees should be killed in honor of any of these beliefs. I do not believe that farmland should be used to plant and harvest such a useless crop. If corn or wheat isn't needed, the trees should be allowed to mature.

I do not believe that mythology should be burdened with the task of teaching the young, and the old, that altruism should be given a one-day annual try-out, because it is so sentimentally "nice."

Ecology, human solidarity and planetary unity all indicate that we should get rid of Christmas. I intend to weaken it a little, by withdrawing my emotional involvement.

The True Meaning of Grinchness

Teresa Hubley

Many people say they know people who are "real Grinches," by which they mean people who do not "like" Christmas, for whatever reason. The truest Grinch I ever met was someone who absolutely adores Christmas and lives for it with unsurpassed passion. Or maybe it would be more technically correct to say she lives for the process of Christmas (what I call "X-mas") and not the content.

The point of view of my "true Grinch," whom I will refer to as "Joan," was well summarized in a conversation with her son, Jack, a close friend of mine, which I swear really took place on one of our holiday visits to his family's home. Jack had referred to something as being, "Just like the Grinch." Joan looked thoughtful for a moment and then said, "You mean that show where he took away all their presents so they couldn't have a nice Christmas?"

"No," said Jack, "That wasn't the point. They had a nice Christmas anyway!"

"To my mind, Christmas is about giving," said Joan.

"No, no, no!" said Jack, "That wasn't the point either! They had a nice Christmas and there was no giving, no presents."

"I'm not talking about television now," Joan replied, "I'm talking about real life and Christmas is about *giving*!"

There in a nutshell is why Jack no longer goes to his mother's house for Christmas.

His brother, Kurt, had tried a more direct approach at Thanksgiving dinner a few nights before as she held court at the head of the table. He informed Joan that she did too much at the holidays, got too stressed out and was always getting sick. "No one wants you to get sick," he intoned, "We come to your house to be with you. We don't care what you *do*. You can serve hot dogs for all I care."

Joan's eyes were teary by now and she declared, in a quivering voice, "Maybe there will be no Christmas next year then. My husband and I will just go out to dinner."

The assembled celebrants were paralyzed, afraid to push Joan over the edge into a crying jag. In the lapsed silence she added, "Couldn't it just be about a mother's love? I just do it out of love for you."

That sentiment came straight from an oatmeal commercial. I overheard Joan talking back to a commercial that tried to convince women they were bad mothers, if they didn't give their children oatmeal in the morning before school. She did not say what you would expect. She was going along with it. "You see? That's right! That's what I was trying to tell Kurt but he wouldn't listen to me. He thinks I'm trying to impress somebody."

Joan seems no more aware that the commercial was taking advantage of her than she is of Kurt's constant and very successful plots to shock her by growing his hair and getting himself tattooed. She just gets shocked. Of course, Kurt probably got his taste for shock from Joan herself who once tried to impress her children with "the *highest* blood pressure" her doctor had "*ever, ever* seen."

Christmas in Joan's house is a major production, something on the scale of an old Hollywood Biblical classic, perhaps even a disaster film with a title like "Towering Turkey" or "Pumpkinquake." The one Christmas I spent there was almost ruined for want of a single can of cranberry sauce. We spent several desperate hours in the dark of Christmas Eve being whisked around by Joan's husband, Arnold, driving as fast as was prudent, while Joan shouted directions, searching for an open grocery store. There *had* to be cranberries, Joan assured us. That was just the way it had to be.

The goal seems to be to sate everyone's appetite beyond the "full" stage and into the "I may need to barf" stage. For example, every year there is enough food to wipe out famine on the planet Earth and every year Joan declares, "I did too much. Well, next year I won't make so much." Everyone gets at least three presents plus money, after which Joan and her mother, Bess, will give the standard lecture about how everyone got too much and no one is ever grateful enough. The way they talk about Joan's grandson getting too many presents often implies that the presents appeared from out of nowhere and their appearance could not be controlled. "He gets way too much," they declare, as if they had no part whatsoever in producing the presents. In the end, they may summarize Christmas with, "Well, it was a nice Christmas...everybody got good," followed by, "We *got* good because we *gave* good," nods of agreement all around.

The pace at Christmas is usually very brisk. Tempers are short and the preparations predictably degenerate into a skirmish or two, usually over something very minor such as the way the tablecloth is placed. There is dashing around, flustered hollering and the constant chirping of the neighbor lady's voice as she comes and goes. Exhaustion sets in for the observer long before the guests arrive. "I like a noisy Christmas!" Joan needlessly declared as she jogged past Jack and me, huddled on the couch, wishing for a cup of very strong, black coffee.

Joan gave me another insight into herself by asking me if my mother "gives a big Christmas." I have never thought of my mother, or anyone, as "giving" Christmas. I always thought of it as something we all did as a family. It's easy to picture Joan with a megaphone hollering directions as the Christmas production gets underway. In fact, with her commanding voice, she needs no megaphone. My eardrums rattle just thinking about her in full voice in the middle of a holiday. This is why Kurt and Jack go unheeded in their insistence that she tone down the production. To her mind, Christmas is *hers* to give, not Kurt's or Jack's to share and enjoy. They are only being ungrateful sons by refusing to take it in exactly the form she dishes it out.

It does not take much insight to figure out where Joan's rigid ideas come from. I recognize them in my own family from stories told about desperately trying to cover up the fact that one's parents are alcoholic. Appearances become everything. The content loses all its meaning and the process becomes the goal. The neighbors are watching. God is watching. The show has to be big and be perfect. That way, everyone will think your family is right as rain, even if they are barely holding together. Joan is giving Kurt and Jack the only kind of family she knows how to give, a scripted production.

This is how a single can of cranberries got to be crucial. It is also why the claim that family is important to Christmas rings hollow in this and many cases like it. This is not a family event, except in the sense that family is present. There is no "sharing," only "giving." Worse yet, it's not even that simple. Christmas has become a package bristling with symbolic gestures and hidden messages. It has become fearsome and stressful, wondering whether one will make the "wrong move" and upset everyone.

Then there is the fact that Joan and her husband live with Bess, Joan's mother. Joan often seems to resent this arrangement and no doubt her daily struggles to remind everyone who is really in charge reflect that resentment. Christmas is just another chance to publicly declare that Joan may live with her mother but Joan is very much in command and can do what is "expected" of her.

For example, Bess works as a nanny to a "well to do" couple in the neighborhood. The blue collar family she comes from sees this as a rejection, Bess' way of saying they weren't good enough. Joan takes it especially hard. Every time Bess begins to praise her employer's family, Joan mutters under her breath and turns away. Bess' employer made the mistake of giving her a lavishly expensive Christmas gift the year I spent Christmas with them. There was an explosion of angry complaints: "That's too expensive!" "I should make her take it back!" The real insult was that they could so casually buy such a thing when Joan and her husband worked all year to launch their annual Christmas fiasco.

Joan really does love her children, which makes it all the harder to cope with the way she overproduces her "X-mas" celebration. If she were deliberately trying to make the children miserable and ruin their holidays, it would be easier. Her family could just tell her to go to Hell and that would be it. As it is, they realize there is nothing they can do to change Joan and still maintain the thread of their family bond. Too much of her identity is now bound up in the thing. The best course at holidays, they have discovered, is to let Joan have her way and be wary of any situation that might lead to tears. It is Christmas in the tense ceasefire mode.

When Jack made his one direct plea to Joan before his last X-mas in her house, she just smiled, shrugged and said, "That's the way it is."

"It's as if Christmas is totally out of control. It's bigger than they are," Jack commented later. In fact, this is exactly the truth. In some ways Christmas gets bigger and bigger every year, not the pleasant event I remember as a child but something like being chased by Godzilla. As Jack and Kurt become more independent, it gets harder to grab their attention and hold it, I suppose.

Jack had told me before the conversation about the "true" meaning of the Grinch, that his mother always hated "How The Grinch Stole Christmas." Her reason, she said, was that the show gave a "bad message about Christmas," though she had never at that time watched it all the way through. While Joan did not elaborate nor would Jack speculate, I presume the "message" was that Christmas can be taken away from us if we are somehow not careful enough. In that sense, she shares the Grinch's belief that Christmas cannot come without all the "ribbons, boxes and bows." This makes her more like the Grinch than people who "hate" Christmas either on principle or because it's "too commercial."

The real irony is that she has accused Jack of being the

Grinch because he wants a different kind of Christmas from the
one she keeps mechanically producing in the name of "family
values." Her children are not allowed to reject a small part of the
package. When they say "no" to any part of the way Joan
"gives" Christmas, they are completely rejecting her and
everything she stands for. Given this unhappy choice, Jack has
chosen to celebrate Christmas on his own and try to spend
Thanksgiving with his family instead, mostly because it involves
fewer dimensions: no presents, only one "feast," a shorter round
of highly scripted visitations from family members and fewer
days at home with a frantic executive producer. Jack argues now
that everyone has a right to their own Christmas and if we want
it quiet, we'll get it quiet. In the end, center stage among the
remaining family, the Grinch still gets her way.

Christmas Compromise

Mary Hartman

"I hurt," said Heart one morning.

The other organs paused in alarm. Was Heart signaling a breakdown?

"Nonsense!" someone grumbled. "Poppycock!"

Engrossed in probing its chambers, Heart wasn't sure which organ had spoken. But it must be Brain; no one else used such a superior tone, such stuffy words.

"I'm really stupid," Heart flashed back. "Everytime I ask for your sympathy, I set myself up to be ridiculed."

"A few more points on your IQ and you'd know that what you get from me is intelligence," Brain replied.

No response.

"Where does it hurt?" Brain asked, trying to sound a bit more solicitous.

"Can't get its pulse," Heart replied. "It's a vague..."

"Vagueness is your 'beat,' Heart. More analysis, please."

"That's *your* field, Brain. Who the hell ever heard of an analytic heart?"

"Ah! At last. Spunk."

"Spunk comes from the backbone," Heart retorted.

"Temper, temper, Heart! Where's the pain? Middle of the chest? Left arm? Shoulder?"

"I told you, Brain, it's not really an ache. Just this overall heaviness."

"When you say 'heavy,' does it feel like a rock's sitting on you?"

"Wet sponge, more like. I feel full of tears, but there's a blockage somewhere. I simply can't break down and have a good cry."

"Oh, good grief, Heart! What is the date?"

"I know the date. I never miss the Holidays."

"Now look who's stupid! I fall for your trap every year, Heart."

"Well, you start it. Thanksgiving shows up on the calendar and you turn into the guru of cranks."

"Hey, don't try to color me with your guilt, Heart. I've never made any bones about my feelings. Soon as I learned to spell, I vowed *never* to capitalize 'thanksgiving' or 'holiday' or 'christmas.'"

"Yes, but don't you dare deny that the Holidays still touch you, Brain. If you weren't losing cells, you'd remember that I'm on the twenty-four-hour shift. I hear your pillow talk; I watch your REMs and observe your dreams. I feel you struggling with depression."

"Ah, but I *win,* Heart. I don't wallow in those god-awful carols like you do. Bing Crosby dreaming of that syrupy 'white christmas.' Sheesh!"

"You liar! You know good and well you don't win all the time. Sure, when you're awake you keep a tight grip on your control. But when you fall asleep, Brain, I hear you mumbling about going to see the grandkids in Missouri. Why, the other night you were trying to figure how you could avoid crossing Kansas' icy highways. Come on, Brain. 'Fess up. You miss those cute little urchins."

A lull ensued, quiet except for Aorta's expansions and contractions and the clicks of Brain's memory index.

"Well, kiddo," Brain said finally, "what the heck is christmas anyway? Christ's birthday? Hah!"

"No, but at this time of year my heartsong is to be near the ones I love."

"Sure, because you fantasize that christmas is angels and santa and packages tied up in bright red and green ribbons that never fray."

"Mere symbols, Brain. It's the love that goes into selecting just the right gift and the imagination that goes into wrapping it."

"Nuts! You really should spend less time with Eyes. You two lollygag around on the sofa all day, watching those old-timey black-and-white movies on AMC. No wonder Doc bitched about your heart rate last week."

Heart "harummphed" stonily, but Brain ignored the message.

"Aw, come on, have a heart, Heart. Let's bury the hatchet and go rubberneck the christmas shoppers at the mall. I'll read their exhausted, harried minds to you. They're not making loving choices; they're scared spitless of pickpockets and trying to forget credit card balances."

"Oh, Brain, I would really *despise* myself if I became so cynical. What about all those sweet mommies and daddies who fish the Santa Claus letters out of the mailboxes and run down to the toy stores? They'd cut off an arm before they'd destroy a child's faith."

"Dear Heart, those parents are making up for their own disillusioned childhoods. If we wanted to, we could rationalize a spending spree, too. Have you forgotten that chintzy plastic eighteen-wheeler? Surely you recall how big and sturdy it looked on the TV screen. Remember what happened the first time we took it on a run?"

"Well, yes. It turned into a nine-wheeler before we got around to the turkey." Heart's beat sounded like an indistinct chuckle. "But they don't all fall apart, Brain. Besides, what's wrong with trying to bring joy to a little child's heart?"

"Joy is elusive; it lets us down. Disappointed children become uptight parents who finally admit they can't work miracles, either. Some spend the holidays in alcoholic hazes; others frazzle themselves, baking cookies, untangling light cords, wasting money on ugly ties and flannel nighties. They'll make everybody happy. Or else. In the long-run, nobody is happy, least of all themselves."

"Can't argue with that, Brain, but what's bothering me — "

"Don't tell me, Heart. I know. You're lonely. Every year, christmas arrives and you still haven't got anyone to hug."

"Right. But I don't want to become a hard-head like you. I want to blubber at *Miracle on Thirty-fourth Street*. Sit in the dark and gaze at sparkling tree lights. Enjoy feeling sentimental."

Heart sent Lungs a "sigh" message.

"You're so smart, Brain, what's the answer?"

All functions paused, awaiting Brain's response.

"Oh, all right, Heart. What if we compromise? I'll be less critical of your emotionalism, and you'll meet me halfway and accept our situation as the best possible. No grandkids, no warm hugs, not for the time being, anyway. Maybe all that will change one of these days."

"One can't help wishing, Brain. But I do hate 'maybes.' I can't turn into a defeatist and never even try to change things."

"Yeah, but we can stop making ourselves miserable about things we can't change. Right now, I'd say we're operating to the best of our abilities. The world does contain people we love, even if they live far away." Brain paused, then spoke softly. "Does that help?"

"I do feel calmer, Brain."

"Good. Let's design a new Christmas card. Instead of 'Merry Christmas' and 'Happy New Year,' let's say, 'Serenity to All.'"

"Say, Brain, do you realize you just capitalized all those words?"

"They're only words, Heart."

"How does this strike you Brain? 'Have a Positive Christmas and a Serene New Year!'"

"Just right, Heart. Just right."

FAMILY

Christmas is a celebration of birth, and therefore a celebration of family. Whereas the story of the first Christmas describes how a family is bestowed with spiritual blessings in the context of difficult physical conditions, today's family Christmases are as often about crises of the soul fought out in arenas of comfort and indulgence. While family is a blessing for many, for some it is a curse. Most of us will spend our entire lives trying to reconcile our muddled feelings about our endlessly mutating families.

Our "Family" chapter is comprised of holiday stories about the shaping of new families and the reshaping, sometimes dismantling, of old ones — with varying degrees of success. Yet with all of this shaping and reshaping going on, there is still a longing for the old forms, even a bitterness at their loss.

If it can be said that no two families are alike, it can also be said that no one family is alike. Only in the photographs does that monster called "family" stand still and present relationships in seemingly clear focus. Apart from two dimensional photos and charts, however, in three dimensions and four, families are messy business. And nothing seems to frustrate us more than exactly this, that such a huge gulf stands between the picture perfect, Christmas postcard, scrubbed cheek, shined shoe ideal of family, and the ragged edges of our true-life experience. No wonder the Christmas season pushes all our buttons, what with Norman Rockwell, Bing Crosby, Currier and Ives, and a whole host of other icons and icon-makers — not to mention the Holy Family itself — seeming to mock our blundering attempts at peace, love and harmony with their very perfection. In this chapter you will find bitter childhood memories of the traditional Christmas gone wrong, seasonal sweetness soured by too much drink, escalating patterns of abuse, the ideal of hearth and home exposed as sham.

The positive message is that even if it is too late to change the families we were born into, what they did for us, or to us, or didn't do, we might at least change our point of view. If we do take the trouble to go home again, we may even learn something new from our own families. And it helps to remember that only gingerbread men are stamped out of the same cookie cutter; real people and real families come in all different shapes.

Christmas Eve

CB Follett

Tearing through night in staccato light-bursts.

I'm in the front seat next to the driver, a boy with red hair and
    a blue uniform,
    the seat belt a tight band across my heart.
I cannot twist to look into the wild theater of the ambulance
    where orange vested people move like eels in a pail.

Between them, tiny as a clothespin doll, my mother on her way to
    unknown doctors, and a cold gurney,
    carrying the relentless hammer of pain down her sternum.

The goose is browning, turkey sputters in the pan
    but she can hold her pain no longer and the siren's
    ululation cuts the night.

This is not how she wants it, disrupting the champagne and
    kisses, delaying dinner, her daughter near tears.
Grandsons uncertain, try to look both somber and joyous
    and to one side, a baby is absorbed in ornaments
    first hung by my mother, eighty trees ago.

ER is crowded and faces in the waiting room defenseless.

We walk in and out among heart monitors, triangles
    of doctors, martialed gasps of pain, x-rays,
    doctors, echo test, ultrasound, doctors, EKG,
    oxygen oxygen oxygen

The Ruby and The Pearl

Marillen Cassatt

Life is like a piece of grass,
Waving in the wind,
Waiting,
    Waiting,
And then it's stepped on.   *Susan B. age 10*

We know she loved us far too much
to want to leave or hurt us.
She who knew pain so well
would not will to cause it.

The small boy knew her caring
he saw it in her eyes,
as she tucked the small stuffed bear
beneath his chin.
"Pretend this is your violin,
show me how you will hold it."

The precocious girl saw reassurance..
and... was it fear in her teachers eyes?
Remembering... what?
"The goal must not be to play flawlessly
but to enjoy...
and experience wonder-filled moments
when you allow the bow to play,
and you become the tone."

The teacher had been too young to understand
when first the Mad-dog Depression bared it's teeth
and pulled her spirit down.
"What have I done?
    Do I deserve this?
        I must do better, try harder,
                            concentrate!"
She fought — willed to pry loose
it's iron grip from her mind.
She ....learned to wear a mask
of self confidence and strength;
covered the scars on her spirit
with humorous cynicism and wit.
She set high goals, reached many,
suffered self-hatred
when she missed the mark.

Discipline
    of the metronome
        ballet bar
developed the attractive and vibrant
appearance and demeanor of the ruby,
hard,
    abrasive
        corundum.
The fragile part of her nature
dwelled deep,
    a pearl
                easily scratched
crushed by the ill-chosen word.

    When she was older she labeled her depression, The Monster,
and she sought to find meaning in her pain.
"For has not God counted our tears, and kept them in a bottle?"
    She searched, and found through studying the
demons of others, that some had learned to use their suffering.

She practiced,
      and taught others,
"to find meaningfulness by realizing creative values, by achieving tasks; to realize experiential values, the Good, the True and the Beautiful; and ultimately, to use the freedom to decide the very attitude with which we face our unchangeable suffering." (Frankl)

She began to use the deep wounds in her soul as reservoirs for empathy and love, from which she drew generous doses of good humor, to place healing upon the wounds and scratches of friends and family, the clients she counseled; and more recently and most happily for her....upon the young lives of her nieces and music students.

She replenished those reservoirs by gathering to herself every kindness and gesture, each friendship she received. On her desk we found them, the pictures, trinkets and letters lovingly fashioned by small hands and large. They looked to her for approval and acceptance, and she reached deep to give each a piece of herself.

"The greatest blessing is to know that one is loved unconditionally, not for what we are, but in spite of what we are." (Victor Hugo)

Nurturing each with wit and wisdom, she imparted to them the meaning of life, "is just to love... and be loved in return".

"In the middle of my journey, I came upon a dark wood," wrote Dante.

We know she loved us far too much
to want to leave or hurt us.
So, what then finally broke
her "will to meaning"
and caused such distress of spirit
that she lost
her orientation toward the future?

Why did her heart cease to beat
on January the fourth,
at the age of thirty-one?

Her talents and gifts were multifaceted
and LIFE awaited, expectantly, her gifts.

"Just" the Holiday Blues:
    Guilt, the depressive's constant companion;
    Denial, protecting Him from the knowledge of debt;
    Generosity to a fault, giving gifts and entertaining friends?
    Procrastination? Unmailed flyers on her desk;
    Despair of feeling unloved? Mom, Spiegals, UPS! Christmas
gifts never arrived.
    Self-loathing? The body that is not perfect, "two
miscarriages, can't tolerate another!"
    Futility? All this debt, buy a house, have a studio;
    Underachievement? "I came to Boston to do graduate work
and six years later I cannot even decide where or what to study."
    Or was it: The knowledge that her husband knew her secret,
that she was "out of control, I'm leaving you, if you do not get
help!"
    "There are things I would rather not deal with!" she cried.

    "Just the holiday let-down?" the downside of an addictive
personality, substance abuse:
    to cure the drearies of ten days of being at home alone, while
He is working on his Masters and new job.
    to cure the guilt of not being prepared for the busy
administrative schedule at school,
    to ease the loneliness of knowing that parents and siblings are
on sun-drenched mountain slopes. She should be, also.
    to combat the allergic reactions of skin flushing, sleeplessness,
and the lack of will-power needed to get "under the light" at six
a.m. and,
              is this heart fibrillating?

She turned on the music, her comfort.
She made tapes of the new CD's, a gift
for her cousin coming tomorrow.
She called the cabin in Idaho, no one answered.
She took more of her anti-depressant, "I must feel better!"
some Benedryl "for the allergic flush,"
a little alcohol, the great remover "...to help me sleep."

He came into the living room at 2 a.m.,
admonished
her for staying up so late,
reminded
her that "it is back to work tomorrow."
Threatened to leave her.

She reacted angrily, he
retreated,
knowing that somehow,
when she was clearer-headed,
he must get her to seek help.
pondered
that puffy rash on her neck.

With the dull light of a winter dawn,
    she quietly drifted away........

As I slept in her house,
in her gown,
in the bed where her heart stopped beating
just yesterday,
she appeared to me,
barefoot and tousled,
standing in this same gown.
She imparted all these thoughts to me.

A healing comfort and good humor radiated from her smile.

With a familiar cock of her head, and clicking her fingers for my
light to come on, "Get it, Mom.... get it?"

I smiled,
somehow relieved I slept,
my will strengthened
for the sadness that lay ahead.

I'm getting it, Sue,
Please forgive us
for the slights you felt,
all so unintended.
Wish we had known
your unshared feelings.
We ruminate and guess.

We loved you so much,
thought you knew how important
and unique you were to all of us,
we saw no signs of danger.
We feel you are making others happy,
wherever you are.

I forgive you for denying me
your beautiful presence,
your mentoring on theater, music and art,
the happiness I always felt when we were together.

You must know that I prayed to
take your unspeakable hurt upon myself
because, I am your mother.

Life is like a chick,
　　　　always in danger,
　　One little nick,
　　　　　　and life stops.　　　　*Susan B., age 10*

A Ticket for My Cello

Carol Weir

They found out in November that the quartet had been booked
for three days in Miami. The timing seemed perfect for Amy and
Martin; three days at the end of December, right before
Christmas. Martin could finally come along on a trip with the
quartet because it was school vacation. Amy and Martin had
been married for five years and this was the first time that
Martin was traveling with the quartet.

"Will your manager get my plane ticket or should I get it
myself?" he asked at breakfast while Amy read the paper. It was
cold and raw outside and he had made a fire in the wood stove.
The room was warm and smelled of wood and coffee. Martin sat
across from Amy at their kitchen table, trying not to get too
excited about the trip. Amy traveled all the time with her string
quartet, but Martin's teaching schedule kept him tied down most
of the year. Amy put down the paper and looked interested.

"Oh, I don't know. I guess we should get our own tickets this
time. We're staying for a week, aren't we? We could rent a car
and drive down to Key West, make a real trip out of it. What do
you think?"

This was getting better and better. Martin hadn't really
thought of extending their stay, but why not? He wasn't due
back at school until after New Year.

"What about Spats?" He looked down at their cat who pressed
himself against his feet and seemed to listen to the travel plans.
Spats had been his cat before they married and he was getting
old. Martin noticed that he spent more time near his feet than he
used to.

"We'll take him," Amy said. "They let pets on planes and

he's too old to leave."

It was all decided then, ten days in Florida. Martin volunteered to go to the travel agent and made the arrangements. He had more time than Amy who was always either rehearsing with the quartet or practicing in the studio. He came home with the tickets the next day, along with dozens of folders about dolphins, conch shells and Key West.

"We're all set," he told her that night, "two tickets for the 20th, returning New Year's Day. I got you a window seat."

Amy was standing at the stove with her back to him, stirring something that smelled mid-eastern and delicious; he could make out onions and cumin. She turned around abruptly, her eyebrows drawn together, her mouth small. "What do you mean, two?" she asked.

Martin smiled at her, feeling very much in control of the whole trip. "We don't need a ticket for Spats. He travels in the baggage compartment. Oh, they'll take good care of him and it's only a few hours," he said. "Don't worry."

Amy raised her voice. "Martin, what about my cello?"

"What about it?"

"It needs a ticket, don't you know that? I always get a ticket for my cello. It can't go in the baggage compartment because it's too delicate." Amy looked angry.

Martin suddenly felt clumsy. "I didn't know. I mean, after all, your manager always takes care of the quartet. How would I know that your cello sits in a seat when you travel? I've never gone with you, remember?" The joy and anticipation he had felt since leaving the travel agent's office was fading.

"Well, it does. You'll have to change the tickets and get three."

"Okay, okay. Tomorrow, first thing."

They ate in silence, Martin feeling foolish and inadequate. All his resentments about Amy's career and the string quartet swirled in his head. When were they going to have a family? He felt as if his life was on hold. He was thirty-six and still didn't have his Ph.D. They didn't stay in one place long enough for him to complete a thesis. Since he had married Amy they had lived in eight different cities, ending up now in Albany where the quartet had received a grant for a year of concerts. He and the other three spouses followed the quartet, the eight of them having become a grotesque imitation of a family, Siamese quads with mates, or worse yet, a gigantic octopus or crab joined at the center. Nothing could be planned without taking the quartet into account. How could he ever go on with his own career when their residence was determined by grants given to the quartet? He had hoped that by now Amy's biological clock would have started to tick and they could plan a child. After all, she was thirty-four. But even if she could be interested in having a child, he thought grimly, the actual date of delivery would have to be coordinated with the quartet's concert schedule.

◇

By the time they left Albany, Martin had managed to put aside his gloom. He had an essentially happy nature, finding pleasure in the smallest of things, a plant on the kitchen counter growing new leaves or the sun shining on the snow outside their window. The planning of the trip had kept him absorbed for days. He loved maps; his collection in the cabinet was well worn with use. Martin himself had hardly traveled at all, but he always followed Amy's trips when she was away. Now he had outlined the road they would take from Miami when the concerts were over, passing through exotic sounding places like Key Largo and Shark Key. Martin imagined a dusty two lane road winding down the Keys, with occasional fishermen's shanties or low slung roadside saloons populated with hard faced men like Humphrey Bogart.

The reality of U.S. 1 was not what Martin had imagined. Fast food restaurants lined the highway, interspersed with warehouse-sized shell stores. Humphrey Bogart was nowhere to be seen. Spats was crying pitifully in his travel cage in the back seat. He sounded hoarse, as if he had meowed all the way from Albany in the baggage compartment. Martin tried to comfort him, looking at him in the rear view mirror. "Spats, come on, be a good cat. You're going to love Key West. There's lots of cats

there. Amy, would you give him something to eat to take his
mind off being in that cage?"

Amy stopped reading the reviews of her last concert and put
a cat treat into the cage. Spats ignored the food and tried to push
her face through the hole. She went on crying until they reached
the Lower Keys where she finally fell asleep from exhaustion.

It felt strange for Martin to be in Key West on Christmas Eve.
Amy loved it; it was her kind of place she said, "funky,"
everybody doing their own thing, totally unconnected. She
sparkled, flitting down the narrow streets. To Martin, the whole
place was too foreign, too much a collection of misfits, people
who had come to the end of the road. He liked it better in travel
brochures, and found himself wanting to go to church on
Christmas, which he hadn't done in years.

It was nine o'clock and he and Amy were sitting at a cafe,
eating salad Nicoise. Christmas carols mingled with guitar
music; a huge cactus glittered with tinsel and lights. All of a
sudden Martin was overwhelmed by the realization that this was
the best they would ever have together, an occasional trip in-
between concerts; that there never would be a traditional home
or child. He looked at Amy; she was taking in the whole street
scene, loving it all. "Let's always come here for Christmas,
Martin," she said, "I mean, if my schedule permits." Martin
didn't answer her. He wrapped up some of his tuna fish to bring
back for Spats who had become more listless since they arrived.

Christmas morning was hot and sunny. Martin got up and
looked at the cat. He hadn't eaten the fish. A thin film covered
his eyes. He was obviously sick, probably dying. What do you
do with a sick cat in Key West, he wondered, on Christmas. As
he showered, a thought came to him. They had toured the
Hemingway House yesterday. Forty-six cats, the tour guide said;
supposedly all of them were descended from the original ones
who lived there in the Thirties. $600.00 per month was spent on
cat food, they were told. Well, he thought, one more cat

wouldn't matter; why not spend $610.00? No one would notice an extra cat in that kind of crowd.

Amy slept heavily. She lay on her stomach, her left hand (the fingering one, he reminded himself) grabbing the pillow. Her bow hand was flung across the bed. Martin picked up the cat and quietly let himself out of the room. Spats lay passively in his arms as they walked down Olivia Street. No one seemed to be up. He passed little pink and gray houses dwarfed with palms and robed in hibiscus blossoms; the town was quiet.

The Hemingway House stood on the corner of Olivia and Whitehead; a brick wall surrounded it on all sides. Martin looked at the wall and gave a stroke to the cat's ears. "So long, Spats. This is better than a last trip to the vet. Good luck, guy. Mind your manners. These are high class cats, literary types." Martin looked up and down the street. Quickly, he lifted the cat up onto the brick wall. The cat stared at Martin, understood what to do, and jumped down into the yard. Martin walked away slowly, hands jammed into his pockets, tears streaming down his face.

Home for Christmas
(Night Windows. Edward Hopper. 1928. Oil.)

Michelle Miller

Anna worked Christmas Eve, amazed at the last minute rush of shoppers buying Peter Max and Van Gogh prints and feverishly constructing frames. At six she locked up the do-it-yourself frame store. The excitement of shoppers, bright faces, laughter coming out of the corner pub filled her with the dual sensation of childish enchantment and a lump-in-her-throat melancholy.

She had put aside thirty dollars and saved the ritualistic purchasing until now, remembering that a great part of Christmas Eve was being elbow-to-elbow with shoppers. In the deli she bought her favorite English strawberry preserves: whole strawberries suspended in a russet — not red — gel. Next, a loaf of fresh French bread in white paper and half a pound of dark French roast beans. At the mall supermarket she chose a carton of eggnog, one Cornish hen, oysters and walnuts for stuffing, two bayberry candles. At the record store she chose the latest Pink Floyd LP for the evening. From the drug store a flask of bourbon, a package of tinsel. Dark chocolate from the candy store. There. Every penny spent from the $30 envelope. Homeward, collar up around her neck, hat pulled down over her ears. She walked quickly, not only against the cold, but in anticipation. She felt a burst of joy that she was doing this and was going to be all right.

◊

Sepia. Cameron stretched his legs out, laid his neck against the sofa back, and stared from one print to another. The light in this room, on the heavy oak furniture, through her cream lace curtains, was brown. Sepia mats and frames on her prints,

57

printed in brown ink. Navajo rug in brown and beige tones, cat tails she had collected from the river last year. Heavy brown stoneware pot with a relief design of a lizard skeleton. Particles of dust crowded the air in a shaft of sun beaming from the window to the floor in front of him, onto his feet, onto his suitcase. Funny, he'd never noticed before that all of the prints in this room were of people alone, staring out at something beyond the frame. A child of indeterminate sex, an old man in a rocking chair, a woman holding a doll. All staring out, longing, remembering. A lonely room full of lonely faces. And now his. Odd, that a room could tell so much about its inhabitants, yet its inhabitants could be so blind to the message.

Cameron resisted re-entry. In the air as the plane had lowered to O'Hare, he thought of this room as Reality. The drive home from the airport had not yet been Reality. He had tried to feel Anna's presence during the drive, like a radio wave emanating from her new neighborhood, but he was unable to evoke her, not knowing exactly who she now was. The thought had occurred, as he had left Lima, that when he reached Chicago, he could drive straight from O'Hare to her place, have the confrontation then. There would be a confrontation; she couldn't walk away from twelve years of marriage without that. He had decided not to go through with it, though, until he had been in their house. He was beyond giving himself rational explanations for these decisions; he was simply going by what felt correct, inside, moment by moment. However, now that he was here, in this room, in his self-imposed definition of Reality, Cameron wanted to change his definition. In the air he had felt distanced from Reality. In fact, for the past three months, he now realized, he had felt that distance. No anguish he had undergone about Anna on the trail at night before sleep could touch the impact of the silence in this room. Peru, the air, anywhere but here, in this room, was Distance. It now came down to this room and this suitcase. The baggage of the last three months. The socks and t-shirts he had packed while she had watched, those poor pieces of himself so naively, trustingly placed in the suitcase, now to be unpacked in the awareness of her absence.

And the internal baggage. The accumulation of thoughts, images, realizations over the past three months. Those things he ordinarily would now be forming into language to communicate to the one closest, the one who gave his experience substance, perspective, meaning. That had always been part of the annual biology expeditions to Peru. The coming home with tales of something she had never seen. The conquering hero, yes. Why not? And the exquisite herbed meal she would have waiting, the wine, the fireplace. The long bath together.

Now his whole existence felt like the trail up the mountain, exposure to the elements, uncertainty, fear. Always before, the flight home from Lima had been relief, the square brick shapes of city blocks pulling him down, reigning him in to the place of no changes, no surprises. To the city of his nest, his home, the definitions of Professor Cameron Stone, as recognized by his community. He needed that stability as much as he needed the loss-of-self in the rain forest. The comfort was gone now. This time there were changes, and he had no idea what to anticipate next. How the house would feel, day-to-day, without her. How it would be at the university. Would there be sympathetic looks? Did they all know already, had they heard she had left him three months ago? It might already be old news to them, his community might already have adapted to the change. He himself had to catch up on his own Reality.

In the air he had felt so close to his death. Descending, looking down on miniature roof tops, the ordered squares and rectangles of arranged earth, he had felt small and vulnerable, in total danger, totally suspended in the Creator's will. He would have liked to talk to Anna about that now, with wine, by the fire. It was Christmas Eve; everything so poignant, close to the bone.

Cameron stood, irritated, crammed his hands into his pockets. That was *her* expression, "to the bone." More than once he had heard her use it, at departmental parties where discussions between two women grew sometimes intense, that urgent nodding of heads as each other spoke, that — recognition. He had envied what they shared. Sometimes he would stand in a conversation circle nearby, pretend to nod to a fellow professor's description of a ski resort, but would actually be listening to Anna's voice, to that urgency she seldom directed toward him.

"That's what I feel I need to do, get down to the bone."

She would slam her fist into her palm, her eyes fiery on the other woman's eyes. The other woman would nod vigorously.

Was this the feeling she had meant?

She always told him this house had a ghost, a woman spirit that came out when he left. Something was here, watching him, waiting for his reaction, waiting for it to begin. All the stages. He had memorized them in Peru. His friend, Joel, whose wife had left him two years ago, had told Cameron all about the stages by the campfire, as they shared a canteen of gin the first night in camp on the mountain. Anna's letter had arrived in Lima the day before, as they began their ascent. Cameron had realized then that she had mailed it before he had even left Chicago. Had bid him farewell on his journey, even knowing already that her "by the time you get this letter" was sealed and in the air.

Disbelief, then anger, blaming self, anger again, blaming her, anger, blaming both, blaming the world, then blaming no one. Resignation. He thought he had gone through all the stages in Peru. It seemed they were to begin again, now that he was here. Disbelief was setting in again. To be here, in their house, to see the objects that brought back immediate memories.

The stoneware pot Anna had commissioned from a local potter after their honeymoon. She had brought back a lizard skeleton she found when they walked in the desert, had wrapped it in tissue and saran wrap and given it to the potter to copy in relief on the pot.

The print on the wall across the room, of a child standing in water, pant legs rolled up to the knee, staring out into the sunset; that one had been inspired by an old photo she had found at his parents' of him at fourteen out at the lake. She had been captivated by the photo, said it made her feel part of him, of whatever fantasies had been going on in his mind as he stood there. Realization that these memories wouldn't be so fast in coming if Anna were here, if all were as usual. When you had objects around you daily, you forgot their source unless someone asked you. Had the objects' histories been poignantly clear to her as she packed, as she made her last tour of the house? For Cameron was sure she had made that tour, had not left quickly, without thought, without some regret. Surely not.

At least in Peru he could avoid this anguish to some degree. After the initial shock, after his anger had convinced him to stay on for the full trip, he had been able to not think of it during the day on the trail, in the camp. Only at night, before sleep. Insomnia. Images of her walking next to him, listening to him, watching him, as if she were a sun that lit his way, gave him life. Her body, torturous images of their sex together. Images of her, across the room, reading, writing letters, staring into space, those moments when he loved her with pain because she kept herself removed, ineffable, making him want her all the more. What he had never been able to discover to his satisfaction was whether or not she actually had deep feelings for him. That question was his constant source of excitement and anguish. Now that she was gone, the question still remained, although her leaving would suggest the question had been answered. But he knew it was not. She was simply gone; the urge to have more of her, the impossibility of doing so, still egged at him. The desire was here, even now, in this brown room growing dark at sundown.

Odd he hadn't noticed before how much of her was expressed in these rooms. Very little of him. Her prints, her choices in colors, pottery, rugs, furniture. His money, her choices. He had agreed with her choices. It had always felt right, felt like home, the realization of an inexpressible part of himself. What he would choose if he could choose.

Now he would have to.

It was Christmas Eve. What was she doing? With friends, with some new lover, no doubt. He poured himself a bourbon. Wandered through the house without turning on the lights. Without turning on the heat or removing his jacket or wool cap. On the stairs, stopped at the landing. No, not yet. Not the bedroom. Not her studio. Too much. Suddenly he felt exhausted, heavy, hungry but with no appetite. Hungry — for what? He crumpled onto the stair, dangling the bourbon glass between his knees, staring at the last shred of light on the living room floor. A vast quiet filled the house and the space beyond the house, a ringing, tinny silence that pushed against his ear drums. Was this where it led, that going to the bone? Two people broken apart? Those tissues so delicate, torn. How could they be so delicate? Hadn't he and Anna built their marriage carefully, for so long? Their marriage should have been stronger than this.

There was no use to it, this going inside the self, forsaking others for that. Cameron didn't like these times, this need in the women in 1978. It had happened to others he knew, their wives suddenly leaving to "find themselves." The expression had become a cliche, an irritant. He heard it everywhere, on television, radio, newspapers. Those women's magazines. One she had picked up mingled beauty tips on how to condition aging hair with such psychological tips as "Don't listen more than once a day to the news. If you watch TV news, don't listen to radio. You can't affect the crises happening around the world, concentrate on *you*, on feeling good." Damn them, their false pampering, the futile build-up of their images, their egos. Not that he was against them having careers, meaningful work. He had supported Anna's art. And what good had it done? He had never stood in her way. She had all day to herself to work while he was at the university. She had whatever funds she needed for supplies. She had total freedom, he would have supported anything she wanted to do with her art. Now she sat snug in her apartment across the city, pointing her fingers at him as the culprit, the one who had stood in her way. In her letter she had written, "...the house is so full of 'us' that even when you are gone it gets in my way." What did that mean? He had nothing to do with that. He was not to blame.

Anger against her rushed through his body. A hot flood, running up his belly, into his chest, through his arms. When it reached his hands, he clenched his fists, slammed them into his thighs. His head went down between his knees and he let out a cry, a groan that ripped the silence with its violence, like silk between his fists.

It seemed hours before Cameron rose, shuffled down the stairs to the kitchen, set the bourbon glass in the sink and ran water into it. He wanted to crush it in his hand, to throw it, to hear breakage, to see blood, even his own. Something to break this immense, screaming quiet, something to horrify that woman spirit watching him in the doorway.

Fuck this. He wasn't going to spend it here. He wasn't even going to unpack. To hell with her privacy, with her needs. He was going over there. And if he came in on some lover, if he came in on some party, then she had asked for it. She was his wife. That was still true. She owed him something. She couldn't just walk away.

The sepia room was now black and grey, lightness. In the dark it didn't evoke any particular feeling or memory. He opened the door, stood staring back inside. Where am I going now? Oh yes, to her place. To the address in the letter. Going to see her. Or something.

◇

He stood on the sidewalk across the street from Anna's apartment building, staring up at the only lighted room. It was hers, he recognized the lace. Everyone else was apparently away for the holidays. His pulse had calmed now in his chest, was subsiding in his wrists. From where he stood he could see only glimpses: a steam radiator, the foot of a bed or sofa, a lamp shade, plants in the window. Beyond that, he could not see into the room. He hoped she would come near the window so he could be prepared before facing her; just to see how she was wearing her hair, and if she was alone. A nice neighborhood.

Brownstones, a grade school on this side of the street. Surreal, it felt, standing here in the snow, staring up at the rooms of his wife, seeing what she had chosen over him, over their mansion across the lake. The anger moved up through him again, clenching into fierce pain in his gut. There was warmth coming from those lighted windows, moving out in rectangular patches of light over the window ledges, cutting through the dark below, just inches away from where he stood.

Did she have a lover, a roommate? That ache returned, what he had felt in the house earlier. It was not really an ache for a reconnection with her. She was a stranger to him now. Her leaving had cut something in him, some cord. That she could do that treachery to him, to what they had built together, made her a stranger, someone he could never trust again. He would never put his life in those hands again. But if she had built a warm place for herself here, he envied that. And hated it, that she could have done so. How fast a person could inhabit a new space. Only three months and, from here, he could feel her rooms held her scents, her colors, the angles of her arranged objects, as if she had lived here ten years. How fast a space could be emptied and filled again.

Then he saw her. Not her face, just her arm, her hip, the backs of her legs, bending over, then straightening, her back to the window. Unaware she was seen, moving slowly in and out of the black negative space between the windows. Recognition of the familiar, how she held her hand out as she bent to pick something up. She had always seemed to over-anticipate her movements — reaching for doors, tea cups, people, several feet away from actual contact, completely focused on that one movement through space, toward that one goal. The particular arch of her shoulder. Hers. Anna's. She seemed to be alone. He sensed it, not so much that he couldn't see anyone else from here, but that her movements were relaxed, the unselfconscious movements of a woman alone in her lighted rooms at night.

◇

"I — wanted to see — so I came."

She stared, folded her arms protectively, withholding herself from him. She looked intruded upon. And scared. Of his reaction. To the letter she had mailed him in Peru three months ago.

"I suppose I should have called first."

(but you are my wife, I have the right to come here) She finished his sentences in her head. "You smell like you've been drinking."

"Yes. Christmas cheer. Forgive me." His voice full of repressed anger, bitterness.

(forgive me for indulging myself, trying to numb the pain you have caused) "Why tonight? It's Christmas. I...had plans — "

"You are alone, though?"

She was dressed in her at-home clothes. That much hadn't changed. The same things she used to wear for an evening at home, when there was no special occasion. The familiar jeans, one of his old flannel shirts, the sleeves rolled up, worn like a jacket over a black turtle neck. Sparkly striped socks. The long, silver beaded earrings he had bought her in Santa Fe on their honeymoon. The usual rings — the long silver and coral, the silver filigree, the six thin bands of ivory stacked on one finger. Not the wedding band. He looked away from her hand quickly. The absence of the ring seared him like white heat.

"Yes. I had plans alone."

"I just flew in from Lima today."

"Oh, you came here from O'Hare?"

"No, from the house. I flew in this morning and drove straight to Milwaukee. I wasn't planning to come here. Once I got there, I...I just couldn't stay there. It being Christmas..."

"I see. Well, come in."

Oh Christ, what to say? Fix him something to eat, like a wife? Offer a drink, like a stranger? Why had he come now? It had been going so well. She had opened her presents, had baked her hen, had a nice glow on from the spiked eggnog. The new Paul Winter album from Garth was in its eighth spin and she had been

dancing, ballet, across the living room when the buzzer sounded.
She had almost not answered, not wanting to break her solace.
The pampering, the peace alone she had so carefully created.
Now she wished she hadn't answered. Cameron. No, not now,
not tonight. Her heart was beating heavily. To her chagrin, his
reaction mattered to her, more than she had expected it to. How
she looked, how the rooms appeared.

Cameron walked in slowly, eyeing everything, searching for
the reason here. He saw the tree, the gift wrapping in wads
around the sofa, half-empty bourbon flask, filmy eggnog cup.

"Christmas alone?"

Anna couldn't explain it to him. So she smiled, shrugged and
resented him for eliciting that much of a gesture. She moved the
gift wrapping so that he could sit, started to whisk away the cup
and bottle, then stopped. *Do not play housewife. Do not
apologize.* She forced herself to sit across from him, in the
rocking chair, wrapping a shawl around her. *Be calm. Give
yourself comfort. This will go better.*

He seemed glad she was alone. He half smiled, looked away.
For a few moments he had her; a superior look. He'd expected
as much, that she would do no better than to spend Christmas
alone. His glance at her meager trappings said he was not
impressed, did not see it as austerity, but as poverty. She forced
herself to ask.

"So, what do you think?"

"It's rather empty. You could have taken — anything you
wanted. I certainly won't need it."

"Oh?"

"I'll move. The house is too big. You said it well in your
letter. 'So full of you and me.'"

"Yes, yes it is. I suppose that's best — " she smiled, trying to
brighten his mood. "What fun that will be for you! A new place
to fix up!"

"Yes, it will be different. I suppose you'll want something out
of the sale of the house."

Anna stood, drawing the lace curtains. She hadn't thought

they'd come to this conversation so soon.

"I hadn't thought about it. I, I guess we'll have to — "

"You don't seem to have thought about much, Anna. Except your *fucking self!*"

His anger spit the words, changed his face and volume so rapidly it frightened her. He rose abruptly, shaking, white, and walked through the room into the kitchen. Running water, the clink of glass. He came out of the kitchen, stood with his legs apart, staring at her from across the two rooms.

"I've — I've done some work. Do you want to see?"

He stared at her, first in astonishment, then away, an ironic half grin, then back.

"Oh, sure, Anna. Sure."

She was perspiring. Guilt. Resenting the guilt his voice invoked. If she could appeal to the friendship between them, then perhaps they could talk about the pain. As she led him to her work table, she avoided watching his face, already regretting having led him into this room, which also served as her bedroom. Behind her, as she arranged the stack of prints, she felt his eyes seeking out every detail.

"Here, these are the most recent."

Cameron moved beside her and slowly fingered the prints. At first his eyes didn't seem to be looking at them, he seemed to be going through the motions. Their shoulders touched and Anna froze, afraid of the implications should she remain or move away. She pretended to straighten one of the prints, moving her arm and turning slightly so that they were no longer touching. He seemed not to notice, seemed to begin to really study the prints. She watched his eyes, finally, then wished she hadn't. It was not artistic appreciation she saw in them, but pain. Seeing her art of the past few months only made the point more clear to him that he was no longer part of her life. His eyes expressed confusion. He searched every line of each print as he had searched the objects of her rooms, for clues.

"Who's this?"

He tapped the print of Garth crouching on the ground over a

map.

"A friend, Garth. He's a geographer at U of C."

"Your lover?"

How easily he said the words. Yet, she suspected, not so easily.

"No, just a friend."

"Of course, it's none of my business."

His voice still held the edge of satire, but bolder now with relief. He turned, looked her straight in the eyes.

"But you have a lover? Or lovers?"

Anna tried to meet his eyes, but the accusation, the fear was too much. She moved away, to the bedroom doorway, her arms folded, turning slowly back to face him. He put the prints down, looked around the room.

"This isn't easy, Cameron. I don't know what you want me to say. I wasn't expecting you, I wasn't prepared for this scene."

"Scene? SCENE? This isn't just drama, Anna. This is our life. Our marriage."

"I can't come back, Cameron."

"I'm not asking you to. I did a lot of thinking in Peru. You've betrayed me. Betrayed us. I could never have you back after that. You've cut the cords."

"Then why are you here?"

"I — I — "

"You wanted some kind of ending? A formal goodbye, perhaps? No — I don't mean it that way. I mean...I just don't know what you want."

Cameron stood stiffly, staring beyond her, somewhere over her shoulder into the next room.

"I — I want..."

Suddenly he began to laugh, incredulously. He cupped his forehead, pushing his fingers into his hairline, laughing or crying or both.

"Cameron? What is it?"

"I want..." He moved toward her, clutching her shoulders, stared into her eyes, bruising her skin with his thumbs, grinding them back and forth along her arms. He spoke in a growl from his throat, his teeth gritting. "...to *hurt* you."

Anna closed her eyes and waited for him to let her go. He did. He pushed her away and walked to the kitchen. She followed, stood in the doorway watching. She realized how drunk he must be, the way he stood with his feet planted far apart, trying to balance himself against his sway. He picked up a bottle of brandy on the counter, opened it and drank.

He turned and they stared into each other's eyes for a long moment. They could. For old time's sake. For apology. For hope. But none of those were possible. Not memory, not forgiveness, not hope.

He stared into the bottle, then placed it on the counter, then moved past her, to the front door.

"You can't drive like this. You're so drunk, love."

He turned to her at the door.

"You said that like — like you cared."

"Of course I care. If I don't seem to, it's just...that I can't do what I have to do if I let myself feel these things."

Cameron leaned his head against the door, shaking it, his eyes closed.

"Oh god, Anna, you don't have to find yourself. You are Anna Stone, my wife. *I* found you!" Cameron rammed his fist into the door.

"Cameron, this isn't the time to talk about this. You're about to pass out."

Anna caught him as he lost his balance, and walked him into her room, awkwardly maneuvering him onto the futon and easing him down. She pulled off his shoes, pulled the comforter over him, and turned out the light. He was no longer conscious. Anna stood in the doorway, watching him for several minutes. This was the man into whose hands she had placed her entire existence for these past twelve years. And yet, here he was, so vulnerable, like a child. He couldn't carry the weight of his own confusion, much less hers. The one thing they both had feared was growth, change. Even after the arrangement was no longer satisfactory, they had repressed everything to preserve it. Because that was the way it had always been. It was known, familiar, safe.

His face now, in sleep, was soft, his lips slightly puffed, his hair in his eyes. A child.

And she, with the discards of her narcissistic Christmas surrounding her: wrapping paper, sticky rim of eggnog circling her cup. Another child. Two children who had set it up to give each other comfort, to keep each other suspended between childhood and adulthood. The seams had just ripped apart, like clothes outgrown. This was what had to be. If she had had any lingering doubts, this confrontation would have brought them up in her. Cameron had brought with him all the emotion and memories, the lure of secure love, and these filled her few rooms like the sharp old-house smell of their Milwaukee home. No, no doubt. She wanted the smell to be gone in the morning.

Anna turned out the lights and lay down on the sofa, leaving the one strand of blinking tree lights plugged in. She stared into the lights.

In the morning she didn't remember falling asleep, and Cameron was gone. It was best that way. What more could they have said? She sat on the edge of the futon he had slept on. He had folded the comforter, smoothed back the sheets. Unexpected crying began, sobs that stressed her sides and scraped her throat raw.

She slept again.

[excerpt from a novel-in-progress]

Replaying an Old Record

Sue Hansen-Smith

The people who live in Walker Street, South Fremantle, love their street. They love the way the street dead ends so there is no passing traffic and their children can play on the road and run between houses safely. They love the way the street is a small community, everyone knowing everyone else, some of the families related, and all congregating in the street on Christmas Eve for Christmas caroling. My two ex-brothers-in-law and their families live in that street. They love it. For me the atmosphere is a little too close.

And yet here we were, my American second husband and I, parking in Walker Street on our way to my ex-husband's family Christmas dinner. My youngest son had called before we left New Mexico.

"Mum, Jim and Julie and Grandma have asked you to come for Christmas dinner."

"Tom, I don't think so. I..."

"Well, I knew you might not be comfortable, and I won't go if you don't want to, but I'd really like to. Dad is away, and Jim and Andrew are pretty pissed off with him at the moment. I'm the only one here, and I sort of feel I ought to keep up our side of the family. Grandma particularly asked if you'd come..."

I said I'd think about it, but I was impressed that Tom, not usually one to think far past his own needs, wanted to improve his father's standing within his family. And it was curious that Jean, Tom's Grandma, had asked me.

She and I had had trouble from the start. Too quiet, too poor and too socially inept, I was not what she had wanted for her gregarious and budding architect son. Soon after we met, she'd

71

asked me a casual question and I had responded honestly and fully. Such an expression of feeling was taboo in that family, and would later be one of many unbreachable gulfs between her son and me. Over the sixteen years of our marriage, she had blamed me for her son's extravagance and thoughtlessness. Many times, insulted, I had vowed never to have her in my house again, and then not only relented but reminded Nick to invite her. When I decided to leave him, I chose to be the one to tell her. Sixteen years of invisibility were waiting to be dumped if she had made the smallest accusation, but she had not. She was sad for her son, but complimented me on how well I had raised the boys. It was, in fact, one of her most gracious interactions with me. And I had somewhat ungraciously reminded her that I'd done a super-human job with Nick as well.

A few months after this, her oldest son, Andrew, turned fifty. The party was held at my old house. I came alone, and cautious. Jean, a trifle tipsy, welcomed me immediately.

"Why don't you come and visit? I never see you these days. We mustn't let sixteen years of love and affection go down the drain."

My mouth had fallen open. Sixteen years of love and affection? What about all those times of being subtly or unsubtly put down, ignored, blamed unfairly, overridden? What about the presents like the floral shower cap that showed every Christmas and birthday that she had never looked at me or listened to me? What about all the meals I had cooked that she had rearranged on her plate and not eaten? What about, what about — the list was long. Her idea of love and affection was surely different from mine.

But it was that remark, and Tom's need to be there, that had persuaded me to go to this Christmas dinner. And I could not use my husband Bob as an excuse to not attend. He was eager to observe this family in action, and felt no discomfort whatsoever. And I, well, I was different now, wasn't I? More self-assured, less likely to be pushed aside, more able to speak up for myself — so we went.

My stomach was not easy as we left the car several houses from the house of Jim, my ex-brother-in-law, and Julie. Much of what had gone wrong with my marriage was embedded in the dynamics of Nick's family. Embedded is the right word: I had pushed my doubts down deep, but full family gatherings never failed to bring them almost to the surface. Invariably I would leave feeling mousy and miserable from hours in the foreign atmosphere of aggression and competition as Jean's three sons vied for their mother's attention.

It was a perfect Fremantle Christmas Day — hot with a cloudless sky of deep and relentless blue. We'd been to the beach in the morning after breakfast, and followed that with a lazy and happy day visiting friends and staying cool. Except my stomach was not cool now, but knotted and anxious. We passed the vibrant blue fence — a fence rivaling the sky in its intensity — of George Haines, the ex-lover of my friend Jan and father of her daughter. Jan was at his house now as we passed, part of yet another strange and extended family. The green leaves of the bushes behind the fence pushed through the bright blue wooden slats so the two colors danced on each other, just as the colors danced in George's well-known and now sought-after canvases. A different dance was going on in the giant sunflowers by George's driveway, a dance of color, motion and noise. The huge yellow flowers, their green leaves and the deep blue sky, already an excessive combination, became impossible with the addition of eight or so pink and grey galahs that were feeding on the sunflowers and talking to each other. These birds, members of the parrot family, fly freely all over the city. Any sighting of them is a gift. There is nothing muted about them, not their voices, their color or their personalities. A friend calls them the bikers of the bird world, noisy, extroverted and exuberant. Bob, new to Australia, Fremantle, and Christmas in the summer, was transfixed. We stood and watched them, their exuberance easing my stomach, until they had had enough and flew on.

We, unfortunately, had to move on too. Jim's house looked much as I had last seen it four years before, a modest timber bungalow in the front and a two-storied rammed earth building behind. We entered the modest section, and found no one until we had passed through to the new. Julie was surrounded by pots and boxes and confusion, but stopped what she was doing to welcome us warmly. She and I had remained friends throughout. We hugged and I introduced Bob. Jim joined us for more hugs. Julie, although more acceptable to Jean from the start, had not had an easy time in this family either. She fully understood the problem I had had, but she had married later than I, and Jim, the youngest brother and with one failed marriage already, had been more adaptable.

Julie and Jim were preoccupied with the logistics of what had to be done, so I took a breath and turned round to say hello to Andrew and his wife Victoria. He was the oldest brother and the one with the most troubled relationship with his mother. At one time I had thought that he and I had some sort of bond. I had spent hours listening to his troubles, his thoughts, his hopes, and more hours trying to comfort various women to whom he had proposed by letter, brought to visit, and then left. In those first difficult and painful two years after the separation, he had only twice made an effort to see me, when Nick was not in town. Others said that Andrew was "sensitive", and, if he overheard the words, his sharp intake of breath and modest look would confirm the description. I knew it was true too, but his sensitivity was for himself alone. It was not until he was over fifty, and Victoria came into his life, that he had learned to live more easily with himself.

I was an easy target in this divorce, the one who had left husband and sons in what had appeared to be a very happy marriage. No one could be expected to know that when we had separated I had wanted the boys to come with me but they had chosen to stay with their father, who was keeping the big house they had grown up in and who, the rejected one, was clearly more in need of their comfort and support. Others could not know either that Nick was a superb manipulator who had consistently and privately won his way for most of our marriage, with means that I now call emotionally and sexually abusive. All I knew was that, despite the huge house, the Jaguar, the trips to Europe and the nice clothes, I was more often unhappy than not. My efforts to talk about this enraged him, and he was a very large man and terrifying in a rage. I began to believe that I was wrong, stupid and did not know what I was talking about. After all, wasn't this the man I loved and trusted, the good husband, the provider of the comfortable life and, most importantly, the father of my sons?

Andrew and I embraced cautiously, and there were introductions all round. No one had met Bob, and I had not met Victoria or her mother. I wanted to like Victoria, but the way she was looking at me was not encouraging. It seemed I'd been judged and convicted some time before. As Andrew introduced me to his mother-in-law, Jean entered. She looked, as always, amazing for her age, with her smooth black helmet of hair and her almost unlined face, although she was nearing eighty. I introduced Bob to her with some trepidation. She had owned an art gallery in the past, and Bob was a sculptor, so I knew she would want to engage him on the subject. Her gallery, where success was measured in terms of sales and prestigious buyers, had been her most successful infiltration into the ranks of the wealthy, and gave her, at least in her mind, considerable authority. Bob was not successful in her terms, and, being soft-spoken, gentle, and unlike her sons, was not how she expected men to be.

I turned away to let them work it out themselves, and found myself in a conversational hole. There was a moment of uncomfortable silence and then I turned to Victoria's mother, Grace, and made a reasonably safe remark, I thought, about how happy Victoria and Andrew seemed. She gave me a frosty look and said,

"Yes, they are very happy. It is most fortunate that they met. They owe that to Leonie, you know. Victoria was introduced to Leonie and Nick, and Leonie thought that Victoria should meet Andrew. They are really beholden to Leonie, and they really love her."

When she finished talking she turned her back on me. It was not a good start.

Leonie, Nick's second wife, had come on the scene very shortly after our separation. Those first years were hard for all of us. Nick needed a woman to run the house for him, yet he refused to consider the separation final. It must have made Leonie's life very difficult, but I hadn't cared about that. My own difficulties were overwhelming enough and I was brimming with unarticulated anger from the years of manipulation. I should perhaps have thanked her for filling Nick's life, but stories from the boys about how she treated them intruded, and I was ruder to her, several times, than I have been to any other person. In recent years the anger has gone, but she remains someone with whom I have no wish to be friendly, despite Nick's insistence. I would like to talk one-to-one with Nick now, about the boys and our past life, but Leonie will not allow this, and Nick feels that to talk with me alone would be taking sides against her. The rift remains. Grace's comments told me exactly how she divided camps and to which camp she belonged. Not much chance of further conversation there.

I could hear Bob and Jean miscommunicating behind me, and turned towards Julie. She told me that twenty-two people were expected, and that dinner was to have been outside, but as rain was predicted, she was thinking of moving everything to the Endeavor building, Jim's workplace. We went outside to check the sky and, sure enough, the previously cloudless sky now had huge and threatening cloud banks, suggesting a summer thunderstorm. A few drops hit our faces as we looked up. The decision was made: the dinner was to be packed and moved. This was a big task, but not as daunting as it would have been for a hot meal. Christmas dinner in Fremantle, in fact in Australia generally, is usually cold.

We began the packing, but there was a diversion. Laughter and noise announced the arrival of friends of Jim and Julie's and of mine too from across the road. They took one look at the somewhat strained atmosphere and suggested that Bob and I might like to visit briefly with them. Julie insisted we go, that she had plenty of helpers. We crossed the road and sat in their huge country kitchen, drinking tea, and talking, a warm, relaxed conversation that roamed over many topics and moved easily around the diversions from their children. Too easily. The time slipped away, and somewhat guiltily we recrossed the road, knowing that the packing of the dinner would be almost done and my bad reputation worsened in certain quarters.

We were in time to help load the cars, and everyone, by this time twenty-two of us, drove in convoy to the huge warehouse where the replica of Captain Cook's Endeavor was being built under Jim's supervision. As we came up the steps to the main working level of the warehouse, the half-built Endeavor loomed above us, rounded sides, beautiful and seaworthy woodwork, already a sense of presence and past in her. But instead of continuing up the next flight to her deck, we were directed to turn off to the offices. My hopes of picnicking on the deck of Captain Cook's ship were lost: we were eating around the long, bare table in the company board room.

There was no need for conversation during the unpacking and setting up of the dinner that occupied the next half hour. The table was covered with a bright red cloth, and places set. The bowls of salads and dressings were arranged down the center of the table while Jim carved the turkey and Andrew sliced the ham. Tom whispered in my ear to know how I was doing and I hugged him and told him all was fine. His warm presence was a comfort, but he didn't look too happy himself. Eighteen is awkward, not adult enough to take his father's place nor young enough to play heedlessly, as his cousins were doing. He, and a couple of his friends whose parents were away, milled uneasily, not quite knowing how to help.

And then, the food ready and the places set, came the awkward moment of seating. No one moved. There was a long pause, and two moved at once, me from one side and Jean from the other. Once we had moved we had no choice but to continue around that table, from opposite sides, until we were next to each other. And not just next to, but securely wedged between the table and the wall, unable to move for the length of the dinner. We made the usual small talk without pleasure, and it was clear that, even if she had invited me, she was no happier about the seating than I was. Passing the cold turkey, the dressing, and the salads replaced conversation with action until the wonderful silence of eating made words unnecessary.

I looked around the huge table as we ate. Tom and his friends were at one end, but none looked relaxed or at ease. Near them was a young German couple, known only to Jim and Julie, who were perhaps the most uncomfortable of all. They were enough older than Tom and his friends to not fit there, and too much younger than Grace, who sat next to them, to manage with her. Grace just looked out of sorts, an unlikely conversation partner for anyone. I wondered if this was her normal expression, or if her words to me or perhaps my presence, had soured the day for her. Next to Grace was her granddaughter, a plain girl a year younger than her step-cousin Tom. She was watching covertly and longingly everything Tom and his friends did, but not saying anything. Victoria and Andrew were on the far side of Jean so I could not talk to either of them. Bob was trapped several seats away from me, and he grinned in my direction. The wretched man looked as if he was enjoying himself as he, too, watched the ill-assorted group. Julie looked frazzled, and Jim, two from me, was instructing his two young sons to behave themselves.

Jean turned to me again and began to tell me about the house Andrew and Victoria were building. It involved a tree that had fallen and that they had built into the structure. She praised the house and said,

"You should see it."

"Why?" I replied shortly and stopped the conversation.

Yes, I thought, she was right, all those years ago. I really do have poor social graces, and I am prickly and difficult. Well, time to redeem myself. Jim was looking down in the mouth, so I turned away from Jean to ask him a simple question about the

Endeavor. It was a cocktail party sort of question, a little something thrown in to push the conversation along. But it didn't work, in fact, it backfired badly. Jim pushed his chair back a little to see me better and launched into a long and technical monologue about the construction of the Endeavor. Instead of a conversation starter, we had a conversation stopper. His voice, loud and allowing no argument, effectively drowned all other talk, as he fixed me with a steely eye and pinned me into my role of listener. The pudding was passed out, but the monologue continued. While eating, there was some relief from the relentlessness of his gaze, but when the pudding was done, there was no escape. The voice punished as it went on and on. Others became restless, but there was no moving from the table while Jim was talking. The teenagers tried a couple of conversations — my ears were primed for anything that might stop the punishing — but none was strong enough to last, let alone to take over. Curiously, Jim did not look happy or animated as he lectured — and he was normally both — but seemed angry or sad. And I was very aware of my own feelings: battered, outsidered, reduced, invisible, and miserable, exactly as I had felt so many Christmases in the past.

It was Julie who broke the monologue. In her brisk way she began to remove plates, and gradually the whole party shifted focus, from eating and talking to cleaning up. The teenagers vanished, and the rest of us organized an efficient washing-up process. As with the packing, the action was safe and comfortable. Everyone had a role within which to act and speak, so there was no need for other speech. Working as a unit, we cleaned the place thoroughly and drifted off into the hot still night, to our separate cars.

The Fisherman's Harbor, into which the Endeavor would one day be launched, was oily and black. The reflections of the few boat lights rippled very slightly, and, gently in the quiet, we could hear the soft, clinking noises boats make when they are almost but not quite motionless. On another night I would have wanted to stay, to walk around the jetties and exchange an occasional greeting with visiting fishermen playing cards on their scrubbed decks. I would have wanted to savor the familiar and comfortable sights, the oily, salty smell with its residue of fish frying, the safe sounds of that harbor. But not tonight. This Christmas night I wanted to get away from there as quickly as possible, to distance myself physically from that family even as I was unable to distance myself emotionally. Jim drove off with his passenger, Jean, who did not drive any more, as Bob and I climbed into the junker we had been lent. Both looked straight ahead and did not acknowledge us.

Bob and I discussed the evening, and his perceptions were enlightening. He had seen Jim's monologue as an aggressive act, which was how I had felt it but, overcome by my past, had been unable to say so. He had seen Jean playing the matriarch, pitting her sons against each other, belittling Andrew and encouraging Jim. He had seen Julie playing the perfect wife, doing most of the work, serving. He had experienced that family, idealized and venerated by Nick and giving me so much distress and confusion in the past, as unhappy. He put into words and images things I had seen but not mentioned to him, secret thoughts censored even from him. And that was some comfort.

It was not until the next morning that I cried. Bob, who welcomes my perceptions and feelings, listened, understood, and held me as I cried. What was I crying for? Certainly not because I wanted to return to that family, and probably not that I had felt a closing of their ranks against me. More likely it was because at that Christmas dinner the growth I had thought strong and irreversible had shown itself tenuous. Whoever I had become away from them vanished as if never known and instead I was the gauche, invisible and unhappy girl who had married into a family who had little understanding of her and for whom she had little understanding. I thought I had seen the last of that girl, but the message of that Christmas dinner was that she was going to be with me, to a greater or lesser extent, forever.

Ho Ho Ho

Donal Harding

Although Gale lives in Atlanta and I live in Washington, D.C., every Christmas we go home for the holidays to be with Mama and Jane, our older sister. Jane never left rural South Carolina; she still lives a few miles from Mama and works part time at the Food Lion. Last summer, Jane married Sam, a disabled mailman who swears his back is too weak to carry a sack of mail to his car, but Mama told Gale she saw him lift a lawn mower into the back of his pickup. Sam is Jane's third husband. Neither Gale nor I have ever married. We both teach high school. Mama retired from the textile plant right after Daddy died six years ago. We all understand the facts of our family and accept them.

Mama's house is way out in the country. She grows dahlias all over the place in summer and sweeps her front porch first thing every morning no matter what season or weather. You can sit on Mama's porch and see the cinder-block coach house that Daddy left Jane, Gale and me. At different times of their lives and separately, Gale and Jane have lived in the coach house. Now, Jane's boy, Jerry, lives in the house with his three children. Each of Jerry's children has a different mother; none of the mothers live in the coach house.

When Gale and I pull into Mama's driveway, Gale almost rams her Honda into Mama's Oldsmobile. Gale can't take her eyes off the coach house. A chain-link fence runs at odd angles down one side of the house. Within the fence broken toys of all sizes and all primary colors lay among high weeds. A refrigerator sits outside the back door with the cord running back into the house. If you look past the fence, a riding lawn mower, rusted so bad you can't tell its color, is parked against a once-fine magnolia tree. Several cars line the drive on the far side of the house. A green Ford with a dent in the door bears the only license plate. A mongrel dog sticks his head round the corner of the house and yaps at us but refuses to leave his safe distance.

Mama comes out on her porch. "What is all this mess?" I ask.

Mama says, "Sush, Jerry might hear you." I don't care if Jerry does overhear, but Mama holds family next to religion. She believes every member of the family has responsibility to get along with every other member of the family. I've heard the lecture too many times to start criticizing Jerry in front of Mama. Gale and I look at each other and shrug. We are happy being together and being with Mama, so we forget about the mess next door and Jerry until Jane arrives.

Gale is getting a little mad that there has been no sign of Jerry, and that Jane has arrived an hour late. "If I can make it all the way up from Atlanta in time for dinner," Gale says, "It seems Jerry could make it across the yard on time."

Jane blows long lines of Marlboro smoke through her nostrils and says, "Jerry had to go to the mall."

"It looks like Jerry has plenty of time to shop. Unless he's too busy turning the coach house into a junkyard," I say.

"Jerry is manager of a club. And what do you mean about a junkyard?" Jane says.

"Boy, that's a life. Jerry is almost forty years old and has never had a real job, excuse me, except in a club," Gale says from behind her iced-tea glass. Then she turns to me and whispers, "Bet that *club* is a beer joint."

Jane stands up and leans toward Gale who is sitting on the small couch beside me. "What did you say?"

"I said I bet Jerry only has to work on weekends," Gale lies, sucking an ice cube from the glass.

We move into the kitchen where Mama is trying to keep the dinner warm without burning anything, and we sit quietly on wooden chairs that go to the dining table. Sam, Jane's disabled husband who I call Sipper because he is always going out to his truck to take a sip, yells from the living room, "Here they are. Santa Claus can come now."

But it's only the three children. Jerry has sent them ahead so he and Tanqueray can finish wrapping presents.

"Tanqueray? Who is Tanqueray?" I ask.

"That's Jerry's new girlfriend. It was her idea to move the refrigerator to the yard," Mama says, sarcastically.

"Mama, you know she put it out there 'til she could get the kitchen painted," Jane says, helping the smallest child out of an orange parka. The middle child stands beside Jane, twisting and smiling. His teeth are the size and color of pumpkin seeds.

Gale stands up and says to the tallest of the children, "How are you doing, sweetie?" The gangly girl switches around and goes down the hall to the bathroom. We hear the lock turn.

Gale sits back down and says, "I try to be nice to her because she fits the profile of a serial killer in development."

"Have you seen Tanqueray?" I ask Gale.

Mama looks around from the sink where she is draining the water off green beans to see if Jane is in earshot. "Wait til you see this one," she whispers.

"Where does Jerry find all these women named after liquors. Last Christmas he brought Sherry, and when I was here last summer, some woman came out and introduced herself as Margarita." Jane pops back into the kitchen. Gale raises her eyebrows and leans so close I feel her lips on my ear. "I hope Jane gave those children tooth brushes for Christmas." I can't tell if Jane overheard Gale, but Jane sucks at her jaws so hard her lips disappear. Mama peers over her glasses at me and Gale; we shut up and ease our way down the tiny hall to the living room. Jane follows.

The children are running up and down the room, making the angel on the top of the Christmas tree shake. There are cookie crumbs and Hershey kisses' wrappers on the coffee table. Gale wads up a silver wrapper and says, "They are on a sugar high."

My nerves can't take much more Christmas, so I say, "Let's

eat. Jerry and Tanqueray can eat when they get here."

Jane fumbles in a shiny gold purse and pulls out a bent Marlboro. She lights it with a green lighter. After the cigarette is going good, she says, "You are the most selfish person I've ever seen. If you don't want to be part of this family, why do you come down here at Christmas?"

That makes me mad. "It seems Jerry is the one who is hesitant about being part of this family." When I start talking, I get even madder. "And while we're at it, I want you to tell Jerry to clean up that pig pen of a yard."

Wanting no part of an argument, Sipper Sam staggers up from

the arm chair and heads for his truck.

Jane says "You don't own that house."

"And neither do you," Gale says. "We own it together, and I vote that the least Jerry can do, since he pays no rent and no taxes, is to keep the yard picked up."

"Shut up, Gale. You think you are so smart. I've never seen a school teacher yet that didn't think their shit don't stink," Jane says.

Mama turns up the volume on the radio in the kitchen. Randy Travis sings *What a Merry Christmas This Will Be*. The front door swings open, and Jerry pokes his head round the door. "Ho, Ho, Ho," he says. "Tanqueray has a headache and had to stay home. Ho, Ho, Ho."

We're at the dining table seated before Mama's good china, six people, six chairs; the three children sit at a card table with the every-day dishes. Just as Jerry shovels down a fork of stuffing, we hear the front door open and close. We all rest our forks and stare at the doorjamb leading from the hall into the kitchen. A woman with blonde hair that scrapes the ceiling appears. When she moves toward us, I can see her hair is bleached with a good inch of regrowth.

"Hey, Babe," Jerry says through a mouthful of sweet potatoes. He jumps up and reaches out to draw the woman closer to the table. She concentrates on straightening the white leather skirt that has gathered in wrinkles around her hips, then fluffs out the frilly collar on the white blouse that floats over the waist of the skirt. "This is my sweetie," Jerry says.

I'm afraid to look at Gale, because I know we will laugh out loud. Mama brings in her sewing chair, and we scrunch up to make room for another place setting. I glance at the children's table. The serial killer is watching every move Tanqueray makes.

Before Mama has time to serve coffee, a chant arises from the card table. "Presents. Presents. Presents."

Gale says, "Those kids need some discipline."

Jane wiggles in her chair. Jerry laughs and drains his tea glass. "Maybe we should send them down to Atlanta to live with you for a while," he says. To keep peace we move to the living room and Tanqueray plays Santa Claus, reading the gift tags and delivering the gifts.

After most of the presents have been distributed and opened and admired, or sort of admired, the serial killer, who has been missing from the living room long enough to rifle Gale's and my suitcases, appears with a gun. I only get a glimpse of the gun because Gale is pushing me forward so she can hide behind me.

"Now, don't mess around, sugar," Jerry says. "Everybody's got on good clothes." Gale and I are pulling back against the love seat. Mama grabs a throw pillow and puts in front of her. No one speaks. In the background some church choir sings *Silent Night* on the radio.

Red streaks run down Tanqueray's blouse. Then it seems everybody is talking at once. Gale and I yank each other up from the sofa and pull Mama up with us.

"What is it?" Jerry asks.

"She's been shot," Gale says. I'm thinking maybe the gun has a silencer like on Miami Vice.

The serial killer is on the floor doubled up with laughter. "Cranberry juice," she screams.

"She is a sick child. Look, she's ruined my blouse," Tanqueray says.

"Let's get back over to the house," Jerry says. "Grandmommy don't allow no fighting in her house."

Tanqueray pushes the children out of her way and is on the porch before any of us can say Merry Christmas.

Before Jerry joins Tanqueray, he kisses Gale and Mama and shakes my hand. Brushing back his hair, he takes a deep sigh and points out a toe. He winks at Gale. "Present from my Babe." We all look down at the imitation snake-skin boots.

Jane pulls on her coat and slaps Gale on the butt with her gold handbag. "I don't know how I got into this family. I believe some nurse switched me at birth," Jane says.

Gale and I follow Jane and Sipper to the door. "Wonder what your real family is like?" We say in unison.

The next morning, I'm packing Gale's car for her trip back to Atlanta. She will drop me at the airport for my plane to D.C. A piece of wrapping paper blows up and floats over my head. At the back door to the coach house a pile of rumpled Christmas wrappings works at untangling itself. The bright reds and greens fit well with the discarded toys, but each piece of paper seems destined to fly away in the morning wind.

Mama comes out to sweep the front porch. A piece of the wrapping paper whirls into her yard. "Where's that trash coming from?" She asks. I point to the fenced yard. Mama crosses her arms still holding the broom. Gale hurries out of Mama's house carrying the sandwich maker Jane gave her. She walks to the coach-house fence and tosses it over, box and all. I left mine in Mama's closet with Jane's presents from Christmases past.

Looking like a toy soldier, Mama marches down the porch steps and across the yard. She bangs on the door with the broom.

"Get out here, Jerry," she says. "We've got work to do."

Opening the door to the driver's side — I'm on the passenger's side — Gale says across the top of the car, "I know they are going to end up on the Oprah Winfrey Show."

Leaning on the car's roof, I say, "Oprah will be out there in a red dress that Marshall Field's provided her, and she will have a gleam in her eyes, like she just discovered a substitute for food."

Gale smiles and nods, agreeing she sees it that way too. "Out will come Jane, Jerry and Tanqueray, if she doesn't have a headache."

We're laughing hard. "They will be followed by the future serial killer, pumpkin mouth, the little one, and Jane's real family, if they can be found," I add.

"And Lord knows what they are going to say," Gale says, losing her smile.

Venus

Natalia Rachel Singer

Just before lunch on the last day of classes before Christmas vacation, Michael Shuga gave Ruth Ann Horowitz a secret note. She was walking out the doors of Riverview Elementary School when he crept up behind her and slipped it into her coat pocket. "After you read it," he whispered, "write me back." Then he hurried off toward the unplowed paths behind the field, sliding as he went, his arms jutting like a gladiator's. Ruth fingered the wax peace sign he'd sealed it with; she knew better than to crack it open in the light of day.

Sure enough, the sound of pelting hailstones warned her that Shirley Spencer — who wore cleats on all her foot apparel, even her galoshes — lurked just to her right. "See you after lunch, Shirley," Ruth said with feigned casualness.

"Yeah, say hi to your grandpappy for me," Shirley said, giggling so furiously that her blond curls shook beneath her furry white earmuffs. Having learned recently that Ruth's mother worked, and that Ruth and her sister Leah went home at noon to their grandfather's cooking, Shirley had laughed hysterically, as though the idea of a grandfather making meals was the funniest concept in the world. As Shirley skipped towards the shiny red car where her ponytailed mother waved wildly and honked, Ruth felt the wind slip inside the baggy sleeves of her coat. She reached inside her pocket to make sure the note was still there.

A big yellow bus pulled into the parking lot and Ruth waited for her sister Leah to descend.

"How was the planetarium?" Ruth said.

"Cool," Leah said. "I'm starving. What day is this? Grease burgers or lamb grease stew with okra slime?"

"Burgers," Ruth said, and they both groaned.

"It's your turn to steal the napkins," Leah said.

"Okay," Ruth said. "Just keep him talking."

They walked past the identical aluminum-sided houses on Fairlane Avenue. "Do you know that the planets are named after the gods," Leah said. "Venus is the goddess of love and she's the rising planet all week."

Ruth considered this and tried not to blush. Lately she had gotten the idea that whatever she was thinking about — Michael Shuga's hands, for instance, or her elaborate fantasies for cutting off Shirley Spencer's hair — was as visible to others as the text bubbles above the heads of cartoon characters. She wondered if this was a normal thing to think. Since they had moved in with their grandfather, her ideas about what was "normal" had been shaken to the core.

"Seeing the planets was cool, but when you're in fifth grade you get to go to the Cleveland Civic Center," Ruth said. "You'll see what the Cuyahoga River looked like before it got polluted."

Grandpa greeted them at the door with wet kisses. Ruth smelled the whiskey on his breath, the lit cigar on the counter, and the parsleyed burgers and onions he was frying which would have been delicious if not for the thick glob of fat he insisted was good for the girls' complexions. His food pantry downstairs was always stocked with countless cases of Crisco, Wesson oil, and lard; the freezer was crammed with butter.

"Give me the coat," Grandpa said.

"In a minute," Ruth said. She rushed to the bathroom and locked the door, then ran the water so that if he listened he wouldn't hear the paper rustling. She sat on the toilet and cracked the purple wax seal with her prize finger nail. The note said:

> Do you like me? Yes. No.
> Do you love me? Yes. No.
> Please circle the correct answers and write me back.
> You have pretty eyes and a nice neck.
> Love, Michael.

"Hurry up, girlie," Grandfather called. "You need some prunes?"

Ruth found an old eyebrow pencil of her mother's in the medicine cabinet and sat back down on the toilet. She circled "yes" twice, scratched out the name "Michael" and wrote "Ruth," and crossed out "a" and "neck" and wrote "teeth." She thought of the way Michael Shuga sometimes leaned into her shoulder as he bent down in the cloakroom to remove his boots, so gently she often wondered if she'd imagined it.

After kissing the note twice, she began folding it. She got off the toilet and turned the faucets to flow full force. The pipes squeaked, which was useful, because Ruth had to stamp the creases of the letter with her boots to make it small enough to hide.

"Leave some water for the fish," Grandpa yelled.

Her coat pocket would not be safe since Grandpa helped them with their outer garments so as to prepare them to marry proper Bulgarian gentlemen. Ruth considered her underpants, but what if it fell out like a mislaid wad of toilet paper? She wrapped a tissue around Michael Shuga's letter, slipped it inside the heart-shaped pocket of her dress, and joined her grandfather and sister in the kitchen.

"Mars can be seen on Thursday this week if you get up early," Leah was saying. "But Venus is in the sky all week. We saw it through the telescope today and it was disappointing how faint it looked. Sorta blue, and thin as tissue paper."

Ruth heard this as her cue to sneak some extra napkins from the counter. She held them behind her back and sat down.

"Then there's Jupiter and Neptune and Pluto," Leah went on. "They're farther away."

Ruth slipped some napkins into her sister's lap. "Don't forget Uranus," she said.

"Don't forget yours either," Grandpa said with a strange laugh. Ruth saw the little grains of meat between his false teeth.

Ruth stared at her burger and tracked the progress of the grease, which dripped like perspiration onto the sliced tomatoes, the olives, Grandpa's home-pickled peppers, and on, in a clockwise orbit along the rim of her great-grandmother Magda's china. Leah talked about the galaxies beyond our own, how it would take until the end of time to travel around the solar system. Ruth chugged her milk and asked for more.

"Speaking of time, Ruth Ann," Grandpa said as he leaned into the refrigerator and the girls quickly drained their burgers, "you gotta play that Old Lang song on piano for the relatives when they come for the holidays from Detroit. And for my poor Mama, who would be eighty-nine this year if she'd lived, I want a little 'Hinky Dinky Parlez Vous.' You know Mama loved Mitch Miller. She said it was the best thing about America." Grandpa handed Ruth her glass and looked at her critically. "She'll be watching you from Heaven if you make a mistake," he said.

"I'm going to do my dusting now so I can watch *Dark Shadows* after school," Leah said. She snuck Ruth her greasy napkin wad and scraped both girls' plates into the garbage can.

"I'll help you dust before I do the dishes," Ruth said, matching Leah's fake convivial tone. She turned so she'd have her back to Grandpa as she walked into the dining room. As Leah opened the bureau to get the chamois cloth they used to dust, Ruth shoved both girls' greasy napkins into the plastic bag she hid in the bottom drawer. Once a week, when one of the sisters accompanied Grandpa to the West Side Market where he bought meat and vegetables, the other would take the napkin collection behind the house to the neighbor's garbage cans. Ruth often wondered if Grandpa rummaged through their mother's used sanitary napkins to see if she got enough use out of them too.

"Aren't you girls forgetting something?" Grandpa said.

"I would have scraped your plate, Grandpa," Leah said, "but I thought you were having seconds." She sprayed the oak bureau and wiped it vigorously with the cloth.

"Ruth Ann?"

"I'll play the piano after I do the dishes," she said.

"Wrong again," Grandpa said. "It's Friday. We have to have

Clubhouse Meeting."

Ruth felt her heart pound down to her stomach as Grandpa approached. "Sit," he said. "Clubhouse Meeting called to order." He nudged them around the dining room table where no one sat except during holidays. "Leah, get the ears."

Leah sighed, reached into the bureau, and produced the three pairs of Mickey Mouse ears he'd sent away for that summer shortly after they'd moved into his house. Grandpa placed the ears on everyone's head and knocked on the oak table with his knuckles. He had borrowed the club concept from the re-runs of *The Mickey Mouse Club* he made them watch so as to be more of a family, except that instead of planning do-good capers to right the world's wrongs, in Grandpa's Clubhouse Meeting the girls had committed the crimes that he, as club president, had to punish.

"I was looking through the trash and I found something interesting here," he said.

Ruth felt her face flush. They were caught. She braced herself for what was coming.

Grandpa opened a bureau drawer and retrieved a crumpled up piece of notebook paper stained with coffee grounds and egg yolk. "What is this?"

"Looks like a gunky old piece of paper," Ruth said.

"Shut your trap Miss Smarty-Mouse! What is written on that piece of paper?"

In terror Ruth wondered if she'd slipped Michael's letter to Leah with the one, above-the-table napkin allotted that Leah had thrown out. It was so hard to keep all the piles straight. She pictured a heart pierced with arrows, saw the words "Michael loves Ruth" smudged with Crisco and ketchup and cigar ashes darkened into a murky jumble of marks. She couldn't breathe.

"Read this, Leah," Grandpa said.

Leah clutched Ruth's hand and blinked. Ruth slipped her free hand inside her pocket and kept it there. Thankfully, the letter was still there.

"'Holidays are here,'" Leah said quietly. "'The snow falls on his spit balls. I wish he would leave.' Then it's crossed out and it says 'Holidays are here. The snow falls on the roof tops. Santa Claus is near.' I'm sorry, Ruth."

"Mrs. Seufert made us write haikus for Christmas," Ruth said. "That was my practice page."

"Haiku is a Japanese poem," Leah explained.

"Piece of crap," Grandfather said. "It's so short. I told you, you gotta fill both sides of a page before you throw it out. House rules. You think I'm made of money, golden girls?"

"Haikus only have seventeen syllables," Ruth said.

"Smart-ass," Grandpa said. "What kind of poem is seventeen syllables long? You got an answer for everything, girlie." He ripped the paper into a thousand little pieces and sprinkled it, like snow, onto Ruth's head. "Now you clean it up. If I see one spec left you're getting the belt."

Ruth crouched low, hugged her knees to her chest to hide the letter, and started picking up the paper bits. Leah bent down to help but Grandpa pulled her up by the hand and pointed to the dust cloth on the table. "You're not the bad girl, Leah. I see a spot there, Ruthie. Good job."

Ruth gathered all the specs in her hem and stood awkwardly to carry them to the trash.

"Watch it girlie," Grandpa said. "You're a leaking box of Lux flakes."

"I could run the vacuum," Ruth said.

"No cheaters allowed in the clubhouse," he said, winking. He was happy again, Ruth could tell. He had found temporary relief from whatever it was that made him need to listen in on her phone calls or throw chairs and spoons at the girls for mistakes they did not know they'd made. She ground her teeth together as she braced herself for his kiss. He missed and hit the mouse ears instead with a loud smack.

"Can I do the dishes now, Grandpa?" Ruth said.

"Play something for Christmas first," he said. He lit a cigar and took a puff.

Ruth and Leah coughed in unison.

"Mom says that we should call them holiday songs, not Christmas carols," Ruth said. "She says the God she believes in didn't put people up on crosses to suffer."

"Ruth!" Leah whispered.

Ruth knew this would set Grandpa off but she didn't care, because she still had the letter which proved that Michael Shuga loved her, and she was on her way to living her real life. She lifted herself up and rose above the blanket of cigar smoke to the ceiling, floated into the living room, and squinted down with faint disbelief at the curtain rods strung tightly with blinking lights, the plastic "child-proofing" draped over the couch, and at the aluminum Christmas tree tipped to its side like a drunk. Outside the window there were naked magnolia trees covered with clean snow. Perhaps by the time they flowered, her mother would have enough money to get them out of there.

"Now you listen to me, girlie," Grandpa shouted. "Your grandma was a Hebrew, but she's dead. And that Jew father of yours is a Commie ignoramus, and if he's so great, why did he run off like that? Your mother and you girls, as long as you live under my roof, are gonna get Christmas whether you know it's good for you or not."

Grandpa followed her to the piano bench. "Play that one about the bells," he said. "That pretty one. The jingle jangle bells. Leah, you get those bells from the Christmas tree and play along. I'll play the castanets." He pulled his mother's castanets from the mantle and began to click them together against Ruth's mouse ears. His rhythm was off by one-half beat but she knew if she didn't match hers to his he'd say she was messing up.

"That's beautiful, honey," Grandpa said. "Now we need the one about the guy knows if youse been bad or good."

Leah jingled the bells behind her. Ruth began playing "Santa Claus is Coming to Town" as mechanically as she could. "This is so stupid," she muttered.

"I bought you that song book!"

Ruth looked up at the grandfather clock and closed the piano, placing her mouse ears on the bench. "Come on, Leah, we'll be late for school. We'll get our coats ourselves."

"What's biting you all of a sudden today?" Grandpa said. He marched to the hall closet and clutched the coats. "Ruthie, the lining of this coat is all shot to hell. If your mother had any sense, she'd be home now sewing it."

Ruth slammed the door behind her and pulled Leah outside by the arm. Grandpa followed after them on the driveway but he slid and almost fell. He coughed spasmodically and spit, and Ruth felt the word "ice hawkers" form in her mouth like a line from a haiku. She saw his knees wobble, saw the snow melt on his red shirt and his slippered feet, noticed how he jabbed at the air to steady himself as he slid. He was an old man, and for a moment she felt sorry for him. His eyes were brown like hers, but they saw things she never noticed. "I'm sorry I didn't do the dishes," Ruth called. "Save them for me."

The first in class, Ruth opened Michael's desk and placed the note on top of *Treasure Island*. Just at the bell, Michael slipped into his seat on her left. "Open the desk," Ruth whispered, her lips clamped tight like a ventriloquist's.

Boldly he laid the note in his lap, read it, and then put it on top of his book report, and made like he was adding a few last words to his assignment. Mrs. Seufert clicked her black orthopedics across the floor and picked up her long pointy stick. *"We are not the only Americans,"* she boomed. "We have neighbors to the South where it is very hot. Who can name a country in South America?"

With Michael's hand on her thigh Ruth gasped "Peru!" His fingers found her pocket and deposited the note. He squeezed her knee as his hand exited her lap.

"Please remember to raise your hand before you speak, Miss Horowitz," Mrs. Seufert said. "Would you like to come up here to the map and point to the major centers of industry in South America?"

"Yes, Mrs. Seufert," Ruth said. She walked carefully up to the front of the classroom, mindful of the note in her pocket, and picked up her stick.

"This is Lima," she said. "Where they have coffee plantations and rubber plants and people ride around on llamas."

"Just a minute," Mrs. Seufert said. "You know the dress code here. That dress is more than one inch above your knee."

"I just grew three inches," Ruth said. "Grandpa measured me yesterday against the cellar door."

"Then you knew without a doubt that it was time to lower your hemlines," Mrs. Seufert said. "I can't believe none of you children brought this to my attention this morning. Let this be a lesson to all of you."

Mrs. Seufert's hem ripper hung from the same chain around her neck as the recess whistle. With a force that knocked Ruth off balance, she tugged down Ruth's hem in one slice all around. Bits of torn, heart-dotted fabric tickled the backs of Ruth's knees.

The entire class watched in silence. After a moment, guffaws and titters began to mount from the back of the room, rising forward to Ruth like waves. With Mrs. Seufert's attention diverted on Ruth's hem, someone had instigated a paper airplane war. One swooped over Mrs. Seufert's head and circled back to the front row of desks, where Shirley Spencer sat. Shirley leaped up and tap-tapped to Mrs. Seufert in her black patent leathers with the paper jet outstretched on her palm. It was labeled *"Public Hairlines."*

"This looks like Robert Fitzer's penmanship," Mrs. Seufert said. "Come up here, young man."

Ruth ran out of the room to the lavatory, where she threw cold water on her face, looked at the mirror, and tried not to cry. She locked herself inside a stall, sat on the toilet seat, and picked at the threads of her hem, hesitating as her fingers felt the pocket seams for Michael's note. Then she made a horrible discovery. Her heart-shaped pocket was empty!

Ruth heard the sound of pelting hailstones and looked out to see Shirley Spencer's shoes. "Ruth Ann? You in here? Mrs. Seufert said it's your turn to read your book report to the class.

She sent me to get you."

"I'm sick."

"I'm sure your mom can fix your dress for you," Shirley said. "It's so pretty."

Ruth opened the stall door and peered out, searched Shirley Spencer's face for clues.

"I'm supposed to walk you back," Shirley said.

"I'll go in a minute," Ruth said.

"Now," Shirley said.

"I have to do something."

"Need any help?"

"I lost something," Ruth said. "I have to retrace my steps." She charged into the hall with Shirley on her heels.

"Your book report?"

"Kind of. Did you see anything in the hall?"

"I didn't know you were allowed to fold them up like this," Shirley said. She waved Michael Shuga's crumpled note across Ruth's face and grinned.

Ruth lunged for it, grabbed a handful of hair instead, and dislodged Shirley's silky lavender bow. Shirley pushed open the classroom door. "Ruthie," she said, "I'll give you the bow if you ask nice."

All afternoon Ruth was made to stand in exile with Bob Fitzer, the airplane perpetrator, at the back of the room. Her swollen eyes blinked. The room buzzed. Ruth was finally permitted to sit down when Mrs. Seufert flailed the stick to conduct the caroling for the Christmas party. Shirley got called on to distribute Mrs. Seufert's home-baked red and green iced cupcakes. Ruth folded hers up in a reindeer napkin to give to Leah. She was careful not to look in Michael Shuga's direction.

As Ruth made her way out the door of Riverview Elementary, Michael Shuga accosted her on the steps. "I would walk you home," he said, "but I have to deliver my papers."

Ruth reached for his shoulder and tugged gently at his scarf, pulling him toward her. She didn't care anymore who saw.

He bent down toward her as if to kiss. "Mail me a letter over vacation, okay?" he whispered. "Maybe we can go skating or something."

Ruth found Leah and glided home. Leah had to run to keep up with her, even though Ruth stopped many times to make nondenominational snow angels on the front lawns.

Before she knew it, it was Christmas Eve, and Ruth found herself in her grandfather's living room with the relatives from Detroit, who were smoking and eating snacks. Ruth and Leah's mother sat by herself on an overstuffed chair dressed in her best office dress and matching shoes. She was reading a novel, and looked vague and a little sleepy, the way she always looked to Ruth now that they were living at Grandpa's house. The room smelled of Turkish cigars and the lamb Grandpa was cooking. Everybody wanted to hug and kiss Ruth and Leah and toss them onto their roomy laps, except for the twin cousins, Joey and Josie, who were pulling each other's hair.

"Eat some candy and join the fun, miss sour-puss," Grandpa said, sticking a handful of butter mints in Ruth's face. "It's time for you to play the piano."

"Not yet," Ruth said.

"Such a slim little girl with such graceful fingers must be a skilled piano player," Aunt Ellen sighed.

"Music is for sissies," Joey said to Josie. "I bet when she farts it smells like perfume."

"Shut up, butt-brain," Josie said.

Great-Uncle Peter began coughing and spitting into a checked hanky.

"Your great-grandma is getting pretty impatient up there," Grandpa said. "It's time."

All eyes were on Ruth. She decided to play a few tunes to appease them, then yawn and say she was tired. In honor of her great-grandmother Magda she played "Hinky Dinky Parlez Vous." In honor of her mother she played "Won't You Come Home, Bill Bailey?" and "The Man on the Flying Trapeze." For Leah she played "Shine on Harvest Moon." All the relatives from Detroit sang along and clapped.

"Now my favorite one," Grandpa said. "Play those jingle jangle bells. Leah and I will help."

"I want the castanets this time," Leah said. "You can have the bells, Grampie."

"Okie, smokie," Grandpa said, but instead of taking the bells off the tree he opened the china cabinet and pulled out a red felt cap with bright gold bells at the end of it, then slipped it on his head with a flourish. "I'm the Christmas elf," he shouted. "Ho, ho, ho! We really got ourselves a Christmas here!"

"I wanna wear the hat," Joey called.

"No, me!" Josie shouted.

"Got any more bells?" Aunt Ellen asked. "We have enough folks here for an orchestra. Can I have the bells off the tree?"

"What kind of balls do they mean?" Great-Aunt Olga asked.

"I think he means the bulbs on the tree," Great-Uncle Andrew explained. "They were Mama's. She brought them from Old Country, each wrapped in big babushkas. They were made by village glass blower. Not like the piece of shit they make now."

"Quiet, Everybody! We gotta play the Jingle Jangle Bells!"

The relatives from Detroit were momentarily silenced.

Ruth felt queasy. She tried to slip off the bench. Her mother nudged her gently back. "Humor the old man," she whispered. "Today's his big day. Next year at this time, we'll be in our very own place."

Ruth mechanically hammered out the song. In the middle of the second verse Grandpa cleared his voice and said, "Now we gotta surprise. I have a special poem to read to youse. You keep the music going soft-like," he said to Ruth, "and Leah, you keep jingle-jangling the bells. We try something new."

Ruth was puzzled. Grandpa had made her read her holiday haikus aloud at dinner on the last day of school, but he had made fun of them for not rhyming. Ruth wondered how the Asian odd syllabled line would match the standard 4/4 time.

Grandpa cleared his throat and began to read. "Dear Mrs. Horowitz and Mr. Spigot," he said. "I am sorry to inform you that Ruth Ann has been writing letters of an intimate nature to a boy in her class when she should be spending more time on her book reports. Enclosed is a recent example.

"'Do you like me? Yes. No. Do you love me? Yes. No.'"

Ruth heard a gasp in the room and wondered if it came from Leah, her mother, or her own throat.

When Grandpa stumbled over the words "intimate" and "composition" no one bothered to correct his English. He tapped Ruth on the neck with the letter and burst out laughing. "We got ourselves a little lovie-dovie girl, huh?" he said, pinching Ruth's cheek. "That's some poetry!" Grandpa laughed so hard he began to wheeze. The choking sounds gave way to hic-cups and soon someone was slapping him on the back. Some of the relatives were buzzing back and forth in Bulgarian and Joey and Josie were still jangling the bells.

"Get him a glass of water," someone said.

Ruth slammed the piano lid onto the keyboard with one fierce hand and whacked *Mitch Miller's Greatest Hits* off the ledge. The discordant cry of the keys lingered in the air while the music book flew to the coffee table, overturning a bowl of mixed nuts and somebody's whiskey highball.

Ruth ran upstairs but her mother stopped her halfway up the staircase.

"How could you do that to her, Grandpa," Leah said.

"What? Do what?" he said.

"I never saw that letter," Ruth's mother said quietly. "If I had known about it, I would never have allowed — "

"If you loved me, you wouldn't make us live here," Ruth said.

"I know he's an old bastard," her mother said. "And he gets worse by the year, but try to be patient with him, and with me. I promise you we'll get out of here."

"When?"

"Ruth, listen. You've got to believe that somewhere in all that crap he gives you is some form of love. If I didn't believe that I would just take us to the housing projects and go on welfare, anything to get you out of here. He loves you girls."

"*Love?*"

"It's true," her mother said. "And my mother loved you, and of course I love you, and Leah loves you, and your father, wherever the hell he is, loves you too."

"You tell the lovesick girlie she's gotta come back down and try on the beautiful coat I bought her for Christmas. That old one was full of holes," Grandpa called.

"I told you she was a sissy snowflake priss," Joey said.

"What's wrong with the girl?" Grandpa said. "This is a holiday. We've got more songs."

"*Love!*" Ruth shouted.

Ruth ran to the room she shared with Leah and shut the door. Leah came up later with a plate of lamb and okra she'd drained, along with an extra pile of napkins, but Ruth wasn't hungry.

It was the Christmas of Ruth Ann Horowitz's eleventh year but she didn't think much of Christmas. Mars went retrograde as Venus rose in the sky. A bluish vapor floated over the city while everyone slept. The untuned piano jingled and jangled through the crack of the door, and Ruth began to sense that there were mysterious forces governing the universe. From now on, she realized, if someone loved her or hated her it was never again to be just a yes or a no. Ruth opened up her notebook and wrote the date. "Dear Michael," she wrote. "How are you? I am fine." She crossed out the last sentence and started a haiku about a girl and boy skating across the Cuyahoga River in a blizzard. She described the way the snow fell in layers like cake frosting. Suddenly a southbound train appeared in the poem and Michael and Ruth ran to hop it. Their skates hit the metal tracks and spit sparks.

There were way too many syllables, enough syllables to write thirty haikus. Even more. She wrote it all down anyway, and kept going. What she had to say to Michael Shuga was going to fill both sides of the page.

Christmas Is Special

Dorothy M. Ainslie

When you're nearing eighty you can stuff a lot of memories in your Christmas stocking. I fit in this age group and my sock is full. Every year I hang up my memory stocking by a clothespin in full view and one by one I pull out its contents.

As a child, Christmas was *Grandma's*. One always made me a new dress. The other one wrote me a letter.

My mother was a teacher. She got store-bought toys and hid them in the closet. Once while she was at work I peeked. That's how I found out about Santa Claus.

During "growing up days" my parents were divorced... but my father always sent a check at Christmas time to my brother and me... even though he didn't seem to remember in-between.

On December 23 in 1930 when I was sixteen my mother was shot in early morning in her classroom in Detroit by a would-be suitor. She was shot three times — bullets pierced through her body, near the heart. She suffered greatly but, miraculously, she did not die. I remember the ambulance, newsboys flaunting papers with headlines, "Teacher Shot," mother's long days in the hospital, the doctors, nurses, and medical paraphernalia... but most of all I continue to see the horror look on my mother's face, her starey eyes, and frantic fear reactions while, in contrast, the city populace was reveling in merriment and celebration. I'll never forget the holiday tinsel and ornaments and music proclaiming this Yuletide season. Christmas was for real that year. In the midst of sorrow and tragedy, the message of Christ's coming was God's way of comforting.

Later: During "bringing up a family days" Clayt and I poured our hearts into Christmas for our own four children. We had real live trees, homemade ornaments, cookies and pop for Santa, presents galore and bulging stockings. We went to church and Sunday school, took part in the plays and parties going on... in church, school, and community. I recall decorating bulletin boards and windows and doors with wreaths and jingle bells, taking pictures and writing hundreds and hundreds of cards.

Salvation Army bells rang every year — even way back then. Downtown Monroe was alive with people shopping. No one seemed to mind walking, even from far, far away. We gathered in the stores and on the streets and with a "hi!" to everyone.

Then in 1963, on November 22, President John Kennedy was shot in Dallas, Texas. Church bells in Monroe pealed loudly. Clayt and I and others attended services. This memorial time was part of what was to be our Christmas this year. Although deeply saddened by national event, with the advent of the festive season we went ahead with holiday preparations. As usual our family tree was special. At this time Richard and Debbie (two of our grandchildren) were with us. I remember on December 22, Clayt bought Christmas present shoes at Yaeger's in downtown Monroe by the bridge. Then, stark tragedy! And so sudden! Death struck at our doorstep. On December 23, 1963 — Clayt died... two days before Christmas.

What memories I have of these compounding events! In tears, we gathered together, bowed our heads and prayed. We clasped each other's hands and asked God's blessing for our loved one (father, grandfather, husband) and for all mankind. This and all my other Christmas experiences combine to make this season of the year a time of remembering joys and sorrows — sharing happiness and seeking meaningful understanding. Through my children and their friends and through extended family I have come to appreciate and respect all persons, families in whatever circumstance, and those of other cultures and religions.

In my growing Christian faith — my brimful stocking, bursting at the seams as it is with the interweaving of "worldly" and sacred memories, I have come to know **THE FULLNESS OF CHRISTMAS.**

At Christmas Time

Mary Ellen Kugachz

Tonight I walked the cold, windy
Upper West Side cement streets
bustling with students, strangers,
homeless men dressed like
prophets in layered blankets

trying not to think of Christmas

trying not to see the tinsel in the drugstore windows
    or the garland hanging 'round the Woolworth merchandise

trying not to see the bunches of pine-needled trees
    piled against wooden rafters fixed with speakers
    from which christmas carols blare,

— but I did,
I saw it all,

smelt the pine as my eyes
bore christmas ball-sized tears,

saw us skating across ice
in Wollman rink last year
you tossing your head back
with a santa laugh
as I wobbled on my blades,

and there I was
walking down Broadway
many city blocks away from you
many months away from you
my wedding band still on my hand
and all I could think of was you

and whether or not
I should call your answering machine
and listen to your voice promise
to return my call as soon as possible
which never seems quite soon enough.

co'c

Christmas, The First

Vicky A. Sigler

All the glitter, all the glimmer,
All the dreams and hopes and fears.
Swirling snow and voices caroling,
Laughter flowing down the years...

You sit alone on the sofa's end,
busily protecting the arm rest, and your heart,
while all around is Christmas.

Looking into your wine glass,
searching for her smile.
Listening for her voice above the crowd,
waiting for her touch on your shoulder.

And Christmas comes with the gently falling snow.
Christmas, the first...

Waking in a cold bed.
No tinsel, no tree, no gaily wrapped packages,
no surprises.

The family tries. For the children's sake they
go on and on.
But somehow, Christmas is over,
in your heart.

Christmas,
the first.

Christmas Past

Andrea K. Orrill

I thought it was the presents.
I was wrong.

It was the way you picked out each one
so carefully —
Just for me.

The way you handed me the packages —
unevenly wrapped, of course —
with a smile and a wink
and said, "Here's one from Santa."

We've got a tree —
I picked it out.
All brightly lit with glowing bulbs and
silver swans —
I won't use the tinsel though.

Those sparkling silver strands
you used to love —
They remind me too much of you.

Don't tell me —
I don't want to know
what you're doing 'special' for today.
You're not doing it with me.

Maybe some day I won't notice that you're missing —
But for now
I only think —
Where's Daddy?

Count on Midnight

Annette Lynch

— Where do you live? she asked behind
my car at Ralph's. When I pointed down
the street, the woman sagged away.
— May I help? called my Christmas mask.

After locking nervous keys
in the car, Jean failed to reach
her husband. She lacked enough
for a taxi, yet had to meet
her lawyer. I rushed her home
for keys and back to the car.

Six months before, the beating
her son-in-law raged on her daughter
led to gangrene, then death.
He had whipped their girls, 8 and 13,
off to his native France. My passenger
could not retrieve her only grandchildren.
Had to push a star legal action.

Jean gave me a red and green
box of macadamias. No stockings
hung, no wreath on her door.
This year, Christmas covered her in dark.

The Christmas Tree

Betty Hyland

He phoned her at seven to tell her he was just leaving the office. "But I'll have to drop in on the party, put in an appearance, shake a few hands."

"Please. Just for tonight you have to come home," she pleaded. "I can't move the tree."

"I'm on my way, Kiddo," he assured her.

"Please."

"I'm on my way," he assured her again at nine, but she heard fun percolating in the background and knew he wasn't.

She begged anyway.

Their five-year-old son was asleep upstairs, confident he would find a Santa-decorated Christmas tree in his living room when he woke in the morning, not the forlorn little fir listing pitifully on the front lawn, its burlap-encased ball frozen to the cold earth.

She had wrapped presents, assembled a puppet show, brought out the decorations, but the tree still sat where the nurseryman had dropped it five days earlier. Buying a live tree had seemed like a good idea at the time.

At ten thirty, she bundled in boots and wools and dashed back out to the front yard. After hacking doggedly at the ground with an ax, she managed to wedge a shovel under one edge of the ball, but still couldn't wrench the tree free of the frozen ground. She sat in the snow and pushed at the ball with both feet. She stood and gingerly reached through the snowy branches. She pulled her arm into her jacket sleeve to create a thick mitten, grabbed hold of the prickly trunk and pulled. Only the top of the tree moved.

109

She looked up at her son's bedroom window, then gazed at the sky as though Santa, himself, might speed down to release the tiny tree with a flick of his magic reindeer whip. But Santa didn't come, nor was there anyone else to ask, isolated as she was from neighbors and without a car.

Then, she had a wonderful idea.

She confidently hauled the garden hose over to the tree and let water trickle under the ball, certain the moisture would loosen the grip. In no time, she managed to turn the soft snow into hard-packed ice.

Tears froze to her cheeks as she walked toward the house picking pine sap from her fingers, certain the tree would be on the front lawn until the spring thaw.

Some time after midnight while she was testing lights, he came home in a taxi. Wondering if he had lost the car again, she pulled on her coat and ran out. He paid the driver, slammed the door and leapt spectacularly into her view. Eyes flashing, tie missing, he enveloped her in an exuberant bear hug.

"Merry Christmas," he bellowed. Tinsel hung from one of his ears. His face seemed to be slipping into his collar.

Good he took a taxi, she thought. It wouldn't be safe to light a match near his breath.

"Why are you standing out in the cold?" he wondered.

"I can't get the tree in."

"How come?" He smiled at the tree.

"It's frozen to the ground."

"No problem."

"Okay. You try."

With one magnificent yank, he wrenched the tree from the ground. A square foot of icy sod hung from the ball. A pit of steaming brown earth foamed where the tree had been. He rushed through the front door with the tree on his shoulder and dumped it into the galvanized tub waiting for it in the living room.

"There we go," he panted.

"The tree's crooked," she wailed.

The top of the tree pointed toward the corner of the room.

He tried to focus through steamed-over glasses. "It'll settle in better as it thaws," he offered, swaying in the direction of the tree. His face was the color of cranberry juice.

She studied his face, wondering if there was a chance he could have a heart attack.

He lay down on the couch, giving himself over to as-yet-unabsorbed scotch, his raincoat bunched around his head. "Wake me in a half hour and I'll give you a hand with that." He closed his eyes as though confident elves would come in the night and transform his home into a wonderland.

Bravely, and because he was asleep, she flung a Christmas ornament at his muddy shoes dripping onto her pillows, then pushed desperately at the gnarled mass of roots, burlap, and earth, sobbing in frustration.

Then, an idea born of desperation came. It was evident that no amount of pushing or pulling would straighten the tree, so she straightened the tub by shoving books under one side. Eventually the tree pointed toward the ceiling.

She put a star on top.

Encouraged, she encased the entire network of roots, dirt, burlap, ice, snow, grass, tub, and books in a white bed sheet. It was a seven-foot grotesque arrangement and only three feet of it was tree. But she was giddy with accomplishment.

Exhausted, she strung lights on the wet branches, then paused, afraid to plug them in.

"Wake up," she said, shaking his shoulder, "the branches are wet and the lights are electric and I don't understand things like that. If I plug them in, could I get electrocuted, could it start a fire?"

"Go away," he snarled, pushing her to the floor, his eyes mean, unfocused slits.

As quietly as she could so as not to antagonize him further, she hung ornaments and tinsel, then collapsed in a chair to wait.

◇

As the white rim of the Christmas sun appeared in the horizon, the boy burst into the room and shook her awake. She watched his eager face as he examined the room, prepared for the worst, but...

"Wow!" he decided. "That's neat. My tree's sitting way on top of a giant snowball." He admired it for a moment, then ran to the couch. "Daddy, wake up, look at my tree."

But his father pushed him away, rolled over to face the wall and didn't answer.

The boy turned to the puppet show, his face solemn. "I don't like Daddy when his mouth smells like that," he told her.

Old Christmas Eve

Don Williams

We three kids came home from school and caught Mama smashing out the window panes of the front door with a high heel shoe. She froze when she heard the screech of the school bus, braking to let us off. Then she just stood there, anguished and lopsided, wearing her other heel. The bus driver stared straight ahead, but our friends looked out from all the bus windows.

Her red hair was undone and her face was black around the eyes, so that at first I thought Daddy had hit her there, but he hadn't. It was just the way her makeup had smeared.

"You all go play," I told Jake, who was only eight years old, and Iris, who was six. Then I went up on the porch and looked in through the broken glass. I saw Daddy's whiskered face dodge back too late for me not to see him standing there with his bottle. I reached in and straight down my arm a shard of glass drew a red line that beaded up, then ran warm between my fingers. The blood dripped onto the floor as I turned the knob, and the door swung open.

"Good Lord, son," Daddy said and set the whiskey on the coffee table. He lifted my arm and stood staring at the blood. I was lucky though. It wasn't as bad as it looked, and the sight of it ended the fighting.

I didn't ask what they were fighting about, or why Mama was trying to beat her way into the house. They fought too regularly for that. You may as well worry why frost gathers on the grass or why the birds fly south. The fighting would pass. We all knew that, just like we knew it would come again. I only hoped we could make it through Christmas first.

The door had been fixed by the next day when we got home from school. Mama and Daddy were sitting on the couch like lovers you see in the movies.

Daddy had shaved. His black hair was combed back and his new sports shirt was open at the neck. He was holding Mama's hand. She was made up like a movie star, wearing stockings and high heels, and her red hair was piled up on her head. She smelled like a flower, and I thought of when I was small enough to sit on her lap all those years ago and play with her earrings. She looked up at Daddy like she was grateful for something.

Me and Jake and Iris stood looking at them, glad the fighting had stopped. Mama and Daddy smiled back like nothing had happened. Nothing at all.

Daddy said, "We're going to go out to eat, maybe do a little shopping. Ronnie, I want you to stay and watch after the kids," he told me. That was my chance to say something, but I didn't ask any questions. "By the way," he said, "what do you all want Santa Claus to bring you?"

"A sled," Jake said. "I want a Speedaway sled," and he began describing one he had seen at Wal Mart. Then Iris told them about the twin dolls and double stroller she had seen on TV.

I asked for the Daisy pump-action BB gun just like my friend Danny Logan's. I had coveted it ever since I first shot it. It had felt smooth and natural in my hands, and as soon as I aimed, I knew I was a better shot than Danny was. I knew how to squeeze the trigger. Easy, like Clint Eastwood in the movies.

About a week later, Daddy came outside where we were playing and called to us. He wore old clothes. His left hand held a pair of work gloves and his right held the axe.

"Pick your coats up off the ground," he said. We looked around nervously, breathless from our playing. "We're going down to John's Bottom," Daddy added. That was where we always got our Christmas tree, down where the evergreens grew thick along John Sutton's good bottom land by the creek. We followed Daddy down Bent Lane. Our shoes scraped icy gravel as we walked, past dried weeds hanging with faded seed pods, past fields of dark cedars that you could smell.

Naked trees cast a web of shadows across the road.

At the big curve, Daddy left the lane and stood by the rusted barbed wire fence that Mr. Sutton had strung years before. He stepped on the bottom strand and picked up the next one, and we three hunkered down and went through. Daddy stepped over the fence, straddling it carefully, and we walked into the field.

A flock of blackbirds feeding there lifted like a new-made cloud and I pretended to catch a bird in the sights of a gun and fire at it with imaginary bullets.

Jake remembered an old family joke. "We're going down to cut a whisker offa John's bottom," he said, and we laughed. We passed Mr. Sutton's herd of cattle, brindled black and dingy white. Daddy nudged me with his elbow.

"Watch out for old Jeremiah," he said as we walked past the big bull with the black face. "Don't look in his eyes. He'll think you're challenging him."

"Ruthie's big," Iris said, pointing. We looked at the calf that had been born in the fall, standing there against her mother's protective flank, then looked away as Jeremiah shifted his weight and took a half-step our way.

Jake pointed to a tree up ahead and ran to it. It tapered into the air like a steeple. Iris danced around it in the weakening sunlight.

"It's perfect, Daddy," Jake said.

"Yeah, perfect," Iris echoed. She had a finger in her mouth worrying a hang-nail as she waited for Daddy's verdict. I pulled her hand down and picked her up, so that my nose was in her red hair. It smelled fresh and clean. My hair is black like Daddy's and so is Jake's.

"Don't you think it's kind of big?" I said.

"We could take the roof off the house," Daddy said, "but then where would Santa land?" Jake laughed and ran off to look for another tree. We found it at the crown of a small knob. It looked too small when Jake first spotted it, but when we got there we saw that it was seven feet high at least.

"Stand back," Daddy said, and his axe struck white chips from it. They flew after each fierce stroke. "Here, try it out." He handed me the axe. I took it, avoiding his eyes. It felt heavy and solid in my hands. I felled the tree, so that it lay hanging by a strip of bark. Daddy made me give the axe to Jake. He heaved two strokes and the tree rolled over at our feet.

We all looked at it, and in the sudden silence I heard the dull thudding of hooves, followed by a snorting sound. Mr. Sutton's cattle had gathered at the base of the hill. They stood in the pocked field watching with gentle eyes, all of them facing our way, and I wondered what it would be like to be so big and yet that quiet.

"Watch out for Jeremiah," Daddy warned again. He motioned for us to follow him down the back side of the hill, then over the fence. On the road, we passed the cattle again and they regarded us silently.

Daddy said, "Grandma used to tell it that if you went over to the barn there after sundown on what folks called Old Christmas Eve you'd see the cattle kneeling, a-worshipping the baby Jesus."

"Really?" Iris asked. Her green eyes were big with the wonder of it.

"That's what Grandma used to say."

That was something I would like to see.

Daddy brought the tree into the yard and stood it up. Mama came to the door. She let out a sigh and nodded. She looked pretty standing there in the doorway.

"It's real nice," she said.

"I chopped it down," Jake bragged, smiling big. He had lost a tooth and his tongue came up to fill the empty space.

"Get a bucket," Daddy said, and I began gathering pebbles in a pail by the garage.

In the living room, Mama had spread out the decorations.

Daddy draped a tangled vine of lights and a shiny yellow rope on the tree, and we began to hang the ornaments. Mama hung the ones that had survived from a time before I was born.

We watched with solemn eyes as she took the tissue from a wine-colored globe that had "Silent Night, Holy Night" written in white on it. She cradled it in her hands.

"This is the first one we ever bought," she said. "Remember, Roy?" Daddy nodded, then she hung it on a sturdy branch above the reach of children. We stood looking at it. It was from another time when none of us were in the world.

The days dragged by. At night after the others were in bed I would look at the growing pile of presents under the tree, searching for the gun, even though I knew Mama and Daddy would put the big gifts out last.

I liked being the only one in the quiet room. Tinsel icicles glistened. The smell of cedar was on the air. The manger scene Mama had crafted from cardboard, paste and figurines was on the coffee table. Three kings brought gifts. A sheep, a cow and a donkey knelt beside miniature shepherds amid bits of brown grass.

"Please Jesus, don't let them fight," I whispered.

On Christmas Eve we sang carols, my mother's rich alto filling the room. I kept waiting for Daddy's sturdy bass to join in on "Joy to the World" and so I sang louder to make up for its absence. We sang "Away in A Manger" slow and gentle, then made our voices deep and strong for "We Three Kings." Mama read from the Bible about the shepherds keeping watch over their flocks by night, and the angel that appeared to them. At bedtime she set out a slice of lemon meringue pie and coffee for Santa Claus.

Daddy took down a glass and poured whiskey in it.

"This is what I would want if I was to fly in on a cold night like tonight," he said, and Mama looked at him. I saw her mouth go tight, then she stood up and led us down the hallway to tuck us into bed in the room we shared on cold nights. She lingered over us, sniffing something back, patting us to show us everything was all right, patting us with her hands white and light as doves' wings.

After she left we lay awake, restless in our eagerness to possess the presents that would come. At last Jake and Iris settled into their familiar easy breathing, but I couldn't sleep. My mind drifted and I remembered what Daddy had said about Mr. Sutton's cattle kneeling in the darkened barn to honor Jesus on Old Christmas Eve.

I got up and pulled on my bluejeans, my flannel shirt, the black and white vinyl jacket with fringe down the sleeves, cowboy boots and gloves. I raised the window beside the bed and stepped through, into the night's cold breath.

I walked down Bent Lane beneath a three-quarters moon. Its reflection shivered fragmented in the creek. I stopped once and looked back the way I had come. The house was small and far away, so that it fit with the rest of the neighborhood. I saw the lights of our living room come on. I knew Mama and Daddy would be laying out the main presents. I pulled my coat tight around me and walked along the shoulder of the road. "Please God," I said.

I saw Mr. Sutton's barn and started to cross the fence to it, then I heard a sound down by the creek and saw that the cattle had gathered there by a mound of hay. Their heads were inclined towards me. I watched them for a long time, hoping for the miracle, not knowing then that the Old Christmas Eve Grandma talked about came later and not on Christmas Eve like we have.

Had I known, I wouldn't have stood there until midnight before I walked away.

As I came close to the house, I could see the yellow window panes of the living room and the silhouettes of my parents. I walked into the yard and heard their voices, and I knew they were way too loud. I trembled as I went to the front door and looked through the new panes of glass.

I saw that the tree was down sideways on the floor, its lights still flashing red, blue, yellow and green. Mama was sitting on the living room rug in her nightgown. Daddy was standing over her, and I could hear the rage in his voice as he shook a new red-checkered shirt in front of her face, tore off a piece of green paper that fluttered to the floor, then grasped the shirt on either side of a seam and began ripping it apart until he held two flannel rags in his fists. Mama covered her face in her hands, and I saw the redness on her shoulder where he had hit her.

My legs began to shake and a tightness came into my chest. When he looked up toward the window, I ran, around the house to the window of my room. I raised it, then climbed in. I kicked off my boots and pulled off the jacket and somehow I got into bed without waking Jake. I heard Daddy's voice rising and falling with his rage, even though the sound was muffled by doors on either end of the hallway that separated us. My breath was coming hard and I realized I had been holding it ever since I looked in the house. By the time I was able to quiet my own breathing, the house had gone silent again.

Then it was daylight and Iris was patting my face and saying, "Guess what, Ronnie, Santa Claus came. Guess what, Santa Claus came. Come see. Come see." I pulled on my bluejeans and followed her into the living room. The tree was upright again, its decorations restored. Only the "Silent Night" globe was gone. Mama and Daddy sat in their house coats. Jake had already taken the ribbon off his sled and had it propped against the couch pretending to ride it down a hill. Mama and Daddy smiled, despite their bleary eyes, as Iris unwrapped her dolls and put them into their double stroller and pushed them through the house.

Daddy handed me the package that held my gun and I opened it slowly, then sat looking at it. It was a Daisy pump-action, just like I had asked for.

"What's the matter?" Daddy asked. "Don't you like it?"

I cocked it and thumped it once into the air. "I'm going off to try it out," I said. I went to my room and put my boots and coat back on. At the door, Mama stuffed Christmas cookies into my jacket pocket. She knelt there before me and as she zipped up

my coat her eyes searched mine to see if I had heard their
fighting, but I didn't let on.

"Be back in time for dinner, boy," Daddy said as I went out
the door. It was a strange thing to say. Christmas dinner would
be in the afternoon, and that seemed like a long time away.

The creek in the pasture was glazed with ice. It flashed in the
sunlight as I walked. Above, the whisper of a thousand blackbird
wings took my thoughts traveling southward.

I pulled the gun off my shoulder and bit two fingers of a glove
to pull my hand from it. Then I tore open the little pack of
pellets that shone with a coppery gleam. I cupped my hand to
form a funnel and directed the BBs into the bore where they
rattled and slid to the bottom. Propping the stock of the gun
against the side of my boot, I slid the compression pump up and
down the barrel until my arm ached and the pump was taut.

I paused on a plank bridge and looked at the cattle scraping
around among the scattered straw across a fence built to match
the contours of creek and field and hills. A dried seed pod from
a mimosa tree floated down the stream and I took a shot at it,
breaking it cleanly in two. Then I looked around for another
target. A stray blackbird had fallen behind the flock. I followed
its low trajectory, gave it some lead time and fired, then chased
its ragged course down the sky, through the limbs of a big
sycamore. I walked beside it as it fluttered along, one wing
grabbing at the ground. I turned it over with the toe of my boot
and pinned its good wing in the dirt. I put the bore of the BB
gun to its breast and closed my finger.

I walked towards home then. I thought of the steaming kitchen
and felt sick at the thought of us all together around the table. I
stopped beside Mr. Sutton's herd of cattle where they stood
among the scattered hay. They stared at me with mild and empty
eyes. I swung the gun towards the black face of Jeremiah,
standing out front.

I cocked the gun and knelt in the gravel. The big bull turned
his head away. Then, when he swung it back, I homed in on the

white of an eye, steadied my hands and squeezed the trigger. The eye closed, and one knee crumpled as if it had been slammed by a two-by-four. Pleased by this response, I fired again. It took two shots to Jeremiah's black face before his other leg gave out so that he pitched forward, uttering a high, broken cry as he went down on both knees in the hay.

"There," I said.

I lowered the gun and looked around to see if anyone had seen me do it. I saw the glitter of ice on the creek, dark cedars on the horizon, the ascending sun. When I looked back at Jeremiah, the parts of his eyes were like bits of candy that had melted and run together and threatened to drip down his face.

I turned my back on him and walked quickly up the gravel road toward home. I held the gun before me. It felt solid in my hands, as if with it, some way, I could change things around.

Family Christmas

Bill Morgan

Inane! Inane! Inane!
Chit-chat of dribble
lips echo father's whips
around the Christmas tree.

My four sisters grew up
under dad's belts of whiskey
leather and Christ. Stringent
bonds of bitter blood.

We're a vampire casket
Catholic family of repressions
loosed with a sip and a slip
at the lips.

Those days of dark
alcohol wife and child
bashing are history. Now
daddy's here, singing

joy to the world of
drinking by the winking
blue lights strung
on a false tree
whose silver-cold balls
disfigure our family
in the smoke filled room.

It's Janet's house.
She's brought everybody here
to witness family peace. Still
she seeks her own from days of old
in a smoke and a drink.
She flits about her Christmas
creche, spilling gin and tonic,
cursing memories
of his pounding hands.

Barbara's over by the couch
with candles remembering mama,
how she loved her and suffered
rejection by our father
who turned the Serpent's tooth.
She's facing him across
presents and drinks
wondering what he thinks
as she drowns her hate
with a tilt of a glass
and a fear of guilt
when he dies.

Peggie's gone away.
She couldn't make it
to the family take-in,
where we'd all frown at her
fawning for father's smiles.
She drinks, smokes, cokes and chokes
in a stale life of trying
to find warmth in men
frozen like dear daddy's been.
We're making fun of her,
the teary-eyed croc.
But who are we? drinking in
a Currier and Ives' gone wrong.

Jean's the youngest of the four-
woman Tomboy lot. Papa's best loved
rotten apple in the bunch
till I was born. Then
bitterness bubbled on her
whiskeyed tongue to be held
back for some eight years
before a hallway attack
with a slam to my back
sent my four foot frame flying.
It was a confirmation
kiss for little brother's
First Communion. Now fourteen years
have passed and we're laughing
together by a Christmas tree
in an eggnog daze.

OK, let us pray —
for more booze
to help forget hemorrhage-making
kicks to the head
of their mother on the floor,
to help forget the lashing out
at his orphanage days'
ghosts of Christmas past,
to help forget his lack
of courage without a bottle.

Now we open The Good Book
where Solomon says bitterness
is all your own.
I quaff mine
every Crosby White Christmas.

HOME: A User's Guide

Dan Dervin

Stories about leaving home, I mean, everybody's got one —
sad and inevitable and slightly uptilted in the end — but never
sadder than stories about *going* home, which is the one I'm
always telling — or almost always — for this time promises to
be different.

It began to be different once I realized all that leaving and
going-back stuff are really the same. The same telephone poles
in the twilight snow, looping down the two-laner, bobbing and
dipping and shooting off a light beam from the tail end of the
somber rose sun, or trailing the moon. Same going or coming.

And beyond, chalky fields of hacked-up corn, a naked cluster
of elm or hickory on a rise, a shabby hulk of stables corralling
frozen muck, finally the farmhouse all decked out in Christmas
bulbs and laced out to a solitary fern over a nativity scene.
Waving.

Where would you be without these desolate hilltop islands that
flit by and remind you how close and then how far you always
are?

Attic windows in half-raised amber shades beckon briefly, and
you're up there plump on the floor exploring all sorts of old
forgotten treasures, accumulated junk, but preciously preserved
— a cradle on wooden rockers, a crate of handmade toys, books,
old magazines, diaries — you whizz by, wondering, what's up
there?

Lost secrets; stories never to be told.

And you refocus on the flickering road because you're going
home or leaving, and all in a sad inevitability with just a slightly

upswinging promise that keeps you going — somewhere. Because if home exists, all other places are somewhere else.

It goes without saying every home has a mom, and at the moment mine is pulling Merry-Christmas flags off a sumptuous fruitcake so unbelievably fruity there's precious little cake, and she's saying, "Sister Lillian bought it at the monastery — must have cost ten dollars." There ensues a discussion of modern nuns who drive Fords and order pizzas and dress like people, but are still the same Sister Lillian who hovered over you in the fourth grade. "If I called her," Mom is suggesting, "would you say 'hello'?"

"*What?*" I was panic-struck.

"Just a 'thanks' — 'the cake is tasty,' or — "

"'Merry Christmas?'"

She smiled encouragingly.

"After forty years?" I should bubble up with small talk to a nun? Then on the other hand, time collapses, you're home and never away at all. You may think you have been away, broken free, grown up, begun a new family, accomplished whatever wherever. But at the moment, you're right here and the fruitcake you're munching is compliments Sister Lillian who glowered over my times-tables, her stiff ruler ever-ready for our tender palms, never smiled, never said, "Play your cards right, child, and someday I'll favor you with a sumptuous fruitcake."

Never. We probably frightened her more than she us — or about equally, and so now I'm to call and with no lisp or lapse, blurt out, 'Hi, Sister; hey — I'm really nuts about your fruitcake'?

"This slice is awfully gummy, Mom."

Indigestion would set limits to maturity. Limits to filial love. Limits to gratitude. Maybe that's why you come home — to rediscover limits — and why you only think you've left.

There was an ice-storm the night I arrived, and since then the sun has been in hiding and the wind-chill factor has sunk to minus minus. Talk of the weather has perked up the town. Up to the minute messages trail like kites' tails along the bottom of the TV screen. Twenty-seven vehicles have crunched up in one notorious intersection. Whole counties are frozen solid. All ponds, puddles, and cow-pastures are transformed into splendid ice-rinks.

In the living-room, I lace up old skates, pump up the hill, and ice-skate on the church parking-lot, which used to be our fenced-off playground at recess. Skating in wide looping swings, I'm peering through the thin ice and dull concrete to the submerged dusty gravel, to the broken crayons and chalky bases, the trading-cards and bubblegum-wrappers, the ribbons and contraband notes. The peripheral girls in spindly legs and midnight-blue uniforms, jumping rope and trading cards and watching a boy smack the ball, skim the bases — but they were sent forth from non-peripheral homes, grew up bent on making new homes, succeeded or failed on precisely those terms, most often ending resigned to send forth a new set of rambunctious kids to round the circle once more.

Carefree, unconstrained play; play within childhood's fences.

Somewhere in that busy playground is Joanie who, amidst all the turmoil, traded me her best-buddy card to save her tomorrow's special-date one. Yesterday I called her: "Let's go ice-skating!"

She vented a mature chuckle.

She was very good on ice, though never with me; now, at the mall where she sells paisley and flower prints to precious young things, she rang off. Doing year-end accounts and putting her home on the market — a rambling rancher dreamhouse won by trading her queen of hearts to a devoted vassal; together they had trumpeted onto the playground of this world five children, four pretty girls and one boy — all coming too late to hold their father home.

He had earlier missed a card in the hand his folks had dealt him, a wild card and, as it never turned up in his own marriage, a year ago he discarded his hand. Joanie needs to sell the house, knowing their fast-growing kids will miss having a place to come back to.

"To hell with 'em!" exclaimed Orville the other night — he's another grown child from the same playground whom I annually visit en route home. Orville then added a stronger epithet to drive the point home; from the kitchen, Fran gasped. The wail of the battered parent. Their son had called from Milwaukee to request his parents not visit him while he was in a Recovery Group for Adult Children of Alcoholic and Dysfunctional Parents. "That really hurt," said Orville, who takes his martinis before and with his meals but was hardly more dysfunctional than other playground survivors. So the kid had been taken ice-fishing in Wisconsin and he whined in the cold and Orville said, "That's enough now, Eric" — and the kid's inner child is devastated?

And your whole adulthood's trashed?

Orville's an architect, and his home is a work of art, but he's putting it on the market, taking Fran to the little bungalow he's designing in the Ozarks, 700 miles from his closest child, guestroom not included. Their married daughter Kim — who ran off with a Greek waiter to Greece, was mistreated, returned remarried to an amiable trucker, blended her children with his, and settled down so she could be close to home — drops by, and I ask her how she feels about her folks moving away. "You really want to know?" I nod. "I think it's really selfish of them."

"Give us a break, Kim," Fran pleads from the kitchen.

"Screw 'em!" Orville concludes on cue.

The kids we once were tore out familial roots and dared return only after we had securely transplanted; now kids still tear off, have second thoughts, get replanted, and parents pack it in.

Looping over the ice, I anticipate the clanging, piercing punctuation of Sister Lillian's black-handled, brass bell. Had she murmured one day as I filed by, "Play your cards right, sonny, and someday you'll get a ten-dollar fruitcake"?

Not so's I remember.

But then I didn't play my cards well. I traded my jack of hearts to Fran's best buddy, who held out for a king of diamonds. Did we gaze past the decorated backs being circulated

— roadsters and waterfalls and thatched cottages — to one another's faces?

Now that little girl's out in Cleveland with her own family, and her original king of hearts, her father Joe, is a spry old widower who computes my mom's taxes with a mild eye to courting. Dying's not what it was, courtship returns, parenting goes on and on....

Last year at this time she drove Joe by to drop off a present, and I caught up with her in the drive. We hadn't faced each other in several lifetimes, but leaning toward the window, I saw that lifetimes never really pass, we never change, one lifetime is never over, and managed to say, "Time evens it up — you got away from me and I got away from Plains."

She sort of gaped at me until Joe came up and then backed out with a lifetime-shedding smile: "Guess we've both had some good and bad luck."

"I don't want to hear about it!" Cry of another shell-shocked, post-traumatic stress-disordered parent — can't mistake it. This one's from Frank, lives across town. Loved to sail, to ski, play tennis. Traded his boat, stored his skis, restricted his tennis to Sunday morning doubles — all for Mary Beth, an irresistible young nurse from Wyoming. In time's fullness they turned up a fullhouse: three boys, two girls. Great kids — themselves now into marriage, relationships.

We're in his basement where he strings rackets when the phone rings and he can tell by Mary Beth's voice it's Andi, the youngest. Calling from backcountry Arizona, needed to dump this beat-up Chevette, but there were problems with the plates. Her ex-roommate Terry — a boy's or girl's name? — had given it to her while she did a masters degree in creative writing at Tucson.

"She wants to sell the car and come home," Mary Beth calls from the top of the steps, "but she's not sure who owns it, so maybe she'll drive it home, but the tires are — "

"I don't want to hear about it!" Frank explains.

"Besides, she wants her Macintosh along to finish — "

Frank delivers his line once more, which had also been mine whenever one of my brood would bring home the latest in heavy metal — I don't want to hear it! — but no, hell, I always bit my tongue. I must have the most bruised, chewed and mangled tongue in creation — can one die from a mouth full of chopped liver? Mourners will review my open coffin and marvel, 'Not a blemish on him anywhere,' and then someone's head will shake and murmur, 'Take a peek at the tongue, poor chap.' 'Bit himself to death.' 'Critter never had a chance.'

"She's writing this novel," Frank muses, calmly resuming the string-job. "It's about her mom's childhood in the wilds of Wyoming — Andi's never set foot in Wyoming!"

He releases one of those sardonic whooping abortive laughs parents use to defend against their children's mystifying turns.

"I guess that allows her to invent it."

"She'll do a lousy job." More mystified chuckles.

"Does she ever ask Mary Beth — ?"

"She doesn't want to hear anything about it. Mary Beth tries, but Andi turns all red in the face and starts shouting."

"Guess it might interfere with her imagination."

"I don't know what it is about this kind of racket," Frank is frowning professionally over his work. "They always pop a string in the same spot — must be a weak spot somewhere."

And most likely it's not one you see coming.

Overall, I think Andi's smart to invent her mom, because you can tell moms are ending operations. Bit by bit, all over the world, the great mom systems are winding down, switching off, shutting down. Stitches from the mending I bring home — once set for a lifetime — now come loose almost immediately. That's the least of it, of course. The arthritis keeps her up every third or fourth night, her steps are short and tentative, as though at any point the floor might open and swallow her.

Yes, we all better get busy inventing new moms because the old ones are closing shop. Andi's onto something and Frank knows but doesn't want to hear about it. Mom is home, home is mom.

"Come on upstairs," Frank is saying with the strung racket next to his ear to pat and ping. "Mary Beth's made a fruitcake."

"Great." We used to have homemade fruitcakes — great dark contraptions that sponged up draughts of whiskey and endured till Valentine's day. Now it's Sister Lillian or abstinence. Moms are going out of business. Not protected by any endangered species act; not included in the sisterhood enterprise. In fact they undermine anyone's liberation trip. Instead, we have primary caregivers, day-care centers, and goddess-friendly workplaces — moms not included. Expect *mom-free workplaces* to be posted. Back home, dads are being trained to mom. Moms are embarrassing — 'excuse me, your mom is showing.' Don't leave home *with* one. Others claim money in moms — dial-a-mom, rent-a-mom. I don't want to hear about it — and don't send us any throwaway moms.

No Mom exits occur along Interstates which lead only to more Interstates. For Mom you need to get on back-roads, watch the sun sink to that unbearably deep rose hue, let the fields come up chalky, pass those forsaken farms, and keep on to Plain City. Then you're getting close.

Plain City — as if the next exit promises Fancy City, not that you'd be fooled. Out on the Great Plains every clunky town is Plain City — it's where we all come from and it's all Mom country.

The rest have passed away or moved on.

My older brother Jack has moved on to Silicone Valley and is due to land any minute. He's a New-Age vegan; I'm an old-hat carnivore — he's getting younger, I'm aging rapidly. Instead of time, we count cholesterol — his down, mine up. Our paths cross in hyperspace. Right now he's in potential reality, closer to Hong Kong, Paris, or Buenos Aires than to Plain City where he is about to materialize. He has two grown-up kids living at home. Girl's separated from her Chicano flower-grower spouse and is turning the house into a day-care center so she and other young moms can go to college. Son's with auto supplies, periodically dismantles and rebuilds his Mustang, fishes, plays guitar with his heavy-metal honchos in the backyard orchard. 'Hasn't turned the corner yet,' Jack will sigh philosophically.

No surprise, Jack's gotta go home, get back in touch. Could be his kids know more than us when we flew the family coop at eighteen. But with a little magic anyone today can go home again: Jack does it via hyperspace. Now that he's deplaned, we press flesh and face mundane icy pavement, known to arrange unplanned meetings between unfamiliar objects in very real space.

At home fraternal space bends out to family space where it takes at least three to make a family, but as long as one is the mom, the rest can be whoever, and although culture is credited with constructing everything from square tomatoes to mail-order moms, I still favor the natural-born kind, scarce as they are.

Basically, we're in a fix.

Like flowers late in the day, natural-born moms over time bend and close in a bit on themselves and peck away at their meager meals like disinterested wrens, though this may be distorted by their growing offspring. As Jack says when he steps out of hyperspace, the streets are narrower, yet the trees are *gigantic*. True for the trees — they've been growing all the while — but not for the neighborhood streets. Sons shoot up, moms shrink.

Home is a very peculiar kind of hyperspace.

On my campus out East, I've attempted to introduce Philosomom studies, translatable as 'love of mother-wit,' but the big guns, wanting none of it, tag it the 'banality of the benign.' In fact, the immortals have been uncharacteristically reticent on the subject of moms. When you come down to it, moms are not very metaphysical, and even physically they dwell in a peculiar kind of hyperspace.

This is one reason when the top guns moan about a 'metaphysics of absence,' they must mean moms. The M-word. It's decentering; it's transgressive; it's subversive — they mean embarrassing. Slide that little signifier under your signifieds in a hurry.

My one disciple is a child-psychologist — colleagues call him a 'child person' — whom I play squash with. He believes most of us start out with 'good-enough mothering.' No argument from me. Moreover, our very first word is formed after we've been humming happily at the breast and suddenly pop away from the nipple: 'Mmmmmmm-m-a-ah! Ma?' And as mom echoes the sound, 'Ah-mma-mma' is right here,' she thereby identifies herself as the 'first semantic object.' It seems that almost every language has its equivalent 'mom' with an initial M. So the buck of the whole 'arbitrary sound-system' called language stops at m-o-m. 'Relax,' they assure us, 'words merely refer to other words, all a game' — ah-h, don't they wish! Not in the beginning, not in the end.

Mom's being there is why we're here.

'Know thyself,' urges the philosopher, but who can the way Mom did? And so when you hear about the mom-shows ringing down the final curtain and no word of their getting their act together and taking it on the road, you have to wonder where that leaves us.

When I once replied to the child-person that 'good-enough mothering,' probably offsets 'bad-enough fathering,' he didn't crack a smile, though subsequently made several wide swoops at the ball. Moms, by and large, do come with dads. Dads are disappearing, too, but that's, as they say, another country, and Christmas, with its candles and wreaths, its carols and cooking, is a feminine feast, a birthday with a glowing virginal caregiver and Joseph the elderly bald chap stooping unobtrusively over his staff in the shadows — 'Call you if we need help, Joe, 'bye now.'

The Irish dad I had contributed a bit more than offering to periodically dose the familial fruitcake with Old Cabin Still. He took me for walks, which is how the subject came up this year at dinner. Mom hadn't picked up ice-cream and was reminding me of the Sunday ritual dessert in days past. True enough, in my memory-bank I had misplaced those childhood walks to Izzy's Market on twilight January Sundays.

During those grim war years, I see my civilian dad incongruously in a fatigue jacket and fedora. I was dreadfully certain kamikaze Japanese would storm over the hill, like howling Indians in a Western, and in fact I knew that hiding out in our attic was a wounded Nazi officer I dare not mention. So what did we discuss on our winter walks? Maybe after twenty-years of psychotherapy I could recover those crucial dialogues and then wouldn't have to congregate in the forest with half-naked fellow savages performing a new-improved father-bond.

I'm sure we didn't discuss the war. Or Dad's work, which was in his service station. Or Sister Lillian as substitute whatever.

"My hands are cold." Whining.

"Well, where are your mits?"

"Jack's got 'em." Lying. Lagging behind.

"Hurry up then." Scampering to keep up.

Dad's gloves are black-leather lined with rabbit-fur, present of an uncle. He doesn't need to grab hold of my red-raw knuckles.

"What flavor we gettin'?"

"What kind do you like?"

"Butterbrickle!" The biggest, tastiest, ha-ha word I knew.

He was unamused. "Your mother will want vanilla to go with a topping."

"Butterbrickle!"

A moral dagger was suddenly unsheathed. The mom I knew — and knew far better — was mad about butterbrickle. There ensued a dramatic plunge into a snow-bank that bypassers might construe as a display of childish temper. A runny-nose, bleary-eyed, teary-cheeked, subdued face. A solemn march to the market, giants negotiating over a high counter, a silent retreat home. The child in his slopping galoshes is sentenced to newspapers by the front-door, while the triumphant dad presents his trophy to the delighted mom.

This segment from my memory-bank may be filed as Life with Father, or How I Lost World War II. Many years later when I was overseas consumed with my own family's comings and goings, he was taken by a stroke; I did not return at once and felt guilty not the least for not feeling guilty. He was the least humorous of men, devoted to the rules of his Church and given over to brooding in his last years over a family inheritance that had by-passed him. Perhaps, he had brooded a whole lot longer; very likely he had. Very likely a case of chopped-liver tongue. There were family farms folding, land leased out West that refused to gush oil, and other disasters Jack and I landed in the path of without warning.

Families are funny places. Chopped liver, the daily special. I have progressed so far as to extract the why from the whine.

Jack and I have just sat through a devastating movie about a family destroying one of its children, while ostensibly celebrating fly-casting in Montana — no whines, plenty whys.

'All is calm, all is bright' on this Christmas Eve, and while sensible families are nestled near their trees passing out candies and kindly thoughts, Jack deems it propitious we visit the old Italian market district, now gentrified and hippiefied. Of course nothing will be open, won't be a soul about, but older brothers must be humored.

So we're treading the icy bricks, passing the darkened shops, and this shape of a man looms up before us: stout and unshaven and hunched inside the grimy green parka of a gas-station attendant.

"Hey, buddy: help a guy out? Need a dollar-fifty for a bus to Miami — "

I start around the bum, but Jack approaches him, peers into his young, but caved-in features and says, "Didn't you hit me for a buck last night?" Jack turns to me. "He wanted a bowl of soup, so I said, 'Let's go. At that price I'm game too.' But the joint was closed. Next he needed some change for a bus to Milwaukee."

"Miami," the fellow corrects.

"You sleeping out in this kind of weather?"

"Under the railroad bridge," he replies with a note of pride.

Jack shakes his head, pulls out a wallet and withdraws a single, glancing at me. I follow suit. The fellow accepts our offering with a merry nod and is soon devoured by the darkness.

"He's an unfortunate Irishman someone didn't do right by,"
Jack nods, affirming the big-brother's inherent edge on things.

And with a further nod, he's ready to go home.

Some ghosts are easier to lay to rest than others.

A new ice-storm has put the icing on our hill as far as getting
to Christmas Mass, which Jack and I have missed anyway for
too many ice-free years to count. "It's not the sin it used to be,"
Mom reassures us about her omission as she sets about cooking
cornbread and catfish, blackeyed peas and brown-sugared yams.

Meanwhile, Jack beckons me up to the attic. In a dim corner
he clears off a cedar chest and casts about inside until he fishes
out a packet of weathered envelopes bound by red yarn. They
are addressed to Miss Mamie Mosley/Yazoo City/Miss. The first
canceled two-cent stamp is postmarked Plain City, 12/23/1927.

Jack nudges me to go ahead, open one. They're our parents'
courtship letters, and I don't dare. Jack takes charge.

"'Dearest Mamie,'" he reads:

'Received yours and glad to read your letter — they are so
nice. Maybe I better not tell you of such cold weather, if it
brings a change down there....'"

"What?"

"He means she may change her mind about moving up here."

"Oh."

"'Sure keep busy selling alcohol — '"

"What?"

"Anti-freeze."

"Oh."

"'You asked about those tonsils etc. Oh I'm feeling fine as silk
and as usual — you know I'm never sick. Gee, didn't you ever
have the measles. Well, you've missed something that I had. If
you get a chance you might as well take them — as once is all
you get them.'"

I glance at Jack sprawled contentedly on the floor.

"'The Will Rogers picture you mentioned was advertised here
but I didn't see it. Saw a whizz of a show this week at the

Paramount. Six acts and they are all good — talk about laugh I'll
say — believe I split a lip.'"

"He went to movies?" This is news to me. "He laughed?"

"He took me to movies, yeah." Jack is sitting more erect.
"Before your time — in the old house — "

"That's right! A Charlie Chaplin — "

"So you remember — ?"

"*The Gold Rush*." Remembering now with pride.

"And he laughed all the way through it."

"Everyone laughed."

"But he laughed with the rest. You were afraid of the bear and
the outlaw."

"The little guy boiled a boot and served the laces up like
noodles — that sort of worried me."

"That really broke him up, remember?"

"I was pretty small."

"We weren't going to take you, but Mom wanted her nap in
peace."

I puzzle over these latest revelations, until Jack gestures
toward the unfinished letter.

"'Baseball's famous clowns were on the bill too and it's a
laugh a second with them....'"

It goes on like that and closes with 'Love.'

He was a guy.

He dressed in suspenders and bow-tie, smoked Wing cigarettes
and cussed over carburetors, played soft-ball and lost his hair...

A guy. Mom's guy.

At Christmas dinner, Jack leaves off our discussion about the
Redskins and the Forty-niners to confirm Mom's maiden name
and her mother's first, which were both the same: Mamie
Mosley. Jack has been struggling to grow family trees.

Neither parent had been very forthcoming about their
childhoods, but their respective losses had perhaps added to a
mystery over ancestry. Dad's mother was barely a mom to him,
having died when he was seven and leaving behind a daughter,
seven husky, hungry lads, six of whom grew into strangely

reticent uncles, producing various aunts and cousins, and a seventh, our dad, producing us. Mom had fared worse: her mother never became a mom to her, dying soon after giving birth. Our momless Mom was raised by a southern-Methodist grandma until Dad could liberate her... and now suddenly being displayed in Mom's open palm is a braided bracelet of light-brown hair taken from her mother, fresh as the day it was cut. The shade was Mom's before hers turned snowy grey; Mom is her mother's ghost.

Home is hyperspace wrapped around time-warps.

And I'm back stomping on those wet newspapers, while Dad slips off his rubbers and delivers the ice cream. 'You scream! I scream! We all scream for ice cream!' But Mom is sounding disappointed. She had wanted vanilla, but here is butterbrickle. A silence follows. Then they are both peering in amusement toward the child confined like a new puppy to newspapers.

Did I forget this part? Am I now imagining?

The bracelet has vanished, it's dessert time. No ice cream. The vestiges of Sister Lillian's fruitcake. Maybe I'll surprise her with a call. Just to say, 'Hello.'

And close with love.

*[Adapted from an earlier version for the **Pikestaff Forum**]*

OUTSIDERS

The Christmas season places a unique strain and focus on the culturally alienated. Those who are already, by choice, by circumstance or by birth, counter to the dominant culture often find their "outsider" experience is sharpened by the seasonal cold as they stand outside the proverbial frosted window, pressing their noses into the holiday view of normalcy, "home & hearth." With longing, disdain, bitterness or perplexity, they stare in, while feeling out.

Standing apart from the customary festivities of the season, whether through emotional distance or actual experience, our "outsiders" take the long view of the Christmas phenomenon. In doing so they provide a clarity of vision often lost amidst the sparkle and glitter. Christmases far from home — from Jakarta to Alaska — provide an invigorating sense of cultural liberation and renewal for two of our authors; in "Earthbound Angel" an alienated artist experiences an unexpected Christmas epiphany. From other contributors we hear the cry of despair, feelings of aloneness and differentness sharply accentuated against the background of holiday cheer.

The poignant, "Solstice," and darkly humorous, "The Spire of Christmas," place us twice removed from the "insider" experience, for stories of Christmas suicides cannot be told first-hand. "A Prison Carol" and "What's A Noel Anyway?" document Christmas in prison. Other tales are not so extreme; but all of these voices — be they homeless, elderly, depressed, grieving, non-Christian, or just plain lonely — remind us of how extra vulnerable many of us are to "the blues" at Christmastime. For some there is no answer but the poetry of lament; others do find a kind of solace, from persons who share unexpectedly, and from creative resources within.

From year to year our outsider/insider status may change, as reflected in "Boston, 1966," further heightening our awareness of what has been gained or lost. Indeed, the outsider's perspective can be the gift of a fresh look at all we take for granted, and a reminder of its transiency.

Exorcism, Christmas

Peter Cooley

Voices paint the streets,
Bells, green, limbs, echoes
in thickening ice.

A long arm of the sun
knits its winter arches
over my ribs.
Under my skin the families of blood,
crossing of pin and web,
weave a groove
to follow me in.

All day I have been listening
to this place inside myself
where no one comes.
How it is written,
how it goes down,
the horizon's shattering breath.

I cry myself
into stones to feed the wind
in this hard place, alone.
Light trims
known signatures of trees, the crowds,
across my face.

Go home, go home.
The tree is sprung
with teeth and hair, the nails
of the living, loving
their long bones out.

You can dance, the dissevered hand,
never allowed to clap.
Plunge your spiny
fingers through needles and sap
to proffer gifts.
A gobbet of skin, the bone rings
of love to bear again.
Amulets against blood, ice,
and understanding.

Solstice

Cathryn McCracken

Christmas day she wakens to the lights, thick, red, pulsing aloud in the forest of the living room. The cats are quarreling. Daylight is only a hovering absence, a remote potential of later sun. The old black mother cat growls at her kitten, who disappeared for two days and returned with a cut like a dirty badge across his ear. The woman supposes he must have the wrong smell now. His mother stalks him from six feet behind, the sound in her throat like the hum of a living engine.

Marta makes the coffee uneasily, aware of the responsibility of this day, aware, below the rumble of her usual thoughts, that a curious inner radio is blaring. Beneath the monotony of that beat she senses trouble, but can't peel enough of the untidy music off to get to it. The coffee is very slow; water takes hours to boil, grounds scraping away into silence, cream falling thick and heavy. On the dining room table even the sugar bowl feels cold, lethargic, the lid a metallic mouth which refuses to open. Cold, heavy, thick, and the glaring red lights are merciless over it all.

It was a morning like this, she thinks, touching idly at the lining between inner and outer voices. Solstice. She takes a breath. It was a morning like this, when the cats were full of bad dreams.

She pours a cup, takes it into the bedroom and sits down on her side of the double bed. Joe is gnawing sleep with little snoring mumbles, angles of arm and leg bisecting the bed. She leaves the orange cup on the table. No help there.

In the living room the presents glow like gaudy underwater

plants, red-glittered fish with ornamental teeth. The kittens use them as an obstacle course, under the full loose tent of the branches, chasing over the bright purple bow of grandma's new robe, wrapped in fancy gold department store paper, behind strings of red lights shoved carelessly into the socket.

On a day like today her sister's heart stopped.

Again she fingers the border, wanting to unwrap the need there, afraid of the still cold of the package, the coagulated touch of three years, the memory of the little urn of ashes which was all that was left for the funeral. Cremation. A red package of flesh reduced to powder, the pump and heat rendered cold and anonymous. Ashes and a photograph, a few lines from Carlos Castañeda printed below it. Life is only a journey. But where to?

Her Buddhist sister had believed in possibilities, but she had only the rounds of the seasons. Solstice and Christmas, though spread apart by the four days between the twenty-first and the twenty-fifth, were much the same to her. The dark time, when death overtakes the earth, layered by the Romans as Saturnalia, covered up by the Christians as the lord's birthday, but celebrated in pagan times as simply the ascendancy of the dark.

Memory: the wedding reception, her sister's witchy mother-in-law, a good California spellcaster who wore black to the wedding. All his relatives in black, poets from San Francisco, and her sister in her long white dress so chic, the sophisticated Chicago people. And above this, superimposed upon it, another memory: her ashes in a little urn, to be put into a paper boat, like the Buddhists do, and sent to China. Over the ocean, over the sea. Did they burn her in that fancy white dress, so her soul could travel in marital bliss?

Tears hover somewhere between San Francisco, where the ashes set out, and the Pacific storms which finally swallowed them. In slow time, in the dark red honeythick streams of the lights, she sees the girl young, her cornsilk hair blowing, the hours spent together in holiday cold while Mother and Dad fought, sees the girl's glasses fly out from her nose, broken when Mother slapped her that time and the blood came out.

Wiping it off: "At least you're not dead." And Mom at the piano later, Wagner without a thought of remorse, chunky Teutonic chords up from the basement. Like living on top of a volcano. *Götterdammerung* in Illinois. Music and violence had circled their childhood.

Absently, she fingers the wrist of her left arm, feels for the beat, the blood rhythm, turned round under fingertips, her slow physical senses fighting in watered pushes against the glassed-in absence of her sister. Turns the radio on, classical station. She goes into the kitchen for another cup, noticing grey as it stretches the windows, avoiding the tree with its glaring lights. Crimson.

A day like today. When the cats quarreled. When the lights were full of red pushes, her arms too thin, too young, the wrist transparent and full of freckles. A girl who had grown into a tall wandering child. In Chicago, at the top of a building, swaying like a lost plant, about to fall. Five stories down to the Loop and then the quiet body.

"Her face was almost peaceful, really," said their brother. The urn, the little grey of ashes, the funeral.

Janice's rooms had been fragrant, graciously absent, with worn polished wooden banisters, and huge, shelved windows holding shiny plants. Pretty things. Dresses, jewelry, perfume. Shoes, lots of shoes. Bowls of earrings. A small, clean kitchen, a refrigerator with no food. No dirt, no sense of struggle.

So unlike her own child, who lived in a cave full of cigarettes, curtained against daylight, wrapped in soft sixty watt bulbs. Or herself, surrounded by windows, no curtains at all, dirty and full of light, guarded by huge falls of fern and ivy, a piano tuned to the childhood mix of the classics. Beauty and pain. But hungrier, full of eating. Remnants of events left in sculptured piles each morning beside the sink. The pagan rituals of physical response. In the dark of the year, turning to any satisfaction remaining.

The coffee is cold. The room holds the red glow of the Christmas lights carefully, stroking the long thin streams of the little bulbs with tenderness. It is cold inside and out. The longest night, the darkest day. A year's worth of regret in small heaps under a green tree.

She takes the cup into the kitchen, pushes the engulfing arms of the spider plant out of the way, turns on the hot. Scalding hot, running her arms under it, thinking of those other arms, the sweeter flesh of that girl. Pours in the soap, enough to see the bubbles swarm, life stretching to the smallest corners. Washes them hot and hot again, the hands red, the arms red. Beats herself red, then, to remember.

Janice's apartment, so clean, so sweetly fragrant, seemed like the setting for a movie, someone waiting in the wings. An actress, wearing a silk kimono, left center stage. Entrance never made. She shakes her head, grabs up the thick SOS and scours a frying pan. Drifts back to the wedding.

The young husband, a musician, part of the props, had smiled graciously at the altar. Black wedding clothes and his mother was definitely a witch. Power and a watching beauty held over her son. He was graceful, her sister's husband, young like a brother, substantial and thin and beautiful with it. Smiling bride and families, all black and white. What is wrong with this picture? Find the ten hidden flaws.

At the funeral, he made orations about afterlives, sincere, insipid, the proper touch of regretful sorrow. Not a hair out of place, the little dog redgold and combed and mournful. The others, his mother, the mourners who came to divide her things, sitting with teacups at the edges of her chairs, as if she herself were peripheral to the story. The entire tale untold, a hovering mist.

As though Janice had been merely an ornament.

She breaks a glass, a sharp cut, surprised in spite of her thoughts. So grateful to feel the pain, to see the red moving, moving. Is this an accident, she wonders, have I had an accident? There is blood dripping on the bubbles. Her wrist has a puckered mouth, an open piece of red, below the thumb. The cut is deep, hurts deep, as Marta stands wondering, at the sink, about reasons, dripping on the clean plates. Remembers the time her sister fell, riding on Marta's bicycle, the blood that time, the ankle torn in the chain, black grease and red. The hollering. An accident, yes, and she holds the new mouth shut, closes it over mysteries inadvertently revealed, heads to the bathroom for a butterfly to keep it that way. Don't let me want to know.

Marta, alive as the daylight clutching the stone walls of the yard, pushes a grey face into the living room, watches the cats wrestle and growl, holding a Christmas decoration in two sets of teeth. Her head is like a planet, round and full, the poles whirling in opposite directions, ice melting at the equator, endless questions plaguing the continents.

The growling cats have dismembered the bauble, torn apart the teeth of chance. At such a time the world stands motionless, caught in the doubled direction of its desire. Music and the endless pull of emotion. Violence, the clean quick satisfaction of departure. The radio is playing Rachmaninoff, the rippling chords like leaves, full of water, full of expansion.

She cradles her hand. Walking quickly to the tree, she jerks out the string of lights, face quiet and determined, allowing the room to sink into the beginning of sunrise. Her wrist aches in its beating. Humming down the hallway, lit now only by grey dawn, she carries her cold coffee, to sit at the foot of her husband's bed, and wait for the day.

O Lonely Night

Harry Willson

Dale was trying his best to fight off the annual bad mood which accompanied the year-end holidays. He wondered whether the holidays *caused* his depression. He questioned whether they were anything more than inept attempts of his confused and dying culture to deal with nearly universal despair. He spotted much that was strained and artificial and insincere in the celebrations, not to mention the cynical commercial manipulations, but his sharpness in identifying and comprehending the underlying desperation didn't lift his mood at all.

He was helping tend a booth at the Annual Christmas Bazaar at the Watermelon School. As a mostly absentee parent, he felt an obligation. The bright young lady who was in charge of the booth was explaining to him what he'd be selling. "No, not *that* kind of truffle!"

"I thought a truffle was a French mushroom, that only a pig could find," he said, truly puzzled.

"No, no — these are chocolate! Here, try a bite." She seized one of the walnut-sized dark brown balls and surgically divided it into eight parts with a kitchen paring knife. She offered him one of the parts on the edge of the knife.

He took it between thumb and finger and popped it into his mouth. His delight must have shown on his face. Susan squealed in triumph. "See! They're delicious!"

"They sure are."

"O.K. Now you can sell 'em, 'cause you're convinced. And you can give these pieces away as samples."

148

"How much are we asking for them?"

"A dollar and a half apiece."

Dale gulped, but said nothing. The days of the "nickel candy bar" were long gone — it was something of a disadvantage to be able to remember them.

He sold some chocolate truffles. He, too, yelped with pleasure as pure delight swept over the faces of some of those taking the tiny samples. Truffles — the ultimate in Christmas candy, if money's no object.

Dale's attempts to interact with his customers at the bazaar were hindered by a loudspeaker which filled all the space in the gym where several dozen booths were located. A revolving crowd of people shuffled through, picking over hand-crafted gifts, homemade decorations, books, cards — while the loudspeaker blared Christmas music. Dale's inner ear rattled. Sales were impossible at certain peak moments, especially when the tape came around again to "O Holy Night." Some guy bellowed it, shrieked it — *"O Night! Divine!"*

Dale shook his head at the people in front of his booth and held his ears. As they wandered off, no doubt wondering why a deaf idiot would be trying to sell mushrooms some French pig dug up for the Watermelon School's annual Holiday Bazaar, Dale wondered himself how anyone could believe that Christmas noise honored Santa Claus, or the Baby Jesus, or God, or whatever. His mood dipped down again.

Susan came back. He shared with her a little of his depression problem, while a quieter voice sang of a reindeer with a red nose. "Oh, I know!" Susan bubbled. "I get into the same state sometimes. And just think of how *other* people must feel at this time of year!"

"What other people?"

"Well, a friend of mine" — she blushed beautifully — "a kind of special friend, just *hates* Christmas."

"Why?" Dale had never put it quite so flatly to himself, but when he heard the words, he knew he hated it, too.

"Well, he finally punched his father *back,* after years of

abuse. This was when we were in high school — here! He was arrested, at his father's behest, on Christmas Eve, and spent the evening in jail listening to Christmas carols from the P.A. system of a nearby church. You can just imagine what this kind of music does to him!" The loudspeaker was blasting "The First Nowell" at that moment.

"Yeah. He hates Christmas," Dale muttered.

Dale shuffled through the next couple of days. Christmas was *not* a busy time for him. He wondered why and how other people found it so hectic and frantic. He found it stupid, and lonely.

It was Christmas Eve. Dale was home alone in his apartment. He didn't have much to celebrate, he felt. He was restless. Nothing non-Christmas-y came in over the television. He tried to read, and couldn't concentrate. He went to the window often and looked out. No snow, but cold. No one moving — no pedestrians, no vehicles. Time seemed to have stopped. What are you looking for, Dale? If you think their celebrations are stupid and superstitious, why does it bother you that you're home alone on Christmas Eve? Why would it bother you, if you were the last human being alive on earth? *Would* it?

Dale was looking for something, but had no idea what. He recalled his friend, Carlos, a former friend, that is, used to be his best friend, maybe, but they had wandered apart and lost track of each other, and when Dale tried, really tried, to find him, the trail was cold. He may not be alive, even, Dale thought.

Carlos had been a missionary to the benighted natives of the villages north of Duke City. He quit that, quit believing it needed doing, and went away, and that's when Dale lost track of him. He remembered how Carlos had come to hate Christmas, and he wished he could find him. Was he alone, too, tonight, somewhere, on Christmas Eve?

Carlos had told him how he had received a Christmas box, the day before Christmas Eve, from a "fat-cat church back East" — that was Carlos' own phrase — full of gifts for those same benighted natives. Carlos had received similar boxes before. He opened this one — and found in it, right at the top, torn and unlaundered used men's underwear! Carlos was already having trouble with Christmas and theology and the very idea of missionarying — and the sight, and smell, of that box caused him to flip right out. He burned the box and its entire contents, without going through them at all. Dale remembered, as he imagined the box and the dirty underwear burning, that Carlos' favorite section in Handel's *Messiah* had always been the part when the bass sings: "For he is like a refiner's fire..."

Dale was bored with Christmas, more out of it than usual. He was more than usually aware of being alone. Where *is* everybody? Christmas is for families, and if you don't have one, you're out in the cold. He fell asleep in his chair, listening to the wind blow cold outside.

He awakened suddenly, with strange dream fragments still in his mind — something about a baby, he could still see the image of a bridge, he could still hear that nonsensical sentimental music.

He went out. It was cold. It was dark — there was no moon at all. He went back in, for a flashlight.

He drove to the bus station. He didn't ask himself where he was going, or why he ended up at the bus station. As he parked his car and walked toward the terminal waiting room, he recalled the end of a long bus trip he had taken the previous summer. The driver was pulling off the freeway and cruising down Lead Avenue across the railroad overpass toward the station, and said, "This is Albuquerque, New Mexico. We'll be here half an hour, while the vehicle is serviced. If you leave the terminal, carry a baseball bat. You'll need it." Dale had travelled over five thousand miles and visited several dozen bus terminals all over the nation, and had never heard such a warning. He had forgotten it, until that moment when he entered the waiting room.

Several people were sitting in the not-very-comfortable plastic chairs. They moved only their eyes, to look him over. Several were slouched and wrapped in blankets, trying to sleep.

Dale crossed the street to the Blood Plasma Center, where they buy blood from the *really* desperate, but it was closed and dark. The parking lot was empty. Christmas carols were blaring from the steeple of a nearby downtown church. Dale thought of Susan's special friend, and wondered about the current inhabitants of the jail. "Joy to the World."

He walked toward the railroad overpass, approaching it from underneath. Several men were huddled around a small fire. They looked up at him, but offered no greeting. Dale said, "Good evening," and walked past them, toward the bridge.

Under the bridge he found his footing more difficult — cans, boxes, the remains of other fires, broken building blocks were strewn all over. From the darkest spot where the bridge comes down to meet the littered dirt Dale heard a voice. Not calling, but moaning, groaning. He went toward it, picking his way with the help of his flashlight. He came to a large cardboard box, the kind refrigerators come in. Inside it he found a woman. She could not, or at least did not, speak. Her moans changed to yells, briefly, and then subsided.

Dale trotted to the bus station pay phone, called 911 and reported an emergency. A firetruck came. The men around the fire scattered. Searchlights brightened the area. The music continued unabated. "God Rest Ye Merry, Gentlemen." The paramedics found the woman — she was giving birth. She never spoke in any language Dale or any of the medics could understand. They took her to the hospital, while the siren screamed.

Dale's ears were still ringing, as he entered once again the waiting room of the bus station. On sudden impulse he called out loudly, "Anyone here named Carlos?" His voice startled him, and the half-asleep occupants of the room. They stared at him, but no one spoke.

Dale went to his car and drove home.

Looking For Christmas

Chris Martín

Neither of us ever thought we'd be in a place like Jakarta! The name has the ring of exotic intrigue, of spy-thriller; of smoky, sweltering bistros, of beaded curtains and hidden jewels; of cool marble hallways and narrow, maze-like, cobbled alleyways.

The first thing to strike me about it is the sledgehammer humidity. At ten o'clock at night, and only seventy-seven degrees, this city is a steambath.

If the humidity is a sledgehammer, the smell is an anvil. Jakarta has open sewers. Three or four feet wide, I-don't-want-to-know how deep, they border both sides of the street, carrying the slimy wastes of eight million people out to Jakarta Bay.

The vendors who back their *kaki-lima* — their three-wheeled sidewalk food-carts — up to the edge of the ditches are so engulfed by the clouds of smoke from their cooking that they probably can't smell the sewer any more. Nor can they hear its disgusting slurping sound for the noise made by the unmuffled motorcycles, the pop music blaring from the speakers of streetside audio shops, and the ear-piercing air horns on the buses rumbling past them on the clogged streets.

Maybe it's the juxtaposition of the food-stalls to the sewers; maybe it's just jet lag and our feelings of other-ness; maybe it's the sweltering heat, or perhaps the sound of the *muezzin* calling faithful Muslims to prayers; but we've been feeling very un-Christmas-y, and that's made us crave some familiar food.

There's a Western-style supermarket up the street from our little hotel, just around the corner, where we go to stock up on home-food and other much-needed items: a loaf of bread, Blue Band butter (in a yellow plastic tub, just like Parkay), some cookies that look like sugar wafers, some vitamin C tablets, toothpaste, and deodorant. It's an odd place, this supermarket. Despite its air-conditioning (the closest we get to a winter chill) and its automatic doors and escalators, it's not your neighborhood Safeway. The produce department has a bin full of huge spiky green things as big as footballs, called *durian*, that emit a smell like the sewers outside. The toiletries department is redolent of more men's fragrances than women's. The signs are all in Indonesian, as are the labels on all the goods, and John has to read the chemical-content lists on a lot of bottles in order to find us some anti-perspirant.

We find Christmas cards written in Indonesian, that betray their secret messages only by the pictures on the front. The muzak piped in through the water-stained ceiling takes us straight to the Twilight Zone: "White Christmas," "Jingle Bells," and "Winter Wonderland," sung in *Bahasa Indonesia*, leaking out through the revolving doors to melt in the tropical heat.

Back at our hotel room I learn why immigrants to my country flock together, starting their own supermarkets rather than relying on things like soy sauce from Indiana, or tortillas from Maine.

We spread out a little Christmas picnic for ourselves on our queen-size hotel bed, and with watering mouths, growling tummies, and Christmas greetings, we butter up some fresh bread, and take a big bite. The bread is flavorless and dry, and the Blue Band "butter" coats our tongues and teeth with sticky, fuzzy tropical oil. The cookies are ok, but the dense humidity has wilted their wafer jackets, turning them into rubber.

At least the toothpaste is sweet and minty, not salty or sour, and it foams up like the head on a cold beer. It has enough fluoride to kill a horse.

The anti-perspirant we bought has turned out to be acne medicine.

We laugh at these small misfortunes, and decide that

Christmas will have to wait. This *is* a Muslim country, after all; and aren't we travelling to learn something, and to escape the ordinariness of our lives? We decide to abandon our homesick yearnings in this very different place, and we board a crowded bus for the small town of Tasikmalaya.

So we're cruising along just fine, if one can be said to be cruising this pocked and cratered road. The bus conductor asks us where we're going, and we tell him "Tasikmalaya." Fine; he collects the full fare, and soon we bounce into what appears to be Tasikmalaya. The man hastily shuffles us off his bus, and we're left in a cloud of diesel smoke and a crowd of minivan drivers trying to charge us exhorbitant fees — to Tasikmalaya, which is actually forty kilometers away. We haggle over fares for a while, disgusted at the duplicity of the bus conductor, and simply wanting to be out of there. I pay the minivan conductor the normal fare, but when we finally get to Tasik, the driver accuses us of not paying at all. A crowd gathers; we tower over these small-statured people, as if our fair coloring were not enough to make us conspicuous, and there is no escaping their displeasure. Shouts, flailing arms, jabbing fingers, all accuse us of dishonesty. I'm getting a little frightened, and at this point we don't trust a soul. I plead our case for the tenth time in my ragged Indonesian, and we drag off, disheartened, to find something to quench our thirst.

We walk fifty meters to a little shop, and buy a couple of warm boxes of this awful pasteurized juice that tastes like sugar-water. And as we stand there, down-spirited, hot, sweaty, dusty, a woman comes up and touches my elbow, beckoning us.

"What now?" I grumble silently. She motions me to follow her, again, and she takes my reluctant hand and leads us to her tiny *rumah makan,* her restaurant. She guides us between plain wooden tables, across the tamped earthen floor, and seats us at the farthest table, a large one worn dark and smooth by hands and hot plates. She gives us cool moist cloths to wipe our faces and hands. A feast of delicious hot and cold food appears on the table, and pitchers of hot tea and chilled juice drinks, and bowls of fresh fruit crowd our places.

Several of the bus mob have followed us; they stand nearby, staring, glowering. She shoos them off with a flip of her towel and a few well-placed words. I look up, and glance timidly around the room. It's filled with women! All women! They look anxiously out the door, and plead with us to stay at their home instead of at a hotel. "No worry," says Mother, in English as poor as my Indonesian. "No men there. No men. No worry. Missus safe." She calls me Missus, in the polite Sundanese custom, and I call her Mami, as does everyone else.

We accept her invitation, and she apologizes for her humble home, which is immaculate and welcoming. We take cold baths in her tiny *mandi*, and when we emerge sparkling and refreshed, there is hot tea waiting for us. We sit around for a while, trying to communicate in two languages and in gestures; and after a traditional Sundanese feast of spicy chicken, cold marinated vegetables, steamed rice and bitingly piquant pickled mangoes, we have some hilarious lessons in English and Indonesian.

I learn that Mami is a widow who lives with her son, daughter, and granddaughter. She and her daughter Susi think I'm beautiful because of my pale skin and little pointy nose. "No," I say, "It's Susi who's beautiful." She is dainty, graceful, with perfect creamy brown skin and liquid chocolate eyes. Susi's daughter Riska is four years old. She watches, with rapt fascination, every move we make. When we all go outside together, a crowd gathers to see us, and Mami says proudly, "She is my friend from America." Little Riska can sing "Happy Birthday" in English and in Indonesian.

That night, I cut a five-pointed star out of the gold-foil lining of a cigarette pack; and gingerly, so as not to tear it, I write on it with a stubborn ballpoint pen, "Merry Christmas" and, in Indonesian, "*Selamat Hari Natal.*" I paste it on a small piece of paper and sign our names: "Thank you. We love you. John and Chris."

The next morning, Christmas Day, we make gifts for them from among the things we've brought from home: a pretty blouse for Mami, an amethyst necklace for Susi, a little toy for Riska that plays "Happy Birthday" in computerese when you press a little button. Mami puts the blouse on right away, and cries and hugs and kisses me. Susi insists on "doing my makeup" as she has learned in a cosmetics class at work, and she slathers my captive face in thick pale pancake and blue frost eyeshadow. It makes me sweat as we walk along Tasikmalaya's dusty streets in the thick noonday heat.

It's so different here, how openly affectionate women are with each other; and to an extent the men are the same way. You never see men and women touching each other in public, except for tiny children. But often you see women or girls hugging, walking arm-in-arm, holding each other, and sometimes you see men together, too. But the women, always. Mami hugs me, strokes me — my hair, my stomach, my breast, my arms — whenever she meets me. I'm at a loss, really, as to why she thinks I'm so great, but she does, and she's clearly happy we stayed in Tasik. So tonight, Christmas night, we'll explain the best we can in this foreign language, how we celebrate Christmas in America, to these Muslim women who rescued us with their sweet open hearts.

[Excerpt from a work in progress]

The Memory of an Alaskan Tradition

Fran Ruggles

In Alaska, "termination dust," the sprinkling of snow on the mountains that marks the onset of the winter season, can often be seen as early as August. By late October, most of the ground is wrapped in an ivory cloak until the break-up of the Nenana River that officially signals the dawning of Spring.

Many of the people living in this great state are years away from their childhood and miles away from the place they once called home. During the Christmas season, when holiday memories are sparked to life, families cling to old traditions, and often attempt to develop new ones which might help to establish roots in their new location so far from the love of family and friends.

Alaska is a beautiful place where enchantment abounds, and where a person, once captured under its spell, could believe that destiny led her there. From the blue ribbons of icy waters that wind through the green valleys, skyward, to the majestic mountains and heaven that is the backdrop for the musical dance of the Northern Lights, Alaska is a wonderland of beauty.

However, this paradise can be a giant, impersonal land in the cold and darkness surrounding the days of Christmas. This chosen isolation, when a person's only connection to family hundreds of miles away is the life-line of the telephone, can trigger longing and sadness at a time when childhood images of the holiday begin to replay in the mind.

One way to overcome the yearning brought about by the separation would be first to accept your fortune and know that Christmas joys begin in the heart. The gratifications of the season are not brought about by consumerism, as commercial images would have us believe. Rather, they come from the unique traditions and rituals which families develop slowly over time, and which eventually become embedded into our memories as fond remembrances we again wish to duplicate.

My family and I spent twelve holiday seasons in Alaska. At first, there always seemed to be something missing from the festivities. We had the tree. The children were young and the opening of presents brought excitement. The elaborate meal preparation resulted in a feast of plenty, but there was always a missing piece of the puzzle, finally discovered in the weeks leading up to our fourth Christmas in Alaska.

My husband, who was from San Francisco, and I, a New Englander, discussed one night the emptiness each of us felt around the holidays. We were grateful for our children, our health and the comforts brought about by financial security, but for us, there was an empty feeling we, at first, could not attribute.

That winter night, we talked at length about Christmas in our respective homes. There were similarities and differences, but the key likeness in both our descriptions was the presence of friends and extended family. It seemed we both missed, not necessarily specific individuals, but rather the din of a home full of people. To us, the joys of Christmas were intensified by increased numbers of individuals who brought with them a unique laugh, a specific talent or a special remembrance of years gone by.

That year, my husband went to his union hall and posted an open invitation to all the men who would be away from their home during the holiday. To our enjoyment, the subdued activities which might have existed in our home were transformed into a merry revelry of friendship and love.

During the next several years, the number of holiday guests increased. There were even those friends who deliberately traveled to Alaska just for our annual celebration. Our near-selfish act of kindness not only became a tradition for us, but also a ritual for many of the men.

My husband and I are no longer a "we," and our children now unwrap needed clothing rather than desired play things, but one memory we all hold dear concerns the years we gave from our hearts and received more in return than money could ever buy.

The Spire of Christmas

Joan Arcari

It's Christmas Eve. I'm watching TV because I want something neutral to focus on. I want to escape all this Christmas spirit around me.

Last year I got drunk and missed Christmas Eve. It started with a little sherry in the office to celebrate the imminent holiday. Then I stopped at Gioelli's to get some fresh fish before it closed.

"Hi, what have you got that's good?" I asked Mr. Gioelli and as he pointed out the fresh and the dried cod, and the flounder filets, I said, "Somehow I've gotten into the habit of eating fish on Christmas Eve."

"Just like the old country. Always fish on Christmas Eve. I have some very special mackerel on sale."

"What do you do with mackerel?"

"It's good, you broil it with a little olive oil, some lemon squeezed, some capers. Perfect." He kissed his fingers as he described it.

I ordered a small piece.

"I give you the lemon," he said as he packed it all in a plastic bag and wished me a Merry Christmas.

It was my first Christmas present.

Bavarian Garden next door looked so festive with lights all over and a kitschy Christmas tree on top of the bar that I decided to go in for a little holiday happy hour. Drinks were half price; the place and the people were full of holiday cheer.

I woke next morning with my clothes put neatly away and the mackerel lying patiently in my bag waiting to be cooked. Maybe

161

missing Christmas Eve is the best way to spend it. Anyway, I took the fish from my bag and cooked it up for Christmas. "Waste not, want not," my mother used to say.

I lost it today for a little while, my cool, I mean. It was about losing the gold and jade bracelet that is mine from my mother's jewelry. I turned my apartment upside down looking for it. Possessions don't mean all that much to me, but sentiment does and there is sentiment attached to my mother's bracelet as well as it's probably the most expensive piece of jewelry I own outside of the diamond engagement ring my father bought her which is not my kind of jewelry at all so it's stashed away in a secret place against a rainy season. Which fortunately hasn't arrived that desperately yet. Not in a financial sense, anyhow.

I don't usually get quite so frantic as I did when I couldn't find the bracelet. If I hadn't been wearing the green sweater because it's the color of a fresh cut Christmas tree, I wouldn't have gone into my jewelry box for the bracelet which has jade stones the color of the sweater. It wasn't that I was going anyplace special, but just out for a walk to buy some last minute gifts in case someone unexpected stops by tomorrow, but I felt like wearing my bracelet.

I'm so embarrassed now because I called my dentist. I was tracing back the last few places I've been and what I wore that might have gone with the bracelet. The last time I went to the dentist, I remembered, he gave me gas. It's kind of fun, really, but I read somewhere that the dentists can do all kinds of things while the patient is happy sitting in the chair inhaling the gas. Things like feeling you up and down. It's kind of hard to believe that a dentist would risk his reputation for that.

At any rate, I began to think: myself being contented sitting there inhaling the gas would be a perfect time for someone to take off my mother's gold and jade bracelet. It's crazy because I've known my dentist for years, but I called him.

I actually called his office. "Russell, is it possible I lost a gold and jade bracelet in your office, you know they're dark green stones, I was wearing it last time I was there, when I had the gas."

There was silence on the other end, and then he said, "Gee, no, Cleo, I don't remember it at all. Are you sure you were wearing it?"

That's what I mean by losing it. What did I expect he was going to say to me? Something like — no, I didn't take it, but I'll ask my assistant. She might have slid it off your arm while you were sitting there happily inhaling the gas and I was drilling that rotten bicuspid. I think she had it on one day. Gold and jade, did you say?

Sure, I can just see him saying that. I'm so embarrassed about calling him I feel like changing dentists.

I'm sitting here in front of the TV trying to relax. Only I don't want to watch one of those dumb Christmas programs about rich old ladies and poor kids and dogs. Always these spotted dogs whining whenever the kid is lost or the old lady is sick, and wagging their tails at the end as the program fades out with a shot of the Christmas tree.

I didn't bother with a Christmas tree this year. Only my Jewish friends are out getting trees tonight. The rest of us are sick of it. I used to have one with Dave, my ex-husband, but I always wound up decorating it myself anyway. He wasn't into it. Sometimes I go up to my brother's house in the country. They always have a tree.

I'm watching the news. It's about the only thing on tonight that isn't going to make me nauseous.

Kaity Chung from Channel 4 is standing out in the street in front of the Presbyterian Church just a few blocks from me. She's wearing a red coat with a matching shawl instead of a collar, it's very festive looking with her black hair. The church is a beautiful old Gothic one, or maybe it's Romanesque, Dave always knew that kind of thing, but the stone could use some sandblasting, it's so dark. I've been to the midnight service there. I went once with Dave before we were married. Just to hear the music. They played the Bach *Magnificat*.

There's a crowd around Chung, and an ambulance in the street. The camera shot is up to the top of the front of the church to what I guess is called the belfry. It's square with four spires rising up from the belfry roof. One of the two columns on the street side looks like it has a gargoyle attached to it, but it's moving, it's a man, a real man in a suit and tie. Isn't that weird? He's hunched over the side of the spire like Quasimodo in a Barney's suit. It's pretty cold out, too. You can see the steam vapor drifting out of Kaity Chung's mouth while she's saying kind of melodramatically, "It looks as though he's planning to jump. He had been up there for at least fifteen minutes before we got here, since the start of the Christmas Eve Service, so he must be vacillating as he sees the crowd gathering down here."

He must have squeezed out of one of the belfry windows and then shimmied up the spire. It's probably easy enough to get a foothold in the fancy carving but he's clearly not dressed for the job. He looks like he might have been sitting there quietly listening to the service and got this irresistible urge to climb up to the top. Or did he plan it all along and wear the suit to the service so he wouldn't look suspicious like he would if he walked in wearing his Alpine rock climbing gear?

It's not clear that he isn't just up there for sheer devilment — like after the office party kind of thing. For all I know, maybe that's what I did last year. Rather than one of the holiday folk beset with a serious depression and toying with the idea of letting go at some special point in the *Magnificat*. If he can hear it from all the way up there. Probably they've canceled the service, though.

It's pretty gutsy of him. I'm getting dizzy just looking at him, and if I even imagine being up there hanging over the sidewalk, I feel a clammy sweat and a sick stomach coming on. If it's suicide, that's not the way I'd ever choose. I'd pass out even just planning it. I can't stand those movies where they have to show you a close up in living color of the blood flowing right out of the bullet holes. I just don't go to them.

My mom was a visiting nurse and her patients just adored her. After my father died, she went back to work and she always worked on Christmas. That was her contribution to the sick and the poor.

"Somebody has to do it," she always said.

"Yeah," I used to say to myself and my little brother, Nicky, while we waited for her. She was a very good woman.

They've just zoomed the camera in for a close up of the man. He has a red tie on, a Christmas tie. Everyone's in red, it seems. I wonder if he knows, if he likes the idea, that the whole fricking country is watching him decide how to spend his Christmas Eve. He looks familiar. I wonder if I know him, maybe passed by him on the street, talked to him in a bar, even. He's fair looking, kind of fleshy faced with light thin hair. He actually looks a little like Dave. He looks a lot like Dave, as a matter of fact. That is really weird. But it isn't Dave. Dave would never do anything like that. He never lost control. And I doubt whether he's changed.

Dave didn't like the holidays, not Christmas or New Years, or even my birthday, for that matter, not that my birthday is exactly a holiday. Dave didn't get depressed or anything, he just always found some way not to be around. There are people just like that. Like my mother. I believe she was like that and that's why she always went to work and her patients always loved her for it which made it work out fine for her. It's better than doing what this guy's doing.

I wonder if the man on the spire has a family. It doesn't look like any of the people milling around are related or connected to him. He looks like a perfectly ordinary guy — like Dave — the kind who would have a family. Somebody is talking to him with a bullhorn, but I can't make out what they are saying. It's probably the minister from the church. Or, maybe a shrink.

Tomorrow I have to straighten up around the apartment. I moved all my heavy furniture today, almost wracked myself pulling out my large chest of drawers, and then the bed across from it, it's a platform bed but the casters are broken so it's a pain and the top gets out of kilter from the platform when you move it. I did all that just looking for the jade bracelet. Then I swept the dust out from all the places I uncovered, but my bracelet wasn't anywhere to be found.

The reason I finally calmed down and of course watching TV helps too, is because I suddenly remembered that I had taken it off at work and locked it in my desk drawer. At least I hope I locked it. The clasp broke so I put it in the desk drawer for safety. I have to take it to a jeweler to be repaired. But why can't I remember for sure?

It's really wild how much that man looks like Dave. Dave used to say, "Holidays don't mean anything to me, I just want to be alone."

And I used to say, "If they really don't mean anything to you, then you can spend them quietly with me."

I thought that made sense. It's strange to think when he wasn't spending Christmas Eve with me, maybe he was scurrying up a church spire someplace. Maybe he really got depressed and contemplated jumping, but he wouldn't tell me. Anyway, he never did kill himself, I would have heard. He's still walking around. But that's all behind me. You can't really dwell on past things. They're over.

The man has climbed carefully down the topmost part of the spire and he's standing on the ledge peering down, and edging toward the other spire. It's kind of scary because he doesn't seem to be holding on to anything. One stiff gale of wind and down he'll go or at least that's the way it looks from where I'm sitting on my couch. Like I could blow him off. They don't seem to have those great round things that you see in the cartoons when someone is stuck on a rooftop in a fire. There is a firetruck on the scene, though. I wonder why. If he falls, what will happen? Will there be a large splat or isn't it high enough for that? Is there any possibility of him living through it?

Kaity Chung isn't talking about those kinds of things.

"We don't have any identification on him yet, do we, Tim?" She's asking the newsman back at the studio.

I'm pretty sure it can't be Dave even though it's uncanny how much I'm looking at him and seeing Dave the way he looked last time I saw him. Wearing a suit and tie. Taller, though.

"Remember the man who dressed like Santa Claus and held the congregation in St. Pat's at gunpoint while he sang 'Joy to the World'? Chung continues.

"Off key, no less," Brokaw answers.

The minister appears and he's saying, "As far as I can tell, this man is not a member of our congregation. I certainly hope we can reach out to him in some significant way. Nothing like this has ever happened at our church before. It is always a great pity to me that a day of such great giving and joy should be the occasion of so much pain to some people. Yes, of course we have canceled the service."

Once I took my little brother to the Christmas service, but it was an awfully long walk there and back so the next year the Websters, our next door neighbors, took us to church with them. They were older and never had any kids.

"You children are so fortunate to have such a giving mother. She embodies the spirit of Christmas," Mrs. Webster said as we were driving to the church.

I don't know why but Nicky and I both hated the service and the Websters and managed to wiggle out of it the next year. After that, we were lazy and slept late. Secretly, although Nicky and I never talked about it with each other, I think we both felt there was something missing in us. We were missing that kind of giving, selfless spirit my mother had and we didn't want to be reminded of it.

Christmas mornings Nicky and I opened our stockings and had hot chocolate and white toast which we dunked into it. I was pretty young and wasn't much of a cook. We saved opening the large presents, the boxes that looked like clothes and usually were, until my mother got home. Nicky didn't much like clothes as a gift, but I did.

Sometimes she might be real late, like if one of her patients was really sick and needed her longer because of the holiday and being alone.

We had really simple meals on Christmas, the kind my Mom could just put in the oven real quick. Once, it was even TV dinners, and we watched a TV special in the living room while we ate them. They were turkey TV dinners with a tiny pile of stuffing under the slice of turkey. And peas. Nicky hated peas. We always had pie. Either my mother made it the day before or her patients would send her home with one. One patient mailed her a plum pudding every year, but Nick and I hated it. I still hate plum pudding. Once, she brought leftover turkey home from one of the homes she visited. Her patients always gave her candy and often they gave her flowers and gifts as well. Even the poorest patient would have a little gift for my mother — like a homemade sachet packet or something. They all loved her so much.

She had some rich patients, too, and they'd often try to give her money, but she couldn't take money and would return it.

"It's unethical," she said. My mother was short and even though she got a little stocky as she grew older, she looked saintly in her white nurse's uniform.

I'd still feel a lot better if I had my jade and gold bracelet with me now. My office is locked up this week or I would have trekked over there to get it, believe me. Just for the security of knowing where it is. I'm very attached to it.

Now Tim Brokaw is in the studio discussing the holiday blues with a guest. They've left the man on the spire for a little while. Between this and the commercial message, we're going to miss the show. I hope he doesn't fall or jump while they're talking about the unrealistic expectations and disappointments of the holiday season. Give us a break. We've all heard it over and over and over. Take us back to the action in the street before something dreadful happens.

And we miss it, and the whole world misses it while we're hearing about the gradual accretion of negative holiday experiences. Maybe the man on the spire has just lost his job. Maybe he can't pay his rent and he'll be out on the street, or maybe his wife is divorcing him; maybe she deserted him on the holiday.

I wish I had a record of the Bach *Magnificat*. I would love to be listening to it now.

At least Brokaw and the guest, I think he's some kind of authority, like a doctor, are not talking as if the man is seriously crazy, but are attributing it to the holidays. It's like when I couldn't find my bracelet — and it still upsets me as I sit here, not having it, even though I'm pretty sure it's safe — I felt like I was going to fall off the edge.

I've decided not to go to my brother's house tomorrow. He doesn't mind. He's got his wife's family coming, and all their combined kids.

"Christmas is for kids," I told him. "There is so much homelessness around the streets, I'm not in the mood for feasting this year. Guess what, Nicky, I bought a turkey TV dinner. Remember them?"

"Why?" he answered. I guess he didn't appreciate the significance.

I've also rented a Japanese film called "Dreams," a really artistic one, and I'm looking forward to watching it. And I bought some champagne, the Spanish kind in the black bottle. If anyone should drop in, I'm prepared. If not, I'm still prepared. I'll drink it myself — with my turkey TV dinner.

I remember the Christmas my mother brought the jade bracelet home. She was really late and I was worried. There wasn't anyplace we could call because she visited so many patients. One was an old Jewish man, who had been a jeweler,

Mr. Kirsch, she called him. I can't remember what was wrong with Mr. Kirsch, I'm not good at illnesses. In fact, sick people turn me off a little which is really uncharitable, I know. Whatever was wrong with this patient, my mom had to help him eat. She had made a tiny tree for him from some branches she found on the street. Each time she visited him, she'd bring him a ribbon or a ginger bread cookie or a candy cane to decorate it. She told us all about it. He called it a Chanukah Bush, but she didn't care. She didn't know what that was.

On Christmas Day he gave her the bracelet. I can't remember ever seeing her so moved as when she told us about it. It certainly dwarfed our piddling little homemade gifts even though she insisted that wasn't so. I remember it was dark when she got home, and we were sitting in the living room in front of the Scotch Pine Nicky and I had decorated. Only the Christmas tree lights were on, and my mother was turning her new bracelet on her wrist.

"It means so much to those poor sick people to be remembered on a holiday like today. You can just see the appreciation and the love in their eyes while you're there with them. Mr. Kirsch was so happy that he had such a special gift for me."

The lights of the tree caught the green stones of the bracelet she was turning on her wrist, and made them shine.

I'm wondering, as I watch this man on the spire, if he has any idea he's providing an evening's entertainment for so many people. People like me. I can see he's responding now to the man with the megaphone, but it's impossible to hear him. Even though it's dark, there are so many lights on him that he has his hand up shielding his eyes. Up on the spire, the cold wind blows his tie out from the suit like a tongue of flame.

The firefighters are running an extension ladder all the way up the front of the church. Another shorter ladder goes up just a yard away from the first. Two firemen are preparing to climb them. One is holding what looks like a wide belt attached to a rope as he climbs the ladder. The other has the end of the rope which he ties to something when he reaches the top. It's probably to guard against an accidental fall or a change of heart, because it looks like the evening is winding down and the man has agreed to their help. They're going to help him climb down to the sidewalk.

I wonder if they've made him any promises. I wonder what made him decide, finally, not to jump.

I feel a little empty watching the man, with the belt around his middle, making his way slowly down the ladder to the ground. It's kind of like I've been disappointed again.

Chung is saying, "All's well that ends well, folks. Have a Merry, Merry Christmas from all of us standing outside First Presbyterian on this cold Christmas Eve. And a Happy Holiday from the network."

There are Christmas wreaths on each of the spires that face the street. They look familiar and when I squint, I think one is my mother's jade bracelet and the man is still standing up there hanging off one of those spires. He's holding on with his left hand while his body slants out from it. The spire looks fragile as a gingerbread cookie and ready to snap off from his weight. With his right hand, as the camera zooms in close, I can see he is waving directly to me, I can see the expression on his face, it's the one Dave always had when I asked him to stick around for the holidays. Kind of pained, like he didn't hear me, or didn't want to hear me. It's all captured on my screen.

The man jumps from the spire, his red tie waving, and I am watching — watching him somersault, as graceful as a snow-flake, toward the earth, the jade wreath following, until he's lying face down on the sidewalk in the middle of a round red pool of blood.

Boston, 1966

Peter O'Grady

The Christmas lights glared, forming a huge bright square surrounding the park in the center of Boston, each store glowing with what seemed to be a maximum and uniform degree of light, as if there might be some law limiting the kilowatts permitted each merchant with which to bathe prospective shoppers during the so-called Holiday Season. A steady stream of people in long coats mentally accounting lists of purchases yet to be accomplished paraded on the slushy sidewalk in both directions all around the park. Santas in their ill-fitting rented red-and-whites were all over, ringing bells or in the department stores, guarding their beards from the kids who might yank. The crisply wrapped packages filled to capacity baskets and arms and back seats of cars. It turned my stomach. The tinsel didn't bother me so much. It was an undefined question: how could all these crowds of people be so unfeeling, so untrue, so devoid of art as to participate in this holiday hurricane, lap it up, ignore it, whatever, but not vomit in the face of it? That bothered me.

As I trudged along the sidewalk, my eyes empty of all but discontent, the snow soaked through my sneakers, chilling my toes. Only lucky that week to have a place to live indoors. Why did I even stay? Oh well, who knows. The lights were kind of pretty. The fir trees in the park were tall and handsome, burdened with new snow, but even their beauty was robbed, lost in the middle of the centerless circus.

Where were people who felt like me, who were too weak or too angry or too bored to laugh along or laugh it off with a hearty "Ho-ho-*ho*"? Where was I going to get food next week? Where did I want to live? Where was spring? How long could I tolerate this horrific depression? Where were the trees not buried in stupid lights? When would I have the guts and the means to

just go there? Where was my life? And when would I find a way
to live in the world?

> *O then I did not know*
> *any sense or answers*
> *to my nameless pain,*
> *knew of no service organization,*
> *category, strategy, philosophy or scam,*
> *teacher, recipe,*
> *invention or book*
> *dealing with my bitter brewing core*
> *shining red like molten*
> *rock in the center of the earth.*
> *Where were the words that would work*
> *to let me know*
> *who I was in the teeming fray*
> *of carnivorous sparkling citizenry?*

And where are they today, the wanderers, now that I've
become what I hated then? Where are they that could keep me
up late tonight with stories of life's coils around them, who now
write poetry on garbage bags? "Can't go. No time. No message
left to bring." Where now is the answer that I thought I had?
Where's my Jesus if not forgotten at the bottom of a pile of
empty boxes neatly wrapped in some holiday window display?
Where is my life if not reaching back to those who are where I
once was, with listening, with caring, with time and food if not
many answers? Where is that lonely army that could fill twenty
hotels if I could gather them to hear their prayers, to give them
space to warm their feet while their sneakers dry by the heater?

Where is that one the Lord would bring me to with such light
as I do have in this home brightened by my wife and children?

> *Please, Lord;*
> *bring me to them.*
> *Bring us together.*
> *Let Your light*
> *(I don't mind sounding trite)*
> *shine through me this Christmas.*

Friends of My Youth

Linda Moore Spencer

The word's out. I'm depressed. So every ugly mood, every painful memory, every sad idea ever entertained by me or any member of my family, all imagine they are invited to my house for Thanksgiving. And, as long as they've attached themselves so naturally to my condition, they think they might just as well stay on through what happy people and depressed alike refer to as the holidays.

Although, to tell the truth, I do not run into large numbers of happy people on the street between November twenty-third and January one. I like to think (in fact, in my darkest moments of psychic disrepair, I fervently believe) that all the happy people are holed up somewhere in one large living room, beside a smokeless fire, sipping hot mulled cider with their sixty-four-year-old mothers who like them (have liked them, for as long as anybody can remember). They chat in a room full of old friends, suspended there inside a comfort I have only witnessed as I walked by outside at night in spitting rain, without a proper coat, in baggy pants and too-thin gloves.

This is the outfit I intend to wear throughout the course of this depression, appropriate down to the toe-hole in my sock, for all the markings of despondency I'd thought to celebrate alone, sitting in the grey mid-winter chill that is my kitchen.

We're back now to the uninvited house guests, these antique injuries who show up, bag and baggage, every time I have more than a little trouble thinking of a reason to get out of bed in the morning (and require a 10:00 a.m. reminder of just what it was that finally decided me). We're back now to the self-invited, those doubts and old distresses that have known me since the seventh grade, when offense was something that I borrowed from my mother and carried with me everywhere.

My house is overrun with them. I go out to my car and find the back seat and half the trunk are full of statues I erected to the memory of my dragon, inadequacy. I erected these statues and then (I thought wisely) left, moving off to a new town with all new people in some entirely different state. Carved in granite to commemorate my failures and unworthiness, these statues refuse to use their seat belts and fall forward whenever I brake suddenly (and I brake suddenly a lot). They either topple forward, fall and smash to bits of powdery chagrin, or they insist that they be carried with me to the supermarket, the dry cleaner. If I set my doldrums down on the counter while I pay the clerk, if I snap my wallet closed, grab my keys and head for the door without my excess psychological baggage, the clerk calls me back.

"Ma'am. Ma'am. Did you forget these?"

Did I forget them.

And "ma'am." People have a meeting on the first of every month when I'm depressed, and say, "Let's call her 'Ma'am'." (To a person, those same people call me "Miss" on days when life seems supportable.)

I drive the statues, fragments and entire alike, back to my house. I cook and clean up and do laundry for a whole houseful of memories who won't even bother getting dressed, in other than vague dread. I slip them small amounts of valium, which only makes them dopey and poor company. I take them on long walks, then home to bed at 4:00 p.m. for naps. By then the valium's worn off, and they bounce on the bed and in my head. If I fall asleep, when I wake up they've rearranged my sensual perception.

So January second (earlier if I can borrow energy from Pat, across the street, who shines the shine on her brass door knocker even as we speak), it's everybody out. "Go home. Go back to Western Pennsylvania, back to Skidmore, back to Buffalo." Just before they go I'm going to slice up my depression, wrap the pieces up in colored cellophane. I'll stick one in each suitcase, tucked inside like so many pieces of a groom's cake, intended to be taken home and stored inside the freezer until some anniversary date.

Next time I'm suggesting we all take separate rooms at some upscale resort, with patterned bed sheets and room service, even in the middle of the night. This idea of houseguests for the holidays has gotten out of hand.

A Christmas Crossing

Gale Swiontkowski

This Christmas as I cross
over the wide Hudson,
the river moves beneath
grey and thick and slow —
as if cold lead
could liquefy and flow;
as if lava could cool
yet ooze as before;
as if icy asphalt
could peak and pour.

Against the vacant drink
of the Tappan Zee,
these great bridge beams shrink
to Erector set scale —
clever but insubstantial;
a train on the bank below
creeps like Lionel cars astray
from a route around a tree;
distant office towers dwindle
to bare metallic boles.

This car, my carapace,
can not preserve me.
The river's endless surface
entrances and diminishes,
baffles my head.
I might jump to embrace it,
but it would smack me dead.
Only a mindless, hollow-boned bird
can light on — and not crack —
a raft of thinnest ice.

My Secret

Jan Nystrom

We are driving down state street on our way to buy a
Christmas tree when I tell my mother I love a woman.

"Mother," I say, "I'm bisexual." This isn't entirely true, but
it's Christmas and I want to give my mother hope for the
possibility of my heterosexual future.

My mother runs off the road, over a phitzer bush, and back
on the road, without showing a single emotion.

"You mean you love women?" she says.

"Yes," I say. "No. I love one woman in particular."

"That's unfortunate," she says, "to be so particular about love
at your age."

I am seventeen. My mother tells me, once again, how at
sixteen she met my father; he wooed her, wed her, and made her
life unbearable. I must be scowling in my side of the car because
my mother glowers in my direction. "Don't think you're so
fortunate," she says. "Don't think you've escaped the romantic
tradition."

"Love," she says.

She turns around and wags her finger at my brother. John,
who is thirteen years old, is staring out the window. His face is
red.

"Look at you," my mother says. "What in your simple life is
going to prepare you for the realities of love?"

◇

When we get to the tree lot, John refuses to get out of the
car. He says he is sick.

"It's Christmas," my mother says. "Be a sport."

178

John shrugs.

My mother looks at me. "Just like his father," she says.

We leave John waiting in the car and my mother tells me if she hadn't conceived John in her womb, carried him for nine months, she would swear his father had been fooling around.

While my mother and I look for Christmas trees, I try to talk about it. Mother doesn't want to talk. It's old news, she says, she has known for years. She tells me it was obvious from the time I was little. She recounts incidents. She reminds me of the time in Sugarhouse park some boys tore Sally's coat. The way my mother tells the story, when I found out I was maternal, ferocious, a wild animal defending its young. I threatened to fight all three boys at once, and I held Sally while she cried.

"Sally was my friend," I say.

"That wasn't friendship," my mother says, eroticizing the whole of my childhood, "that was love."

I think of the agony of touching Laura for the first time and being so unsure. I think of all the secrets my mother has kept to herself. Love, she calls it, keeping us together.

"I'm not bisexual," I say.

My mother gives me a vague look. She is holding one of the cheap five dollar Christmas trees. It looks like every Christmas tree we've ever had.

"There's no chance I'll ever, ever, ever love a man."

"Of course not," she says, "it was never in your nature."

◇

I am sitting on the sofa watching my mother and John decorate the tree. It's as steeped in tradition as my family ever gets. My mother has electric bells hanging in the archway to the kitchen. They play Christmas songs and each bell represents a note so they light in turn, B-flat, C, A-sharp.

John is hanging lights on the tree. They are tiny and white. Without my glasses on, they look like fuzzy angels. Mother's interfering. John wants her to wait to decorate the tree until he's finished hanging lights, but she won't. She drapes tinsel from the branches — every year we have hundreds of tinsel-strings and in

May we find them floating between the cushions of the couch. John steps around her with the lights. She keeps telling him to be careful; she doesn't want to be wrapped up with the tree.

"Come help us," Mother says, but I just want to sit and stare at the tree and think of Laura. Laura has lived across the street from us with her mother and her three brothers for two years. This is the first Christmas I have had a lover. I think of inviting Laura over for Christmas Eve.

"You know her," I say.

"Who?" my mother asks.

"My lover. You know my lover. You too, John. You know my lover."

John acts like he doesn't hear me. My mother is self-involved, humming to the Jingle Bells, hanging icicles. I think of Laura. I look at my mother draping her silver threads and I think that I too have my secrets. I know what Laura looks like when she steps out of the shower in a steamy room. I know how she gestures, how she perches her toe on the edge of the tub and rubs each calf and thigh briskly with a towel. I know Laura's face close to mine, her wide open eyes and lips, I know the taste of those lips tasting mine. And I know that Laura has never been loved before by man or woman and when I run my hands over her, I feel such power in these fingers, such power that I can touch lips, breasts, hands and I can make Laura happy. It makes me feel like some queen or something, I feel that good and strong and powerful because I have it, Laura gives it to me, I have the power in the tips of my fingers to make Laura smile.

I've never been so happy in my life.

"I want to invite her over for Christmas."

"Who?" my mother says.

I wonder if my mother is trying to drive me crazy. I want to tell her it's working.

"John knows who."

My mother looks at John. He has finished hanging the lights and is sitting on the sofa.

"Do you know what your sister's talking about," my mother

says, "because I don't."

Sometimes I feel sorry for John. "Give us a break, Mom," I say. "Laura. My lover. I want to invite Laura over for Christmas."

My mother stops hanging icicles. "Not Laura," my mother says, "That's not fair. Don't tell me it's Laura."

I look at John, but we're alone in this. He looks like he's ready to bolt.

I shrug and stand up. "I'm getting drinks."

My mother follows me to the kitchen. "Not Laura," she says, "that's not fair." My mother tells me that Laura's not like me, to love a woman is not her nature; I have played on Laura's insecurities, reduced her to the needy state of love; I have wormed my way into her heart, turned her head, complicated her life beyond all reason.

My mother delivers her monologue while I mix three rum and cokes. I make them extra strong. My mother follows me back into the family room. I'm enjoying this because, probably for the first time in her life, my mother doesn't know what she's talking about. She doesn't know Laura. She doesn't know that Laura is just like me.

When my mother pauses, I begin. "Let me tell you what it's like being with Laura," I say. I look at John. His face is red. I stop, reconsider. That's my secret. "Let me tell you how it started. What Laura said to me."

"I know how it started," my mother says. "It started with Laura's insecurities. It started with Laura's mother. It started with your seduction. It started..." Our voices are rising. I realize we are yelling and the bells are singing and suddenly John stands up. "You piss me off," he says, "both of you. You piss me off." He walks out of the room taking his rum and coke with him and calling the dog Willie from under the sofa.

My mother and I look at each other. She looks down at her hand and notices she's still holding a fistful of icicles. We look at the doorway where John disappeared. I tell her to sit down. I sit down beside her on the sofa and put my arm over her

shoulder and then I begin to laugh. I can't help myself. My
mother starts laughing too. I think that she is laughing at John
and at the two of us sitting on the sofa, but I am laughing
because I have my secret. I have been smitten with the sameness
of Laura's body to mine and the infinite particularities that are
her difference. I know something my mother does not know. I
laugh until the tears come and I can't breathe. I look at her.
There are tears in both our eyes. I look at my mother's face and
feel, on the back of my head, her hand caught in my hair.

Family
(From one without one)

B.A. Cantwell

Greeting card
embroidered with
moss threads
tiny guilt-hidden phonelaughter
when the others are
upstairs
"Imissyou!"
holiday melodies
hidden in couches
spill into messy rooms
in song ribbons
untied
in the rich stream of commentary
of cashmere hours.

December Afternoon

Joan E. Sullivan Cowan

Here I am again, alone, except for our dog. There's just the two of us out here walking on the mesa. I hadn't planned to be here now. I had planned to be at the museum making star decorations.

The museum newsletter came a few weeks ago. In it was information about a special holiday program. Part of it was making star decorations from different countries. That's a good idea, I thought. We all need to realize we are citizens of the world. What a good way to do that. So I asked my husband and daughters to go with me. We would do this as a part of our holiday celebration.

But, some time ago in another newsletter I get, there had been an article on places that didn't use pesticide. I remembered that the museum was listed as a place that didn't use them. Since last August, when I unknowingly walked around on the ground where pesticide granules had been spread and then ended up in bed, I have been more cautious. I decided to call the museum to be sure they didn't use pesticide. The first person I talked to didn't know and told me the person in charge of the building had left. So then I talked to, I believe, the assistant director. She was kind to me, but I sure didn't want to hear what she told me. The museum did use pesticide. She put me on hold and tried to find a copy of the pesticide contract so she could tell me how long it had been since the museum had been sprayed. When she came back she told me they didn't use a commercial company, the custodians did the spraying. She didn't know when the building had last been sprayed. I asked her if the area where they were

184

going to be making the stars was sprayed and she said yes. I thanked her for her time and for the information. I told her I would have to think about it.

Well, I thought about it. I thought about the headache and muscle pain I had last August. I thought about the time I had spent in bed. I decided not to go.

So we aren't making stars at the museum this afternoon. Instead, here I am just like every other day. Out here, where there is no pesticide. I'm walking on the mesa with our dog and being alone.

[Ms. Cowan reports that the museum, after receiving a copy of this story with her cover letter, adopted a new method of pest control and is now safe for her.]

Earthbound Angel

Zelda Leah Gatuskin

"Rockin' around the Christmas tree... At the Christmas party hop..." When Sabine noticed herself singing along, she put down her paintbrush, stomped over to the radio and angrily spun the tuner dial. It was hopeless. One Christmas song after another — country-western, classical, rock'n roll, forties, thirties, rap, chipmunk chorus, dogs barking — assaulted her ears as she searched for some inoffensive background music. Just when she thought she had found an acceptable station and was returning to her easel, the music faded into hysterical day-before-Christmas sales pitches. Sabine moaned and clicked the radio off. There. Silence.

The abandoned paintbrush was still moist. Sabine dabbed some color onto the canvas, then swished the brush in a can of turp and wiped it on an oily rag. She stepped back to examine her work. Something was off. The color. Yes, the background was too flat; that blue was dead. "I thought the background needed to be very neutral," Sabine muttered to herself as she squeezed some cadmium yellow light onto her palette, "but it just doesn't work. Something needs to be going on back there." She squirted some viridian green next to the blob of yellow and then some cobalt violet next to the green.

Like a dancer positioning to commence the ballet, Sabine arranged herself at her easel. Perching on a high stool with a padded swivel seat, she layered her paint rag over her right knee and reached over to pull the tiered supply caddy closer. She picked her widest fan brush out of a bouquet of brushes in a coffee can, dipped it into her secret recipe oil-and-turp medium

186

and wiped it almost dry again on her rag-draped knee. With a deep breath, she took the palette in her left hand which she rested against her left thigh and touched the brush bristles to the pigments. The wide brush was able to pick up all three colors at once, and Sabine applied these to the still-wet, dense blue background of her painting in a short arcing stroke. The effect was that of a prism of light falling across a darkened room. Carefully, Sabine applied more such three-toned strokes, meticulously cleaning and priming her brush between each one to keep the colors from muddying. As she settled into her work, a feeling of serenity washed over her just as it always did when her hands and eyes joined in that magical visual communication that bypassed conscious thought. Placid and empty, Sabine's mind amused itself with random melodies. In the quiet of her studio, with only the sounds of a dripping faucet and the scratching of brush bristles, Sabine smiled and began to sing under her breath, "Rockin' around the Christmas tree... at the Christmas party hop..."

Sabine stopped swiping at the paint rag on her knee and bit her lower lip. She put the palette and brush on the caddy, then swiveled away from her easel and slid off the stool. There was a shoebox full of tapes in her car; she had meant to bring it in earlier, with the other stuff. Impatiently, Sabine pulled off her apron and wiped her hands on it. She grabbed her keys and her parka and slammed every door — studio, third floor landing, second floor landing, foyer and front — on her way to the street. The blast of cold air that greeted her was really what she needed. By the time she had walked around the corner to where her car was parked, and back with the tapes, Sabine was feeling refreshed. She let herself back into the building and jogged up the stairs, noticing how quiet the place was. A lot of the artists who rented space there were out of town, or staying close to home for the holidays. By contrast, Sabine had brought her overnight bag and some groceries so she could camp out at the studio on Christmas eve. Alone. Maybe tomorrow night too. It was better this way, she thought, putting on her old Abbey Road cassette and turning up the volume.

She avoided looking at her work-in-progress as she hung up her parka. Obviously she had been due for a break, and it would be good to go back to the painting with fresh eyes. She was dying to look, to see what the prism-like swirls did for the painting, but instead she busied herself tidying up around the couch where she would sleep and unpacking her meager gear. "Might as well get comfortable." Sabine took off her shoes and put on a pair of slippers. She opened a bag of potato chips and fished a beer out of the mini refrigerator under the sink. "Thanks, Brian!" Sabine toasted her sort-of boyfriend. She and Brian were in the process of trying to decide if it was worthwhile turning their friendship into a romance. "Thanks for leaving me a beer." Brian had brought a six-pack over yesterday afternoon when he came to wish her a happy holiday. He was heading south for the long weekend, to see his parents in North Carolina. Sabine was not only glad for the beer, but glad that Brian had gone out of town. That saved a lot of awkwardness. 'People get so sentimental around the holidays, relationships seem to be under the microscope. That's the last thing Brian and I need right now.'

The tape clicked off. Sabine jumped. She hadn't meant to take that long a break! But she had eaten almost the entire bag of potato chips while sitting on the couch in a daze for half an hour, thinking about Brian — and Christmas. Sabine washed her greasy hands and mouth at the paint-stained sink and probed in the fridge for another beer. 'No luck; or good thing, depending how you look at it.' Sabine poured a tall glass of water, put on her apron, and flipped the tape. Head bowed, she prowled over to the far wall and turned to look back across the studio to the canvas on her easel.

"Shit." Sabine did not like what she saw. The balance was all off. Now the background was so vivid, with its arcs of yellow-green light against violet shadows, that the subject made no sense at all. The single female figure, rendered in Sabine's trademark elongated style, looked like a cartoon character surrounded by soap bubbles. The woman's coloring was too pink against the now green-tinged background, and her spaghetti-like limbs and neck had a supernatural appearance. "It almost looks like a damn Christmas card! The holiday is insidious! I haven't read a newspaper, watched TV, or gone shopping in a week and still my sensibilities have been taken over by the Christmas aesthetic. I might as well turn this thing into a Madonna and Child and be done with it!"

Sabine walked up to the easel and confronted her creation eye to eye. "I think I'm tired of you. I know you got me into my first gallery, and won me some decent reviews and enough sales to keep painting, but look at you now. You're a formula, a cartoon. It's my fault. I should have been more sparing with you, always kept the concept in the front of my mind when I painted you. When you got to be easy to paint, you lost your power. How could something that started out to be so fluid, that was a manifestation of fluidity, get to be so rigid?" Sabine found a short palette knife on the caddy and tearfully scraped away the elongated female figure and some of the blue-green areas behind her. She flung the partially dried globs of paint into the trash can. "Yep, might as well just surrender and turn you into a Madonna right now." Sabine was mad. The second side of the tape clicked off and she switched back to the radio, tuning in to a non-commercial station. They were playing what sounded like a Mass; she decided it wouldn't be too bad, so long as she didn't have to listen to any advertising.

White. The new figure needed to be white, Sabine decided. Fresh; pure. More an angel than a Madonna. Yes, an angel. Sabine found a giant tube of titanium white and squirted a couple of tablespoons worth into an old teacup whose delicate flower pattern had long been covered over by white fingerprints and drips of paint. After stirring in a splash of medium, Sabine stabbed a half-inch flat into the cup and attacked the canvas, not bothering to hike herself up onto the stool. She worked to the sacred music. And as she brushed a white angel to life, wings and all, she dared herself to find some inspiration in Christmas.

It was her holiday too, after all, culturally if not religiously. Nothing could be more all-American than this mad, effusive, compulsive, capitalistic, slobberingly sentimental rite of winter. It was a multi-media, high-tech affair, an orgy of generosity, an opportunity to decorate homes, selves, streets and lawns as if each and every individual could for one month be a Hollywood director, creating a perfect vision of harmony, love and happiness. "Or a Michelangelo painting heaven." Sabine stepped back from her work. "Pure self-indulgence, that's what Christmas today seems to be about. Even the whole charity thing comes off self-serving. I wonder why." Sabine was now talking to the ghost shadow of an angel. There was no question that she was indulging herself. She had painted a beautiful kneeling woman in classical proportions, just for fun and to see if she could still summon her old art school techniques. "I think it's because having children is self-indulgent. Completely egocentric. Mother Mary may have been a martyr, but God the Father was definitely out to further his own cause. What do you think?" Sabine scooped a little more white paint onto her brush and made her angel's stomach a bit rounder. "Everyone talks about Christmas being for the children, but it's very much for adults also, to feed our fantasies of being both perfect children and perfect parents — the Virgin Mary, the noble Joseph, the baby Jesus. Father, Son and Holy Ghost — only a mind mature enough to feel divided can long for the unity of God."

Satisfied now with the angel's contours, Sabine carefully painted an aura of light emanating from the kneeling figure. A ring of pale gold intensified through shades of ochre, melon and rose as it radiated from the angel and was absorbed into the blue background, where the prism streaks suddenly suggested stained glass. With a translucent glaze of zinc white, Sabine smoothed out the foreground so that the angel appeared to kneel on the reflectent surface of polished marble. Stepping back to appraise her work, Sabine felt the hairs on her neck rise as the music of the Sanctus swelled. The image she had constructed almost by formula had assumed a depth of character that was completely unplanned. The supplicant posture, the glowing roundness of mid-pregnancy, the strong uplifted wings, presented a surreal, all-in-one representation of woman: child, mother, lover, angel. Sabine chugged some water in an attempt to swallow the lump that was forming in her throat. She knew that the church had a long history of patronage of the arts, that the church was to thank for fostering the brilliance of the world's greatest painters and composers; but until now she had never stopped to consider the effects of the content of the work itself on those old masters. Just because they were creating on spec for the church wouldn't mean they were not inspired by their own souls, and spiritually nourished by their sacred works. 'In a peculiar, perverted way our capitalistic elaboration of sacred ritual is just an expression of a universal desire to participate in holiness. We artists like to turn up our noses at the tasteless, mass-produced look of the Christmas and Easter seasons. And where the aesthetic is more refined, we complain that the spirit behind the presentation has been replaced by status-seeking. Pretty elitist thinking. Artists are no more the sole protectors of the right way than the priests.' Sabine returned to work, picking out her finest brushes with which to render in meticulous detail the folds of the angel's tunic, feathered wings, loose tawny curls and soft, pliant, pale-rose skin. Again she addressed her subject:

"I expect fewer and fewer people will be learning to paint like this. Computers, scanners, photolithography, laser printing — art is no longer the domain of the select few. Same for music. Anyone can buy a keyboard that can be easily programmed to compose and play music well beyond the expertise of the operator. Welcome to the twenty-first century! Art is for everyone. I still get to have my tastes and preferences. I can be a snob if I want. I can be a snob about art, a snob about spirituality, a sexist snob, a leftist snob... But I don't see what that will get me except a constant state of disdain and displeasure. No one's stopping me from painting; no one's putting down what I choose to do, how I choose to express myself. It seems I even get to have a spiritual experience tonight

— in spite of hating Christmas." Sabine applied one last minuscule sliver of violet to a feathery eyelash and then used the same brush and the same violet mix to label her painting across the bottom in quarter-inch block letters: THE ARTIST GIVES BIRTH TO HERSELF — SABINE — 12/24/93

She stepped back and chuckled as if at a secret joke. There was still some work to do, she saw, but they needed to rest for a while, she and the painting. Once the oils had set, dried on the surface, the final touches would be easy. This had been the hardest lesson for Sabine to learn, knowing when to stop and let the painting rest. But tonight the work had been so intense, she was ready to clean up, eager to shake off her strange mood. She spun the dial on the radio and found the same song playing that had riled her in the first place. "Rockin' around the Christmas tree..." Sabine looked at the clock, it was already midnight. Enthusiastically she sang along with the radio as she gathered up her dirty brushes and dishes and took them to the sink. For the first time all day she pulled the shade on the window next to the sink, giving it a sharp snap so that the roll of yellowing plastic spun around and around at the top, pull-string slapping wildly. Sabine looked out at a patchwork display of the season. In the distance, the civic plaza glowed under carefully arranged, energy conserving strings of white lights; up the street, office building and shop windows were the settings for snowy, tinselled fantasy worlds; and just below, a cluster of taverns and fast food joints had punctuated their usual neon with flashing red, green and blue bulbs. "Codey's" seemed to be doing a brisk business. Sabine's stomach rumbled hungrily as she soaked, soaped and rinsed her brushes. She felt like company now, food, maybe a beer, or better yet, an eggnog. She had a feeling she just might run into one or two other artists from her building at Codey's. Surely there were others like her who found themselves on the fringe of the Christmas festivities yet felt celebratory in their own way. They could sit under the blinking lights and smile warmly, without feeling the need to talk much, and drink a silent toast to the happy, impossible circumstance of being at once alone and together, ever child and parent, always of spirit and flesh, past and future, perfection and fallibility — in short, human.

"Merry Christmas," Sabine said to her angel, turning off the radio and the overhead light. She left on the floor lamp next to the easel and got ready to go out. It would be nice to come back later and sleep into the morning, under the radiant aura of the angel, with the building and street super quiet because of the holiday. "The artist gives birth to herself," Sabine tested the title out loud and grinned. "I wonder if anyone will get it but me. Oh well, it doesn't matter. I've had a great time." At the last minute, Sabine moved the easel, painting and floor lamp in front of the window, facing the street. Her own contribution to the spirit of the season.

She could see her angel from the entrance to Codey's. You had to look for it, up on the third floor, fifth window from the left, but it was there. Inside she went right up to the bar and asked Jen for a grilled cheese sandwich and an eggnog, which cracked Jen up. She wrote it up though, and passed the ticket to Jarrett, who was waiting tables. As Jen put the eggnog and some other drinks on Jarrett's tray she said, "Duster's here. And the only empty chair in the place is at his table — he's got his foot up on it and growls at anyone who tries to take it away."

"Nice of him to save me a seat!" Sabine followed Jarrett to Duster's table. A lanky, shaggy-haired man looked up as Jarrett placed an eggnog opposite him. Seeing Sabine, he shoved the chair out from under the table with the foot that had been resting on it. Sabine sat.

"Bad day in the studio, huh?"

"You just wonder sometimes..."

"I know what you mean." Sabine told Duster about her disillusionment with the elongated women, how she had given them up, starting tonight. Duster commiserated. He was sick of the unique finish his metallic sculptures were known for. Maybe he didn't want to work with metals at all for a while... They fell silent. Sabine finished her sandwich and touched the rim of her glass of eggnog to Duster's beer bottle before drinking the last of it.

"Crashing at the studio tonight?" Sabine nodded as she put a ten on the table and reached for her coat. "I'll walk you back. Been sitting here too long anyway."

On their way out, Jen mouthed a "Thank you" to Sabine behind Duster's back. They were on last call and she didn't want to be the one to have to kick him out at closing on Christmas eve.

After saying goodnight to Duster in the lobby, Sabine realized that she had forgotten to look up at her angel on the way over and point it out to him. "Probably just as well. I don't think he's really into that sort of thing; but then, neither am I, as a rule."

Sabine marched wearily up the two steep flights of stairs, and was soon asleep on her studio couch. She dreamt that the angel tried to fly out of the window, but her belly was too big and weighed her down. Sabine tried to comfort her by saying, "You may not be able to fly, but you can still dance." And they did the jitterbug together to that song: "Rockin' around the Christmas tree... At the Christmas party hop..."

A Prison Carol

C. M. La Bruno 62097

My life is on hold I'm searching solution.
It's Christmas, and time for confession of confusion.

In explanation I'll be both fair, and precise.
I'm paying my dues, at fate's exorbitant price.

> On the first year in prison
> Christmas wrung my heart
> as reflections mirrored
> indiscretions which tore
> my life apart

> On the second year in prison
> I became a nervous
> churning mass; waiting,
> breathlessly in vain, for
> the sense of sin to come then pass

> On the third year in prison
> I prayed on bended knee:
> Christ's day, it was, when
> God offered an only Son
> to begin HIS family tree

> On the fourth year in prison
> my loneliness would not cease;
> wife and child misery, caused

wild promises, promising
dedication, in lieu of release

On the fifth year in prison
Christmas brought me little peace.
I was trapped deep within,
myself; with me my own keeper
in eternal atoning of sin

On the sixth year in prison
I could no longer see my face
in her eyes, where once
a candle brightly burned,
in memories kind embrace

On the seventh year in prison
bitterness and rage slept,
deep and hard, at my side
while quite alone I lay bereft
as time idly crept

On the eighth year in prison
I began slowly to disappear
with only seasonal recognition
reminding me, at Christmas time,
tears had dissolved another year

On the ninth year in prison
not remembering what I'd done,
forgetting who I was, brought me
closer in fading, to the manger's
fruit, the blessed, risen, Son

On the tenth year in prison
all is gone now, no more family.
Hope is taken hostage by despair,

and in trying to cope, Oh God!
what's to become of me?

As all life's questions with no answers — what's to say?
Except time in a final judgment will one day, in my slumber,

absolve this body of its sins and ordained shame
and then by GOD what a march; — in glory to a name

divested
of its number

[EDITOR'S NOTE: La Bruno sent us this poem in March, 1993, with permission to publish it. When we wrote back to him in September, 1993, to tell him we had accepted it, our letter came back marked, "Deceased." We tried, through the prison system, to find out more about La Bruno and his death, but received no response to our queries. La Bruno's poem was accompanied originally by this note: "For Father O'Brien who asked me to write a Christmas poem for reading to his prisoners at Bordentown's Christmas mass: From a prisoner's perspective, of course, and on short, short notice, 12/23/88..."]

Reviving Pearl

Jennifer Lynn Jackson

"We think Pearl might be dead," says Goldie. She stands at Beth's door, trembling. "It might be meningitis, or even a stroke!" Her eyes are magnified and alarmed behind her glasses. She is crying and grasps a worn Kleenex in her tiny hands.

Beth groans. She just finished wrestling with the bread dough she'd decided suddenly to make to defy her mother's expectations. She has never made bread before. She eased the sighing loaves into pans, and just put them in the oven when Goldie knocked. She is annoyed, impatient, because she would rather sit in a chair and watch the loaves rise through the oven window, but this is her first apartment, not her family, so she has to be polite to her neighbors.

"Who's Pearl?" she asks, watching Goldie's feet shift back and forth in pink fuzzy slippers. And what am I supposed to do about it? she thinks.

"Oh, she's the nice older lady at the end of the hall. She hasn't been doing well. Oh, dear. I'm afraid for her. Oh."

She takes Beth's hand and holds it tight and they walk out into the cold, florescent hallway. Beth's door shuts behind her, and locks instantly.

"Damn," Beth says.

Goldie looks at her. Soon Beth will smell the bread burning in her locked apartment from the hallway, the Christmas bread from the recipe her mother had left under a banana-shaped magnet on the refrigerator door. The footnote on her mother's recipe said: *Braided Christmas Bread: A little flour on your nose never hurts. Young fellows like a girl who can bake.* Her old-fashioned mother.

Goldie squeezes her hand tightly. "I'm glad you were home, honey," she says. "We're not sure what to do."

The stringy, tense woman who lives at the end of the hall stands in her doorway chewing on something. She is dressed only in a floral housecoat, her arms crossed, a fork in one hand.

"Good evening," she says tersely. "We seem to have a slight problem here." She points at what apparently is Pearl's door, and three day's worth of newspapers on Pearl's welcome mat. The door is chained from the inside.

Pearl is an old, old woman, Beth knows. Most of the people in Olentangy Village are old, but Pearl is older than most of them. She must be in her eighties at least, and still living alone. Beth has seen her coming home with groceries in a wire cart from the Home Market, two blocks away. "They're all like little children," Beth tells her mother on the phone. "They shuffle around like they're afraid they're going to trip and fall or something." But her mother only laughs.

Her mother had liked the complex when they came to look at the apartment a month ago.

"It will be quiet and safe and normal," she decided, inspecting the mint-green walls in the bathroom for cracks or holes. "Yes, you'll like it here." She peeked into the closets. "It will be good for you." She spoke into the oven, checking for cleanliness. "Since you insist on having your own place," she said, finally looking at Beth.

Her mother knew the woman in the rental office, Shirlee Petersen, from high school. When Beth started to sign the lease on the dotted line, her pen ran out of ink, and her mother uncapped a new Bic and slipped it between her fingers.

"Just sign there, dear." She smiled at Shirlee. "On the dotted line, honey."

Beth felt sentenced even before she was really free.

The hallway is cold, but the air feels good on Beth's cheeks, since she'd kneaded the bread twice and punched it down three times in the past two hours, and since management insisted on keeping the apartment building thermostat at an even eighty-five degrees in the winter, good for Ft. Lauderdale or some resort in Arizona, but not for a little efficiency apartment in Ohio. She is wet under her arms. Her mother had made her think that bread was easily produced and with a certain aesthetic. She remembers her mother's clean apron. It seemed like her mother never, ever got messy. Beth looks at her nails. Dough is stuck underneath, yellow and crusty.

On Pearl's door is a wreath made out of molded plastic. Stuffed fabric letters spelling "Joy" in red, green and white gingham are sewn inside it. A strange mixture of smells wafts out: mothballs and something old people eat, like bean soup.

Beth steps forward and looks in, as far as she can see. There is an owl-shaped mug sitting on a coffee table, the handle turned towards the couch. She squints to see if there is any steam rising; maybe Pearl is playing a trick on her friends, crouching in the kitchen, ready to pop out and say, "I sure fooled you all." There is a crochet comforter on the back of the couch, in shades of orange and green, and the feeble glow of a floor lamp is the only light on in the room.

"Have you tried calling her, by phone?" Beth asks Goldie. She thinks this must be an appropriate question.

Goldie nods, puffing and sniffing. "Sylvia did," she says.

"I let it ring ten times," Sylvia says. "I pounded on her wall from my bedroom. I called through the door. I even used my rape alarm." She holds up a tiny plastic siren and shakes her head. "But nothing. And she's in there all right. I mean really, look at all those newspapers. Pearl *never* goes out of town." Her curlers are so tight they raise her thin eyebrows to an extreme angle. She looks possessed, one hand gesturing with her fork.

"Well, the police, someone should be notified, right?" Beth says. "With a possible dead person here in the building?" She watches Sylvia chew. Her jaw muscles bounce and tighten.

"She has a son," Goldie says softly, and she grabs hold of Beth's arm with her other hand. "We could call her son, couldn't we? She's talked about him. I think he lives in town. I think."

Her voice trails. Goldie wears sweatshirts with her grandchildren's photos transferred onto them. She vacuums her carpet three times a week, Monday, Wednesday, Friday. Beth can hear the vacuum, anxious and insistent through the walls, back and forth, while she's doing step aerobics with the video her mother gave her.

"What about maintenance?" Beth says. "Maybe they can do something about this chain." She can smell her bread beginning to bake, all the butter and flour and yeast and water and salt combining and growing together in her oven, inside her locked apartment. Interesting as a science experiment, this bread baking.

The idea of Pearl dead in her warm apartment is also interesting. Old people are a mystery to Beth. What could have happened? Maybe Pearl killed herself. Maybe old age was too depressing for her, the aching bones, the sagging skin, the endless days of creamed corn and jello salad and talk shows. She wonders if Pearl has a gun, or poison. What if Pearl has put her head in her gas oven? How much strength would an old woman need?

Beth calls the maintenance emergency number from Sylvia's kitchen phone. There is steam on the windows, a casserole full of unidentifiable food on the stovetop, and cat chow in a dish on the floor. She explains to the gruff voice on the other end of the phone that there is this old woman, a chain on the door, concerned neighbors.

Fifteen long minutes pass before Ted from maintenance finally arrives, groggy and aloof, and sheds his worn parka so that it drops on the floor. He has a spurt of gray hair over each ear. He smells like cigars and gasoline, and his blue shirt says "Ted" in embroidered letters.

"Well, ladies!" he exclaims, looking at the chain. "We can take care of that."

He pulls an enormous pair of shrub shears with green handles out of a bag that rattles with other various tools. Goldie and Sylvia gasp, and Goldie tightens her grip on Beth's arm. Ted pulls open the shear handles, and then he clips the chain like a

thread. Pearl's door slowly creaks open. Warm, still air drifts
out from her apartment.

Ted gives a short, proud laugh. "You see, ladies, those chains
don't do squat to protect you, take it from me. Anyone can clip
them, if only they have a pair of these babies." He holds the
shears in the air, admiring them himself.

Goldie shakes her head. "Poor Pearl," she says. "Oh dear,
sweet, poor Pearl!" Her voice trails off to a whisper. She puts
her head on Beth's shoulder. Sylvia has stopped chewing in her
doorway. She puts her fork down and picks up her cat, who has
been meowing for a bite of whatever she's been eating. The cat
nuzzles under her chin and sniffs at her mouth.

Ted looks at Beth. He has put the shears down. Up until now
he acted like he had seen this situation many times before. But
now his face is completely blank, and his hands hang at his sides
as he stares at Pearl's apartment.

"Is everyone just going to stand there?" Beth says. Her voice
is loud, and everyone looks at her.

Goldie's eyes are dark and enormous behind thick lenses. She
lets go of Beth's hand and backs up against the wall. "Well, I
can't do it," she says. She shakes her head and cries again,
quietly. "I'm her best friend around here. I just can't do it."

Ted stands next to Goldie, pats her arm awkwardly, taking on
a job: comforting. "Don't worry, ma'am. I'm sure everything
will be all right," he says. Goldie rests her head on his shoulder.
Sylvia grips her cat and her face looks even tighter.

Out of impatience and urgency and curiosity, Beth walks into
the apartment. She hears Goldie suck in her breath.

"Young lady," Ted says. "Young lady, you don't have to do
that." But he makes no move to stop her.

Beth ignores him. "Pearl?" she calls, looking around. She
blinks to let her eyes adjust to the dark. "Are you in here?" Beth
hears her own voice echoing off the walls as if the apartment
were empty. Her voice sounds different from her mother's —
there is a quick force to it, an edge, she believes — in the
darkened apartment. I don't know this woman, she thinks. Just

what would I do if I did find her dead? What if she's blown her brains all over the bathroom walls?

The kitchen is very clean, and a countertop light is on. Beth sees a small package of chicken, two drumsticks, sitting out on the counter in a puddle of water. A can of Del Monte peas stands next to it, and a single plate with silverware and a paper napkin gathered in the middle, like there had been a small dinner for one planned.

"Pearl?" she calls. She sniffs at the chicken and gags. Rancid meat. She walks into the living room and puts her hand on the owl mug sitting on the coffee table. It's cool. Peppermints are clumped in a bowl shaped like a piece of holly. She steals one, unwraps it, and guiltily pops it into her mouth, like she did when she took mints at her grandmother's house. Her heart beats faster.

She walks down the hallway toward what appears to be the bedroom, where blue television light glows under the door. Pictures line the walls — Pearl and a small grandchild, Pearl and a wedding couple, a family picture posed in rows on a sunny lawn, the oldest people sitting in chairs in the front row, holding the tiniest babies. She walks slowly, sniffing the air for the smell of an old lady who's been dead for two days. She thinks of death as a smell. The peppermint sticks to her teeth.

She pushes the bedroom door open with one jab of her index finger. There is a window, a braided rug, a television, power on, sound down, a bedside table with a lamp. Everything is neatly arranged. And then Beth sees her, barely visible in the tangles and piles of sheets and quilts on the bed. A little body, an old lady with high cheekbones and shapely, large ears, stretched earlobes. Her blue lips fit tight together, and she has soft, white hair. Her eyes are closed. Beth holds her breath and doesn't blink for a second. The lady is so small and beautiful, and she looks so comfortable and still. Beth holds her breath because she is afraid of smelling what seems clear now: Pearl is dead, and she doesn't look so bad.

The only dead person she has ever seen is her grandmother,

who was caked with a lot of make-up and red lipstick and laid in a satin-lined casket. *She* looked dead. She stepped up to the casket with her mother at the visiting hours. Her panty hose itched — it was the first time she had ever worn hose. "Stop squirming," her mother said. "Go ahead. Touch her hand." She watched her mother lean over and kiss her grandmother, on the cheek. But Beth just couldn't do it herself.

"Pearl?" she says.

And just barely, there is movement. A knee, an elbow, some sharply-angled joint shifts, and Pearl's eyes open a bit, blind. Her eyelids flutter. Beth suddenly thinks that she is entering where she isn't wanted. Pearl has been sleeping. She has been getting her rest before the holidays. Maybe she is just getting her rest.

Beth spots a pair of blue plastic-rimmed glasses on the bedside table and picks them up, opens them. She tries balancing them on Pearl's face. The glasses fall crookedly to one side. The apartment is warm and muggy, almost tropical, and the glasses steam up. Pearl blinks, brown-eyed, through the steamed lenses.

"I'm so thirsty," she says. A windup alarm clock ticks on the bedside table.

"Do you want some juice?"

Pearl nods. Beth almost floats to the kitchen. She pulls down a glass, and finds some red liquid in a container in the refrigerator. She heads back down the hall with the glass. When she is almost to the bedroom door, Ted calls loudly, "Everything okay in there, young lady?"

She jumps. "Everything's fine," she says. "Pearl's fine."

"Is Pearl in there?" Goldie calls. She sounds soggy and loud.

"She's alive; I've got juice." Beth stands in the bedroom doorway, still amazed at the sight she sees. Pearl watches her, cozy and bewildered in her bedclothes.

"Thank God," Goldie cries. "I'm going to try and find her son's number. He should come, quick as he can." Her voice bounces and fades down the hall. And from where she is, Beth can hear tall Sylvia's door click shut.

"Ma'am?" Ted knocks on Sylvia's door. "Ma'am? You okay?"

But Sylvia bolts her door firmly shut. "I've done my fair share," she says through the door. The sound of her television clicks on and blares loudly.

Beth carefully props Pearl's head up with one hand, and tips the glass with the other. Pearl closes her eyes and drinks the whole glass of juice, a hummingbird at a feeder, using her long, gray tongue and swallowing loudly. Beth looks away, at the silent television. A rerun of "Newhart" is on.

Pearl says, "This tastes so good." She slurs her words and smacks her lips. "This tastes *so good*." Listening to Pearl drink makes Beth thirsty. She swallows, and her own throat is dry. "More," Pearl croaks. Beth pours her another glass. The juice seems to fill in the caving-in parts of the old woman's face. The red coloring stains Pearl's lips and gives her a pinkish moustache, the look of a smile. Pearl's eyes fix on something across the room. Beth follows her gaze. A ceramic Christmas tree stands on the dresser.

"Do you know what day it is?" Beth asks Pearl.

"Friday."

"No, it's Sunday. You've been in here for almost two days. You've been asleep the whole time?" Beth's eyes sting with tears then, at the thought of Pearl sleeping away what little life she has left, the T.V. silent, blinking through its daily schedule, beaming its radiation onto her little body.

"Didn't you hear Goldie and Sylvia calling you?" Beth asks. She grits her teeth, like she's talking to a child. "Goldie and Sylvia have been worried about you. We even called you on the phone. Didn't you hear the ringing?"

Pearl looks at her. "Who are you?"

Beth is caught off guard for a second. At first she isn't sure how to answer. She realizes with slight panic that she's forgotten her name. She looks down at her doughy nails. "Um, you don't know me," she says, very slowly. Then, "I'm Beth. I live down the hall."

"The girl. The new one. You're a quiet girl. Don't see you much." She coughs softly. The cough becomes louder, so she raises a small fist to her mouth.

Beth kneels on the floor with the glass of juice and feels very strange — half-nauseated, half like she's been running. She straightens Pearl's crooked glasses, and brushes her white hair back off her forehead. "Don't you worry. Everything's going to be fine," she tells her. She pours more juice into the glass, and for the first time she can smell alcohol. She sniffs the glass and pulls back. "What is this stuff?" she asks.

"Ohh." Pearl licks her lips, and her eyes focus. "I think it must be the Cherry Bounce I put away for Christmas Eve. Grain alcohol and Michigan cherry juice. Very good." Pearl's hand reaches toward the glass. She is waking up.

Ted and Goldie appear in the doorway then, so that suddenly it is crowded with people. "I called the squad," Ted says. "They should be here in a minute or two." He is careful to look at the ceiling, hands in his pockets, as if he is embarrassed.

Goldie is crying not too quietly. "How are you, dear?" she sniffs, settling on the edge of Pearl's bed, next to Beth, and picks up Pearl's hand. "Oh you poor, poor thing." Pat pat pat. The old woman's eyes shift slowly, blinking, from face to face, in her small bedroom. Beth thinks the old woman's pink Cherry Bounce smile is natural-looking, better than the red lipstick and make-up of the dead.

Red and blue lights of emergency squads flash into the window. Beth backs against the wall and stays out of the way. The three paramedics stand over Pearl and peel her blankets away and gently lift her onto a stretcher. They hook tubes into her veins and strap her down.

"Meningitis," one of them says to Beth. He'd seen this before: the stiff neck, the short coma. "It's a good thing you found her when you did," the young man says, and his smile is nice enough.

"Does she have any family?" he asks.

Goldie shakes her head sadly. She says, "Pearl's son is out of

town, golfing in the Bahamas. But I'm her best friend around."
She hiccups and holds the same Kleenex. "So I'll be her family."
And she puts on her coat and locks her apartment and climbs
into the ambulance with Pearl, forgetting she is still wearing her
pink slippers.

Ted and Beth watch from the hallway window as the flashing
lights fade. "Something's burning," Ted says, sniffing.

"My bread," Beth says. "I'm locked out." They go to her
door, and Ted unlocks her apartment with his master key. In the
oven are two hard, black, shriveled loaves, and she pulls them
out and sets them on the counter. "Damn," she says. The kitchen
is hazy with smoke, and Beth waves her hand in the air.

"Sorry about your bread, young lady," Ted pulls on his coat.
He turns and winks at her, then steps out, shutting the door as
he goes. "Remember to lock up. Goodbye now." Beth locks the
door after him, and lets the chain dangle. She throws the
blackened loaves in the trash can.

She sits at her kitchen table. No snow like there's supposed
to be this time of year. Outside it is deceivingly clear and calm.

What's a Noel, Anyway?

Claude Tower

And what is he in for, you want to know, right? Did he hurt somebody? You wonder. Is he a kingpin? A lifer? You are eager to believe we all deserve this, and want to assure yourself about me. Put me in a context so what I say can be measured against it. That's about it, isn't it?

We do this ourselves. Your cellmate gets released (we are at double capacity here, two to a one-man cell.) You get a new one. Hi, my name's Breeze. Mine's Fingers. *What are you in for?* For sixty percent of us federal inmates the answer is "drugs." The jolly old Drug Enforcement Agency has made the Bureau of Prisons a dealer's convention. The old line crooks, the Mafiosi and bank robbers, the kidnappers and con men, lament this endlessly. "These dopers are nothing but a bunch of snitches and bitches," they sneer. The established hierarchy puts the dopers down with blind beggars and sleaze wheedlers. Hit men are the most exalted. Yes, it is a topsy-turvy world here in your Bureau of Prisons. I saw a poll that ranked dealers with journalists and elected officials, that is, at the bottom, in the public's esteem. Odd, because at least a third and probably half the population uses illegal drugs, or legal drugs in an illegal manner, some of the time.

So here we are, at the bottom of everyone's list. There, I gave it away. I'm a doper. I've been clean for nearly five years, one of them locked up, as far as using goes, but a pot dealer nonetheless. I'm doing sixty-eight months at the Federal Correctional Institution at Oxford, Wisconsin, a medium security prison, for conspiracy to distribute marijuana and psilocybin mushrooms. Oh, and carrying a pistol while doing so. I had heard there was a stickup man operating in the area where I was busted, ripping off dealers, so I had a .38 along that day. Bad luck. Carries a mandatory five, federal.

There are one thousand or so of us inmates. That's the new euphemism for convict. Even the convicts, at least the dopers, use it. So here I'll stay for sixty-eight months minus fifty-four days a year good time if I am good. Four years and ten months of fucking my fist. The inmates are unfortunately all men. This makes life extremely simple — not a bad thing — like a Western novel. No women, no complicated relationships, just simple, straightforward guy stuff. Still, I keep thinking of the big sailor in South Pacific who sang, "We get letters doused wit' poifume, we get dizzy from the smell; what don't we get? You *know* damn well!" That is all part of the punishment, of course. Probably the worst part if you're young, which I'm not. Of course the gays aren't feeling any pain, unless they like it that way.

Besides sex we are sitting out the entire delicious maelstrom of shoving and acquiring and fighting and drinking and doping and avenging and squabbling — life — which so resembles that island of rhesus macaques at the zoo. Many here are in a funk too deep to conspire or strive, hardly acting or being acted upon, except by a trivial schedule, subsumed with TV and card games and flipping through skin mags. We are the poor in spirit, Walt Whitman's

"Downhearted doubters, dull and excluded,
frivolous, sullen, moping, angry,
affected, disheartened, atheistical.
I know every one of you. I know
the sea of torment, doubt, despair and unbelief."

Some assuage their despair and unbelief by going to the weight rooms (there are four) til they could juggle Sumo wrestlers. Some are as enterprising as ever, conducting businesses which provide for almost any need, from placing a bet to building shelves in your locker to giving tattoos.

Some practice religion. It's a big department. There are three full time ministers — a Catholic, a Methodist, and a Nazarene.

The Indians, a large contingent in the B.O.P. because all crimes on the rez are federal, practice their religion religiously, complete with drums, wood fires and a sweat lodge. There are meetings of two Muslim groups, one of them angrier than the other. There are a last few Jewish mobsters who keep kosher, although it's getting tough because there are a lot of black Muslims in the kitchen and they fuck up the food. There is Bible study, Alcoholics Anonymous, which is treated as a religion and is to some people, and a single Zen Buddhist, a doper of course.

They lit the first Advent candle in the chapel today. It is the beginning of the church-calendar Christmas season. Of course the shopping stories on the news began two days ago. Thereby begins the duality of Christmas, sacred and profane.

"On Saturday, December 17th, Sunday, December 18th and Christmas Day, December 25th, the Athletic Club will have a Santa Claus in the visiting room. If you want to have pictures taken of Santa with your children, you may want to plan ahead to ensure that you have a sufficient number of photo tickets." (Notice on guard's office, Nov. 29.)

"And so I greet the vile season with a disgusted sigh: And now Christmas is coming again, as if we hadn't enough to put up with." — *Phillip Larkin.*

The sacred, the profane, and the cynical, I should say.

Dec. 1. I might as well tell you the emotional gamut around here mainly runs from anger to despair and back again. That's typical of the chemically dependent anyway, who tend to be a lot alike no matter what their drug of choice. Of course the alcoholics have been recognized as having a disease. Anybody on something else is a criminal and war is waged upon him. We are the prisoners of that war. Your vast gulag of drug offenders has made us the nation with the highest percentage of its citizens under lock and key. The land of the free has become the greatest police state, and the federal Bureau of Justice statistics extrapolates *twice* as many P.O.W.'s in eight more short years. And will there be any reduction in drugs and violence? Do you need me to tell you there won't be?

You see, the person who resorts to dealing, the street-level, gun-toting, crack-handling rooty-poots who account for ninety percent of drug arrests, have already despaired. They have no hope for a straight life, and no amount of punishment will deter them or prevent their immediate replacement. The straight public keeps thinking, "If we just give them more time, they'll stop." Wrong. People who have despaired are immune to further misery. They have already been saturated with it.

But, ah, Christmas approaches. This is my first as a convict, so I wonder what it will be like. I always found Christmas on the outside to be more pain than pleasure. I am relieved to be relieved of it. Having been a cultural dropout, it's to be expected that I lacked Christmas spirit. Along with most other kinds. I think I may like it here. Christmas, I mean. I appreciate the idea of not having to buy anything, go anywhere, see anybody, or pretend to work up any enthusiasm. I can just let the whole thing pass unnoticed and not a person here will care or say a word. Cynicism carries no consequences here.

"Blessed are the poor in spirit, for theirs is the kingdom of heaven." Matthew 5:3. Yeah, in about one million years.

Dec. 4. The government is going to be giving us gifts. For Christmas. I find this baffling. The government has gone way out of its way to, first, create an intense and effective propaganda campaign to generate hysteria about drugs.

Then it let the Constitution become a cliché as its mandates were waived in the name of "winning" against drugs. The Supreme Court turned its head because there was a war to be won.

Everyone here will talk for as long as you will listen about how unscrupulous the police, prosecutors and judge in his case were. And it isn't all bullshit.

The cons and the system regard each other as evil, dangerous and detestable. Sometimes I think they're both right. And now here comes the enemy with gifts and amenities. It must be hard to accept them, I would think.

Of course they live with the specter of riot. Conditions must be kept tolerable, if they can be. The extra help to enforce intolerable conditions gets expensive.

This must be what the gifts are for. We, the alienated, agree.

Dec. 5. I may be the wrong guy to cover Christmas for you, because I've been kind of a Scrooge.

There was a time, though, when I had a thrilling Christmas. I was small, and turgid with anticipation the night before. I got an electric train, as ordered from Santa. It worked beautifully and everything was perfect. *A* time.

The next distinct memory I have of Christmas is of opening presents with mother demanding that I show some appreciation. She shot me an index finger, nudged father and said, "Look at him! He doesn't even appreciate what he got for Christmas." He gave me a glittering, resentful look. Guilty as charged, though. I *tried* to be grateful, but by then (ten years old or so) I was a cynic. The whole production of tree, enforced carol singing on Christmas eve — forty years later when I found those song books in mother's desk I put them out in the snow with the trash — they just made me angry.

I remember watching my mother's mother and even she softened at Christmas: had her annual small glass of Danish cherry wine, got a little glow on and appeared to feel a little kindness and *bonhomie.*

Our Christmases were abundant, splendid productions in every detail, but nothing was more indicative of how wrong things had gone with me than how I felt about them. I resented being expected to be grateful with a wild, searing anger that I couldn't even conceal. It was as if a few material items were supposed to wipe the slate clean for the rest of the year. They didn't.

I began to dread it as an ordeal of failed attempts at hypocrisy, of exposure to naked resentment in turn for being an ingrate, of having to go through an entire routine of shopping and buying and wrapping and giving about which I felt nothing but annoyance and ennui. Why didn't everyone just buy himself something and save the overhead, I wondered.

It just became hopeless. But it was unavoidable. The whole process had to be seen through in every detail, every time. I have repressed it so thoroughly that of all my growing up Christmases I have exactly those two distinct memories, the day and eve of the train, and the accusations of unthoughtfulness the other time. The rest I do not recall. Oh, I remember that we had those song books and put up those trees and ate those turkeys, but don't recall any specifics. I have pushed them away so fiercely I can't find them anymore.

Dec. 8. We are arranged into living units here, which are ten separate buildings of about a hundred men each. There are fifty cells arranged on four hallways in each unit. There are three T.V.'s in separate rooms: one kept on movies, one on sports, and one for everything else. There are two phones with a fifteen minute time limit and no collect calls allowed. There is one washing machine and two dryers. There are laundry services available, but they are unreliable. We have one microwave, a soda machine and a vending machine with candy, pastry, peanuts and microwave popcorn. Smoking is allowed only in the cells, but lots of them are sneaked, smokers being the addicts they are. Showers and toilets and sinks are communal. The showers give hot, abundant, unchlorinated water. There is an ice machine and a pencil sharpener, and a guard's office. There is a guard on duty twenty-four hours a day and he or she hands out the mail, issues passes and handles supplies such as soap, shavers, pencils and paper. Oh, and they enforce the rules, too. The guard is unprotected by any barrier and lives among a hundred cons as a matter of course.

Everyone has a job, and must report to work. If you refuse to work, you live in solitary.

We can go to the gym, chapel, library and crafts and arts rooms til 8:30 p.m. when everyone is recalled to their living units. I was coming back from the library tonight and watched a bunch of young guys from the living unit next door. They had built a snow woman, a huge thing, with even huger breasts, of course, and had the unit photographer out there. You can buy tickets from the commissary for two dollars, which are good for a Polaroid photograph. Each unit has an appointed picture taker. The guys next door were embracing the sculpted female for their photographer, hamming it up and hollering, zapping each other with snowballs and generally showing some spirit.

A lot of them were Indians, who seem to bear up pretty well. They travel in groups, pick each other up emotionally, all wear headbands (the only people allowed to do so) and have their section of the chow hall, where no one else sits.

Someone, at least, is capable of play and high spirits.

I came into my unit and there was a stack of pamphlets on the ice machine. The pamphlets have green covers and eight pages of holiday-related text, from the warden's holiday message urging us to share dignity, respect and kindness in our thought, words and actions inside the front cover to, "Have a Fun-filled Holiday Season" on the back cover. Thanks.

Christmas menu: Oyster stew, Cream of Mushroom Soup, Sliced Roast Beef, Maryland Fried Chicken, Whipped Potatoes, Candied Sweet Potatoes, Raisin Dressing, Giblet Gravy, Whole Kernel Corn, Lyonnaise Green Beans. Salad Bar Including: Carrot/Raisin Salad, Waldorf Fruit Salad, Giardiniera Salad and Parker House Rolls, Pumpkin Pie, Assorted Sodas, Hot Coffee.

The food here ain't bad, considering. The chef's school on campus (for this is a campus. Grassy open spaces, four-year degrees from the University of Wisconsin. It just has a fence around it. And no women.) issues associate degrees in food preparation and the students who work in the kitchen do what they can with whatever food doesn't somehow wind up in the hands of the microwave cooks in the living units.

There will be tournaments of every description in the recreation department, several groups of what look to be cute carolers coming to chapel, *beaucoup* food and free Christmas cards. Well.

Watched the morning news for holiday input. The lead story was about shopping, of course, followed by one on letters to

Santa Claus. I was shown her letters to Santa Claus by the girl across the street when I was five. She had found them — hers and her sister's — under their mother's mattress. I went straight to our kitchen where my mother and her mother were canning green beans. I asked them if there was really, really a Santa Claus. Their eyes got big and innocent and their heads bobbed in unison; yes, there really, really was, and he came down the chimney, too. I went away very angry. These were the people who had me beaten for lying.

Following the shopping and Santa stories was the news of Pablo Escobar's murder by Columbian government employees. Some representative of the U.S. war on drugs came on saying how Escobar had "brought a lot of misery" to the United States in the form of cocaine. Those people were miserable already. They just thought cocaine would help.

Look. People do drugs to *treat their pain.* In a culture with a single message — "acquire" — the general level of hurt from unfulfilled greed is immense. There is no escaping the mechanism: Greed-Pain-Medication.

The news this morning — Santa, shopping, Pablo Escobar, nurses. Greed-Pain-Medication. Are we to expect to break the cycle after people have begun using medication?

I always think of the Coneheads relative to this issue. Those naive aliens have distilled the content of our civilization, "consume mass quantities." The core of humor is always a baleful truth.

I hate to be the one to tell you, but heroin will be the next really big trend in self-prescribed pain medication. The war on drugs has been so successful in drying up the supply of bulky, mild marijuana, that dealers will only take risks for more concealable, higher profit substances.

The entire greed-pain-dope causality and the opposition to it have become entirely ruthless and I am almost grateful for having been taken out of it. I know the way out of the maelstrom. It is spiritual growth — loving yourself and others more and more effectively. That is what I have turned to here.

I thus represent the dichotomy of Christmas.

The spiritual, the selfless, the love of your enemy, was brought to the West at Christmas. The paradox of Santa Claus and Christ is about as extreme, and amusing, as it gets. People never stop being fun to watch.

Dec. 16. As the rest of December passes, I see spirit building. The chorale groups who visit to carol with us are well attended, and the singing is enthusiastic. Decorations appear in all the housing units and workplaces. A lot of them are elaborate and represent serious effort. There is a competition between "living units" or dormitories, for the best decorations. I myself get in the spirit, surprisingly. I start helping decorate the unit, making red and white paper chains to hang in all the halls. One of the guys helping with it tells me about his try at hanging a stocking. Two years ago he hung a stocking on his door (we have wood doors here. They are never locked.) The next morning someone had stolen the stocking. That sounds about right, I thought. Stubbornly, the next year, last year, he hung another one. In the morning it was full of candy and fruit. I want to believe him so I let myself.

What is getting into me here? Am I so contrary that I must just always buck the trend? Will I now become upbeat and enlightened here, on the scene of general anger, resentment and bitterness? It is almost a certainty.

Dec. 17. The season is hardest on the men with little kids. That is who Christmas is really for, the little 'uns. It is so easy to be hateful about it as an adult, and I have been. But even I once had a wonderful, magical Christmas as a little kid, where I stayed awake late trying to catch Santa and got an electric train. The fathers of little kids feel keenly that they are missing their chance to see and create those chimerical early Christmases. It hurts.

As the 25th approaches I call my son, the pilot, to chat. He inquires about visiting procedures. "You just show up," I tell him eagerly. "Can you give me a tour?" he asks. I laugh.

He's going to come and see me! I now know how badly I

wanted a visit, and only a visit, for Christmas. All the denials, all the sublimation through decorating and singing, all the casual indifference, is blown. It is a sham. I *want* something for Christmas. I want a visit. The wheels of karma have now informed me of how keenly he wished for my appearances when I used to visit him. I've been cast in the helpless, waiting situation, and taught how I've been needed. I've now been instructed in remorse. I had no idea what others were feeling then because I was simply suffering and drinking to kill it. But now I need him. He can make my day, month and year, by just coming. Visits are really the best things that happen here, the only really good things for most of us. I fell asleep late and not too soundly.

Dec. 18. Sat. I worked at my desk most of the afternoon, and the guy across the hall sang the line, "Chestnuts roasting on an open fire" every few minutes for hours. About four o'clock he added, "Jack Frost nipping at your nose," once, to complete, finally, his Christmas haiku. This little melody, randomly repeated, was more poignant than the whole three-hour carol fest with the Quakers yesterday, or anything so far. At times this place almost seems like home — you tend to accept whatever is customary. You must to stay sane, if anyone is sane — but the image of those chestnuts, a flagstone fireplace, the coziness, the aroma, the sensual, intimate little good time, say with a buxom redhead. And a little tear to enjoy it with, I had for myself.

Dec. 20. I work in the dental lab where we make false teeth for this and twenty other prisons. We erected a plastic tree in the lab today. The branches look uncannily like pressed marijuana buds. Everyone noticed it — the techs are all dopers, except for one bank robber. We gathered around laughing, ringing the bare little five footer. "Hey, Jim, let's fire up one of these branches!" we were joshing like that. A huge Jamaican detached one of the limbs and passed it under his nose, as he drew a belly-deep inhalation with his eyes closed and quietly exclaimed, "Ahhhhh, *Ind*ica!" It was a fun fantasy and a light note provided by the season, albeit inadvertently. The boss put on Nat King Cole's caroling tape. It is the best of them. It had "Chestnuts roasting on an open fire" on it.

Dec. 22. The guards inspected, or shook down, an entire living unit for alcohol today. They sent six guys to the hole for making alcohol. They'll be there til way after Christmas. Thirty gallons of wine, called "hootch" were found a'making. The other nine units are good to go, I guess.

Dec. 23. There are seven of us out in the main hall and lobby working hour after hour to decorate the area, mostly with bells, chains, and snowmen, all of paper. It looks at least somewhat festive, for here. We have even decorated the ice machine to look like a brick fireplace, and come up with a little tree.

Dec. 24. Our gifts arrive. They are a wool scarf in army green which smells as if it had been stored since before I was born, a knit cap to go with the one we already have, an apple, a pear, a big navel orange, a little address book (crucial to record all our new acquaintances and important appointments), a couple cups of microwave macaroni and beef and an insulated coffee cup, small. At least no one's expecting me to be grateful. I had been hoping for some gloves, as they aren't available through the commissary here, and the issue gloves are thin white canvas and nearly useless when doing laps on Wisconsin winter days. Besides, they have very unfashionable large black numbers printed on the backs; clumsily printed, with smeary edges on the numbers and crooked lines. My cellmate still had his Christmas package unopened from last year, when they got gloves, and loaned me some black knit units that will serve just fine. We are not allowed to conduct any purchases between ourselves; it is against the rules for any inmate to receive anything of value from any other inmate. Such a prohibition could be taken seriously only by something as impractical as a government, as economic activity is common to all human beings in all times and places, and can no more be successfully forbidden than breathing.

1:00 P.M. Everyone is sitting around the unit. It is a day off work. The guard comes down the hall. She hollers, "Tower!

Tower! You have a visitor!" loud enough to inform the whole wing. Yeah, holler the roof off, you big-mouthed bitch, I love it! Feeling like a fully formed celebrity, I head past the indolent inmates with my coat.

Down to visiting, get let in. Strip in a booth, raise arms, stick out tongue, pull ears forward, raise testicles, turn around, show soles of feet, spread cheeks, get dressed, go out to the lounge, and there he sits. I've been sober and drug-free for almost five years continuous, I've been meditating for almost two years, and am finally able to feel affection. I'm not sure it's a good thing — everyone is afraid of change — but it sure is a rich vein when it is answered.

He stayed almost three hours. Brought me a hundred bucks. I can buy a radio! It was good. I didn't even notice who else was in visiting, but they all noticed me. They came up later and said "Was that your son the one who's a pilot?" "Those were all nine of my kids - good looking bunch of Americans," I said to a Mexican who looked perplexed. It was all an overwhelming relief, to not be abandoned. This year. Friends become scarce as time goes by, though. They stop writing. Wives drop away. Children become alienated. The con becomes a pariah.

Not many of us had visitors. The Mexicans did best; they have good families. Other Hispanics, too. We have coherent groups of Puerto Ricans, Cubans, and Colombians, and I guess a few Dominicans. But from what I could tell at our living unit only about a third, at best, had people come. The blacks took a beating. They are nearly half the inmates, but were only about twenty percent of the people in the visiting area.

I could tell the men who didn't get visits were sad. They were gruff and didn't show it much, but they were bummed. I would have been, too, if I hadn't gotten one, but my son saved me from turning against at least this one Christmas. I had actually wanted something and gotten it.

So how was our Christmas? It was the same as yours. The scale was different, the amounts involved, the expectations were less, but our feelings were the same, because we are the same, you and us: we are all serving sentences.

Were you curious to peek into our lives, to assure yourself that you are different? Your awareness of separation is an illusion. Ninety-nine percent of the involvements you have, your thoughts, deeds and emotions, concern yourself. You feel the same greed and anger we do; you are the prisoner of your ego with its insatiable demands. You think of your mind as yourself and instead you have let it become the master of yourself. Your desperation is as real as ours.

You lock us up to be safe in your possessions while your billionaires rob you unmercifully. You lock us up to be safe in your homes, while your television is corroding your family, your values and your very sanity. You lock us up to be safe in your soul, while your preachers tell you that you are less than God.

To avoid being a victim you must become a student of your own life. Blaming us won't solve your victimhood. We are not separate from you. If you are not at peace with yourself you are in a prison, too.

As long as you think that anything you can see, taste, hear, touch, smell, think about or obtain will satisfy your incoherent longings, free you of fear or bring you the peace you really want, you are doing hard time, buddy.

Merry Christmas.

STUFF

*Other cultures have a periodic orgy of gift-giving, called a potlatch, in which status and honor accrue to the extent that the giver impoverishes himself, giving everything away. What we do at Christmas looks a little like that, but it doesn't work because in our culture a person's worth is quite literally tied to the abundance of things he or she possesses. So our potlatch is in reverse. It is gift **getting** that interests us, and troubles us.*

Everyone complains about the commercialism of Christmas. It's almost a tradition in itself. Somehow the complaining helps us endure. Because even though we all readily acknowledge that the finer spirit of Christmas has been overwhelmed by merchandizing, we just keep going along with it.

"We do it for the children," is a popular refrain, as if children can't see when something's being faked, or overdone. Several of our contributors point out that the worst part of getting something for Christmas you don't want, or that comes at too high a price, is having to act grateful for it. More acting; and now you're just as bad as the rest of them. Guilt and gifts seem to go together at Christmas.

"We do it for the children." Maybe the children we're talking about are ourselves. As Joseph Barda wrote to us: "Is it really honest to cover something up, disguising what truly lies beneath the surface? In terms of gift giving, yes; in terms of relationships, no. Maybe this is why Christmas is for children and adults should learn to act their age and not play games."

The season of pushing our finances, schedules and good humor to the limit brings into sharp focus ways in which we've failed to take care of ourselves during the preceding year. Our relationships are also subject to scrutiny as we apportion emotional and material resources that never seem sufficient. The Christmas list has become part scorecard, part balance sheet.

*At Christmas we confront the scariest question of all: "What do I want?" Realistically we can only wish for tangible things; inside we long for so much more — security, beauty, companionship, love, health, hope, freedom. Why are we so reluctant to admit to these deeper needs? Amidst the avalanche of Christmas "stuff" it should be liberating to recognize that the **really** good stuff doesn't come gift-wrapped; it still comes from within.*

Presents

Sparrow

The saddest thing about Christmas is the presents. You break open their wrapping — which always looks like every *other* wrapping — and inside is either something you want or something you don't — and the unwanted gifts are always made of *wool* — often *tan*-colored wool — and the things you want are obvious and mundane, like the rest of the junk you have — another *Bob Dylan* album — and after all these manifold disappointments, you must kiss the gift-giver, while smiling, or be branded a *misanthrope*.

Making a List and Checking It Twice

Joseph A. Barda

Presence for presents was not an equal exchange, but rather Sylvia's cry for help the day before her gift giving. I looked at all the unwrapped Christmas presents she bought for her family stacked on the dining room table, and realized we had our work cut out for us.

Since my birthday was only five days after Christmas, I thought Sylvia's presents for me might be there as well. While she went to her room to drop off her jacket and briefcase and change into sweatshirt and jeans, I made some room on the table and laid down the bags of wrapping paper, labels, and tape. I sat down and snooped through the plastic bags, boxes, and tissue paper, wondering who each present was for. Since Sylvia recently graduated college and was now working full time as an accountant, this was the first Christmas she could afford to buy presents for everyone in her family; all thirty-seven. When Sylvia walked back into the room, I deliberately looked mischievous with my hands inside of a large Carson's bag. Although I knew she saw me, she didn't say anything. It was obvious, therefore, that what I was looking for lay elsewhere.

"Where do you want to start?" I asked.

Sylvia looked at the overflowing table and quickly put her analytical mind to work.

"Okay. We have presents on this side and wrapping paper over here. The trick is to merge the two together."

She put the five fingers of her left hand to the side of her forehead and said, "I hope we have everything. You start unpacking and I'll get the list so we can see what's what."

I remembered Sylvia telling me she spent five dollars for every child and ten dollars for every adult. She wanted to make this Christmas special, but the total added up quickly and this was all she said she could afford. Having dated her for over two years I knew everyone in her family fairly well from the numerous birthdays, holidays, christenings, and family get-togethers. As I emptied the bags, I wondered who would get what. It was easy to separate children's gifts from adults, but beyond that I was just guessing.

We wrapped the bigger gifts first in order to clear the table and make more room for ourselves. Pedro and Miguel each got a "Where's Waldo" poster-board, Alex got a Bulls hat, Maria got a maternity blouse, and pre-packaged boxes from Carson's and JC Penny's went to Melissa, Hugo, Bertha, and Sylvia's mother. The remaining toys, crayons and children's books even had Sylvia wondering who got them. Since we knew none of them got the set of hangers, I started wrapping that gift while Sylvia wrote the card out to her sister Zelda. While I started folding in the corners to make a triangle, Sylvia looked over at me and stopped her search for the list beneath the scraps of paper.

"No, no, no. You have to fold it like this."

She turned the package towards her and refolded the first corner so that it was more angular and proportionate to the other side. I sat back and watched as she repeated the same technique for the other two sides. After the last piece of tape was pressed into place, she lifted up the gift and showed me the result.

"See what I mean."

I shrugged my shoulders. The result of my technique would have looked almost identical.

I responded, "I guess."

"You're doing a good job," she said, handing me another gift to wrap.

The next gifts were those of Emily, Jesse, Olivia and Eliza. Looking at her list and arranging different items on the table Sylvia formed four different piles.

"Let's see. Crayons for Emily... no. Crayons for Eliza and Olivia. Perfume for Emily and glitter nails for Jesse. Wait. No. Emily doesn't like perfume. Okay. We'll give the glitter nails to Emily and the perfume to Jesse. Each of them also gets a barrette and a wiggly Christmas pen for school. Now, we've got crayons for Eliza and Olivia. Socks for each. Two necklaces. Eliza will like this one. Where's the other necklace?"

We spent the next several minutes going through discarded boxes and bags, looking for the misplaced item. Sylvia found the receipt and was surprised to discover she bought only one. I leaned back in the wooden chair and watched as she recalculated the children's presents.

"I guess Eliza gets one and Olivia doesn't."

"You can't do that," I replied. I jokingly made a noise like a police siren and said, "Favoritism, favoritism."

Sylvia looked at me and smiled and then returned her questioning eyes to the four piles that restlessly occupied the table in front of her, as she tried to decide what to do.

I handed her the necklace from Eliza's pile and said, "Why don't you just hold on to this for now; save it for another time."

She held the necklace in her hand for a few moments before coming to a decision.

"I guess you're right."

"Do you have any boxes for these?" I asked.

"No. We'll have to get by with what we have."

Sylvia took the scissors and cut two large squares, one for me and one for her. After putting the paper back on the chair next to her she turned to me and confronted my puzzled look.

"Come on, be creative. You do Eliza's and I'll do Olivia's."

As we laid the presents on the paper, we looked back and forth at each other's work, taking the best hints the other's technique had to offer. Tissue paper was used as stuffing to offset any revealing bumps. The act of disguising contents was something we both did well. Although we each had a different colored paper and folded our corners differently, the final products looked fairly similar. We wrapped Emily's and Jesse's presents the same way, as we hummed to Christmas songs on the all-request radio program where everybody got to hear what they wanted.

On Susie, on Marcos, on Jill, on Betty.

On Elena, on Joyce, on Drena, on Patty.

With only a couple of presents left our conversation became quiet as we concentrated on our individual efforts. Our technique had improved to a quicker pace, our actions became more mechanical. We had been wrapping presents for nearly two-and-a-half hours and the job I never thought would end was quickly coming to a close.

"Are you sure we're done? It doesn't seem like we wrapped thirty-seven presents."

"We didn't," she answered.

I thought she would continue, mainly because I didn't know what she meant.

"You said you were buying presents for everyone in your family. I don't remember seeing anything for Tim or Allan."

"I didn't buy them anything."

While Sylvia continued picking up the scraps of paper, I found myself spacing out, caught in a diligent effort to make sense out of what she had said. It appeared that a line was drawn between those born into the family and those who married into it. But didn't marriage make them part of the family? Aren't they always there for her, and wouldn't they buy her presents? Thinking further, I asked myself where I fit into the equation. She felt me staring at her, stopped, and looked up.

Evidently she mistook my confusion for tiredness. She snapped her fingers close to my face, "Hello! Anybody out there?"

"I'm okay, I was just wondering why."

"Why what?"

"Why you didn't buy anything for Tim or Allan."

"Because I spent over two hundred dollars as it is. I couldn't buy something for everybody. I bought for all my nieces and nephews and all the people in my family."

"Tim and Allan are in your family. Did you buy anything for

Bob, Ladel, or Marta?"

"No, just my brothers and sisters. I had to draw the line somewhere. Come on, I'll fix you a cup of coffee to wake you up. I don't want you to fall asleep while you're driving home."

While Sylvia made the coffee, I sat on the couch listening to the Christmas music and reviewing the presents. I reached down and picked up one of the packages Sylvia had wrapped. It was red, and red was her favorite color. She used the cellophane wrap to enclose the contents and tied it off at the ends with white ribbon so it looked like a giant piece of candy; a piece of hard candy. Although I didn't remember what the present was, I knew it wasn't candy. Sylvia had disguised it well.

She returned from the kitchen with a tray containing two cups of coffee, a pint of amaretto cream, and a plate of Christmas cookies she made the other night with her nieces. She had the habit of filling my cup about an inch and a half below the rim because she liked to put a lot of cream in her coffee. She watched me as I stared into my cup.

"Oops, I'm sorry. I forgot. You don't like things too sweet, do you?"

I shrugged my shoulders and said it was fine.

"I think I'll have it black tonight. Just give it to me straight."

It was my opinion that black coffee was stronger and that adding cream or sugar only lessened its strength. I took the coffee pot from her and finished filling my cup, sacrificing my sweet tooth for the honesty of the dry, bitter taste.

After Sylvia poured her coffee, we each took a gingerbread cookie from the plate and sat back on the couch. The cookies she told me that she made the night before didn't look like gingerbread men. I couldn't help but think her nieces and she ate the best and left the rest for whomever. I took one bite from the misshapen lump and her handiwork fell apart in my lap.

"What time do you want me to come over tomorrow night?" I asked after swallowing the remaining crumbs I picked off my pants.

"Tomorrow night?"

"Yeah. What's for dinner?"

"Oh, you think you're coming for dinner," she responded with a playful smile.

"Well what time does the party start?"

"We usually eat around seven by the time everybody gets here. That usually lasts a few hours with seconds, late arrivals, new dishes, dessert, and so on. Then we open presents around ten and leave for midnight mass around eleven. So if you want to come over around — eleven?"

Even though her body was positioned slightly sideways on the couch, I felt Sylvia looking at me with troubled and expectant eyes, waiting for my response. A quiet moment passed, as each of us took a sip of coffee to cover our indecision.

"I'd invite you to come earlier, but I think you might feel uncomfortable, just sitting back and watching everybody else opening gifts."

In the past I had watched members of her family open presents almost every time they had a family party. For some reason I didn't know why Christmas would be different. Since we spent a lot more time with each other over the past year, I was really coming to think of myself as part of her family. I was going to suggest that we could exchange our presents on Christmas Eve, but kept the thought to myself as I took another sip of coffee.

The holiday season was supposed to be a time for giving, not just of presents but of ourselves. Last Thanksgiving was the first time I spent that holiday away from my family. Since there are only four of us, my absence was sharply felt. But I wanted the holiday to be special and was willing to do whatever it took to be with her, so I spent the day with Sylvia and her family. I was hoping my sacrifice would not go unnoticed, and that our relationship could grow stronger as a result. I was out of town last Christmas, but we had spoken on the phone to wish each other well. When Thanksgiving came around this year I waited to see what would happen. Nothing did. We spent that holiday with our respective families and made the customary late night phone call like it was just an ordinary day. Even as Christmas was approaching, she never made an inquiry into what I was doing on that day. I, too, seemed to let it pass without offering an invitation to join my family for dinner. Perhaps it was because I was afraid she might say no, that she would choose her family over me. Whatever the reason, I knew this Christmas would be different. It would have to be.

Sylvia's family did the majority of their celebrating on Christmas Eve with the ritual culmination of midnight mass. My family did their celebrating on Christmas day itself. I couldn't think of an easier way for two people to balance their time between families. Many married people often find this to be a stressful situation. If we ever reached that goal, we could sigh with relief at being able to balance out a Christmas schedule that was fair to both families. This foresight gave me the courage to speak out even after the late arrival time I was given for her Christmas Eve.

"Do you want to come over on Christmas day for dinner?" I asked with a confident and impassioned voice.

"Oh great, now I have to buy your mom a present."

Her response was sharp and direct. After having spent the last few hours wrapping presents, I could understand the apprehension she might have at any extension of the ordeal we just finished.

I put my hand on her arm and spoke in a calming voice. "You don't have to bring any gift, just bring yourself."

Sylvia took a sip of coffee and then responded, "What time do you want me to come over?"

"How about eleven, or make it noon? That way you can sleep in a little bit."

"What time are you eating dinner?"

"Probably about two thirty."

"Well what am I going to do for two-and-a-half hours?"

"I don't know, maybe talk to my parents and my brother, enjoy their company. You could talk to me. Come on, you haven't been over to my house in a long time."

"Can I come at one-thirty?"

"How about two?"

"Okay."

"Better yet, why don't you just drive by and leave the car running? We'll pack a carry out bag for you."

Although my wry smile was loaded with cynicism and disbelief, Sylvia mistook my comment and briefly giggled. Even though I sensed her discomfort with the situation, I pushed the conversation further, sensing the greater need for resolve.

"Is it really asking that much?" I pressed with a look of concern.

"I feel uncomfortable when I'm at your house. You don't have any sisters. You, your brother, and father spend most of your time drinking beer and watching sports on TV. I don't like beer and I don't understand sports."

"Why don't you talk to my mom?"

Sylvia took a sip of her coffee and rolled her eyes away from me. "I feel uncomfortable talking to your mother. A lot of times she doesn't understand me. I can tell she gets frustrated talking with me."

For the first time I saw deep similarities between my mother and Sylvia. I saw two people who shied away from communication so as not to burden the other, preferring to be sealed off and wrapped up in themselves.

"It's true my mother lets her deafness get the better of her, but she acts the same way with me, my brother and my father. You need to be patient with her. You need to at least try. It's really ridiculous you know, two people who could share a lot, but refrain from doing so, in order not to inconvenience the other. You don't have to discuss the theory of quantum physics; just talk. You could at least try to communicate. Is it really asking that much of you?"

"You don't have to jump down my throat."

My words did come out strong and quick. I joined Sylvia in a brief period of silence to think about what I had said. Sylvia put her mug down and folded one of her legs underneath as she repositioned herself on the couch. I sat on the corner of the coffee table directly in front of her and caught my strained expression in the large mirror which hung on the wall behind the couch.

"How do you think I feel when I talk with your father? His heavy Mexican accent? His slurred speech from the stroke? He's almost completely blind. You have to admit, it's kind of creepy watching him stare off into space wondering if it's you he's looking at or not. Sometimes I'm not sure if he's all there when I'm talking with him. But the thing is, at least I try."

Sylvia had her head down, but raised it to flash a hard cold stare at me before returning it to focus on a few loose threads in the cuff of her sweatshirt.

"Comment?"

Sylvia quickly lifted her head and folded her arms in a way that told me her sweatshirt was really of no concern.

"I don't like it when you say my dad is not all there. Can't you see that?"

"I'm sorry. It may have been a poor choice of words, but let's face it, your father is lucky to be alive after all he's been through. You've said yourself that he has occasional memory loss and even forgets what he's talking about within a conversation."

My apology or explanation seemed to fall on deaf ears. She wiped a tear and hardened her presence as if it had been overcooked like the ginger bread cookies.

"One o'clock. Fine. I'll be there."

It seemed hypocritical to follow through with our ill-conceived plans and pretend like nothing had happened. We had done that before, and much too often. As we sat there in silence I reached for my mug to take another sip of coffee, but found the well was empty.

I stood up and went to get my jacket. When I returned I found Sylvia with the same expression on her face; lost in herself. I stood in front of her dressed for the cold weather outside and said, "Maybe I should stay home tomorrow with my family. We usually have pizza and open our cards afterwards, I haven't talked to my brother in a while. Anyway, they say it's supposed to start snowing late in the afternoon. It's a long way to drive, you know."

Walking me to the door, she said once again she would see me at one o'clock on Christmas day. Her mannerisms were so businesslike I thought she was going to shake my hand or pat me on the back. Our revealing conversation seemed forgotten, or lost. Sylvia turned the tricky knob on the large wooden door and I passed through the storm door while keeping a careful foot on the icy steps. Once I was down the steps and outside in the full bluntness of the cold December air, I felt the instinctive need to zip my jacket, put my hands in my pockets, and protect myself in some way. Instead, I turned and walked back up the steps. Sylvia had rubbed a small hole in the frosted pane window so she could see me on my way. Whether she was able to see through it or not, she gave me a look of surprise when I pulled the door aside and exposed her to the cold air.

"I don't think you should come over on Christmas. I think it would be best if we stayed with our own families. After all that has been said, we need to talk about a few things, and Christmas is not the day to do it."

She paused in silence for a second and her face changed to a look of concern.

"When will I hear from you?"

"I don't know. I need time to think, to sort things out. I'll see you later."

After getting into my car, I quickly pulled away from the curb, not letting the car heater sufficiently defog my windows. I made a list in my mind of the good and bad in our relationship, and went over it again and again. Things cleared up just as I entered the expressway, and it became apparent to me that I might not ever see Sylvia again. Driven to recall my insecurities about our relationship, I thought it might just be best to move forward with my life.

When I got home, I went straight to bed, not bothering to talk to my parents or even tell them I was home. Although it had been a long day, I tossed and turned for over an hour. I figured if I stayed in bed, I could sleep through Christmas and wake up the day after. That way my mood could coalesce with everybody's holiday hangover. Maybe in that sense I would belong. Nobody would have to know I had a bad Christmas. I rolled over like a dead fish and stared at my present for Sylvia sitting in the corner all wrapped up. As I closed my eyes, I started to count sheep and wondered if Sylvia could hear me somehow. When I neared forty, I finally dozed off.

Gimme

Coral Calais Suter

In the dark
round the corner
at the far end of the hard blonde floor
something shines out there like aquarium lights
steadily
blue beneath a pine bough
orange against a brittle green sphere
red shooting up at a spun glass reindeer
which twists slightly
astir with the dawn.

This golden waiting.
All night we have huddled
awake
not wanting to breathe too hard.
Gimme morning.

Scrambling down the hall.
Gimme stuff, new, now
ripping through the papers, tossing ribbons.
Gimme what the ads promise:
curvy bangs, sweet pout, tight jeans.
I wanna Barbie. I wanna pert little nose
and teeth formed from pearls
wanna charmed life
water in the desert
manna.

Don't wanna
orange
taking up raw space at the toe of my stocking
where the pretty chocolate pieces could otherwise
cluster and hide.
I won't eat it
gonna feed it
to the dog.

Gimme fire
Gimme power, wild will, forked thunder
a forearm, bold and muscled, rising from the steam.
Gimme back that ray gun
better gimme that back;
you're gonna break it, make it ugly, make it old.

Mamma
lemme out
of this flat afternoon, long and hopeless.
Lemme live back there
where we never go to sleep
always wanting.

Has the best happened yet?
Let me not know now
in a golden morning
in a golden land.

Give me some last gift
hidden low in the branches
gleaming.

The Christmas Special

Kenneth Ellsworth

At six-thirty p.m. on Christmas Eve, Jerry Silver leaned back in Frankie's chair and extended his legs. With both heels, he scuffed the surface of Frankie's custom-crafted desk. He sipped Frankie's bourbon from a chrome tumbler as he looked beyond the rain-soaked streets of Freehaven, New Jersey, at the large, luminous Christmas tree in the center of the distant town square. He listened to the peculiar quiet that permeated the office. No phones were ringing. He was alone, waiting. Waiting for a phone call. Waiting, he thought, because the boss, one Frankie St. fucking Germaine, would probably call promptly at seven to see if there were any "numbers on the board."

When there weren't any numbers, it would be Jerry's fault. Even though "The Christmas Special" was created and shoved up everyone's posterior by the sole owner of St. Germaine Enterprises, Jerry prayed for just one bastard to sell one God damned ad. A single sale would let him off the hook for the holidays with Him.

It was only yesterday afternoon, Jerry recalled, the eve of Christmas Eve, when Frankie had birthed his latest marketing motivational tempest, totally derailing Jerry's plans to escape from the office for the holidays. He had been counting on a little R & R (rum & roulette) this particular year with Adrianne and the kids, for Christmas and New Year's fell on Wednesdays. Leave it to Frankie, though, who could purge all pleasure from a wet dream.

Frankie had been sitting behind his tall, ebony-colored desk in

237

his black leather custom-designed chair cranked high, like a barber's seat for a child. Jerry had been slumped onto the black leather couch, gazing out the window at the light rain. He focused at the large white cross planted on a hill beyond the Freehaven square.

Frankie should be happy, Jerry thought, with all the great gifts he had received. Homage from his sales force that pillaged from border to border and coast to coast. A Spread 'Em Magazine Calendar from Harry Ford. An autographed copy of Willie the Dweeb Lomax's best seller, "How To Cheat and Beat the Vegas Odds." A gold and diamond studded chest chain with a medallion that read, "# UNO STUD." Lou Ford, Harry's infamous brother, had even traded a book cover ad for the office Christmas tree.

Frankie's tentatively cheerful mood had twisted rabid when Dooley inflated and popped an indigo-colored French tickler, part of the "Dirty Dozen Exotic Twelvepack" Jerry had bequeathed Him for the yuletide. An hour later, Jerry was answering the phone while Frankie played with a pewter replica of a '57 T-bird.

"Who's on?" Frankie asked.

"Thompson."

"What'd he write?"

Jerry held up his hand, looping the index finger and thumb until they touched, producing a circle.

"Lemme talk to that fucker."

As Frankie picked up his phone, Jerry, still on the line, heard a click. Frankie slammed down his receiver so hard that the black plastic base split.

"What do the rest of the numbers look like?"

Jerry looked out the window at the rain, which was falling harder. "The same."

"Chicago? Atlanta? Dallas? Los Angeles? Ft. Lauderdale?"

Jerry repeated "same" after each territory in question. The silence that followed was more frightening than the usual Frankie St. Germaine tirade. Jerry gripped the leather of the couch, prepared for a verbal torrent, and then snatched the offensive.

"Look, Frankie, it's an impossible situation this year. Not one limp-dicked business proprietor or weeny principal or monseigneur or sheriff is gonna be around until the Monday *after* the first."

"What the fuck are you gonna do about it?"

"What can I do?"

Frankie leaned forward and pointed his finger at Jerry like a saber, aiming directly between his eyebrows. "You're my fucking general manager. What are you going to do about it?"

Jerry shrugged. "Put the answering machine on till the sixth of January and take the wife and kids to Atlantic City. You know Adrianne's been planning this forever. What are your plans, Frankie?"

Frankie stood, strode around the desk, and hovered above him. "You don't get it. I'm not going to shit away two fucking weeks of business."

"Look, Frankie, why not relax? Take your wife and kids to L.A. Disneyland. Maybe see that broad in Memphis. Get the biz out of your system for two weeks. Tell you what. I'll set up a shift of managers to check for important messages, the mail, make deposits daily, okay?"

"That's it?" Frankie screamed. "I'm paying you all these fucking greenola bars and that's the best you can do?"

Jerry stood and shouted back. "What the fuck would you do?" As soon as he uttered the challenge, Jerry had an uneasy feeling fill his stomach. Rule number three, he thought. Never challenge Frankie. Never.

Frankie paced, darting like a caged, hungry rodent. He stopped and looked out the window. Then he laughed, which sounded like bursts from a machine gun. Pivoting, he gave Jerry one of those cocky 'that's why I'm the boss and you're the fucking employee' looks, and proclaimed, "The Christmas Special."

"The what?" Jerry said.

"The Christmas Special. For the salesmen, every ad written

daily — meaning check in hand, not their meat — over a two forty-nine is worth an extra twenty-five fucking bucks; anyone writing a grand per day, an extra fifty bucks; anyone writing two thousand per week, an extra C-note; and, *and,* high man for each week *over* twenty-five hundred gets a week's stay *for two* in my condo in Florida, including flight to and from. Car rental, meals, booze and broads, they buy. How's that sound, Jerr?"

Jerry scratched his mustache. "Incentive for the reps, but, let's face it, how you gonna sell when there's no one to sell?"

Frankie snapped his thumb and middle finger. "For the businesses, every ad they buy over two hundred dollars they get a fifty buck discount; over five hundred, a hundred dollar discount. And that's good only for this Christmas Special which expires on Sunday, January fifth. Well?"

"But Frankie, half our people don't have no accounts to work. The parishes and schools and chief law enforcement officers are off for two weeks..."

"Any parish," Frankie said, and paused, as if he were dictating a letter. "Any parish which signs up and opens during the Christmas Special receives its choice of the following bonuses: color TV; 35mm camera; video tape player; collector's decanter filled with Jack D. How can they say no? How the fuck can they refuse?"

Jerry shook his head, wondering what language to employ that could possibly persuade Him.

"But Frankie, who the fuck they gonna sell?"

"That's your fucking problem. I'm sending every manager into the field. Same bonuses apply to them. You, you man the phones from nine till seven every day. Except Christmas and New Year's and Sundays. Saturdays you're here, too."

Jerry felt his spirit sag as he collapsed onto the couch. First he flushed from embarrassment. Then he blanched from fear. What am I going to tell Adrianne? he thought. Jesus, when she hears, Jesus Christ. She'll put my balls in a garlic press.

"But Frankie, I, we, the family, had plans for the break. Adrianne, you see..."

"Cancel them. You're my G.M. And don't give me no shit about the reps taking the day off. Call every one of those lazy fucks at home and pump them full of the Christmas Special. I'll handle the rest of the incoming calls."

Great, Jerry thought. Every time he handles calls, I lose two or three reps. Naturally, it's my fault.

Jerry didn't want to make those calls. But better me than him, he thought. He was no longer in any rush to go home. Didn't want to face Adrianne, whom he had *promised* to take on their long-delayed vacation.

The phone rang. Jerry speared the receiver before Frankie could mess it up.

"Who's that?" Frankie asked.

"Lou Ford."

"I'll take it. You make those fucking calls."

◇

The sun had set an hour ago in the city of Confidence in western Pennsylvania. Snow had fallen all day. It had taken the salesman three hours to make the "hour" drive from Pittsburgh.

Should have quit an hour ago, he thought. But Big Lou Ford never quits. Hell, shouldn't't've even started. Can't sell no one if there's no one to pitch. If it weren't for them mother-fuckers. Threatening to send me back in the field, full time. Fuck 'em. Jerry. Frankie. Fuck 'em all.

He shuffled along Main Street feeling winter bite through his thin leather driving gloves and hundred-and-eighty buck Italian shoes. All of the store lights were out except for the dim beams displaying the appearance of security. As he crossed Robert Frost Boulevard, he glanced to his right and saw it. Two blocks down. A store brightly lighted. "Fuckin' A," he said, as he jogged towards his destination. "But what do I say?" It had been two hours since his last pitch. The last three had all been "no's," a rarity. Not that he could blame any of the prospects for not buying, not trusting him this time.

He was within twenty feet of his target when the neon sign of Frugal Florists faded. "Shit," he muttered, trudging ahead until he reached his destination. He cupped his hands above his eyes like binoculars, pressed them against the window, and squinted. He couldn't see anything through the windows, glazed outside, steamy within. Kiss this day good-bye, he thought, jerking his tie loose with such force that he popped his top button free.

For the hell of it, he turned the door knob. It opened. Eureka! he thought, and entered to the sound of door bells jingling.

A man stood in the part of the store still lighted, behind the cash register at the end of a gauntlet of greenery. Lou approached and stopped before the cash register, stomped the snow from his shoes, and removed his gloves. As he blew into his hands, he saw his reflection in the rose vault to the right of the register. He wore an open beige trench coat over a gray two piece suit. The loosened tie made him appear disheveled. The pure, glistening whiteness that frosted his hair was melting. His face seemed on the verge of rage or tears.

Rage or tears, he thought. Either gives me the edge for the sale.

The man gulped, arched his neck, and spoke in a cheery tone. "Yes, sir, what can I do for you on this fine Christmas Eve?"

Lou looked down at his prospect. The man was a foot shorter and sixty pounds lighter than himself, like thousands of other men he had sold. The florist wore a frizzy red cardigan sweater over a faded blue long-sleeved shirt with a worn collar. His thick black glasses were held together with a strip of masking tape adjacent to the left lens. A large family photo of the florist, a woman, and two adolescent boys occupied the wall above and behind him. Next to a "Charles Dickens" calendar, the month of December. Above the dates was the sketch of a lame-looking kid leaning on a crutch, who said, "And God bless us each and every one."

Just what I need, Lou thought, as water dripped onto his forehead and neck. Either this guy's got no dough or he's a cheap fuck.

"You, uh, the owner of Frugal Florists, Inc.?"

A half smile twitched onto the man's face. "Yes, sir, I am."

"Sister Candace of St. Monica's Parish asked me to stop by. I know it's late, but it's important." Lou removed a portfolio hidden inside the fold of his trench coat. He stuttered, stumbling over his words. "Sister's having these book covers printed up for all of the kids books at St. Monica's. With her school seal in the official freshly squeezed orange juice orange school colors, of course. And, and she would appreciate it very much if you — Frugal Florists, Inc. — would join her on the cover."

The florist grimaced. "Look, friend, I'm closing, and frankly, the last thing I need is advertising."

"You don't wanna know what it costs?"

"No."

"You don't?..."

The man slashed the pitch short with an arm gesture.

Lou still hadn't discovered the florist's hot button. He wondered what "frugal" meant. Was it another guilty Catholic word?

"Okay, but Sister's gonna be disappointed, friend. Very, very disappointed."

When the florist's jaw dropped like an elevator after its cable had snapped, Lou continued along the guilt line.

"You at *Frugal* Florists didn't give a fair hearing of her program."

The florist scowled. "How do I know Sister Candace sent you?"

Lou grinned. "I have a letter of authorization signed and sealed by the Sister herself..." He searched his vinyl case. "The letter. Christ, the letter." He dumped the case upside down onto the counter. Papers, tape, and scissors spilled out. "Must have left it, oh, God..."

Water trickled into his eyes, irritating them. Lou slipped and fell to his knees. He moaned, trying to rub away the stinging streams of water. He looked up and saw the florist standing next to him, offering him a hand filled with tissue papers.

Lou grabbed them. "I'm sorry, mister, but it's, oh, you don't want to hear my problems. On Christmas Eve and all."

The florist didn't respond.

"You gotta family?"

The florist looked away.

Lou blotted his eyes. "Go on, go on home to your frugal family. You don't wanna hear my problems."

"I've got a few minutes, friend," said the florist, helping Lou to his feet.

"Well, normally I'd take these two weeks off, you know? I mean, I know that the last guy you want to see right now is me. But my youngest, youngest of six." He removed a billfold and showed him a color photograph, dulled with age, filled with children. "That's him, right there. Him. Uh, little Timmy — he got in this accident three months ago and the insurance ran out and if, if, if we don't get help, oh, dear Lord, I just don't know, I just don't know."

Lou ran his hand over his hair and rubbed his eyes, pretending to sob. "My little Timmy, oh, my little Timmy."

Lou caught him glance at his family photo. Then the florist placed his hand on Lou's shoulder and guided him to his feet. "Want to talk about it, friend?"

"Well, maybe, if I just talked to you about it. I'm not looking for no charity, you know? But it would help me and Sister and you. Help her help you with the Christmas Special, follow?"

"The Christmas what?"

◇

Fifteen minutes and I am outta here, Jerry thought. And Adrianne's happy for another year. Sure the bastard will call me, drill me another asshole, but at least then I'm outta here for twelve fucking days.

The phone rang. Jerry's mouth felt as dry as the crust atop hardened snow.

"Hello, toll free," he said.

"Jerr?"

"Big Lou Ford? Where the hell are you?"

"Saint Monica's, western P.A. And it's Sir Lou Ford to you. Just got a two ninety-nine. *In hand.*"

"A what?"

"You know, a three forty-nine less the fifty buck Christmas Special discount."

"How, how in the hell?" Jerry paused. "This afternoon you didn't have an account. I tried to open up Saint Monica's last week for your brother Harry. Wasn't Sister Suck My Dick out of town until next year?"

"Yeah, well, that's a fact. But Saint Monica's, remember, is a renewal near Pittsburgh."

"So how did you do it?"

"Yesterday I calls in and that mother fuck Frankie reams me with this riot act. So I'm visiting Harry for the holidays, you know? And now I gotta work or else, Frankie tells me."

"Or else what?"

"I lose my fucking overrides and go back in the field full time in January."

Shit, Jerry thought. Frankie's fucking with everybody. Every single body.

"So get this, Jerr. Sister's on retreat, I improvise and open the account up like a can of prime tuna."

"Without a letter?"

"Yeah. All by myself. I just show the prospect a sample of last year's book cover and make stupid like I lost her letter."

"Yeah?"

"Yeah. And this fucking florist gives me a dozen long stems for my little kid in the hospital."

"Your little kid? Lou, you been?..."

"Whoa! No little Ford fucks I know about. Look, I flashed this pic of my family when I was sixteen. Bottom line, pal, is it worked. Maybe I can make some coin this break. Pay off some debts. Keep you and Frankie happy."

Jerry was relieved, but still in shock. His ass, though, was covered. For the moment.

At seven o'clock sharp, Jerry flicked the lights off. He placed the key in the door. Shit, he thought. Left my wallet on his desk. When he returned to Frankie's office, the phone rang. Like

Pavlov's mutt, he grabbed the receiver.

"Jerry? Give me the numbers."

It was Frankie. Fucking Frankie. But *no problemo*, he thought, I'm covered.

"Lou Ford just wrote a two ninety-nine — you know, the deal, a half front cover less the fifty dollar discount."

"No!"

"Yes!"

"No fucking shit?"

"No fucking shit. He even did it *without* a letter."

"Anyone else?"

"Nope."

"But it worked."

"Yeah, a fluke. Lou said he needs some bread to cover the ponies. I've got it all set. He's with Harry in Pittsburgh and I'll call him both Fridays from Atlantic City..."

"No, you don't. You call every goddamned rep and tell them how Lou Ford fucking did it."

"But Christ, Frankie, I need time off, time to get away from here with Adrianne."

"What the fuck do you want? I gave you Hanukkah off."

"That was on a Sunday."

"I'll check in with you Thursday, *here*. And Friday. And Saturday. Take Sunday off. But Monday, be *here*..."

Jerry gazed out the window as he listened to Frankie repeat the days of the week, the days he would be expected to man this office, this cell, waiting for the calls that wouldn't come, fearing His daily call, as the outdoor temperature plummeted, rain burst into wet snow flakes that struck the road, and slush hardened into black, jagged patches of ice. He stared at the glistening well-lighted Christmas tree and then at the cross, its crooked, shadowy arms reaching for him. He shut his eyes and beheld Adrianne, a sack of spikes, and that cross. He opened his eyes and stared out the window, not wanting to view the place where he'd be spending his holiday days, twenty-four hour days.

Christmas Blues

Claudia Thompson

Fond memories do not abound,
although there was one
Christmas Monday when
the tree looked beautiful,
having been personally
cut down two weeks before,
and one Christmas Wednesday
when the Barbie Dollhouse and
the mechanical walking dog
welcomed us into the room,
and one Christmas Saturday
when Donna brought over
Christmas Stollen for our
hungry stomachs, and we
sat down and ate it all.

But one Christmas Tuesday,
everyone assembled before
the tree, under which no
presents were to be found,
except one multicolored
handknit sweater for me
and one blue handknit
sweater for Paula, and
and one beige handknit pair of
slippers for Dad,
Mom having worked hard for

the family to have Christmas
this year, despite the
financial crisis we were in,
her smiling face making us
grateful and guilty,
there being no present under
the tree for Mom.

And one Christmas Thursday,
hours after the few gifts had
been opened and the coffee
cake had been eaten,
as I played with my friend,
I watched as Debbi showed me
an unending supply of Christmas
gifts, a typewriter, a stereo,
a bicycle, a dress, a shirt, a robe,
that she had received,
embarrassed that I was
wearing all of mine, one boot
on my left foot and one
on my right, feeling ashamed
and hurt and envious.

And one Christmas Sunday
the hour drew late,
as both my sister and I
tried to feign sleep for
as long as we could,
each isolated in separate
bedrooms, but connected
enough by our mutual fear,
of having to face yet another
Christmas, with this family
of ours, always feeling the
obligation to provide a

Christmas celebration, and
always letting that obligation
show, making enjoyment
next to impossible and
shame and hurt feelings as
predictable as the number
of presents we would find
under the tree.

But one Christmas Friday
was the best one so far,
it was the first Christmas
away from home,
without the need to repeat
the travesty of celebration,
even though not doing so meant
no presents, but also no
shame, no hurt feelings,
and no guilt, except that
the feeling of loss continues
to raise its ugly head,
making the choice of no Christmas
a hard one to make, still
making it a day to be gotten
through, although less painfully
than in days long ago.

The Stuff of Life

Elizabeth Templeman

It happened again: my mother, an eternal pessimist, has managed to bring about what was very nearly a natural disaster. And disaster is just the right word for it — "dis-aster:" a failure of the stars, and so, related to ancient and compelling forces of faith. Despite my best efforts to rationally consider such phenomena as weather, superstition — all tangled up with stubborn traces of Catholicism — keeps on haunting me.

For months we'd been making plans by telephone. And each time my excitement would burst forth into evidence, she'd puncture it with dire storm predictions. "We can hardly wait to see you," or, "You'll get to see Nicole's school concert with us!" I'd say, trying to end our conversation on a high note.

"Well, I'm not going *anywhere* if it's storming," she'd quickly retort. The down-side wins again, I'd think to myself, but she'll see, once she *does* get here, that things work out just fine.

The worst storm to hit the northeast in fifty years, we heard on one news account on the morning she should have departed from the Portland, Maine airport. She was flying out to meet her newest grandson, and to spend Christmas, and her birthday, which falls on Christmas Eve. My children were thrilled, and so was I, despite the heap of other feelings that rode the crest of that thrill.

Since October, parcel upon parcel arrived at our already cramped rural post office. Her frenzy of Christmas buying may just be her way of releasing anxiety wrought by the season. Or maybe it's natural for a child of the Depression, born eighth in an immigrant family, who grew up with so very few possessions.

◇

My own uneasiness about stuff must, indeed, be wrapped up in tissues of superstition, floated down to me from the generations, or up, from troubling perceptions of issues surrounding us in the 1990's. It's now a year since my mother's Christmas visit, which did come to pass, despite airline delays caused by flukes of turbulent weather, or fate. This Christmastime, again, I find myself thinking about my family values, wondering if we derive too much from our material possessions and clutter; too little from our spirits and our relationships with one another. I worry about my own fondness for every little plastic trinket that, for as many as thirty-five years, has served to reflect Christmas for me. Throughout December, conscious of my doing so, I carefully unwrap these various glittery wreathes and brass angels, aiming to create the sense of Christmas our children will carry forth into their lives, subjecting spouses and offspring to the same.

◇

I wonder, perhaps more than a normal person should, how we would survive a house fire. What would we do if suddenly we found ourselves with nothing but the clothes on our backs? What would we remember to mourn? What would we struggle to replace? Would a certain freedom of constraint balance the sense of loss — the grief displaced by a lightness of being (to quote the heavy book I have not read, but which rests amongst a weighty collection of books I suspect I would be years grieving)? Once, in the summer months between my freshman and sophomore year of university, a box of my stuff was stolen from the dorm closet where I'd arranged to store my things while I was at home working. Even now, more than twenty years later, I find myself wondering if a particular volume of Aeschylus might have been in that box. I'm not sure if that slow burn of vulnerability and unspent anger will ever lose its heat.

I think that what I would miss most is what we have created. I fear for my word-processor, and for the words it stores for me in our uneasy partnership. I would weep for the drawings my kids have done over the years, and for the cards they've made my husband and me, and each other, and for the baby book we all made for James. The baby pictures of our kids, of us and even of our parents — well, I don't know quite how I'd feel about them. What they really reassemble for me is carried forward in the individuals: the funny way that Andrew always seemed about to catapult himself through the camera lens, the round-faced, round-eyed sweetness of Nicole, the impishness of James. I love having those photographed images cluttering the bookshelves, always in view. Yet I could love this family without them, too, and I could remember the phases of that love from the stories we tell.

The house we live in, all wood and rock and glass, has been my husband's creation. It, too, is irreplaceable. He's probably a better designer now, certainly a more competent builder. So he could, indeed, build a new home, and it would be superior in many ways, stark and clean, freed of our possessions, and with a broom closet actually as tall as a broom, and perhaps enough cupboards and closets for the clutter that we would have lost. Yet, for all that, it wouldn't be right for years. We *do* seem to take the shape of our homes and our stuff, or maybe our homes and our stuff evolve in trails and piles according to some scheme of personal or family identity.

◇

Last fall I made a quick stop at the Safeway on the way to pick up my kids for swim lessons. I'd forgotten their snack. Looking for something tasty and even a bit entertaining to hold them for the forty minute drive home after, I searched for animal shaped fruit snacks. Should I look by the candy, or chips, or cereal, I wondered, aware that each passing minute of my search would proportionally reduce the time left to change from school clothes to swim suits, increasing the frenzy of an already wild time.

A store manager, apparently responding to my frantic, harried look, stopped to help. He sent me to a shelf over the frozen vegetable section, beside beer-making equipment. To my parting comment on the illogic of the organization, he replied, looking harried himself, that the profusion of new products and varieties pretty much defied systems of organization.

That left me thinking. The nineties are often characterized by the information explosion. That may well be, but perhaps every bit as extraordinary and even more insidious is our explosion of *stuff.* I don't remember fruit snacks from my youth, yet today we can choose from at least five brands. We can have bear snacks, shark snacks, dinosaur snacks, rolled snacks, or puzzle shaped snacks, cherry, orange, cola or tutti-fruity snacks, natural fruit or simulated fruit flavoured snacks, number or letter snacks, spaceship or Ninja snacks.

Any more, it's hard to imagine what might *not* be found in a grocery store. Looking for quart sealers the other day I went past raincoats, socks, toboggans, goldfish paraphernalia, best selling novels, hubcaps, and potholders. When, I wonder, will we be compelled to protest such mindless and overwhelming stimuli immersion? When will we notice that in the name of convenience, our grocery stores span city blocks?

It's ironic that those of us who clamour for simple foods only add to the situation. Chemical free vegetables now crowd the four kinds of mushrooms and six varieties of fresh won ton wrappers. Corn flakes, rather than dropping out of circulation, hold their place in three name varieties, not to mention two generic brands. Beside them are Astro-flakes, Cocoa Pebbles, and Pro Stars. Up the aisle live the plain, unadulterated oats — quick, instant, rolled, slow-cooking, porridge, wild, and even apple-cinnamon flavoured. And that's nothing compared to the cola story!

When will the ridiculous cease to appear so normal? When will we refuse to be attracted by the glamour, and actually see the clutter of our own surrounding culture? The pressure for eco-sensitivity has only complicated matters. The eco-sensitive products, boldly labelled in their recycled containers, compete for space with eco-callous goods, labelled "new and improved."

Do we substitute more choice for better sense? Does this
profusion of stuff result from pride in our technological capacity
to produce it? Or is it simply an inability to conceive of
restriction of choice as a possible choice?

◇

This Christmas, our older children left Santa letters with the
butter tarts and carrots and apple and rootbeer. Nicole, now
eight, retains a staunch belief in all the magic of this season. She
uses her logic to wed fantasy to faith in the mysteries of life.
Her letter reads:

"Dear Santa Claus, I hope you have a fun Christmas. If when
you come to our house, you're too full to eat anything, take the
stuff we leave out home. My hamster, Dasher, died [Santa's gift
three long years ago]. I was very sad, But he was old. If you
ever see Jesus, wish him a Happy Birthday for me. I don't really
care what I get, because I don't know what I want, give me
anything. So far I'm having fun skiing. I made you a picture.
Love Nicole. P.S. please give all the poor people nice presents.
MERRY CHRISTMAS."

Her brother is three years younger and more sure and easy in
his belief. His letter, a sticker in its upper right-hand corner to
match the sticker his sister uses, comes right to the point:

"To SANTA — I want a new skiing snow ball. From
Andrew."

His faith may be casual, but so is his perceived need: The new
skiing snow ball he requires would belong to a set sent by his
Nanee a couple years back, another of so many decorative
trinkets she insists that the children have.

"They're just little things, worthless really, that make them
happy," she retorts to what I intend to be mildly discouraging
comments — my feeble, and quite futile effort to stem the tide
of material excess that seems to engulf us. And here's my son,
one of the children my mother feels to be so fun-deficient,
asking Santa for another "worthless" skiing snowball — a
dimpled plastic ball decked out in red skis and a striped toque —
to replace the one that just happened to lose its ski when flung

on the floor by the self-same child, two years back.

The possibilities latent in that very circle of needs and wishes seems greater than my own ability to comprehend them. I'm struck, not for the first time, by the wisdom of my mother's irritating ways, and by the strength of what tugs between the Nanee and the grandchild. She knows him in ways I simply do not — knows how to delight him with the very stuff which threatens to overwhelm me. He responds with the simple love of delighting in that which she sends in the nooks and crannies of her parcels. And Santa, of course, will work the magic to repair the object that provides the glue in their relationship.

◇

This season, once again, the family spends most of a surprisingly satisfying day pulling down the decorations, wrapping God knows how old tarnished and pleasingly fragile tree bulbs in God knows how old scraps of tissue and paper towels, packing box after box, making a game out of ferreting out the one last ceramic choirboy resting amongst magazine and plant, packing and labelling and finally handing boxes up to Dad, who will stack them in the storage area above the back entranceway. The ladder gets carried back through the house, the unusualness of that fascinating our baby. One child pinches up tinsel from the wool of the carpet, while the other proudly discovers one last felt Rudolph hung on my rowing machine. We chase away the impending post-Christmas gloom with loud rock-and-roll and hot chocolate with marshmallows. My feelings? Tremendous relief, but also a sense of accomplishment. Once again, we emerge intact and somehow enriched by this time of beauty and magic, with its underlay of excess and sham.

Spinning The Holiday Wheels

Terrence E. Dunn

As the days started pouncing one on top of each other and I prepared myself for that one day alone again, I couldn't help but think of that cold December night back in 1970 when I first realized that my idea of the gift and the gathering — and my idea of aloneness, itself — might be changing forever.

I was in forth grade and we were at my grandmother's brownstone in upstate New York visiting for the holidays. My brother Mike and I had just snuck out of our roll-away beds and were busy in the living room rummaging through the presents. Mike found a big, blue heavy one, lifted it to his ear and then shook it a few times, trying to figure out what might be inside. "I bet you this one's the skates that I wanted," he told me as he sat himself down on top of another large wrapped box. "No way — why would you get skates for where we're going?" I told him back, "There's no ice rinks over there, you know?" And then we laughed and sat there a bit in our warm cowboy-print pajamas as I stared at the snow falling past a dark window and at the lights on the tree as they flickered on and off, on and off.

"Look," Mike said as he broke the silence and reached back behind the tree, "Eileen got the bike she wanted." And then he lifted a small red bicycle — complete with training wheels — out over the presents that surrounded us. I looked at the bike, noticing how small it was and how the lights from the trees melted in with the red paint on the frame, and then I reached down and grabbed one of the training wheels, which was sticking out over the edge of a present, and gave it a good spin.

"We leave in a week," I said to my brother, "and then Dad

leaves from there two weeks after that — right?" And then Mike shook his head in a silent, slow nod of approval. I looked up again at the snow falling in the dark night and watched as it floated down past the window and noticed how it almost didn't seem real, as if I was watching a TV version of snow instead of the real thing.

"I wonder what it'll be like over there?" I asked, not really thinking I'd get an answer. "Well, Dad says," Mike started to say as he gave the training wheel a spin for himself, "that Hawaii is just like where he's going — just like Vietnam — but...well, you remember the pictures from the other time he was there, right? They were all green and jungle-like and Mom thought it looked sorta' pretty... Well, Dad says that both places are kinda' the same, but actually not even close to being the same...or something like that..."

"Oh..." was all I could say and then we both sat there in our pajamas and I stared at the spinning training wheel as I remembered my next door neighbor, Susie Hollander, from the army base we had just moved from and I remembered her Dad — tall, dark and broad shouldered, like my own — and then I remembered how he too had gone off and how he had never come back.

And then I listened to the silent sound of the snow and I knew I didn't care about the presents around me and I knew I couldn't think of the future, so instead I thought about the big meal we were going to have the next day and how nice it would be and how full I'd get...and then unfortunately I wondered how many more holiday meals our family would be able to have with all of us together. And then I bit my lip to keep my emotions in and I gave that wheel one more spin. And it went around and around. And continues.

Just What You Want

Lee Webb

A mutter of voices drifted into the hallway from Grammy and Grandad's kitchen. A brocade-covered fainting couch nestled into a corner of the stairwell in this hallway and a tangled pile of winter coats lay heaped on it. They gave off a slight aroma of pine and cologne. Among the coats sat a small girl.

It was chilly in the hallway because the door at the end of it did not hang perfectly within the frame and unseen eddies of cold breathed in through the cracks.

A soft draft moved across her skinny legs, causing the girl to wriggle deeper into the pile. Her red petticoats, carefully ironed into brittle fullness with sugar water, crackled like thin ice with every squirm. She knew very well that she shouldn't be crushing her petticoats, that they would be flattened and spoiled, but she didn't care because she hated wearing them. They prickled her skin awfully. Their stiffness made it difficult to do anything but sit still, which, the girl suspected, was the whole idea of having her wear them.

From her vantage point on the couch, the child could see the tall, ornament-encrusted Christmas tree through the archway that led into the drawing room. It glittered like a night-time carnival. Points of candy-colored light reflected off the stacks of fancy packages laid under its branches.

When are they ever going to stop talking? thought the girl.

Bored with teasing herself, she slid down from the couch and trudged into the den where her cousins were watching TV.

"Hey Lisa, you're missing the best part," said Rose, stuffing another piece of divinity into her mouth. Rose and her younger sister Beth were dressed identically to Lisa in green taffeta with red petticoats. Beth sat daintily on the edge of a footstool so as not to muss her finery.

Several bowls of fudge, divinity and ribbon candies were set out on the coffee table. It was entirely possible that Rose had licked every piece, so Lisa ignored the candy. She plopped down beside her cousin on the love seat and sighed heavily.

On the TV screen a crowd of animated elves bustled in their workshop. Rose's eyes never left the screen, but she poked Lisa and said, "So what did you ask for this year?"

"I want a B-B gun and a chemistry set, one of the big ones like in the Sears catalog."

"Eeeuuw!" said Rose. "That's stupid." She reached for a piece of fudge. "I want a Betsy-Wetsy and I want all her clothes. Miss Princess over there —" Rose jerked her head toward Beth, "— wants a Barbie Vanity Table."

Lisa did not reply. She knew better than to provoke Rose because Rose had been raised by a woman who wanted revenge on people she hadn't even met yet. Even Lisa's grandparents were afraid of Aunt Carrie.

Beth piped up. "I know I'm going to get my Vanity Table. I saw Grammy hiding the box upstairs." She bent forward, crackling delicately. "And I bet you're going to get switches and coal!"

Before Beth could scramble off the stool, Rose darted out a chubby hand and pinched her sister hard in the soft place behind her knee. Beth began to scream. It was a thin sound, but piercing and in two seconds Grammy appeared at the door, closely followed by Aunt Carrie.

"What on earth's the matter?" asked Grammy.

Beth ran to Carrie and sobbed into her skirt.

"Lisa did it, we were just sitting here watching the TV and she just came in and pinched Beth for no reason," exclaimed Rose. She pointed a finger smeared with fudge at Lisa.

Gathering Beth up into her arms, Carrie shot a look of purest malice in Lisa's direction, then carried her sniffling child out of the room.

Grammy knelt by Lisa. In low tones, she said, "Now why'd you want to do that? It's Christmas, sugar. You two just stay here in the den and behave. Ol' Santy Claus'll be here any time and he might not leave anything for little girls who don't act right."

Grammy returned to the kitchen and Rose went back to watching the TV as though nothing had happened. Unable to interest herself in the cartoon program, Lisa watched the fire in the fireplace and considered her situation. She was not upset with Rose for blaming her. Rose did it all the time, that's just the way it was. Right now Lisa had more important concerns.

A B-B gun and a chemistry set are not either stupid, thought Lisa. She'd been trying to get them for the last two years, but it was as if nobody could really hear her. The Christmas before this one, she'd only hinted about them. *Careful, be real careful. If they see what I really want I won't get it for sure.* The hints hadn't worked at all. Instead of a B-B gun or a chemistry set or even a Bowie knife, she'd gotten a big baby doll with a crib and a play kitchen set. Sometime around last March, her mother put the doll and play set out in the storage shed, still pristine in their cellophane wrappings, and once in a while Grammy asked what she'd named her doll and Lisa said she hadn't decided on a name. Desperation made her bold and this year she'd said plain out what she wanted.

Just last week, they'd come over for lunch. Grammy slid two hot fried salmon cakes onto Lisa's plate. "You know what you want Santy Claus to bring you?" asked Grammy.

Lisa's fingers trembled a little as she reached for the catsup. "Yes, ma'am. I want a B-B gun and a big chemistry set, the kind where the case folds out from the middle." The grownups didn't say anything, so she continued. "Like the one in the Sears catalog. Want me to show it to you?"

Grammy chuckled knowingly and looked at Lisa's mother. "That's all right, sugar. You've been pretty good this year, I'm sure Santy will bring you just what you want."

Just what you want, just what you want. It was like an echo in her head. Any minute now the sleigh bells would jingle from somewhere outside of the den and they'd run out to the tree, light bulbs flashing, and broadly displayed under the tree would be just what she wanted. A worm of avarice tightened around her stomach and made her giddy.

The green china clock on the mantel chimed eight times, then the sleigh bells jingled. Grabbing one last piece of divinity, Rose shoved it whole into her mouth and disappeared into the drawing room. Lisa hung back, afraid to go out, afraid to stay behind.

Grandad shuffled into the den. "C'mon, sugar. The other kids are already opening their packages. Don't you want to see what Santy brought you?" He gently shooed the reluctant child out the door.

A large Victorian divan sat akimbo to the tree, partially hiding the spread of presents from Lisa's view. Approaching carefully, carefully, at last she took one long step to see a bride doll standing in white lace splendor. It was horrible.

For a minute, Lisa had the most awful feeling that she was going to throw up, all over the tree, all over her cousin Rose (who was clutching her Betsy-Wetsy while clawing through the rest of the gifts, looking for anything with her name on it), all over everything. Lisa's mother, who was sitting on the divan, saw the child's face go pale and said, "What's the matter, babe? Do you feel all right?"

Lisa nodded. Somebody put their arms around her and hugged her. Very close to her ear Grammy said, "Isn't she a beautiful doll, sugar? She's a Madame Alexander and she's even got her trousseau with her, see?" Grammy nudged her in the doll's direction. "Beth is going to hand out the rest of the presents, so you go ahead and play with that pretty doll that Santy brought you. Go on now."

The doll's trousseau was laid out behind it against a doll-sized trunk. Kneeling beside the trunk, Lisa took each item, the little dresses and jackets and shoes, and put them on the doll-sized hangers and into the doll-sized drawers. When the last piece was put away, she shut the trunk and placed the doll on top of it. *Next year, I won't tell them,* she thought. *It's too hard. I won't ever tell them again.*

In the car going home, she sat in the back seat listening to her parents talking. Her mother said, "This happens every year. It's all the excitement and all that candy, she just gets too wound up and it makes her sick."

"Yeah," agreed her father. "But Ma and Pop get such a kick out of doing it, I hate to say anything."

Her mother sighed. "I know what you mean. I just wish they wouldn't make it into such a big deal."

They pulled into the driveway, then Lisa's mother opened the car door. "Come on, Miss, we'd better get you to bed."

When Lisa awoke the next morning, she almost forgot what day it was. She lay in bed, gazing sleepily at her red patent leather shoes that were set out in front of her closet door. *Is it Sunday already?* she wondered.

A warm smell of bacon and cookies wafted into her bedroom, accompanied by her mother. "Well, sleepyhead, Santa's come and gone. You'd better go see — " Lisa was already out the door.

The tree at Lisa's house was not so grand as the one at her grandparent's, but she liked it better because it had blown-glass ornaments in the shapes of animals and houses, and lights that bubbled. She knew each ornament by heart.

"Here's your stuff, sweetheart," her father said.

An assortment of packages was arranged in front of the bookcase, but that wasn't all. Behind them sat a wide orange case with a picture of a microscope printed on it. She pulled the case from its place of honor and unlatched its cover. There was a microscope and little test tubes on a little rack. Rows of mysterious substances waited in their various bottles and packets. She touched the wick on the alcohol burner and knew satisfaction.

Later, Lisa and her father took turns looking at things in the microscope while her mother packed food to take over to her grandparents' house for Christmas dinner. The bride doll and her trousseau already languished in the storage shed, covered with a plastic cleaner's bag.

On Christmas Day, even the children could eat at the big table with the grownups. Lisa sat near Grammy at the head of the table. As Grammy put a helping of gummy noodles on Lisa's plate, she said, "Well, I guess ol' Santy must've figured you were a good girl this year. He sure brought you a bunch of nice things, didn't he?"

From across the table, Rose interrupted, "He brought me everything I asked for!"

Grammy smiled at her while looking sideways at Aunt Carrie and said, "That's because you were a good girl, too."

Lisa surreptitiously pushed the noodles under her creamed peas. She thought, *Maybe you can't ever get everything you want. Next year maybe I'll ask for a B-B gun again. Sometimes people listen. You never know.*

The Man Who Hated Christmas

Jeane C. Gottsponer

He hated Christmas from a child,
    when Mother, shopping,
Lost her purse to a thief, and came
    away, empty-handed.
It was, he said, the only time
    he ever saw his mother cry.

He hated Christmas from a man
    when wars and alien lands and tongues
Made of the day a mockery —
    of tawdry tinsel and hollow gaiety,
Raucous laughter and the sour taste
    of too much liquor.

He hated crowds that thronged the streets,
    and elbowed fiercely in the stores,
As he purchased, dutifully, the lingerie
    for her, every year,
Inevitably, in the last week before
    Christmas Day.

He hated carols that blast the air
    from radio, in mall and store.
The garish lights, the dusty wreaths,
    the dripping needles of long dead trees,
Were, to him, the despised essence
    of Christmas.

Last year, as usual, he purchased the same
   gifts for her in the rush of
The week before Christmas, hating the crowds,
   the lights, the noise,
And the dropping needles of long
   dead trees.

Then, suddenly, he, too, was dead —
   with Christmas still two days away.
And we who loved him have
   always wondered —
Did he die of the cancer, or
   was it Christmas?

Some Assembly Required

Marion Abbott Bundy

"Let's give her a doll house," I suggest the night after Thanksgiving. James and I are tucked in bed, brainstorming on Christmas. We're streamlining this year. One meaningful, well-made gift per person. No junk. An old-fashioned Christmas is what we're after.

Surely the toy shop down in the village will have a wood structure in our price range, big enough for four-year-old hands to maneuver within, yet small enough so we won't have to buy a new house to accomodate it.

Sipping tea the following Sunday afternoon with my friend Lucy, I relate my shopping saga: Plastic, plastic everywhere. "Not only that," I tell her, "my hand got stuck in the door of one house and the surly saleswoman had to extricate it."

"Have you tried garage sales?" Lucy ventures. Her wince tells me she knows this is a feeble suggestion.

"Nobody holds garage sales in December. They're too busy accumulating stuff to put in them next summer."

"I guess you're right. But you know what this means."

Over breakfast the next morning, when I casually mention to James I'm having trouble locating the proper doll house, he mentions a store. "You don't mean *Mrs. O'Hearth's* do you?" He wants *me* to go to a *hobby shop*? Soon after Alice was born it became obvious that I would never qualify as a Full Service Mother. There are some things I simply won't do, and constructing models is at the top of the list. How can he be so thick? "Thanks, I'll try her."

I drag on my jeans and a black turtleneck and rev up the

266

station wagon for the trek across town. I worry this will be the kind of place where women will be wearing hand-knit sweaters with little deer bounding over their mountainous breasts under a banner of HO! HO! HO!

The fifth time I round Mrs. O'Hearth's block, chanting *Parking, Park-ing, Park-ing*, I spy back-up lights. Oh. Sorry, just straightening it out, the driver pantomimes. When I finally enter the overheated store, my senses are assaulted by tinkling sleigh bells and the cloying scent of mulled cider. The place is decked to kill: doll houses in every style and size, unadorned or outfitted with crystal and chandeliers, flocked wallpaper and mini-antiques. All natural materials — nothing fake, shabby or petroleum-derived here. In kits or ready-to-wrap. Not only is this place too pricey, it scares me.

I had hoped it wouldn't come to this, but Lucy warned me: It's Toys Я Us or Bust. I hit the freeway, accelerating out of the cloverleaf for a smooth transition into the northbound lane of rushing — *stalled* — cars. I punch POWER ON and SCAN to hear a dizzying medley of *ngle bell, jingle bell rock... oh holy night, the stars... hark! the herald angels sing... Claus is coming to... I'm dreaming of a... red-nosed reindeer, had a ve—* POWER OFF.

Cruising down Aisle 13, I marvel at the display models, pausing before one that doesn't look too complicated. Brick Colonial. Two stories, central staircase. Flower boxes. Why, it's almost tasteful. A few simple screws (included) and Alice will be ready to move in. Best of all, the price is right.

At the checkout stand I surrender the bar-coded card, congratulating myself for getting the very last one. I scrawl my name across the credit slip and head for Customer Pick-Up. Anything bigger than a breadbox here comes in an ominously flat cardboard box you collect around the back. "Merry Christmas!" I call to the clerk at the loading dock as I slide the box into the wayback and slam down the hatch. He makes a check on his clipboard and waves me off cheerily.

Hoping to avoid pulling the traditional Christmas Eve all-nighter, I plan to put the doll house together the minute Alice is in bed the night of the 23rd. At 7:45 I creep out to the garage to retrieve the parcel, envisioning a Norman Rockwell scene of a cozy work session before the fire. We'll play Ella Fitzgerald and sip hot chocolate. We'll finish by nine, early enough to get a decent night's sleep before the serious bustle of Christmas Eve descends.

"I thought you said Colonial," James calls from the living room. He's rattling the box, flipping it over.

"I did."

"This says Victorian."

"Oh, well — Colonial, Victorian, Tract — who cares? It looks easy, that's the point." The microwave shrills to alert me the chocolate is ready. I load two ceramic mugs onto a tray and join James fireside. He's pushed his glasses up on his forehead to zero in on the fine print.

"Some Assembly Required."

"Let me look," I offer. Once the box is in better light the bitter truth is revealed in frilly pink ink: *Authentic Gingerbread Victorian House Kit, Scale Model Number SST-553-924-7b, Collector's Edition, Dolls 'N Dreams Series.*

"We're screwed," I announce heavily. "I'm going to kill that sucker!" I leap up, smacking my fist into my palm, pacing the room while visions of dismemberment dance in my head.

"Sounds like *he* wasn't the sucker," James sighs. He doesn't have to remind me of the numerous times I've brought home an incomplete Chinese dinner ("No rice?") because I didn't bother to examine each of the little white cartons. "What now?"

I try to remain upbeat. "We could go back..."

"Right. The day before Christmas. I'm sure they'll have a terrific selection. Maye we can trade in the Victorian for something Greek Revival since this is turning into such a tragedy."

"... or we can start in. C'mon, it'll be fun." He groans, draws his Swiss Army knife and in one sharp sweep slits the carton wide open.

The box pictures an elaborately decorated edifice not unlike those featured in coffee table books on San Francisco's Painted Ladies. Inside we find twenty-four main plywood parts: foundations, walls, floors. Twenty-nine component parts: windows, shutters, railings. Twenty-two trim pieces. An arsenal of small nails. A plastic bag containing hundreds of cedar shingles the size of my thumbnail. I stash the bag behind a chair.

"Ah, directions," I say. "Wow, ten typed pages with exploded-view diagrams." James glares. I decide against sharing the manufacturer's admonition that "*by taking your time you can create a family heirloom that you and future generations will cherish forever*" and simply lay out the parts.

Since James won't take seriously my suggestion that we just throw the whole kit and caboodle into the fire, I retreat to the kitchen to dump the chocolate and pour two scotches. Our eyes meet as we clink the amber-filled tumblers. "Let the hammering begin."

Construction goes along swimmingly until we discover a curious misalignment of the front door and the stairway opening. They're supposed to be parallel. "What is this, the Winchester Mystery House?" James hisses.

"Didn't you read the Note, right here on Page 4?" I refer to the text. "'*Make sure your stairway opening is in the correct location.*'? Obviously, the second floor is in backwards. If you had bothered to read, this would never have happened. How do we fix it?"

He replies by yanking apart the four pieces we've painstakingly nailed, glued and allowed to dry in place over the last hour.

Next we attempt to insert the room partition. It is somehow too tall. "How could they be so sloppy? This is off by a quarter of an inch!" I cry, outrage and remorse mounting in equal measure.

"That must explain the sandpaper," we lament in two-toned harmony. When it is all used up and the partition still buckles the second floor, James abruptly scrambles to his feet and heads out the front door. The chilly wind fans the fire and I wonder if James could possibly be the kind of husband who takes out the trash and keeps on going.

But he does return, armed with the neighbor's saw, two metal files and something called a rasp which looks more like a giant cheese grater than a woodworking tool. I can't stop myself: "No axe?"

After much mutual hurling of expletives, followed by my renewed offer to stoke the fire, we carry on. Midnight: aching back, major headache, scratchy eyes. Desperate for sleep. We haven't spoken for the last quarter-hour, not since I stepped on the porch railing while retrieving a towel to sop up the drink James inadvertently kicked over.

"I'll just freshen these up a bit." I rise and stretch my arms heavenward, lifting the tumblers overhead like sacrificial offerings. We're going to need some stiff ones to get through the rest of this.

Onto the dormer roof. *On, Prancer, On, Dasher, On, Donner, On, Blitzen* — yes, that's what we are now: blitzen.

"What's next?" I ask brightly, leaning over dear diligent James to consult the directions, hoping that body contact may warm up the atmosphere. The fire has died down to a few embers and poor Ella spins endlessly around the turntable, her glassy voice replaced by the hollow click of the phonograph needle bumping against the record label.

"Shingles. Where are they?" While he gropes, I see that Page 9 is a lengthy treatise devoted to the finer points of shingling. Do we really need this?

"Right here. Take a handful," I giggle, filling James's outstretched palm. "Get up. Turn this way." He looks at me quizzically, then a lascivious grin overtakes his face.

"You know you want to." Slightly unsteady on our feet, we prop each other up.

"Ready . . . aim . . ."

Cedar burns so brightly. And it fills the house with the most wonderful old-time scent.

REMYTHOLOGIZING

Some decades ago there was a movement among Christian theologians to adapt their teachings to the modern world, and the buzz-word for a brief time was "demythologization." The idea was to remove the element of myth, and get down to the basic message. The message became elusive and vague, something about loving your neighbors and even your enemies. The movement fizzled, but not before many began to see that there was no avoiding myth. Joseph Campbell was helpful. "Remythologizing" became the new project, albeit briefly, among doctrinaire Christians.

"If you have Christmas Blues, if Christmas is a downer for you, one transforming experience is to re-invent Christmas. Shape Christmas traditions to your liking..." Raymond Crippen included these comments with his own collection of re-done myths. We chose the one about the origins of "Santa" and follow it with two pieces that take literally the widespread confusion about the identities of Jesus Christ and Santa Claus. We then offer a Christ Mouse and a Christmas Worm, to counteract the excessive sweetness of the season, clearing our palates for a taste of some new myths and traditions in the making.

A modest Christmas village display gets out of hand, and then the basic values creep back into consciousness. The Navajo have their own way of handling this time of year. Kwanzaa is a new myth just now taking shape.

The pair of birth stories that close the anthology suggest that the myths are rewriting themselves all the time. One way to counteract the Christmas blues is to invite the mythical, mystical and magical into our lives throughout the year. Then, when we approach the holiday banquet table, we can be less needy and more selective — able to choose what truly nourishes while avoiding the poison.

Sissy Pfunder-Pui: The True Story

Raymond Crippen

Santa Claus is a fraud, a hollow legend, a bit of make believe. Everyone must know this.

The story of how Santa came to be is a dear story worth telling once again in this Christmas season.

It has been several centuries now since Sissy Pfunder-Pui began making her rounds on Christmas Eve. Sissy lives (all the world knows) on a tiny South Pacific island where palm trees sway gently in warm zephyrs and where each sunrise and each sunset are a spectacle of glory.

Sissy's name (everyone knows) is Evelyn. She is called Sissy for the fact that she is the eldest of twenty-seven sisters who busy themselves through all their days making toys for distribution to good children on the eve of every Christmas.

The difficulties for Sissy and her sisters came about two centuries ago when publicity began to make life stressful for Sissy. As always she would load her Polynesian canoe to overflowing with gifts. Then her extraordinary Fourteen Porpoises would lift out of the sea, raise Sissy's canoe on their backs and begin to rise and dip gracefully through the air, all around the globe, stopping briefly at every home which Sissy designated.

Kids began waiting up for Sissy. That was a part of the problem. Kids wanted to see her, wanted to tell her which toys they wanted most of all. Parents also would wait for Sissy; they wanted to discuss toys and other gifts with her. Newsmen pressed for interviews. One year both Lisbon and Copenhagen scheduled giant Sissy festivals. They plunked Sissy into a carriage at both cities and had her leading giant, joyous Christmas parades.

"This whole thing is becoming very difficult," sweet Sissy told her sisters. "There are so many interruptions and there are so many demands on my time. If the world grows by another one hundred twenty-seven children I'm not going to be able to make my rounds before the dawn of Christmas morning."

Some said it was Sister Sauce and some said it was Sister Sue Sity who first came up with the idea of Santa. Sissy said all of the sisters had the idea at once and all of them deserve credit. What one of the sisters, whether Sauce or Sue or Sissy or some other said was:

"We need to find some big, good-natured drone who will be willing to claim credit for delivering the gifts of Christmas Eve.

All he will have to do — it will have to be a man — all he will have to do is sit around granting interviews, talking with kids, ho-ho-hoing at parents and looking like a million dollars. Assist with deliveries. He can be front man for the operation. Then we can get our work done without interference."

The sisters undertook an international talent search. It was Sissy who remembered the jolly old elf of the North Pole, a little fat man with a red suit and a white beard, who "really doesn't have a thing to do all day long but count snowflakes."

Sissy persuaded Jolly Five-by-Five to take his suit to the cleaners and then to begin a triumphal world tour, taking loud and conspicuous credit for himself for the mysterious goings-on of Christmas Eve. (The jolly elf's name was Santab Gbrgh. It was Sally Pfunder-Pui who said, "That will never do," and it was Sally who came up with the name of Santa Claus.)

A time came when Santa could not meet all of his Christmas publicity obligations. "Find an assistant. Deck him out in another red suit and let him do some of the chores," Sissy counseled. Santa did as Sissy said.

By this age, of course, there are Santas to be found on nearly every street corner. All credit to them; the chores of meeting and greeting the children of the world and their parents and the news media people, of eating cookies by the ton and riding in cold weather parades is not one of the great jobs of all the ages. The Santas earn their pay to be sure. It is also they who read the mail and pass along the word to the South Pacific. Sissy's sisters give encouragement when Santa's morale sinks with the winter suns.

But when Christmas Eve comes once again this year, as in all the long years gone by, it will be Sissy Pfunder-Pui and her porpoises who bring gifts in a mysterious way to the children. It will be Sissy, in her original chic but practical orange and yellow and brown costume, who will glide effortlessly through the silent night and who will call out in a melodious voice here and there all across the dark sky:

"Merry Christmas! Merry Christmas! Merry Christmas to all, and to all a good night!"

For Santa...

Chaibou Elhadji Oumarou

Your Christmas is white
of snow and chilly wind,
But a forgotten sheep
is wandering alone
In Thy kingdom
facing the Unknown.

A lonely heart
is throbbing in the cold,
Its freezing blood
needs warmth inside
But Thy sheep are gone
even when it needs them most.

Jesus Watered in Glory Hole

John Brand

"Then a second Adam to the fight,
And to the rescue came."

Adam wanted to know what Jesus wanted for Christmas but was afraid to ask his father, who would have said, "Cats. Jesus loves cats."

"Not my cat," said Adam.

"Especially your cat. 'What I wouldn't give for the fur off that cat's back,' Jesus told me. It's so cold at the Pole that he needs a new coat, so he's coming to Glory Hole where he's heard about a very fat cat." His wife said he was being sacrilegious, he said he hoped so, then sprayed Lysol around the Christmas tree where Fatcat had peed again. During dinner, Fatcat had stood on hind legs and nibbled kernels of popped corn strung around the tree. "Cat," Adam's father had said, "Cat, I'm talking to you," the man said rising. Fatcat looked straight at the man, lifted his bushy tail and squirted the tree behind him. After he heaved the cat outside Adam's father had said, "It's Christmas Eve and there's no more shopping days left until Christmas. At least Jesus won't have to shop long for a new cat."

While his parents dressed for a candlelight church service, Adam took his mother's coffee cup and wiped it clean with his sleeve. He filled it with Pet milk and listened to them quarrelling over a droning hair dryer. His mother said this was the last time she'd ever say Jesus was coming for Christmas — "But that's what they're saying this year. They're saying Jesus is coming soon." She turned the dryer on High.

Adam didn't know what else to do while he waited. He already had peeked under the tree and knew he was getting Addidas and a set of junior weights. He didn't want to be trim like other boys. "I want to stay fat like Fatcat." He carved frost flowers on the picture window behind the big tree. He carved through frost until his fingertip almost touched the pink nose of Fatcat, who perched on the snowy ledge outside the window. After tiptoeing to the door and letting the cat back in, Adam led him to the tree and the cup of Pet milk hidden between the legs of the tree stand. While Fatcat lapped his milk he sunk his spreading claws into the red felt skirt Adam's mother had purchased at Niemann's in Denver, then arranged tidily around the stand. Tired of saving electricity, Adam plugged the Christmas lights back in. "Hold your breath, Fatcat," Adam said because of the lingering Lysol fumes. Then he told his cat it was safe to purr. "Jesus likes cats, but he won't like you this year and take you away."

"Take who?" his father said as he came back into the room straightening his tie. It was tight at the collar.

"Not my cat," Adam said.

His mother came next. She tucked in his button-down shirt and clipped on his tie. He squinted while she sprayed his blond hair. She dug a wet, cold Q-tip into his ears. His father said his fingernails passed inspection.

Before the family left for Christmas Eve at the church, Adam closed the fireplace flue so Jesus couldn't get in.

At church Adam's father was not impressed with the towering tree standing over the empty manger. Hanging from its limbs were snowflakes made of paper doilies. The flakes made the green tree look frosted. Adam's father reminded him in a loud whisper that he'd waded through waist-deep snow to cut the family tree. "Just about froze in the crotch. Haven't had a good pee since." He smiled until he remembered what Fatcat had done under the tree. "A man's house ought to be his house," he said.

His wife shushed him. "We're in God's house now."

"Is that what they're all saying this year?"

People in the pews around them were beginning to notice, but Adam went ahead and asked if they were getting a divorce. His mother stroked his hand with her gloved fingertips. "If Jesus is born tonight," he asked, "he won't have time to grow up and come to my house, right?"

She asked him how he liked the gold cross his father had given her, with its matching gold chain. Adam was confused because his mother, after breaking another fingernail just last week, had said all she wanted from Santa was a new set of nails.

"Where's Jesus right this minute?"

"Hush," his mother said, squeezing his fat thigh. "Jesus is almost here so be still."

Adam covered his face with his hands; then, when he hoped it was safe, he spread his fingers and saw blue hay in a blue manger. He wondered if Mary and Joseph wore crosses. When they bent over the Baby Jesus in the manger Adam decided not to be a good boy. He swung his legs and kicked the seat of his pew with his heels. He dropped his hymn book. He slouched like his father, digging his hands into his pockets. He hoped Jesus and his pack of snarling reindeer would get tangled up in telephone wires or get hit by a jet. "There," he thought, "now I've been a bad boy."

At home while his mother fixed sandwiches and hot chocolate for Jesus, she told Adam this was a hard time for his father, so Adam would have to help her take care of him. The man stood at the lighted tree. Fatcat purred and nuzzled his leg, then got brushed off by a foot. Adam's father shook a present and said, "All these presents I can't use." His wife offered him fresh coffee, beans from Niemann's she had ground herself. "It's the hazelnut you like," she said.

"You want me to drink coffee at bedtime? You know what coffee does to my kidneys." He got himself a Corona and came towards the tree, behind which Adam hid with Fatcat. Adam had done as told and gotten into the Christmas pajamas his grandparents had sent him, but now he hid, watching his father open his Corona. He tossed its cap into the tree, where Fatcat pawed at it and almost gave away their hiding place.

"Corona's the beer they piss in, you know," his wife said over the man's shoulder. She had a leer on her face Adam hadn't seen before.

"You just love to kill my joy," the man said.

"This is the last Christmas I'll ever try to keep happy for you."

"Last Christmas you decided we needed to 'get centered' and filled up my house with your chanting. This year it's Jesus."

After she left for the bedroom Adam's father took several swallows without putting the bottle down. He drank standing, and every time he opened a new bottle, he tossed its cap into the tree. "This is Christmas?" he asked. "First she won't let me use real icicles on my tree. Those plastic icicles, they blow off every time the heat comes on." He belched. "This is Christmas? Then she makes me open my main present on Christmas Eve."

Adam watched the lights blink on and off in his father's glasses. The man whined, "Then she gives me a digital watch. I wanted a watch with a face on it." He tried again to get a drop from his empty bottle, said he needed a good watering trough, then went to the bath without closing the door. He didn't flush the toilet. "Only good thing about this Christmas is a good pee."

His wife was already asleep when he got in bed with her.

Adam and Fatcat were sleepy but wanted to stay up. Fatcat sniffed at the steaming thermos that had been filled for Jesus. Adam poured Fatcat's coffee into a cut-glass bonbon dish. After adding Pet milk and sugar cubes to the coffee he said, "Let it cool." Adam served himself hot chocolate, which he thickened with Readi-Whip from the cabinet where his mother had hidden it. Adam let Fatcat lick Readi-Whip off each cup of hot chocolate, then watched him lick his white whiskers. Soon the Pet milk and Readi-Whip were gone, and significantly reduced were the coffee and hot chocolate and sandwiches of salami and Port wine cheese. Adam left the crusts for Jesus. Now there was nothing left to do but wait and guard Fatcat.

He got sleepy and yawned with his jaws set. He needed to pee but was afraid to leave the tree. He lay down at the rim of the felt skirt. A striped bow from a present tickled his nose. The room was dark except for the lights blinking up and down the tree. Heat came on and blew several icicles. Fatcat sniffed at a frosted ornament. Adam opened his robe and let the cat in. Fatcat turned once, twice, then settled.

Adam woke up burning between his legs, and when he tucked his knees close to his double chin Fatcat squirmed and Adam almost wet his Christmas pajamas right then. He prayed he wouldn't wet himself, but knew Jesus would never answer the prayer of a bad boy.

Then he was there, Ho-Hoing and scratching his furry red sides, licking his beard of Readi-Whip away until he exposed scraggly brown cheeks. The sack he took off his shoulders turned into a huge can of Pet milk, perforated all around and spewing foamy arcs into the waiting mouth of Fatcat, who drank while on his back, paws folded against his white tummy. Every creamy jet of milk hung in the air over Fatcat until he opened his mouth. "I love cats," Jesus said.

"Not my cat," Adam said.

While he scratched his furry red sides, Jesus counted the presents under the tree. "All these presents I don't need," he said.

"You can't use a good cat, can you?" Adam asked. "Don't you want some gourmet coffee?"

"You know what coffee does to my kidneys," Jesus said.

But Jesus loved hot chocolate, and with marshmallows. Adam knew he was in trouble. The thermos was empty, and Adam had scarfed the marshmallows before dinner, after finding them in his mother's crowded sweater drawer. The can of Readi-Whip was also empty. "Would you like some Pet milk?"

"Never touch the stuff," Jesus said.

"Just try it this once," Adam said, and showed Jesus how to get down on the floor, like Fatcat, on his back with his hands curled under. Jets of milk again streamed from the perforated can and the three drank, Jesus, Fatcat and Adam. Adam heard Jesus swallow. He heard Jesus' stomach gurgling. Jesus finally stood up and groaned. Adam stood too. "You don't need a good cat, do you?" he asked, squirming and clutching his groin.

"What I need," Jesus said, "is a good watering trough."

"Both my parents have bathrooms."

"Which one's nearest?"

As he walked down the hall, Jesus almost bumped into Adam's father, who veered into the bathroom and closed the door. Instead of going on down the hall to the other bath, Jesus went back to Adam, who was afraid he would wet his pajamas right there. By this time both of them squirmed and pressed their knees together. "Right there is where Fatcat goes," Adam said, pointing to the red felt skirt at the base of the tree. Jesus fumbled at his thick black belt and said he didn't know how to get out of this outfit. "What's this?" he asked Adam.

"It's your zipper. Want me to show you how it works?"

Adam looked away as soon has Jesus got his fly open. He finally said, "Fatcat's in trouble for whizzing on the tree."

"Then that'll make two of us," Jesus said.

Tears came to Adam's eyes, but instead of crying he opened the fly of his pajamas. He sprayed the tree. So did Jesus. Sprayed branches and lights and jiggling ornaments. Almost hit the lighted star at the top. Fatcat joined them, with his tail raised and his backside to the tree. Jesus sighed. "Glory, glory," Jesus said. "There's nothing on this earth quite like a good pee."

He took longer to finish than the other two.

"Do kids ever tease you about being fat?" Adam asked.

Next morning Adam's mother had to rouse him from his sleep at the foot of the tree. Adam went back to sleep. "Heavy sleeper like his father," his mother said. She bent over and picked bits of red felt off Adam's pink cheek. "Lawrence," she called out to Adam's father, "Where did you put the Lysol?"

The Christ Mouse

Bruce Ferguson

Nobody believes in visions, but that is where the truth is. I know because I see visions. I see visions as clear and awesome as any of those seen by Isaiah or Daniel or Ezekiel. I've stood in the court of God. I've watched myriad fire-breathing horses and flaming chariots charge from clouds of silver and gold and opal and pearl against the stinking, slinking hosts of hell. I've witnessed endless choruses of sword-wielding, shining beings wrapped in glittering robes raising, in eerie harmonies, hymns to the blinding light they came from, and at whose compelling will they throw themselves against a writhing unknown of gnashing and wailing and deadly threats.

Who am I going to tell? Most people are so unspiritual, Biblically illiterate, and crass that the only visions they see are on television. But I have to get the word out. I know something that will rock the economy of the western world, something that may call the integrity of the Christian Church into question. I've had a most incredible revelation! The world has been living a lie for almost two thousand years: Christmas is a mistake.

It came to me the other night. I realized there was someone in my room, but I couldn't see or hear anybody; no breathing, no rustling of clothes, no movement. I sat up and looked around, trying to see in the darkness, and I gradually became aware of a very dim light. It had the vague outline of a person, but I couldn't see any arms or legs, or even a face. I was scared. It's always that way with these visions. I never think at first that I'm caught up in a vision. I always think someone has broken into my house and wants to kill me for my money or something.

283

I finally got brave enough to say, "Who's there?"

The light didn't move, and there was still no sound. Then I heard a voice, but it didn't seem to come from the light; it came from somewhere in my own head, I thought. It wasn't exactly a whisper. In fact, it didn't seem to have any volume at all. It was more of a sensation in words, if you can understand what I mean. For some reason, I never thought to turn on my bedside lamp. I just sat there in bed, in the darkness, staring at this dim light — sort of greenish, as I remember — and being aware of words being said from someplace.

"Do not be afraid," I heard in a hollow, low-pitched sound. "We are going on a journey to a far-off place and a time of long ago. You will not be in any danger. You must pay close attention to everything you see and everything I tell you. You must not question. Just believe and remember. You will know what to do."

The light came closer and got brighter. For a minute, I couldn't see or hear anything. It was like I was in the depths of outer space, or else sealed up in a tin can. I wasn't scared any more. I didn't feel anything. All of a sudden, I was in this place that looked like it might be some kind of garden. It seemed hot, and I thought I could smell something that might have been mimosa. There were trees around, old and gnarled, and in front of me was a cliff with some big holes in it. There were also some big rocks that looked like they had been put there on purpose, maybe to cover up some of the holes. It was late in the day. In fact, it was beginning to get dark here in this little valley.

I heard some shuffling of feet and voices murmuring, and I looked toward the sounds. I saw four or five men carrying the body of another man and a couple of women walking behind. The men were grunting and sobbing, and the women were crying openly. They were making their way toward one of the holes in the cliff.

"My God!" I said as it dawned on me. "They are burying Jesus! But how can that be? It happened two thousand years ago. "

Then I remembered what the voice had said about a journey, and that I should not ask questions. I looked around for the light, but I couldn't see it anywhere. It didn't matter. The people paid no attention to me, and I assumed they couldn't see me. I followed them, but I wasn't aware of the sensation of walking. It was like I floated when I moved. I could see and smell and hear, but I couldn't feel.

Sure enough, they went to one of the holes in the cliff, which by now I realized were tombs, and took the body inside. A slab had been carved out of one of the sides of the hole, or cave, and they put the body on it. Then a funny thing happened. One of the people — disciples, you know — saw a mouse's nest against the opposite wall. He pushed at it with his foot, and a mouse ran out. Instead of running toward the mouth of the cave, it went toward a back corner where it could not escape the man, and he stomped on it and killed it. Then he kicked the nest outside, but he left the mouse where it lay.

Almost immediately, one of the women began to berate him for killing the mouse; he could have simply run it outside, she said. "After all, we're burying the one whom we believe to be the Lord of Life. It seems wrong to be the instrument of death as we lay him to rest."

"What difference does it make?" I heard the mouse killer say. "The Lord is dead. It would be a sacrilege to leave a mouse alive in here to nibble at his corpse."

He said this very defensively, and I could sense some remorse in his manner. A pall seemed to fall over the group after that incident, which drove them even deeper into sadness, and they left the tomb. Together, and with great difficulty, they rolled a nearby boulder before the mouth of the cave to prevent any molestation of the body until the women could get back the next day to embalm it properly.

I did not follow them as they left, but lost myself in thought as I contemplated that strange little episode with the mouse. How odd, I thought, that a person who followed some guy who

promised a renewed life should so cavalierly snuff out a life —
and with such a sanctimonious excuse! The guy is dead. What
difference does it make what consumes the corpse, microbe or
mouse? I wondered if there had been baby mice in the nest that
now lay on the ground outside the tomb, but I decided not to
investigate, since there would be nothing I could do except to
add to my own feelings of regret about the scene.

The boulder and the mouth of the cave were not a perfect fit,
and as I stood there in the darkness, I saw, through the cracks
where the two didn't meet, a brilliant flash of light, and the
boulder was dislodged from its place. It was like an explosion,
but there was no sound. This feeling, like a vibration, ran
through me, and I felt that something had happened here that
was too much for me, so I didn't approach the tomb. I waited,
expecting to hear weird music like I've heard before, but there
wasn't a sound. All was dark again.

What happened next is a well-known matter of record. Some
time passed, of course, but in visions there is no such thing as
time. It's just that your mind can't process everything at once.
It was now getting light, and what I saw was a couple of women
coming toward the tomb carrying their embalming paraphernalia.
It hadn't occurred to them how they were going to get the
boulder away from the opening, so they were both relieved and
perplexed when they found it had shifted enough that they could
get past. They went in and were back out in an instant, white as
ghosts themselves and terrified. "We've got to find the men,"
one of them whispered, and they were off, leaving their
wrapping cloths and spices behind.

Then there was a bunch of men around, searching the ground
for tracks and examining the boulder, which they had pushed
further aside to let more light into the cave. Two or three of
them were staring at the now vacant slab, and one, the mouse
killer, began glancing around, looking for the dead mouse. He
acted puzzled and dropped to his knees and started crawling
around the floor of the cave, but the mouse's carcass was
nowhere to be seen. The only evidence that there had ever been

a mouse was a small spot of dried blood where it had met its end. Whatever had happened to the dead man had happened to the dead mouse, too.

At that point, my guide, the dim, greenish light, appeared beside me, and I was aware of words being said. This is what I heard:

"In a way that was, and still is, absolutely mysterious, the disciples of Jesus came to know that their leader — their Lord — had been raised by God from the dead. At the same time, the disciple who had killed the mouse became convinced that the same thing that happened to Jesus happened to the mouse. He worked very hard to persuade other disciples that God had resurrected the mouse to show sovereignty over all life; not just humans but all living things. That it was also a convenient justification for his having killed the mouse in the first place lent vigor to his crusade, and several people were convinced."

Then, I began to hear that strange musical sound that I usually hear in my visions, but I could also still hear the words that were being said.

"From the beginning, the disciples of Jesus realized that their belief in the resurrection and its message set them apart from all other religions, and it became the focus of their worship and their one annual celebration, coinciding with the Jewish Passover. The believers in the mouse's resurrection wanted to celebrate that, too, but they realized they could not detract from the celebration of the Resurrection of the Lord. The best alternative was the winter solstice, when many religions — and even the non-religious — celebrated the return of the sun, new life, a new year, new hope. What better time to celebrate the resurrection of the mouse as a symbol of God's power over all life. Now, the language of the day was Greek, and in Greek, the word for mouse is *mus*. And so the day, coming about a week after the winter solstice, when the resurrection of the mouse was celebrated, became known as Christosmus Day, Christ Mouse Day.

"Christosmus Day immediately became very popular among

the earliest adherents to the new religion. It was a day when they could share their joy with people from other religions. One way they shared their joy was by exchanging live mice. White ones were especially prized as gifts, and joyful rivalries sprang up over who would end the day with the largest number of mice. People from other religions often joined in the practice. The mice were in no way venerated, and when they became too numerous they were sent, with prayers, to join the mouse that started it all."

Suddenly, I was back in my bed in the silent dark. I lay there, numb with disbelief. There isn't a breath of any of this in any Christian writing I've ever heard of. Then, somehow, it began to come to me why that is. When the Christian Church began to get organized, and rules and explanations began to replace faith, Church leaders got uncomfortable with the idea of Christosmus Day. It did not neatly fit into their concepts of who Christ should be. They began to look upon the Christosmus as sacrilegious, if not idolatrous, and they set about systematically and thoroughly to wipe out all traces of it.

The first thing they did was to forbid any mention of the word, 'mouse,' in any religious context whatever. Maybe you haven't noticed, but the word, 'mouse,' does not appear in the New Testament. There are plenty of birds, fish, sheep, goats, snakes, and even scorpions, but no mice. Then, they supplanted Christosmus Day with the Feast of the Nativity of the Lord. The leaders' campaign was successful; not right away, though. We know the Nativity of the Lord didn't gain what you might call official acceptance for three hundred years. Check this out: Neither the first Christian writer, Saint Paul, nor the first Christian Gospel, Mark, says a word about the birth of Jesus.

And think about this. In England, the midwinter feast came to be known as 'Christmas,' which etymologists have mistakenly taken to be a corruption of *Christemasse*, Christ Mass, which is silly because every mass is a Christ Mass. What happened is that the Greek expression, 'Christosmus,' had been preserved, and I'll bet the Christ Mouse tradition had been, too. Can't you see carvings of mice, rag mice, clay mice, and even stuffed mice being among the gifts that were joyfully exchanged as logs and candles burned to celebrate the victory of God over the hardships of life?

The driving of the snakes from Ireland by St. Patrick, true or not, shows him to be a folk hero and a champion of the Christ Mouse. Why? Because snakes eat mice! The symbolism is obvious. The snake recalls the Garden of Eden and the Fall of Man; mice represent that one mouse in the tomb of Jesus that signified God's ultimate control of the destiny of all things and the promise of mercy represented by resurrection. St. Patrick's accomplishment was an acted-out parable, which everyone at that time could understand.

I suspect the Middle Ages saw the end of Christmas as the commemoration of the resurrection of the mouse. The Black Plague, which devastated Europe at that time, was known to be carried by rodents. I think Church leaders seized upon this popular knowledge, declaring it to be the judgment of God against the unholy practice of observing the resurrection of anything other than a human.

And yet, vestiges remain of the legend of Christosmus. A couple of examples: Clement Moore's poem, *A Visit from St. Nicholas*, not exactly Christian literature, contains a reference to a mouse, and although this is in the context of Christmas Eve, the observation is made here that nothing was stirring. Doesn't that make you think of death — of a tomb, maybe? Perhaps he somehow knew of the Legend of the Christ Mouse and wanted to acknowledge it. Perhaps that is why the poem was first published anonymously; because Moore feared that if someone picked up on the allusion, it could mean his being labeled a pagan cultist.

Also, did you ever reflect on what made Walt Disney decide upon a mouse for his Steamboat Willy character? Have you ever pondered why this mouse has become the pervasive American symbol of family, friends, fun, fantasy? Can you accept the possibility that our collective subconscious still holds onto that two-thousand-year-old scene in a Judean tomb, however vigorously suppressed?

It is crystal clear to me that I have been called on to give back to the world the miracle that Christmas originally represented, to proclaim the resurrection of the mouse, the Christ Mouse. Christosmus! Theologically, it's rock solid: God of all creation! The history of Christmas has been a steady downward spiral from the sublime to the ridiculous. For a long time, its message of God's involvement in creation has been at best secondary to its importance as a sales promotion device, however desperately preachers preach and choirs sing. But abolish Christmas, the Church's big day, with all the emotional and financial investment that has been loaded onto it? It means going against two thousand years of religious teaching and the retail establishment of the western world. Where to begin? Who will help me — who will believe me?

I must be crazy. There is no way a weird visionary from nowhere is going to change the world.

["The Christ Mouse" is an adaptation of a chapter from a novel in progress.]

Christmas Worm

Peggy Garrison

God rest ye merry Dickens imagery,
Marley dragging his chains,
and Tim the tiny; a heinie-shaped roast
o' grouse n' bevel — the devil take
Christmas and give it back with Manhattan
for 25 dollars and a bottle o' rum
hum hum (wax paper over a comb,
that's a poor man's harmonica).
The girls in dark skirts and light blouses
sing carols in the darkened auditorium,
Away in the Manger, O Gloria
while snowflakes fall on the charming
red-brick pharmacy; Adeste Fidelis,
Aurora Borealis, the star and the 3
wiseacres puffing like Groucho; Perfecto
Garcia with a ribbon around the box —
my father's favorite cigars.
The prettiest tree of all is
the big one with blue balls
flocked in the picture window, flogged
in the town square — the Christmas worm
is at it again trying to make us
throw out that holiday as though it were
a rotten apple. Marley's chains are heavy;
the old Christmas ghosts will appear
on Channel Memory tonight, that unstable
cable — through the hi fi Mahalia
wandering vibrato, Dad on the green couch,
Mother at the green table …

The Christmas Village

Brian Skinner

Lorraine sits at the kitchen table and stares at the sludge in her coffee cup. It doesn't seem like Christmas. She tries to remember the last time she was in a holiday mood — ten years ago.

Howard pushes open the kitchen door with his foot, his arms laden with fluffy rolls of cotton batting. His hair is dusted with snow. He smiles; there is a bounce in his walk. He squeezes through the doorway to the living room, whistling "Joy to the World" so off-key it is unrecognizable — except to Lorraine, who has been listening to it for months.

She shoves herself away from the table and pours another cup of coffee. She slumps into the chair in her pink fuzzy bathrobe and warms her hands on the steaming mug. Lorraine wishes she could go back and nip Howard's obsession with Christmas in the bud. With the clarity of hindsight, she knows exactly how it started — and it was all her fault.

The twinkling lights from the living room swim in the dark liquid abyss of her mug. She stirs the coffee into a whirlpool that sucks down each of the colored reflections, pulling her down into a melancholic recollection of Christmas past.

Ten years ago, Howard did not even shop for his own undershorts. Lorraine suspected something was afoot when he agreed to accompany her to Ralph's Discount World the week before Christmas. Howard pointed out each tinsel-draped display of marked-down Christmas items, every glittering gewgaw and cheap stocking-stuffer, as though he were visiting from a small village in Eastern Europe. They lingered particularly long in the aisles crammed to the ceiling lights with Christmas decorations, even though their attic held enough lights and ornaments to festoon a forty-foot Douglas fir without cheating a single branch or needle of its cheerful burden.

Howard stopped as if a wad of chewing gum anchored him to the floor. "Look at those," he called to Lorraine. "And they're on sale, too." He stood in front of the shelves laden with cheap little made-in-Taiwan cardboard houses, the kind that one would arrange into a circular village beneath the Christmas tree on a fluffy skirt of cotton batting to represent snow, with one bulb from a string of lights stuck into the round hole at the back of each house to show that miniature families lived in them.

Lorraine thought the toy houses looked especially cheap that year. The glistening mica snow had been sprayed at angles from which no storm could approach unless it had descended out of a whirlwind, depositing a blanket of snow even on the underside of the eaves. The spongy lichen trees had been glued to the bases in postures leaning into the make-believe blizzard rather than away from its blasts. The cellophane windows had been stuck on so haphazardly they could have been designed for miniature fun-houses. The church steeple slouched at a precarious angle, and the small shops were marked with crooked signs announcing "Candies Shoppe" and "Toys Shoppe."

"You can't be serious, Howard," Lorraine said, moving aside to let the bottle-neck of shoppers pass around them. "They're ugly, and cheap-looking, and they're probably a fire hazard. See? They don't have any UL stickers on them."

Howard seemed disappointed by her remark. "But the price is certainly right: $9.99 for the whole village. Come on, Lorraine. I never say a word about how you spend our money. Are you telling me I can't get one lousy little Christmas village for ten bucks?"

"It's not the money, Howard. It's how cheaply-made and tacky they are. What on earth would you want them for?"

"Because I had one as a kid. I like the stupid thing, OK? Do

I have to sign a voucher or something?"

Lorraine relented, deciding that $9.99 was not worth an argument one week before Christmas. That was her first mistake. She told herself at least it will be *under* the tree. She had enough long, spiralled icicles and spread-winged angels to conceal a model of Manhattan beneath the lowest branches.

Howard's impatience with the rest of their shopping caused Lorraine to suspect that her husband had got what he set out to find once the "Olde Tyme Xmas Village" had been loaded into their cart. She also suspected that, back at home, she would find a wrinkled, dog-eared page in the Sunday advertising supplement with just such an item in it, though photographed from the first models to roll down the assembly line rather than the tired little houses churned out by the weary Taiwanese trying to make a few extra yen in overtime before Christmas.

She wondered what they thought of the odd little trinkets they made, such as Pez dispensers and Groucho Marx glasses. After making all these Christmas villages would they think that every American house had a huge round hole in its windowless back side? What would they imagine it was for?

That year's Christmas presents — mostly electronic gadgets in large boxes packed with molded styrofoam — did not allow enough room under the tree for Howard's village, so the shops and houses were set up in a Main Street straight line on the mantel. Howard removed the clock, the brass candlesticks and Lorraine's paperweight collection, setting the village up on fresh rolls of Red Cross cotton.

Lorraine considered Howard's arrangement suitably festive, so she raised no strong objections. She did not care for the effect created by the portraits of Howard's grandparents hung above the mantel, the old couple staring down sternly like disapproving deities plotting an assortment of natural disasters about to befall Howard's cheerful village, but she let all of that pass. She doubted the Christmas village would survive the summer in their hot attic. What didn't fuse together in the August heat would probably come unglued. She needed only to worry that the discount stores would again carry the cheap cardboard shops and houses. Maybe she could write a letter to Underwriters' Laboratories informing them of the potential hazard.

The holidays over, Lorraine looked forward to having an uncluttered mantel for the next eleven months. Howard did not give her that long, however, to take a holiday away from the thought of his village. That June, on their vacation trip through the Ozarks, Howard stopped at every gift shop and tourist shack selling handicrafts. Unfortunately, he hit it lucky at the first such shop, a ramshackle addition to the gas station, where he found a pair of popsicle-stick log cabins with papier-mâché fir trees.

The miniature cabins had been intended as holders for salt and pepper shakers. Howard planned to drill holes in the backs of the log cabins large enough for a seven-watt Christmas tree bulb and asked Lorraine if she had any use for a couple of extra salt and pepper shakers.

She did not say the first thing that came to her. "Why not make snowmen out of them?" she said instead.

Howard heard none of the sarcasm in her suggestion. "Great idea!" he said, and was then on the lookout for a drugstore to buy more cotton. Lorraine and the kids stayed in the car, sipping their warm milkshakes.

In late June it had not been so difficult to put aside thoughts of snow on the roof and Howard's village coming down from the attic. But by the end of October, around the time the first stores began putting up their Christmas displays, Lorraine could not avoid the subject. Howard brought out the boxes he had stored in the hall closet and began unpacking his summer's worth of acquisitions in miniature real estate. He even drew up a blueprint for the layout of his village.

It became clear to Lorraine that the boom-town Christmas village would no longer fit on the mantel. Howard set to work out in the garage, building plywood extensions to the mantel. She said nothing, having learned her lesson with her fanciful suggestion to turn salt shakers into snowmen. Her sewing basket had been ravaged and now the button-eyed miniature snowmen stared at her from across the room.

Each holiday season the village grew, as though land developers had descended upon the bucolic tranquility in speculative hordes. Howard spent their vacation trips and three-day weekends scouting garage sales, flea markets, and church bazaars in search of more items for his village. The miniature houses were no longer his main concern; he had dozens still to be unpacked and worked into the snowy setting. He now needed all the things that went with village life: the streetlamps, mailboxes, doghouses, cars, pedestrians, skaters, sledders, carolers, and snowmen.

Lorraine had been dropping hints to their relatives and friends not to buy any more miniature items for Howard. The village had expanded to cover all three windowless walls in their living room, reaching upwards on additional shelves nearly to the ceiling, and downwards two more shelves practically to the floor.

But Lorraine's request was ignored. It was easy for people to shop for Howard. They didn't have to think about what to get him and he liked what he got. He could always use a few more streetlamps, especially the battery-operated kind that did not need to be wired up.

Howard and Lorraine tended to get more company during recent Christmases than they had been used to. Howard's village became an attraction, while Lorraine's Christmas tree — as meticulously decorated as ever — was all but ignored. Howard's village became the reason people visited. They never got further than the living room, content to gaze at it for hours on end, delighting in finding scenes they hadn't noticed on earlier passes.

Their enjoyment puzzled Lorraine. The village was cute and clever only from a distance. All the magic disappeared for her upon closer inspection. Nothing matched the style of anything else. The scale of things was way off. There were streetlamps from an old train set that towered above the church steeple. There were sledders so huge they could only have fit into the houses through the large round holes at the back. The skaters had come from so many flea markets and were of such unmatched sizes and periods of dress that they seemed like a freakish carnival skating across the glitter-dusted mirror. There were toy cars unable to fit in any garage and pedestrians tall enough to look face to face with second-story occupants gazing out their crooked cellophane windows. To Lorraine, it was as though Charles Dickens and Rod Serling had collaborated on a theme park.

Didn't anyone notice all these discrepancies, Lorraine wondered? Were they simply dazzled by all the blinking lights? Try as she would, she could not manage to see the charm of

Howard's Olde Tyme Xmas Village.

Now there was less and less of each year that Lorraine did not have to look at this surreal concoction of cardboard, plastic, wood, and ceramic pretending to be a normal village. Last year it had taken him until the middle of April to put everything away and allow Lorraine to reclaim the living room.

This year, Howard had told her he planned to get a head start on setting up his village over the extended Labor Day weekend. Out came the boxes and rolls of cotton, the plywood shelves, and the stapling gun.

Lorraine had wanted a quiet barbecue in their back yard with just a few friends over. She could hardly get Howard to take ten minutes away from his project.

"Howard, please come out here and mingle, will you?" she called.

"In a minute, dear. Just let me finish up this one string of lights."

"All right, but then that's it. This is a holiday."

Howard eventually came out to the patio. It had been a long string of lights. The hamburgers and chunks of Italian sausage were indistinguishable from the unlit briquets at the edge of the barbecue kettle.

No tactic Lorraine could devise ever got Howard to give up or delay his project. She did vow to herself, however, that it'd be over her dead body that the Christmas village would be allowed to sprawl beyond the living room. It was the only time she'd put her foot down.

By Halloween, Howard had the shelves installed in the living room and began setting out the first houses according to his numbered and color-coded master plan. He relinquished part of one evening to carve a jack-o'-lantern, and then went back to rolling out the cotton. On Thanksgiving, Lorraine had to enlist her sister's husband to carve the turkey. Howard had become entangled in the public works project that would bring light to Main Street.

Janet and Ricky rarely brought their friends over once their father had started setting things up in the living room. It was not so much his peculiar obsession that embarrassed them. Rather, their friends became so engrossed in looking at all the miniature scenes and in watching their father set up a new neighborhood that they hardly paid attention to Janet and Ricky.

Ricky now let his girlfriend wait on the front porch, ever since she had got so caught up making suggestions about how to place a row of houses on a terraced hill of cotton that she and Ricky missed the movie they had been looking forward to for weeks. Ricky wished for a father with more normal pastimes: one who watched every football game broadcast and simply grunted in response to all remarks and questions.

"Hand me that hardware store over there, will you, Ricky?"

"Pop, where's it all going? I mean, don't you ever stop? It's like you're still playing with toys. Here."

"Thanks. It needs a new bulb. The box is under that roll of cotton. I guess I never thought of it that way: playing with toys. Maybe you're right," he said, chuckling.

With that single remark, all the air was let out of Ricky's argument. You just couldn't insult him enough to get him to give it up. The whole family had tried.

This year, Howard added a new feature to enable the children and shorter adults to see how those on the upper tier of shelves lived. He built a wooden platform with three steps. To the high railing at the front he attached a small telescope. Lorraine and Janet and Ricky knew at once from where Howard had drawn his inspiration: from all the scenic overlooks with stubby, coin-operated telescopes at which they'd spent a few moments during their vacation trips to gift shops.

The living room furniture was clustered in the center of the room, sofa and chairs back to back, with the viewing platform at one end of the group, nearly equidistant from the three walls. As a touch of authenticity, Howard placed a hand-lettered sign, "Please Watch Your Step," on each of the three risers. Janet's calligraphy set had been nearly depleted of inks before her father got the lettering just right. He had chosen Old English script, in keeping with the holiday theme.

The whack! whack! of Howard's staple gun awakes Lorraine from her depressing reverie, driving the thought of Christmas into her. Whack! It is nearly ten o'clock and she's still sitting in her bathrobe. She intends to keep the few remaining Christmas customs that Howard has not ruined for her, and hopes she has enough energy and enthusiasm left to make at least one batch of rum-balls.

The steady tramping of visitors up the walkway has not been impeded by the heavy accumulation of wet snow. If anything, it seems to add to their enjoyment of the season and their appreciation of Howard's village, which they can view in all its snow-blanketed charm without having to shovel any of it.

Lorraine grows tired of answering the front door. She is getting nowhere with her Christmas baking. She scrawls a note and tapes it to the door, asking visitors to let themselves in. She sets out two boot trays and unrolls plastic runners from the entrance hall to the observing platform. If they had charged only a quarter per head, Lorraine figures, they could have paid off the mortgage. But Howard objects to the idea. It doesn't coincide with his notion of the spirit of Christmas.

What *is* Christmas about, Lorraine wonders? She had once looked forward to the holidays and enjoyed every minute of their brief stay. Howard's stupid village has ruined all of that for her. She now dreads the holidays and overlooks any reminder of their coming as handily as she tucks away and tries to lose her dental check-up reminders. Why can't she get into the spirit of Howard's innocent pastime? Everyone else seems to enjoy it, even the strangers steadily trudging up their unshovelled walkway. What is she missing? What's wrong with her?

Every Christmas tale requires its King Herod or its Ebenezer Scrooge, just for contrast. Lorraine has somehow been cast in the role without ever trying out for the part. She vows to change that. After all, conversions are an integral part of Christmas lore, too. She takes her last tray of cookies out of the oven and makes herself a pot of tea, which she laces liberally with the liquor remaining from the batch of rum-balls. Nearly a quarter of the bottle spills into the teapot.

Lorraine settles on the sofa next to Howard, allowing the glimmer and glint of miniature streetlamps to sparkle in her blurry vision. The Christmas warmth spreads through her like a viscous fog. She is a little drunk and begins to feel sorry. She takes hold of Howard's hand and squeezes it. Not feeling up to words or apologies at the moment, she leans against his shoulder and hums, getting sleepier and cozier with each sip of tea.

The periphery of her vision suffers a rum-induced collapse. Lorraine can no longer focus on the room or the furniture. She sees only the village, sparkling with tiny lights and mica-crusted snow. It's like being outside in mid-winter without the inconvenience of a bulky coat and sound-damping hats and scarves. The blasts of pelting snow cannot touch her.

The doorbell rings in the middle of her reverie. Howard pulls himself up from the sofa and opens the front door. A six-year-old boy has come to see the miniature village. His snowsuit looks as though it has been pumped full of air. He waddles along the path of plastic runners, the snow slipping from his head and shoulders in muffled thwumps.

Howard helps the boy out of his hooded snowsuit. An oval of bright red skin lights up the center of his face.

"My mom says I can only stay till six. We're going to open all our presents after supper."

"We'll let you know when it's time," Howard assures him. He takes hold of the boy's hand and helps him climb onto the viewing platform. "Watch your step."

Lorraine extracts herself from between the sofa cushions. She feels as though she has been swallowed up in a snow bank: a deep, warm, sleepy pile of snow. She brings out a plate of her cookies and a glass of milk for the boy. He hesitates, as though he doesn't know whether to admire the cookies or eat them. He takes a bite of a sugar-sprinkled butter cookie and puts his eye up to the toy telescope.

"Neat," he says, swinging the telescope around and nearly toppling from the platform.

"Why not come down for a minute?" Howard admonishes. "You'll be able to see the streets on the bottom much better. Just don't touch anything."

"I won't." The boy walks around the room, leisurely viewing one tier at a time. Lorraine follows him with the plate of cookies and a cordless vacuum.

"What's your name?" Lorraine asks.

"Michael."

"Well, it's almost time to go, Michael. You wanted us to remind you."

"Oh. But I don't really have to go home. Mommy and Daddy are fighting again, so I always go outside to play when they fight. I just came over here 'cuz I got cold. I saw the Christmas town last week. Can I stay a little more?"

"We'll have to ask your parents," Lorraine says.

"OK," Michael replies, and recites his phone number to her as if it were a commercial jingle.

Lorraine goes into the kitchen. Her tongue has grown a little thick. She can hardly think how to phrase what she wants to say to the boy's mother.

The woman on the other end of the line sounds distraught. Her voice is all in her nose, as though she has a terrible cold, or has been crying.

"He talked about that toy village of yours all week," the woman says. "We're not quite ready for Christmas yet. But I don't want him getting in your way. Just send him home when he gets to be a bother."

"But it's dark out," Lorraine reminds her.

"He knows the way home. Just tell him when you've had enough of him. Thanks for your trouble. And Merry Christmas."

"Merry Christmas," Lorraine echoes. She holds the buzzing receiver; she isn't quite sure what's been decided on. She gets herself a cup of black coffee and sets the dining room table.

When Janet and Ricky return from last-minute shopping with

their friends, they say nothing about the extra place setting and the little boy who announces to them, "This is where I'm gonna sit." When their father sets Michael on his shoulders, straddling his ears, and takes him on a close-up tour of the upper terraces of the village, Janet asks her mother what's going on.

"Your father keeps busy with his hobby," Lorraine says. "Here, bring the casserole along, will you? Maybe I have too much time on my hands. Maybe I need a hobby, too."

"What, taking in under-appreciated kids?" Janet asks.

"You gotta be kidding," Ricky says.

"Well, why not? You two are pretty much on your own. I've got the time. I could call the Volunteer Center. There are plenty of kids out there who need a little extra attention. I could always become a Den Mother or something. Please go call your father and Michael in to supper. The food's getting cold."

Throughout the meal, Janet and Ricky stare at their plates in silence. No one has to worry about keeping a conversation going. Michael does enough talking for everybody.

After supper, Michael grabs hold of Janet with one hand and Ricky with the other, and hauls them into the living room. He takes them on a guided tour of The Olde Tyme Xmas Village as though they might not have noticed it before.

"I don't get it," Ricky tells his sister. "Are we from another planet or something? I really don't get it."

"Me neither," Janet says, lurching forward as Michael tugs on her arm.

The boy keeps them in tow, dragging them along with the enthusiasm of a real estate agent who suspects the young couple might have inherited some money.

Lorraine settles back in the sofa cushions. It is still early on Christmas Eve — plenty of time, she thinks, for a couple more conversions. The miniature lights sparkle in her eyes.

The Olde Tyme Xmas Village glows with renewed effort, too, as though conjuring up one last trick on behalf of the hard-hearted.

Keshmish Blues

C. M. Topaha

A blue hogan wakes with laughing sunrays
The Wind Brother's expression, an audible smile
Sounds of yearning, my grandmother at work
Long winters of empty ceremonies
Old, black, moccasins worn
Coyote walks on tender soil
Prestige wrinkles, no longer noble
Meat of the four-legged, cries of hunger
Only sounds of yelps across dry river beds
Whirlwind Logs, a displacement of balance
Magic logs seeks grandfather's medicine bundles
My oval tears need Athapaskan satisfaction
Winter feed lost to angry skies
Sandstone hearths lying awake at midnight
Pinon trees shed no Keshmish lights
But grandfather still holds my little hands
And we "walk in beauty" to blue hogan skies.

Southwest Indian Claus

C. M. Topaha

No gender Claus sweats in cedar canyons
A plan of survival walks their paths
They produce a new winter language
"Exchange new truth," the elders said
A Southwest philosophy, a gesture
Square windows of slabstone, leans east
The visions of happiness, to seek beyond
Dream thinking, this new gift from the past
Keshmish spices flavors symbolism on canyon walls
Oral tradition on painted mesas
A pride to honor the elders, a respect of gifts
We invite Coyote too, Coyote waits for verbal twist
The impossible glyphs notes winter message
Strange echoes blink to cosmos
Indian Claus, a transformation of the Southwest.

The Seventh Night of Hanukkah

Lemar Rodgers

On the seventh night of Hanukkah, which was also the night before Christmas and two nights before the start of Kwanzaa, Mrs. Dranoff sat in the back of her car, cranky and annoyed. She was annoyed at herself for waiting until the last minute to buy presents for her sister and her sister's family, knowing that the store would be horrifying. She was annoyed that her husband had been called out of the country on business, during Hanukkah, with almost no notice. She was annoyed that her son had just met another girl in Miami and could not bear to be away from her. If only he had met her three weeks earlier! If he had, he would be ready for some "space" by now. The really intense affairs never lasted more than a month.

She was annoyed that she would have to go to her sister's house for the last night of Hanukkah alone. It made her feel like a poor relation on whom pity was being taken. She was cranky that she was thinking like this, and because her driver was driving too slowly. "Can't you go a little faster?" she almost whined. She was tired and already wanted this shopping trip to be over. The driver looked back at her in his rearview mirror, with a rather cold glance, Mrs. Dranoff thought, and replied, "It's not so easy driving in all of this mess, Mrs. Dranoff. I don't want to get us both killed, especially not *tonight*." Mrs. Dranoff didn't know of anyone who could put a spin on a word the way her driver could. He had made it clear, very subtly and respectfully, of course, that he would rather be at home with his children on Christmas Eve than taking her shopping, especially since his wife also had to work. She saw the look again in the

306

mirror. Really, she thought, he could be so difficult sometimes. What was she supposed to do with her husband and son out of town? Call a cab? In Manhattan? At night? And he was always the first to say what a terrible driver she was. She would never be able to do it in all of this snow.

Pooh on him and his evil look! That look she knew all too well but with which she had never quite grown comfortable, even after all the years that they had been together. Still, their sparring generally ended with Mrs. Dranoff winning, getting her way.

She encouraged all of her employees to speak their minds, to say what they thought no matter what. The catch was that Mrs. Dranoff had been captain of the debate team at Bryn Mawr during her time there, and had only grown sharper and more adept at verbal combat in the three decades since college.

Her driver, thank goodness, was the only one of her employees who seemed to realize that silences bothered her more than verbal confrontation. Whenever her driver was upset about something and was sure that Mrs. Dranoff knew where he stood, he would be silent and give her "the look." "Is there a problem?" she would ask. He would always say, "No, *ma'am*," with the "ma'am" spinning all over the place, and the look would continue. This drove Mrs. Dranoff crazy. She told herself that the driver could not tell how much this drove her crazy and that she would never give him the satisfaction of knowing. So as she sat in the back of her car on the seventh night of Hanukkah, being driven through Manhattan in the middle of a snowstorm, she avoided his eyes, staring out the window at the heavily falling snow, and was cranky and annoyed.

Snow? What on earth was it doing snowing like this in Manhattan? Where was the greenhouse effect when you needed it? she wondered. With a sharp pang of guilt, Mrs. Dranoff, a Greenpeace member, shifted uncomfortably in her seat. Her mood was deteriorating more and more with every foot that her car crept along Fifth Avenue.

◇

Finally, her driver pulled up in front of Lord & Taylor. Mrs. Dranoff took a deep breath, preparing herself to do battle with the multitude of last minute shoppers, as her driver got out of the car to open the door for her. She had her eyes closed, summoning strength, when the driver slipped on the ice and hit the pavement hard; she didn't see him go down. Earlier that year her car had been featured in television ads that showed how soundproof it was; boom boxes, jackhammers, car horns, none of it could penetrate into the luxurious interior of the car. Neither could the sound of the screaming chauffeur. Mrs. Dranoff didn't hear him yell out in pain as he hit the ground.

After many seconds she opened her eyes when her car door wasn't opened for her. She peered out into the night, seeing only the heavily falling snow and the lights from the festively lit store. Only after someone approached her car and knelt down did she notice her driver writhing on the ground.

◇

Mrs. Dranoff was secretly pleased at the turn of events that had her driving her own car through Manhattan in a snowstorm. What a wonderful opportunity to show her driver just how good a driver she really was. Outwardly her face was drawn tight in what seemed to be concern for the man who sat across from her on the passenger side of the car; inwardly her heart soared with glee at the excitement. How long had it been since she had done something important, anything that really mattered? She loved the power and control and was lost deep in a fantasy of being an ambulance driver when the chauffeur called out in a panic, "Mrs. Dranoff, look out!" Their ride a few blocks to the hospital, where the driver's wife worked as a nurse, was colored with exclamations such as these. He tried to get Mrs. Dranoff to drive more slowly and be more careful, all the while grunting and groaning in pain. She would only sigh and look his way whenever he called out, hoping that she was executing "the look" properly.

She finally spoke up when he called out her name in terror as she hit a patch of ice and the car went sliding a few feet.

"Really," she said calmly, "do I yell at you when you are driving?" She hadn't had so much fun in ages.

The driver was relieved when they finally got to the hospital. Good Lord, he thought to himself as Mrs. Dranoff gingerly made her way to his side of the car to help him out, if I don't give this lady some driving lessons she's going to kill herself one day in this thing.

As they entered the emergency room Mrs. Dranoff wondered why big men always act like such babies when they are in pain. This always amazed her. She settled her driver into a chair and went about the business of getting some help for him.

The driver leaned back in his chair, cradling his arm and letting the pain wash over him as he heard Mrs. Dranoff cry out, "Excuse me. Young lady, excuse me." He shook his head and wondered how he was ever going to get any help if Mrs. Dranoff started treating people like lazy counter girls at Macy's. His wife was a nurse in this hospital. She had told him how some of these people could behave when you made them mad.

Surprisingly, Mrs. Dranoff hadn't made anyone angry enough so that they wanted to ignore him just to spite her. Before too long someone came to take him for an x-ray and he thanked Mrs. Dranoff as he was wheeled away.

As he vanished around a bend in the corridor Mrs. Dranoff became acutely aware of where she was. She didn't like it. Everyone looked so... despondent? People in pain, miserable people. She sat down on a hard plastic chair, pulling her mink coat around herself to keep warm, and wondered how long she was going to have to wait.

She could feel the eyes on her. Why do they always stare, she wondered. One or two even glowered. She returned their looks. One underfed woman with tangled hair, wearing a vinyl jacket that couldn't possibly be keeping her warm, got up from her seat and sat next to Mrs. Dranoff. She sneered through rotting teeth, reached out to touch Mrs. Dranoff's coat and said, "Nice coat, lady. How much it cost?" Mrs. Dranoff stood and moved away from the woman. She turned once to look back. People were

watching her. She knew what they were thinking. "Rich b—.
Snob." She grew angry and walked quickly down the corridor.

She stepped outside telling herself it was to get some air, but
she knew she wanted to get away from this place. It was the
seventh night of Hanukkah, she should be home with her
husband and her son lighting candles, saying prayers, having
dinner and opening presents. Several hospital employees walked
joyfully past her. They were free at last. They were going home
to fireplaces and parties and presents. They called out to one
another as they parted to find their cars in the snow, "Merry
Christmas! Merry Christmas!" A tall Black man yards away, just
a ghostly, dark figure in all that snow, yelled back at them all,
"Happy Kwanzaa! Happy Kwanzaa! Happy Kwanzaa!!" But there
was nothing happy in his voice. It was bitter and almost in a
rage. His words sounded more like a curse than well wishes, like
a petulant incantation to cancel out the hopes for a Merry
Christmas. Mrs. Dranoff shuddered and went back into the
hospital.

Typical, she thought, that Black people would now want their
own holiday celebration in December; and that was fine with
her. She just could not figure out why. Christmas is not enough?
God knows you certainly cannot avoid it. She had tried.

Mrs. Dranoff was not like other Jews who had not only given
up in the struggle against Christmas but who now wholeheartedly
embraced it. She reasoned and often reminded herself that as a
Jew this celebration of the supposed Christ child's birth was
nonsense, at best, since the Messiah still had not come. At
worst... oh, never mind. She just wanted to know if it would kill
the Switzenbaums if they called their presents to their Christian
friends Hanukkah presents instead of Christmas presents. Well,
would it? And how many Christians go around saying, "Happy
Hanukkah!"?

◇

"Merry Christmas, lady!"

Mrs. Dranoff had been walking the halls, thinking mean
holiday thoughts, going in and out of elevators, up and down

corridors, and had wandered into the pediatrics ward. She turned to see a little urchin wearing worn Snoopy and Woodstock pajamas who was brimming over with holiday cheer. She looked down at him, armed with the usual smile and reflex response of "I am Jewish," but she didn't get past the smile. She knew that to the sickly child her Judaic heritage would be no reason for her not to have a "Merry Christmas!" She said, "Thank you, sweetheart," touching his gaunt, sunken cheek. "Shouldn't you be in bed? It is cold out here in the hall."

"He sure should be. Let's go. Back into your room," said the nurse, a familiar face to Mrs. Dranoff. It was her driver's wife, who had just seen her husband in Emergency and was now returning to duty.

"Merry Christmas, lady!" sang out the urchin. Mrs. Dranoff followed the nurse and sickly boy into the hospital room.

The room was full of people and presents and Christmas. The families of the other young occupants had filled the sterile room with noise, color, wrapped packages, cards, balloons, goodies and their own presence. The urchin walked over to his corner of the room, which was a lot less exciting than the rest of the room, and turned to face Mrs. Dranoff.

"Do you want me to tuck you in?" she asked. She was a mom; she knew the look. The urchin nodded yes and crawled into bed. Mrs. Dranoff pulled and smoothed and straightened and tucked and fluffed; she was an old pro at this, and made such an event out of it that the urchin felt safer and cozier than he had ever felt in any bed before. "There!" she said. "Now you are ready."

The urchin looked up at her with true urchin eyes and said softly, "Merry Christmas, lady."

"Merry Christmas, sweetheart," Mrs. Dranoff said, looking down at him and wondering what in the world he had to be merry about. She tucked and fluffed him a little more before kissing his forehead and leaving the room.

"Mrs. Dranoff, I didn't realize you were so good with children," the nurse said with a lilting accent, her English influenced by Ghanian speech.

"I am a mother," said the other lady offhandedly. The nurse didn't respond, but she had been working with infants and children long enough to know that being a mother was no guarantee that one would be good with children.

The nurse's husband was dozing in a lounge downstairs. He had been x-rayed, set, plastered, and tylenol-codeined and was comfortably drifting while waiting for his wife's shift to end so that she could drive Mrs. Dranoff and him home.

Mrs. Dranoff accompanied the nurse as she went about the business of wrapping up her shift and preparing herself to go home. They were headed to where the newborns were kept; Mrs. Dranoff had asked to see them after learning that the nurse worked with them.

"Aren't they beautiful?" Mrs. Dranoff sighed amidst a small crowd of cooing, gurgling men who were congratulating one another and wishing one another a merry Christmas.

"Yes, they are," responded the nurse. "Would you like to see the really special ones?"

◇

The room was, at once, both large and small. Its actual dimensions made it a large room, but it also seemed small and cramped to Mrs. Dranoff because of all the machines.

Whereas the other room was filled with crying and cooing and gurgling within and without, from the babies and their admirers, this room had an odd stillness about it. The predominant sound was not the wailing of children complaining of hunger, but the whirring, clicking, beeping, wheezing and humming of a vast collection of machines whose noise and size and relative animation gave the children in this room an appearance of being secondary, inconsequential.

"Oh, how terrible!" Mrs. Dranoff said of the special babies. The room was filled with drug addicts and HIV carriers; most were both. Mrs. Dranoff noticed that the babies either lay very still, apparently uninterested in a world so new and as yet unexplored, or they twitched and shook nervously as if this new world were just too much for them and they wanted to go back to a safer place.

There was a nurse in the room, on duty, holding a former crack addict in her arms, walking slowly to and fro. The former crack addict didn't care that it was being held close to a warm, soft breast that smelled faintly of lilacs. It didn't know what lilacs were. The wife of Mrs. Dranoff's driver said, "I call these children special because every day that they live is a miracle." She reached down amidst a veritable forest of tubes and wires and clasped a shaking hand with her thumb and forefinger. As she gently rubbed its palm, the HIV-infected child was still; when she released her hold, it began to tremble once again.

◇

In one corner of the room a cozy little nook had been created by keeping this small area free of machines and nursing paraphernalia and by cramming it full of baby necessities, simple toys, mobiles, and artwork in dramatic black and white patterns — such as bull's-eyes, spirals, and checkerboards — which didn't overly stimulate the narcotic-ravaged brains of the children here. There were also three rocking chairs, and classical music played very, very faintly. Mrs. Dranoff was seated in one of the chairs across from the nurse, wearing, as the nurse was now, sterile clothes and hair coverings and holding in her arms, as was the nurse, a small, newborn child weakened by lack of prenatal care, the physical demands of crack-cocaine, a difficult birth and most recently the price that's paid to free the monkey. "Awful, aren't they?" the nurse asked, watching Mrs. Dranoff closely.

"Yes," she replied, "And beautiful."

The two women held the children and rocked slowly in their chairs listening to the baroque Christmas music: Bach's Praetorius: *In dolci jubilo*. Mrs. Dranoff wasn't too sure the child was enjoying the rocking because it lay very still and quiet in her arms, staring at her vacantly; or perhaps it was focused inward on its pain, with its eyes set in her direction but fairly unaware of her attentions. She pulled the child closer to herself.

She could have crushed it with her hands. Instead she gently snuggled the baby closer, lightly laying her hands on it.

The nurse began to hum a tune softly to the child she held, competing with Bach. An odd tune, Mrs. Dranoff thought. She asked the nurse what it was. "It's a Kwanzaa song," said the nurse, "A happy song for a sick baby."

Mrs. Dranoff did something akin to snorting. The nurse, having a curious look on her face, was told, "There was an angry man in the parking lot yelling about Kwanzaa at people who were wishing each other a merry Christmas. That song does not sound like something he would have sung."

"Kwanzaa isn't an angry time, Mrs. Dranoff," said the nurse.

"No? That's funny, because whenever I hear anyone talking about Kwanzaa it sounds as if it is some kind of rebellion against the *white* man and *his* holiday. Not that I could really blame them for wanting to celebrate something besides Christmas."

The nurse responded, "That may be true for some people who don't truly understand Kwanzaa, or embrace its spirit. Kwanzaa is a wonderful time to celebrate one's culture and heritage. It brings us together to reaffirm the bond of unity in a seven day celebration starting on the twenty-sixth of December. Its origin is as a harvest festival; Kwanzaa means 'first,' and in this instance 'the First Fruits.' It's a time to take pride and joy in one's community and history. It's a very special time with special practices. The *Vinbuziis*, the stalk of corn which represents the offspring of our children, is placed in the *Kinara*, a candle holder not unlike your menorah, which symbolizes the source of our origin and holds seven candles that represent the 'seven principles,' on the *Mkeka*, a straw mat that symbolizes our traditions."

Mrs. Dranoff had stopped rocking. She was silent, thinking. Resettling the child in her arms she said finally, "It is so unusual to hear a young person speak about tradition these days." She continued rocking. She said, "Tell me, what *are* the seven principles?"

The nurse, slightly surprised, but pleased at the question,

answered: "*Umoja* — unity; this signifies togetherness in the family, community, nation and race. *Kujichagulia* — self determination; each person determines his or her own destiny. *Ujima* — collective work and responsibility. *Nia* — purpose. *Ujamaa* — cooperative economics; by being true to the other six principles we may create financial strength and independence. *Kuumba* — creativity; being self-sufficient, not relying on other people to create things for us; and *Imani* — faith; believing with all our hearts in our people."

Mrs. Dranoff sat rocking and listening intently. Why on earth, she thought, did it surprise her that this holiday was... was what? Beautiful? Was that the word she wanted? How about real? No, that was her son speaking. "Real" was one of Dave's words, not hers. She didn't know what she thought about Kwanzaa. It certainly made sense that it, like all major cultural celebrations around the world, was based on important, beautiful concepts, significant ideas, time-honored customs. But when was it that she had last heard someone speak so seriously and with genuine pleasure of the origins of Hanukkah or Christmas? Certainly never before about Kwanzaa. It pleased her to think of her driver and his wife lighting candles in their home as she did in hers. But no candles would be lit in her home this year, no prayers said. Only a last minute, frantic race to Lord & Taylor to buy presents for people who will not need the things she buys and probably will not want them. She asked the nurse, "Is this holiday as important to all your people as it is to you? I mean, is it the same for others? The respect for tradition, the understanding of what the holiday really means?" She paused, "Does that make sense to you at all?"

"Hmmm... yes. I think it does. Mrs. Dranoff, Kwanzaa is by no means a magic time. Just like Hanukkah and Christmas, you get out of it what you put in." Mrs. Dranoff nodded. She understood.

"When I was a little girl," the nurse continued, "I had a wonderful, favorite little doll. I had had the doll forever. She was old and worn but I loved her intensely, the way little girls

always love their dolls. Well, as I said, the doll was old, and
finally one year, during Kwanzaa, she broke. Right at the neck.
It just snapped right off. Poor thing. I cried and cried, holding
the body in one hand and the head in the other. My father
promised to get me a new one *especially* for Kwanzaa, but I
didn't want a new one so I cried and cried.

"Well, it was the tradition in our family to pick one person
during Kwanzaa and do something very special, very personal
for him. My mother used to call it 'the gift of love for
Kwanzaa.' We kids called it 'the assignment.' We were always
looking for a chance to get it over with so we could just enjoy
the holiday. We weren't allowed to give our gift of love to
anyone in the family unless it was something extra special. My
little brother saw an opportunity to get his assignment out of the
way, so he took the two pieces of the doll and wrapped this
horrible tape around and around the doll's neck... You should
have seen her! She was sticky, she wobbled and her head wasn't
even totally facing the right way... It was awful! So, of course,
when I saw her I cried and cried even more than before and
threw it at my brother, ran to my room and wouldn't talk to
anybody.

"When I was hungry enough to re-surface, I was still mad at
my brother. But he said he was sorry and he had really fixed it
this time (with my father's help, I found out later). He presented
my little doll to me very gallantly and asked me if I would
accept his gift of love for Kwanzaa. He was being so sweet and
had fixed the doll so nicely that I was really touched. I guess I
knew even then that they all thought I had been over-reacting,
but I didn't care because the doll was very important to me.

"I just received a package from my little brother who now
lives in Ghana. I can't open it until Kwanzaa starts, but I have
a feeling it might be a doll. He's given me twelve of them, over
the years, at Kwanzaa. Beautiful dolls from all over the world
that he packs with a roll of masking tape and a note that says,
'Just in case it breaks.'

"That year our assignments stopped being assignments and

became gifts of love. I think my father would be pleased because now we all really do go out of our way to make a difference in someone's life during Kwanzaa. I've started early; this little child and the others here are getting special attention from me as a gift of love for Kwanzaa. They need so much more but it's all I can give them and they don't get much of it from their own mothers. Happy Kwanzaa, little one," the nurse said, her voice both sad and hopeful. "Happy Hanukkah, Mrs. Dranoff."

Mrs. Dranoff looked at the nurse, "Happy Kwanzaa, dear," she said, still rocking a now sleeping child in her arms. "And Merry Christmas to you," she said to it, although she knew the baby would not hear her. She rocked it slowly and told herself that she would have to ask the nurse when visiting hours would be tomorrow.

Silent Night

Miriam Sagan

The year my heart was broken in Boston I lay on the floor of my apartment and looked at the catalpa tree outside my window. I learned little about the catalpa, still less about my heart, and when I emerged from my desire to die I promptly went and got a job on the drug and suicide hotline.

Hello, Hotline, hello, Hotline. I sat in that drafty warehouse that smelled of piss and old coffee in styrofoam. Eating the remains of a jelly donut in sugary paper I sat in an old easy chair and watched four black phones — coiled, ready to strike, hello, Hotline. It's an old woman wanting to know if she can drink a glass of wine on top of an antihistamine — it's Christmas Eve, after all, and celebration is in order. The next caller is a guy who wants to know what color my underpants are, and who then asks — do you mind if I masturbate? Our masturbators are polite, and some staffers will talk to them. But I say, no, I don't talk to masturbators. My friend Howard says this means I cannot converse with the entire human race; but still he has not been able to talk me into bed.

But it's mostly quiet here, the late afternoon of Christmas Eve. It's snowing lightly, the South End is covered in snow, Back Bay with its brick, the river with its frozen bridges. The lines are swelling outside the shelters and the street people who fear the shelters more than the cold have settled down over the steam vents from the T. I want to go out myself, my blue velour dress is rolled in my backpack and I have a date with Howard.

The phone rings again. Hello, Hotline.

Hello — is this the hotline? It's a man with a thick Yiddish accent.

Yes?

My wife, she is in trouble.

What kind of trouble?

You're Jewish, Miss? The man asks me.

Yes. We usually won't give out personal information but I *am*
Jewish.

Well, listen. We come from Russia recently, to Brookline.
We are — how shall I say, very observant...

Orthodox?

Yes, you understand. My wife, she is a good wife. She keeps
a kosher house, looks after the children, always has a smile now
that we have left Russia. But tonight....

Yes?

It is America! All this Christmas, lights, music on the radio.
What kind of country is this? At least in Russia we were spared
this. So, tonight my wife thinks she is Jesus Christ.

Excuse me?

She thinks she is Jesus Christ. She lies on the clean linoleum
and says tomorrow is her birthday. She is waiting to be born.
She will not get up. 'Why should I make dinner?' she asks,
'When I am the son of God?'

Oh, I say. And then, what do you want me to do?

Do! Take to the hospital, he rages.

I give him the number for the psych unit at the Beth Israel,
murmuring something to him about the needs of recent
immigrants. Besides, the B.I. is kosher.

When I get off the phone I want to laugh. I'll tell Howard
about it and he'll claim he saw the same thing in a Woody Allen
movie. Still, I'm lonely too. I think how Howard will take me
to the No Name restaurant on the pier and buy me fried calamari
and lemon meringue pie. Then there is a knock on the door. I go
and unbolt the heavy piece of wood across it and let in a woman
about my age, bedraggled in a shapeless beige coat. She smells
crazy, with that peculiar metallic smell. Besides, her hair needs
washing. Wearing sneakers in the snow, she is nine months

pregnant.

I need to crash, she says.

It really isn't our policy at the hotline to let people stay overnight, only in exceptional emergencies, which we define as middle class runaways. But I ask her name.

Mary, she mumbles.

Mary, you can't stay here, I'll call one of the shelters...

No! I won't go. They laugh and they stare. And they...Besides, I've been banned from the women's shelter.

Really?

Uh huh. Someone tried to rip me off and I stuck her with my scissors.

Oh...

I look at her but now she has taken off her sneakers and is stretched out on the couch, covered with her coat. In a moment she is snoring, almost convincingly.

I want to go out to dinner. But I can't bring myself to evict a pregnant Mary on Christmas Eve. Maybe this drafty warehouse will serve as a manger and isn't every child a savior. I am filled with the flush of virtue; besides, I am leaving in five minutes. I go into the funky bathroom and perform a spot sponge bath from the cold water faucet, spray on some Charlie cologne, and don the wrinkled blue velour dress. Someone has quoted an Elvis Costello song on the bathroom wall about how love is like a tumor.

My replacement comes in — a small curly haired woman in social work school. She regards my sleeping madonna skeptically, but lets her lie.

I go out into the pale snow. Howard and I eat on the pier and then go to Christ Church for midnight mass. The church is a small white jewel with crystal planes. The seats are red, the windows are blue with night. We sing the songs of redemption, two Jews staying up late to watch someone else's savior get born. We come out and it's snowing harder, the commons are whited out, the windshield is a small tundra. Howard says to me — well, here we are, the family with the terrible sex life. I know that if I take him home there will only be trouble, the kind of trouble two newly divorced people share. But it is Christmas Eve. So we go home to my bed and make love. Howard says — this is so comfortable, it reminds me of being married. The trouble is already starting.

The next morning I get an irate call from the hotline. Mary — now referred to as my client — woke up and attempted to strangle the overnight counselor. The cops ran her in to Boston General and a few hours later she gave birth to a baby girl. I will have a lot of explaining to do. But today the streets are unplowed, and outside my window the catalpa tree is weighed down under snow.

Stolen

Jeanne McDonald

Coming into town, we see the sign sprouting up out of a fan of frostbitten weeds: *Careyville, Population 612.* Somebody has tied a red Christmas ribbon around the post. "They haven't changed that in forever," Jimmy says. Now that he is close to home, he lapses into the easy country language he used when I first met him. He casts me a sidelong glance and grins, waiting for my reaction. "They didn't even subtract a number when I left."

Numb, I stare out at the unwelcoming fields, bare frozen pastures, a few peeling farmhouses. Jimmy pats my knee. "Doing okay, Paula? You've slept most of the way since Richmond."

"I'm homesick," I say, then feel his arm stiffen against me. Silent now, we turn onto Main Street. A skinny weatherbeaten rope of tinsel loops across the intersection and red plastic bells swing from the telephone poles.

Jimmy slows down for a couple of Christmas Eve shoppers coming out of the catalogue store and nods toward the car bed in the back seat. "Have you checked her lately?" he asks, knowing I haven't, knowing that most of the time I leave it to him to change the baby, to feed her, and (oh, yes, I have known him to do this) to see if she is still breathing in the middle of the night. He is so much better with her than I am. I feel awkward holding her, and she senses that, somehow, and cries harder when I pick her up.

The baby, three months old now, is still without a name. The psychiatrist who is supposed to be helping me over my depression says it's because I haven't accepted her into my life. So for now, she is Baby, just Baby.

Jimmy worries. Not just because I can't name the baby. He worries about my crying, the fatigue, the sleeplessness. What I really want is for everything to be the way it was two years ago when we were married. It was my first year as copy editor for a fashion magazine, and Jimmy had just been accepted as a junior partner in an accounting firm. We were paying off his college loans, and we figured that in three years we would be able to buy a house and take the trip to Europe we had always dreamed about. Having a baby had never been part of the plan. I wasn't ready for that.

And certainly I am not ready for Christmas in Careyville with Jimmy's parents. I've never even met them. They didn't come to the wedding because they don't like crowds, Jimmy says. They are simple country people. And Jimmy has reminded me that I had promised a long time ago that if we spent our summer vacation with my parents at the beach we would come here to have Christmas with his parents on the farm.

But that was before the baby. When I found out I was pregnant, everything changed. "There are other options," I told Jimmy.

"Not for us," he said. "There are no other options for us."

It didn't seem fair that during the summer I was so big with the baby that I couldn't even wear a bathing suit, and I was tired and uncomfortable. And now here I am at Christmas in this ugly little country town, on my way to spend Christmas with people who are virtual strangers to me.

I think of Christmas at home in Richmond as if it were a memory that belongs to somebody else — the tree with icicles twirling like silvery winter rain, glass balls gleaming against the lights with their star-struck halos. And in the kitchen the tangy aroma of cranberries, lemons and oranges and mincemeat hot from the oven. Shortbread, fruitcake — all the yeasty baking smells blending with the earthy sweetness of balsam and the

biting fragrance of pine and the spicy tea my mother stirs with
cinnamon sticks and pours from a silver teapot.

My brother will be there with his new fiancée and my sister
will come home with her husband and children and on Christmas
morning when they open their gifts my mother will cry because
this year there will be nothing from me. Not even a card. This
year my heart is cold, wrapped in a wintry layer that separates
me from everything and everybody I used to love.

Jimmy turns off the main highway onto a dirt road lined with
bare trees. Beyond is the house, a two-story white frame
structure built on sturdy brick columns. The roof is tin, edged
with copper-colored streaks where rain has run down and clung
to the lip of the metal and finally turned to rust. There are
chickens under the porch, pecking at the frozen ground.

Jimmy turns off the ignition and looks at me. "Promise you'll
at least *try* to be cheerful," he says. "For my parents' sake." He
squeezes my hand. "Okay, for *my* sake."

I pull away and take a deep breath. "Turn back," I say. "Tell
them I'm sick."

He leans his head against the steering wheel and sighs. "They
know about your trouble, Paula. I told my mother last time I
called."

"Why? Why did you tell?"

"I had to. They'll see how you are. It's better that they know
you're getting help."

"They must hate me," I say, trying to swallow the lump in
my throat. "How could any decent mother not want her own
baby?"

Just then his mother steps out onto the porch, hugging her
arms against the cold. She wears a rough brown sweater over
her cotton housedress. Her gray hair is pulled back into a tight
knot. Though she must be the age of my mother, who always
dresses in silk and soft wools, she looks much older.

I sit stiffly in the front seat while Jimmy opens the back door
and lifts the baby out. When the cold air strikes her face she
wakes up and begins to cry.

"Get something on that child's head," his mother calls. She runs down the steps, takes the baby from Jimmy, and whisks her into the house. No hello, no greeting for me.

"Dad's probably out in the barn," says Jimmy, taking packages and suitcases from the trunk. "You go on in, Paula. I'll get these things."

Inside, everything seems bleak and chilly. My parents' house is furnished with Oriental rugs, deeply cushioned sofas, and rich paintings, but here the floor is bare and the lamp shades wear crinkled plastic covers. Under the narrow windows in the parlor sits a stiff gold damask sofa that looks as if it has never been used. The only other furniture is a green wooden rocker with a faded print pillow, a brown naugahyde lounge chair, and a television set.

There is no Christmas tree in sight.

The kitchen is better. Something spicy is baking in the oven and the windows are fogged with a silver sheen. Jimmy's mother lays the baby on the table and unzips her snowsuit, crooning to her in a singsong voice. When she notices me standing in the doorway she shakes my hand with a solid grip and then looks down at the baby and smiles. "She has Jimmy's nose," she says. "I'd know her anywhere." She slings the baby over one hip and leads me up the uncarpeted stairs. "I've put Jimmy's old crib in the front bedroom for the baby. The two of you can have the room next to that. I know it's chilly right now, but it'll warm up in a couple of hours. We usually keep the upstairs rooms closed off."

Swallowing tears, I follow her as she shows me the old-fashioned bathroom with its claw-footed tub and then our bedroom, with its metal bedstead and thin sagging mattress. The only pretty thing in the room is the quilt, stitched with colorful squares of the family's history. She points them out to me — the blue square from Jimmy's first coat, black serge from her husband's wedding vest, a yellow print pocket from one of her mother's aprons.

In the front bedroom she hands the baby back to me. She

frowns for a minute, as if she has just recalled an unpleasant memory. "I'll warm her bottle up," she says briskly, and then at the door she turns back. "Have you named her yet?"

"We haven't decided," I say.

She stares at me and bites her bottom lip, then comes back to touch the baby's downy head. When she disappears down the stairs, I carry the baby over to the window and look down at the driveway. Jimmy is leaning against the car, staring out over the pasture. I lean my forehead against the windowpane and the cold seems to enter me there and run slowly through my body. Beyond the glass I see the first flakes beginning to fall.

Snow for Christmas.

I can't help crying. The baby looks up into my face, her eyes as clear as blue glass, her cheeks flushed pink from the cold air. She struggles against me and arches her back. Why do I feel so separated from her? Why does she feel so alien — blood, bones, heart? For a second I *do* think I see the resemblance to Jimmy's nose. But there is nothing at all about her that seems like me except for the tears.

When I lay her in the crib she settles down and makes noises, but so far I have not learned to speak her language. I pull the sleeves of her sweater over her hands to keep them warm and go downstairs to get her bottle. I hope to retrieve it without conversation, but Jimmy's mother motions with her spoon toward the turkey she has been stuffing. "Look at old Tom," she laughs. "Lo, how the mighty have fallen."

"Who killed him?" I ask.

"Me. I killed him. I always liked him, too, poor thing. But on a farm you learn to give up things. Priorities. Is that the right word? You learn when to give in, too. Makes you a better person, though it hurts."

I grab the bottle and hurry out. The last thing I need is a lecture. By the time I get back to the bedroom, the baby is screaming. She gulps at the bottle hungrily as I hold her in the rocker. She falls asleep with the nipple in her mouth, and I burp her and lay her in the crib, wrapping her in the pink quilt.

Occasionally she skips a breath and sighs or, dreaming, abruptly jerks an arm or a foot. This is what she must have done in the womb, I think. Even then she was protesting. Suddenly a door slams downstairs and her eyes fly open and she begins to scream. Nothing I can do will quiet her this time. I would call Jimmy's mother, but I don't know how to address her. Mrs. Springer? Clara? I can't call her *Mother*. "I want to go home," I chant to myself as I walk the howling baby back and forth, "I want to go home. I want to go home." The snow is thickening now, covering the roof of the car and dusting the gravel on the driveway.

Finally the baby drops off in exhaustion and I lay her down again and cover her with the quilt. I feel so tired. I'm always tired these days. When I open the door to our bedroom, cold air strikes me like a sudden slap. I slip off my shoes and crawl under the patchwork quilt and pull it up over my head. The tent of the quilt fills with my own warm breath and when I wake later it is almost dark outside and the house is deadly quiet. I sit up and listen, but hear only the wind, sighing under the sill, and the stutter of frozen branches against the roof. The light is blue and watery and the shadows are lower, stretching across the faded old carpet. Outside the evergreens droop, fat with snow, and the fields are filling up with white. Silence folds itself over and around everything in the house. I open the door to the hallway, but there are no voices downstairs, no sound of any kind. Then I tiptoe into the baby's room.

When I open the door, my heart stops beating for a moment. The crib is empty.

I feel panic, confusion. What if Jimmy and his parents had left, gone for a walk, while I was asleep, and someone came in — a drifter, maybe, and took the baby? It would have to be a stranger, a man, someone unfamiliar with babies — otherwise, why would he not have taken her snowsuit, which is still flung across the chair where Jimmy's mother left it? Or the pink quilt, pushed up against the rungs of the crib?

My breath catches between my throat and lungs, clenching

itself into a hard knot that stops somewhere in the middle of my chest. I run to the stairway, lean over the banister, and call. "Jimmy? Mrs. Springer?"

When no one answers, I hurtle down the steps, rush through the empty rooms. Gone. They're all gone.

And someone has taken the baby.

I try to remember her face. How will I describe her to the police? Flushed cheeks. Blue eyes. And, oh God, yes — Jimmy's nose.

I run back up the stairs for my shoes, my coat. No, no, there's not time for the coat. Wait, it's there, on the ladderback chair. I push my arms into the sleeves, dash once more into the baby's room to make certain she is really and truly gone, and then hurtle down the stairs. I run out the front door and across the porch, falling on my knees into the snow. I get up and whirl around. Where do I think I'm going? I stand in the driveway and call, but my voice is muffled against the thickly frozen ground. "Jimmy, Jimmy!"

Then I notice the crosshatched soles of footsteps in the snow, heavy, deep, veering off across the yard and away from the house. They are too big for Jimmy's shoes. The wind picks up, the snow blows into my eyes, and I remember that my baby's snowsuit is upstairs in the bedroom. I'm running again, lurching into the hollows of the footprints, stretching my legs to match the long stride. The sound of my own pulse pounds in my ears and my throat sears with pain because my mouth is open. I am crying, calling. Suddenly, in the white swirling air, I make out the shape of a barn. The footprints end here, the last one under the fanlike scrape in the snow where the door has recently been pulled open.

I look around in desperation and find a rusty pipe in the stiff weeds. I pick it up and push open the door just enough to slip inside, not daring to breathe or make a sound. I ease inside and lean against a cattle stall.

And then I see him, a big man in a plaid flannel shirt, his heavy boots planted firmly in the hay. I pull back and tighten my grip on the pipe. Then I realize he is murmuring something. I peer through a slat of the stall and watch as he lifts the baby's hand and places it gently on the nose of a cow that is nibbling at the hay in one of the mangers. "See, little sweetheart?" he says. "It was a cow like this that watched the baby Jesus in the barn hundreds and hundreds of years ago." He guides her fingers over the velvety nose, and the baby makes a soft, contented sound. I drop the pipe into the hay, realizing that this is Jimmy's father and that my baby is safe.

He hears the thud and turns. "Who is it?" he asks, and I rush forward — grateful, relieved, but angry.

I want to pound my fists against his wide solid chest. "Why didn't you tell me you had her?" I scream. "I thought she was stolen! I thought she was dead! I was terrified!" And then I am crying so hard, I can't say another word.

"Come here, girl," he says, shifting the baby to his shoulder. All this time she has been wrapped inside his fleece-lined jacket.

I walk closer and reach out to touch my baby, to press her tiny hand against my lips. Jimmy's father folds his arm around me. "Thought she was stolen, did you?" he says softly. "Well, I believe that now you have finally found her." He looks down into my face and smiles. "See, Jim and his mother walked out to the woods to cut the tree, and I didn't want to wake you when I brought the little one out to see the animals. I always did this with Jim on Christmas Eve. They say the animals talk then, you know. That's why I took the baby. I never imagined you'd think she was stolen." He squeezes my shoulder. "Well," he says, "I guess we never know what we have until we think we've lost it." He hands me the baby and whispers, "Merry Christmas, girl." I lean into his broad shoulder, still crying, but my tears are tears of relief because I realize that suddenly I am better. At last it is over.

"Another thing," Jimmy's father says, wiping his eyes. "She has a name, whether you like it or not. I named her here in this barn a little while ago. It's a Christmas name — Joy."

"Joy," I whisper. "It's a good name. Thank you."

Then the barn door opens and Jimmy's mother, her face mottled with cold, comes in carrying a canvas sling filled with greens — mistletoe, holly and pine boughs. Jimmy follows, pulling a fat blue spruce. The Christmas tree. When he sees me with Joy and his father, tears spring to his eyes. "Jimmy," I say, laughing and crying at the same time, "the baby has a name now. It's Joy."

As Jimmy's arms close around the baby and me, I'm aware of a rich, exotic smell. Maybe it is the sharpness of the freshly cut spruce. Maybe it is the steely smell of the winter air or the musky odor of hay. No. It is the sweet fragrance of the baby. I can sense these things now. Already, I am falling into my appointed role. Joy looks up at me with wide eyes full of trust and I tuck her snugly inside the front of my coat, knowing that because she had been stolen from me for a while, I must be the one to carry her back to the house.

The Editors

Multi-media artist **Zelda Leah Gatuskin** is the author of *The Time Dancer,* a novel of gypsy magic (Amador Publishers, 1991) and *Ancestral Notes: A Family Dream Journal* (Amador, 1994) which she also illustrated with her original collages. She is a native of Wilmington, Delaware and a graduate of Emerson College in Boston. Zelda followed the sun to New Mexico in 1983, where she has resided since, establishing "Studio Z" near downtown Albuquerque as her workshop, office and gallery.

Michelle Miller is a novelist and playwright. Her fiction collection, *Hunger in the First Person Singular: Stories of Desire and Power* (Amador, 1992) won the New Mexico Press Women's Zia Award. Her plays have been produced by the University of N. M. and N. M. State University. Miller co-edited the 1991 New Mexico Anthology, *The Spirit That Wants Me.* "One blue Christmas Eve I decided 'someone' should do a book on the down side of Christmas, to document this significant social phenomenon. My colleagues agreed. Hence this collection."

Harry Willson is a mythologist and writer. Four books of his fiction have been published, including *Duke City Tales, A World for the Meek, Souls and Cells Remember,* and *This'll Kill Ya: the Last Word on Censorship.* He has contributed essays to various alternative press publications. His special interests include equality and respect for all cultures and preservation of the Biosphere. He is editor-in-chief of Amador Publishers, which specializes in fiction and biography of unusual worth and appeal, outside the purview of "mainstream" publishing.

The Contributors

Retired elementary school teacher **Dorothy M. Ainslie** has published poems and articles in newspapers, books and magazines. She lives in Monroe, Michigan and is the mother of four children.

Joan Arcari is a fiction writer living in New York City. "I've done paste up work, teaching, and telemarketing. In my real life I have raised kids, I travel frequently, I hang out, and I write."

Joseph A. Barda has published non-fiction, poetry, fiction, and literary criticism. He is currently finishing his masters degree in English at Northeastern Illinois University where he is completing a collection of short stories for his Master's thesis.

D. C. Berry has published widely and teaches at the Center for Writers in Hattiesburg, Mississippi.

John Brand teaches literature at the University of Northern Colorado. "Jesus Watered in Glory Hole" is part of a novel he is finishing: *Winter's Child,* on the deaths of children.

Marion Abbott Bundy recently co-authored *Talking Pictures* (The New Press), an oral history of early filmmakers. She celebrates Christmas with her family in Berkeley, California.

B. A. Cantwell is the author of *Waters of the Manitoulins* and has appeared in metropolitan, *The Wayne Literary Review, The Maryland Poetry Review* and *Amelia.*

Marillen Cassatt is the pen name of Marilyn Bauman, a native Idahoan best known for her writings on religious Ecumenism and governmental issues affecting human rights and the environment.

Peter Cooley has five poetry books in publication, the most recent being *The Astonished Hours* (Carnegie Mellon, 1992). He teaches creative writing at Tulane University in New Orleans, Louisiana.

Catherine Couse is a state government research scientist in the child welfare area, living in Albany, New York. Her short stories have been published in *The Little Magazine.*

Joan E. Sullivan Cowan, chemically disabled (pesticide exposures), is Executive Director of Education for R.E.A.C.H., International, Inc. (Research, Education and Action for the Chemically Handicapped). A free-lance writer, this is her first anthology publication.

Raymond Crippen, a Minnesota native, worked at *The Daily Globe* for 35 years and was editor for 20 years. He now does freelance writing.

Dan Dervin lives in Fredericksburg, Virginia, and teaches at Mary Washington College. He has published several short stories and poems and won awards for *Interstates,* a play.

Terrence E. Dunn earns his living as a Production Accountant on motion pictures, but keeps his sanity by writing short stories, poetry, and occasional non-fiction articles.

Kenneth Ellsworth's Sales Fiction is part of a series that occur in the world of Frankie St. Germaine. Publication credits include: *Atom Mind, Caffeine, Esc!, Farmer's Market* and *Pacific Coast Journal.*

Karen Ethelsdattar is a poet and creator of women's liturgies who lives in New Jersey and works in New York City.

After a career as a technical editor, **Bruce Ferguson** earned a Master of Divinity degree and served as a minister for five years. He now lives in New Mexico.

CB Follett's poems have appeared in *Calyx, Green Fuse, Without Halos* and many others. Her collection, *The Latitudes of Their Going,* was published by Hot Pepper Press. She lives in Sausalito, California.

New Mexico artist, **Mark Funk,** a published writer, performance poet, muralist, sculptor and greeting card artist, has an interesting story to tell but not enough beer money to tell it.

Peggy Garrison's work has appeared in *The Literary Review, South Dakota Review, Poetry New York* and *The Bridge.* She is currently teaching writing workshops at New York University.

Geraldine Gobi Greig, a native Texan with a Rice University degree in German, has been published in various literary magazines. She lobbies for the Mongolian Relief Effort.

Jeane C. Gottsponer has had poetry, short stories and essays published in several national magazines and local newspapers.

Australia-born **Sue Hanson-Smith** completed graduate studies in education in Hawaii and New Mexico. She now lives in Chicago with husband Brad and teaches teachers. She has three grown sons.

Donal Harding's first novel will be published by William Morrow in the spring of 1996. He won the 1994 Southwest Writer's screenplay competition and the Parris Afton Bonds Award.

"Christmas Compromise" is **Mary Hartman**'s first published fiction. She has published two non-fiction books and numerous articles in national magazines.

Teresa Hubley lives in Maine with her husband and two cats and works for the State of Maine as a research associate.

Betty Hyland writes often on mental illness and alcoholism. CBS developed one of her stories into a teen special, directed by Diane Keaton. She is a member of PEN Center USA West.

Jennifer Lynn Jackson, previously published in *Passages North*, was awarded the Roy W. Cowden Memorial Fellowship while in the MFA program at University of Michigan, where she currently teaches.

Mary Ellen Kugachz [a.k.a. Ugactz] lives in New York City and is a Literature-Writing major at Columbia University. "At Christmas Time" is her first published piece.

C. M. La Bruno, an active member of The Poetry Society of America, was published over one hundred times during the last five years of his 14-year imprisonment. He died in prison in 1993.

Annette Lynch, long-time college English teacher and literary magazine editor, has had many poems published in journals here and abroad, including her chapbook, *Ways around the Heart*.

Chris Martín hosted KUNM-FM's Women's Focus from 1983 to 1994. She manages the Mesa Verde Plant and Wildlife Refuge in Albuquerque with her husband and six cats.

Cathryn McCracken lives in Albuquerque, New Mexico. Her poetry has appeared in *Blue Mesa Review* and other journals. Presently a graduate student at UNM, she is working on a novel.

Jeanne McDonald, an editor at the University of Tennessee in Knoxville, has published short stories in magazines, journals and anthologies. She is presently working on a novel.

Bill Morgan was graduated from UMASS-Boston, and served as assistant editor of *Dorchester Community News*. He was taught by poets Martha Collins and Lloyd Schwartz.

Jan Nystrom has completed her first collection of stories, *Women Who Fly*. Stories from this collection have been published in *Indiana Review, North American Review, Prairie Schooner* and other journals.

New Mexico artist, **Claiborne O'Connor**, is also a calligrapher and graphic designer. She owns See O See Studios, and is Art Director of Amador Publishers.

Peter O'Grady lives with his family in Petaluma, California. He's a general contractor and a counselor in a youth home, and is starting a writers' group.

Andrea K. Orrill is a freelance writer for magazines, newspapers and other journals. She is completing a collection of writing on the subject of eating disorders.

Chaibou Elhadji Oumarou is a native of the Republic of Niger, and currently a dissertator at the Department of African Languages and Literature, University of Wisconsin at Madison. He has won numerous awards for his poetry and essays.

Linda Pinnell is a life-long resident of West Virginia where she teaches English and Creative Writing. She recently published an introductory theater text through National Textbook Company.

Lemar Rodgers writes and lives well with AIDS in Dallas. This is his first published story.

Fran Ruggles worked as a free-lance photo-journalist and in public relations and marketing during her years in Alaska. She is currently working on a collection of short stories.

Miriam Sagan's books include *The Art of Love: New and Selected Poems* ('94), a novel, *Coastal Lives* ('91). She co-edited the anthology, *New Mexico Poetry Renaissance* ('94).

Vickey A. Sigler was raised in the shadow of the Appalachian Mountains and credits her talent to their enduring strength. This is the debut of "Christmas, The First."

Natalia Rachel Singer is an Assistant Professor of English at St. Lawrence University. Her work has appeared in *The North American Review, Harper's, Creative Nonfiction, Ms,* and many other magazines.

Brian Skinner is co-editor and illustrator for *Chicago Quarterly Review.* His work has appeared in *The Grasslands Review, Civilization, Viet Nam Generation, Magic Realism* and *Other Voices.*

Jesse Evan Smith, age 6, has a marvelous imagination, loves drawing, stories, spooky things, making stuff, video games and computers. Sometimes he looks a little like the canary-eating cat.

Sparrow is a poet living in Manhattan with his wife Violet Snow and their daughter, Leiba. Sparrow has not watched TV since 1971. As essay of his will soon appear in an anthology about James Dean.

Linda Moore Spencer's work has been widely published in the U.S., Canada and Great Britain. She lives in Northampton, Massachusetts with her husband and two sons.

A published author of fiction and non-fiction books, **Jo Stevenson** was film actress, *Joanne Duff,* who performed on Broadway, off-Broadway and in Sydney. She hosted *The Late Show TV-7* in Melbourne and worked in TV in New York City.

336

Coral Suter's poems have been published in numerous magazines. She was completing her first volume of poetry and had begun a novel about women and Wyatt Earp. She died in November, 1994, at age 40.

Gale Swiontkowski lives near the Tappan Zee region of the Hudson River north of New York City and teaches modern poetry at Fordham University.

Elizabeth Templeman lives with her husband and three children on a farm at Heffley Creek, British Columbia, and teaches at the University College of the Cariboo, in Kamloops. Her essays have appeared in *The High Plains Literary Review, Mothering, North Dakota Quarterly* and other journals.

Claudia Thompson is a survivor, a writer, and a paralegal living in Los Angeles and finding herself in her poetry.

Navajo poet, playwright and anthropologist, C. M. Topaha lives in Farmington, New Mexico. Her publication credits include *National Library of Poetry, Yahoo Press* and *Hayoołkááł [Dawn]*, a forthcoming Navajo anthology. "Poetry is my sleeping consciousness of endless landscape and freedom."

Claude Tower writes poetry, fiction and nonfiction. His art furniture has been showcased in commercial galleries and group exhibits at the Milwaukee Museum of Art. He is father of four and a practicing Zen Buddhist.

Betty Wald, retired college counselor, has published essays in local newspapers and an article about facing retirement in the *Bulletin of Psychological Type*. Her family includes eleven children, ten grandchildren!

Lee Webb lives and writes in Los Alamos, New Mexico. She recently placed in the Southwest Writer's Workshop writing competition with a suspense short story.

Carol Weir lives in Bloomington, Illinois, where she teaches English Composition at Illinois State University.

Don Williams is an award-winning columnist and feature writer for The Knoxville News-Sentinel, Knoxville, Tennessee, and a 1992 University of Michigan Journalism Fellow. He is at work on a novel and a book of stories.

Early Reviews of *Christmas Blues*

Christina Rossetti wrote, "Love came down at Christmas, Love all lovely, Love divine." This multifarious collection of writings — poems, short stories, remembrances — makes vividly clear that the true significance of "Love coming down at Christmas" for a multitude of people has been the breaking of hearts and severe depression. Instead of angelic singing of great joy, we are led to hear carols which give voice to melancholy and despair.

"The history of Christmas has been a steady downward spiral from the sublime to the ridiculous," one the contributors to *Christmas Blues* writes. And the ridiculousness of what has become a Christmas masquerade is revealed in many ways throughout the book. It is a theatre of the absurd, the trivialization of what might be a theologically profound message.

But "ridiculousness" and "trivialization" are terms which are much too weak. Outwardly trivialized, conventionalized, commercialized — yes. But when these authors each remove the "Holiday Mask," we discover an inward reality which is tragic in the extreme. What we need is not an angelic choir proclaiming joy and peace, but an army of angels of mercy capable of ministering effectively to a large portion of today's population who have been victimized by an annual event in our culture which is "celebrated" for several weeks, and cannot be escaped by those whose response is one of severe pain, and who must shudder when the common sentiment is uttered: "Wouldn't it be wonderful if the spirit of Christmas could pervade each day of the year!"

Christmas Blues should be required reading for all Christian clergy, and for anyone who "celebrates Christmas" without understanding its horrible dark side.

— Fred Gillette Sturm, Department of Philosophy
University of New Mexico

*Christmas is inescapable. This important book provides the faces, the life stories, behind the mask of convention — "the rest of the story," a phrase I often invoke in clinical conferences when we discuss a difficult medical case. **Christmas Blues: Behind the Holiday Mask** is a disturbing book. It will not be found in the greeting card section. It does not come gift-wrapped beneath the perfect tree. It is more like what we needed than what we wanted for Christmas. And it requires a very special, insightful Santa Claus to dare to bring it!*

It is a gift of the private face behind the public facade. It is about the "other" meanings of Christmas, about dashed and different expectations, about what one does and how one feels when the "Miracle on 34th Street" does not happen at home. It is about the pain we are not supposed to feel — or even to acknowledge as existing — and what the writers did with their anguish. This anthology also shows how literature not only supplements science (even "human science"), but helps keep it honest, true to experience.

The editors and writers are to be congratulated for confronting us with Christmas' unsettling particularities. In place of dogma and correct performance, the reader of this anthology encounters a rawness that makes me think that realism, translation and authenticity might still be possible, even in this "post-modern" world. Despite the diversity in stories and poems, there was not a one that felt so alien that it could not have also been my own. In telling their personal histories through story and poem, the contributors give us back and help us reclaim our own. I cannot think of anyone who, if able to read superb English, should not read this book.

*The editors did far more than "collect," "select," and "assemble" a book. Like thorough anthropologists conducting fieldwork, they found that the contributions fell into recurrent categories or themes. This taxonomy became the organization of the book, the **tableau** of contents: Tradition, Family, Outsiders, Stuff and Remythologizing.*

*__Christmas Blues__ is not only a successful antidote to standardized, stylized, sentimentalized, falsified, stale Christmases; it suggests the disturbing thought that, if we were honest with ourselves, Christmas might be better understood as casualty than victory, something to be recovered from. It is an immensely **healing** work.*

— Howard F. Stein, psychoanalytic anthropologist
Department of Family Medicine, Oklahoma Health Sciences Center

This compilation of short stories and poems, generated by an open invitation to submit short pieces on the subject of Christmas, is not likely to arouse a warm inner glow in the mind and body of those who look only for traditional Christmas love and happiness. What, on first reading, was a tale of emptiness and coercion to submit became, on the second reading, a longing for what once was, and an expression of anger over the loss. These are stories of reality, and as in reality, there are more sides to this melange, another truth in love which bears to tell the other side of pain. Many of the writers have come to terms with reality, and found it good. Many of the stories and poems are beautiful, using Christmas merely as the background in exaltation of spirit, sometimes in despair, sometimes in the dawn of a new day. Life, and the return of the sun, can be reason for shared joy.

— William J. Turner, MD,
Professor Emeritus of Psychiatry, Stony Brook, NY

I laughed, I cried, I was often touched, I was sometimes depressed and occasionally disgusted, but I was always absorbed as I read this charming anthology. I knew I would be recommending it to clients, to friends, or to anyone who has ever experienced, either temporarily or permanently, that disgruntled feeling during the 'Holidays.' This book doesn't provide answers to the incongruities of Christmas, but it's provocative. It provides 'food for thought' and, in the end, hope.

— Katie Fashing, Counselor/Therapist, Albuquerque, NM

AMADOR PUBLISHERS
P. O. Box 12335
Albuquerque, NM 87195
505-877-4395
To Order: 800-730-4395

ORDER BLANK

# of copies   **price**
____CHRISTMAS BLUES   @ 15.00_____
____HUNGER IN THE
        FIRST PERSON SINGULAR   @ 9.00_____
____ANCESTRAL NOTES   @ 10.00_____
____THE TIME DANCER   @ 10.00_____
____DUKE CITY TALES   @ 9.00_____
____A WORLD FOR THE MEEK   @ 9.00_____
____SOULS AND CELLS REMEMBER @ 8.00_____
____THIS'LL KILL YA   @ 6.00_____

Subtotal_____

Shipping [$2.50 per order]_____

Total, enclosed_____

Send to: Name_____

            Address_____

            City, State, Zip_____